ABOVE AND BEYOND

OTHER BOOKS AND AUDIO BOOKS
BY BETSY BRANNON GREEN:

HAGGERTY MYSTERIES

Hearts in Hiding

Until Proven Guilty

Above Suspicion

Silenced

Copycat

Poison

Double Cross

Backtrack

Christmas in Haggerty

OTHER NOVELS

Never Look Back

Don't Close Your Eyes

Foul Play

Hazardous Duty

ABOVE AND BEYOND

a novel by

BETSY

BRANNON

GREEN

Covenant Communications, Inc.

Cover image "Men in SWAT team attire exiting vehicle" by Paul Edmondson, © 2008 Getty Images/Riser Collection.

Cover design by Jessica A. Warner, copyrighted 2008 by Covenant Communications, Inc.

Published by Covenant Communications, Inc.
American Fork, Utah

Printed in Canada
First Printing: October 2008

15 14 13 12 11 10 09 08   10 9 8 7 6 5 4 3 2 1

ISBN-13: 978-1-59811-714-1
ISBN-10: 1-59811-714-9

*To my maternal grandparents, John and Ruth Walton—
quiet people who lived simple lives full of hard work and sacrifice,
leaving their posterity a legacy of love*

ACKNOWLEDGMENTS

Words are not adequate to express my appreciation for the love and support and encouragement and sacrifice that I receive from my husband and children. Writing books is a time-consuming, heart-wrenching, emotionally draining experience, and I am grateful beyond words to my family for sustaining me through yet another creative process.

Also my debt of gratitude toward the incredible staff at Covenant continues to grow. My editor, Kirk Shaw, is talented, intuitive, and resourceful. I am thankful for him and his determination to strive for excellence. The art department and marketing people are the best in the business, and I'm glad to be a part of their team.

I continue to be grateful to all the readers who buy and recommend my books. It is a great honor to claim a few hours of your time.

And as I complete another installment in my Hazardous Duty series, I want to honor the servicemen and women who sacrifice so much to defend our country and protect freedom and liberty everywhere. May God bless and protect you all!

PROLOGUE

AFTER SIGNING AWAY ownership of her row house near Capitol Hill, Savannah McLaughlin left the lawyer's office for the ride back to Ft. Belvoir. Her bodyguard, one of Hack's seemingly endless supply of grim-faced men, accompanied her out into the cool December night. The new black Yukon she'd purchased at Hack's insistence was parked by the curb. As she slipped into the backseat, she saw that Hack himself was behind the wheel.

"Evening," he said with a smile.

Savannah smiled back. "What brings you here personally? Did Dane send you to spy on me?"

"Dane didn't send me," Hack replied.

Savannah hoped he couldn't see the disappointment on her face. Because of their business relationship, she saw Hack frequently, and Doc stopped by often, but she hadn't seen Dane since they left his cabin over a month before.

"I call him every day," she confided. "I leave him messages, but he doesn't return my calls."

Hack didn't comment. Whether this was because he had no excuse for Dane's behavior or if he just refused to speak ill of his former commanding officer, Savannah couldn't tell.

"I guess if he really wants me to quit calling, he'll change his number."

Hack remained silent, and Savannah decided to drop the subject. Instead she stared morosely out the window at the rain. Her row house had ceased to feel like home months before, but selling it was still more difficult than Savannah expected. By giving up the house, she felt like she was closing the door on her past. It was hard to let go and more forward.

She'd accepted General Steele's offer of employment and was now a research assistant for his staff. She and Caroline had a nice apartment at Ft. Belvoir, and as an additional safety measure, she'd hired Hack's firm to provide round-the-clock protection. Since she wasn't ready to let Caroline go to school yet, she'd found a tutor. General Steele had arranged for a supply closet to be converted into a school room and playroom for Caroline.

Savannah felt settled into her new life and basically back to normal, except for her freshly broken heart. Maybe Dane had been right to keep his true feelings from her for so long. It was certainly harder now, knowing that he loved her and just couldn't live with her, than it had been before when she'd thought he hated her.

"Doc's babysitting for me," she said to Hack. "Caroline is probably driving him crazy."

"Short trip," Hack muttered gruffly.

Savannah smiled. "I won't fall for that again. Doc's saner than the rest of us."

During the ride to Ft. Belvoir, Hack asked questions about Caroline and the events of the past week. Savannah knew he was trying to distract her from painful thoughts about Dane and the fact that she'd just sold the only real home she'd ever had. He was mostly successful.

"Almost there," Hack said, slowing the vehicle as they approached the Tulley Gate entrance to the post. One of the MPs stepped out of the guard shack and held a flashlight to the DOD decal displayed on the front windshield of the Yukon. After a cursory examination of their military IDs, he waved them through and retreated into the booth.

Just as Hack began to accelerate, a specter moved in front of the vehicle, and he slammed on the brakes amid a flurry of curses.

Savannah leaned over the backseat and stared at the young, rain-drenched girl swaying in the illumination provided by the headlights. Her hair was wet and a brassy blond thanks to a terrible dye job. The girl's clothes clung to her thin body, emphasizing the bulge at her midsection that indicated impending motherhood. Her round, frightened eyes were fixed on the Yukon with determination.

Hack opened his door and stepped out into the rain. "Stay inside," he ordered Savannah. "This could be a trick."

Savannah did as she was told but lowered her window a crack so she could hear what was being said. Three MPs and Hack all approached the girl.

"Help me," she cried.

"She's just a vagrant who's been hanging around the entrance all day," one of the MPs told Hack. "I warned her that if she didn't leave, I'd have to call the police. Apparently she didn't believe I'd keep my word."

The MP pulled the girl more roughly than Savannah thought necessary toward the guard shack, and Hack headed back to the Yukon.

Savannah watched in morbid fascination as the girl twisted away from her captor and called out, "Please, Mrs. McLaughlin! I'm here to see you! I've waited all day!"

"Hack," Savannah began as the big man opened his door.

"No, no, no!" the giant said, anticipating her request. "It wouldn't be safe to talk to her. For all we know, she may have been sent by Ferrante to kill you."

Savannah studied the girl again. "She certainly doesn't *look* dangerous. Maybe you could search her first. If she isn't carrying a bomb or a weapon, I'll listen to what she has to say. Then we'll decide whether or not to call the police."

"I don't like it," Hack said.

Savannah decided to appeal to his softer side. "Oh, Hack, she's been waiting all day in the rain."

He glanced back at the girl, and Savannah knew he was weakening.

"Please," she coaxed.

Hack was still frowning, but he nodded as he walked toward the guard shack. "You stay here until I've checked her out."

When Hack returned to the Yukon, Savannah lowered the window, ignoring the rain that pelted her face. "No weapons or bombs?"

"None that we found," Hack admitted.

"So I can talk to her now?"

"I guess." Hack glowered at her. "But I've got a feeling I'm going to regret this."

"I'll be careful, Hack," she promised as she climbed out. The last thing she wanted was to put herself or her daughter back in danger. "But I have to find out what she wants."

He nodded with resignation. "I know."

Savannah hurried through the rain. "The girl probably needs medical attention."

"I already called Doc, and he's on his way."

"Who is watching Caroline?"

"I told the men I had posted outside your apartment to go in until we get there. And I sent over a couple of MPs for good measure."

Caroline had gotten used to Hack's large, mean-looking guards, but she wouldn't be particularly comfortable in their care. Savannah wondered if this was Hack's way of ensuring that her interview with the girl was completed in a timely manner.

She followed Hack to the MP station. When they reached the door, he stepped back, allowing her to precede him inside. The girl was seated in one of several wooden chairs lined up along the far wall. The three MPs standing guard all moved back when Hack entered the room. There was no question about who was in charge of this interrogation.

Before any questions could be asked, a well-preserved, old Bonneville pulled up outside. Savannah watched through the rain-splattered windows of the MP station as Doc climbed out carrying a cardboard box.

When the small man appeared in the doorway, Savannah announced, "We've got a patient for you."

"So I heard." Doc examined their guest from his position by the door.

"What do you think?" Savannah asked.

"Malnourished, dehydrated, exhausted, and on the verge of hypothermia," Doc diagnosed.

Savannah was impressed. "You can tell all that just by looking?"

Doc nodded. "And she's about seven months pregnant."

"Eight," the girl whispered through chattering teeth.

Doc crossed the room and put the box on the floor by the girl's feet. He placed a blanket around her shivering shoulders. Then he used a towel to dab her wet hair.

Finally Hack lost patience with Doc's ministrations and stepped forward. "We need to ask her some questions."

"Not until she's had something to eat," Doc replied with surprising authority. He drew a microwaveable container of tomato soup out of his box and handed it to the girl. He watched while she took a few sips, and then he nodded. "Okay, you can ask your questions now."

Savannah sat in a chair beside the girl. "Let's begin with the basics. What's your name?"

"Rosemary Allen."

"And how old are you, Rosemary?" she asked.

"Twenty," Rosemary replied.

Savannah was pleasantly surprised. She would have guessed fifteen. "And what brings you here?"

"I'm in trouble."

Savannah's eyes dipped to the girl's distended abdomen, but Rosemary shook her head.

"I don't mean the baby." Rosemary clutched the sides of the blanket with clawlike fingers. "It's something worse. Much worse."

Savannah leaned closer. "Tell me about it."

Rosemary took another sip of soup then faced Savannah. "My mother died when I was very young. I barely remember her."

This seemed like an odd place to begin an explanation of why the girl found herself in her current circumstances, but Savannah nodded encouragingly.

"My father was gone a lot, so I was raised by a series of nannies and housekeepers. I never thought Father was neglectful," Rosemary added. "Just busy."

Hack sighed impatiently, and Savannah gave him a cross look. "I understand," she assured Rosemary.

"My father was protective—obsessive even—about my safety, so I didn't have a lot of freedom. I thought when I started college that would change, but it didn't. He enrolled me at George Washington University, just a few miles from our house. If I was ten minutes late getting home, he'd send someone to look for me." Rosemary's face brightened. "Then I met Chad."

"He's the father of your baby?" Savannah guessed.

Rosemary nodded. "And my husband. My father was furious when he found out we got married behind his back. But when I told him about the baby, he calmed down. He remodeled part of the house to make us our own apartment and even gave Chad a job at his company. I thought everything was going to be fine. But then Chad said they were trying to get him to do things at work that were wrong. Things that were *illegal.*"

Savannah felt a prickling of uneasiness.

"Chad was desperate to get away from my father and arranged for us to live with his parents until he could find another job. But when we told my father, he laughed. He said we weren't going anywhere. He took away our cell phones and our car keys. He withdrew me from school and made Chad ride to work with him every day. We were prisoners."

"Who is your father?" Savannah forced herself to ask.

Rosemary answered with obvious reluctance. "My father is Mario Ferrante."

Hack stopped pacing, and Doc's fidgeting ceased.

"That's it," Hack bellowed. "I'm calling the police."

Savannah held up a hand to stop him. "Not yet." Then she addressed Rosemary. "Do you know that your father helped kidnap my daughter a few months ago?"

Tears seeped out of Rosemary's eyes. "Yes, Chad told me. I'm sorry."

Savannah patted Rosemary's cold hand. "It certainly wasn't your fault."

Rosemary looked nervously toward the windows of the MP station. "Yesterday I ran away. Chad was supposed to come too. We were going to change our names and make a new life for ourselves where my father couldn't find us."

"But something went wrong?" Savannah guessed.

Rosemary's expression was bleak. "I had a routine doctor's appointment scheduled, and we decided that was our best opportunity to escape. While I was waiting to see the doctor, we'd slip out the back door and be gone before my father's driver got suspicious. But when the driver came to pick me up for the trip to the doctor, he said Chad had been delayed at work."

Savannah frowned. "But you escaped anyway? Alone?"

"Yes!" Rosemary sobbed. "Chad made me promise to go on alone if I had to, for the baby's sake. But I didn't really have a plan. Chad was supposed to be there to help me! I walked for hours, trying to stay in large crowds. Then I realized that I needed to change my description, so I found a drugstore and bought a bottle of Sun-In. I guess I used too much, because my hair keeps getting lighter." She lifted a damp, yellow lock. "I hope it doesn't fall out."

Savannah studied the splotchy mess, thinking that starting over might not be the worst that could happen to Rosemary's hair. "Let's not worry about that now," she recommended.

"I've got to help Chad and my baby, but I don't know how." Her lips quivered. "Finally I decided to come to you. You've defeated my father once, and you know how it feels to be separated from someone you love. So I hope you'll help me."

Hack shook his massive head. "Mrs. McLaughlin can't help you. She'd have to be crazy to take on your father."

Rosemary kept her eyes steadfastly on Savannah. "I don't have anyone else I can turn to for help."

Later Savannah wasn't sure what tipped the scales in Rosemary's favor. Was it empathy for the girl and her situation? Was it a desire to get some revenge against Mario Ferrante for the pain he'd caused her? Or was the excuse to see Dane again just more than she could resist? Smiling at Rosemary, she said, "I can think of one person crazy enough to take on *anyone.*"

Hack and Doc both stared back at her with amusingly horrified expressions.

"Hack, will you take us to my apartment? Rosemary needs a shower and some dry clothes. Caroline and I need to pack. Then we'll head to Dane's cabin."

"No," Doc whispered.

Hack kicked a chair.

"I strongly discourage you from this course of action," Doc tried.

Hack was less tactful. "Are you *crazy?*"

"Yes," Savannah admitted, too happy to be offended. She was going to see Dane, and under the circumstances, she knew he wouldn't turn them away. "Will you drive us, Hack?"

"What, you think I'm crazy too?" the big man demanded.

"I think craziness is a prerequisite for working with Dane." She turned to Doc. "You're invited too."

The frail man wrung his hands. "Savannah," he said sternly, "this is a mistake."

She laughed. "I've made so many mistakes. What's one more?" She took Rosemary by the hand and pulled her to her feet. She led the way to the waiting Yukon, confident that Doc and Hack would follow. They didn't really have much choice. All for one and one for all.

CHAPTER 1

SAVANNAH WAS LESS sure of Hack and Doc's commitment to their new cause once she and Rosemary were seated in the Yukon. Hack remained in the guard shack, conferring with the MPs and Doc. Savannah smiled over at Rosemary, who was shivering beside her.

"They are probably just working out some security details," she proposed as a possible explanation for the delay. "They'll come any minute."

Rosemary nodded uneasily. "I hope so. Chad needs help soon."

Savannah patted Rosemary's cold hand. "Don't worry. We'll rescue him."

Several more minutes passed before Hack and Doc exited the MP station. Hack walked around the Yukon to open the door by Rosemary.

"Please get out, Mrs. Allen," Hack requested. "Doc is going to take you to the hospital and have you checked by a doctor."

"That's not necessary," Rosemary assured him. "I'm fine."

"We won't know what's necessary until you've been to the hospital," Hack replied, respectful but firm.

Doc stepped up and ducked his head in to the vehicle. "You've been under a lot of stress lately, and you missed your last doctor's appointment," he reminded Rosemary. "While you're at the hospital, you can take a shower and eat a hot meal. I'll find you some dry clothes, and you'll be much more comfortable."

Rosemary turned to Savannah with frightened eyes. "I want to stay with you." Rosemary leaned closer. "I *trust* you."

"Mrs. McLaughlin is going to have to try to convince the Army to get involved in your personal problems," Hack answered for Savannah. "She'll get started with that while you're at the hospital."

Savannah wasn't thrilled with the adjustments Hack was making to her plan, but she knew his cooperation was essential, so she decided to embrace his alterations. "You can trust Doc," she told Rosemary. "And I think seeing a doctor is a good idea. That shouldn't take long, so we'll be together again in no time."

Rosemary was frowning as she scooted toward the open door. "They'll bring me back to you when we're finished at the hospital?"

Savannah nodded. "Of course."

Rosemary climbed out of the car, and Doc led her gently to his Bonneville. As Doc pulled out onto the street, two cars driven by Hack's men moved to follow him.

"How did you arrange an escort so quickly?" Savannah asked Hack.

He slid under the wheel. "A couple of phone calls while you were listening to that girl's sob story."

She ignored his unkind description of Rosemary's situation. "Now if you'll take me to get Caroline, we'll be ready to drive out to Dane's cabin as soon as Rosemary is through at the hospital."

If possible, Hack's scowl increased. "Maybe we should talk to General Steele before we bother Dane with this."

Savannah didn't think she'd have any trouble convincing the general to help Rosemary, but she couldn't be sure he'd assign the operation to Dane. Since Dane's involvement was essential—both in terms of ultimate success and her personal satisfaction—she had to approach him first. Once she got a commitment from Dane, they could talk to the general together.

Choosing her words carefully, Savannah said, "Dane wouldn't like it if we went behind his back. He'll want to decide for himself—not be told what to do. Even by General Steele."

Hack considered this for a few seconds and finally nodded. "Okay, we'll get Caroline and head to the cabin. But I can't guarantee you'll get a warm reception."

"There are no guarantees where Dane is concerned," she agreed. "But I do want to ask you for a favor."

He glanced over his shoulder. "Another one?"

She smiled. "This one's easy. Just don't tell Dane we're coming. I want it to be a surprise."

"You're afraid if he has advance knowledge of your visit that he'll leave," Hack accused.

She didn't deny it. "I do want to surprise him—but he does tend to avoid me, and I can't ask him to take the case if he's not there when we arrive."

Hack nodded, and she wasn't sure if he was promising to keep her secret or just agreeing that Dane avoided her. As they drove across Ft. Belvoir, some of her happiness dimmed. Maybe the whole thing was a catastrophically bad idea. But she wanted to see Dane, so she pushed her doubts aside as they pulled in front of her apartment.

Caroline was glad to see them, and the child's mood progressed to ecstatic when she found out they were headed to Dane's cabin. After Hack had motioned for the guards to join him outside, Caroline asked, "Are we spending the night in his guest room so I can see the sunrise?"

"If I can convince Major Dane to work on a new case, we are," Savannah replied. "Come help me pack."

"Where's Doc?" Caroline asked as she watched her mother take an overnight bag out of the closet. "Is he coming too?"

"I met a sick girl tonight, and Doc took her to the hospital," Savannah explained briefly. "He'll join us later."

"Is the sick girl coming with him?"

"Yes."

"What's her name?"

Savannah led the way into Caroline's room. "Rosemary."

"Can I play with her when she's feeling better?"

"She's not young like you. She's an older girl who might not want to play." Savannah removed clothing from Caroline's drawer and placed it in the bag. "Her husband is lost, and I'm going to ask Major Dane to help get him back."

"Major Dane found me," Caroline pointed out.

"Major Dane is very good at finding people," Savannah confirmed with a smile. "That's why I'm hoping he'll help Rosemary's husband."

Caroline followed her mother into the other bedroom and chattered ceaselessly about fishing at Dane's cabin and her Christmas gifts. While Savannah packed her own overnight bag, her thoughts were on Dane and their upcoming confrontation, so she had difficulty concentrating on Caroline's continuous flow of words.

Finally the bags were packed, and they were ready to go. On the way to the door, Caroline paused beside the Christmas tree. She pointed at her gift to Dane and asked, "Can we take this to Major Dane now?"

Savannah frowned. Their uninvited presence was going to be awkward enough without a gift he would be unprepared to reciprocate. So she shook her head. "Let's wait."

Caroline looked disappointed, but she left the gifts and joined her mother by the front door. The rain had stopped but the night air was still damp and cold.

Hack was standing on the sidewalk in front of their apartment, consulting with four of his security guards. When he saw Savannah and Caroline emerge from the apartment, he dismissed his men. He walked over to Savannah and said, "Let's get you settled in the Yukon." He reached down and relieved Savannah of the overnight bags.

Once Caroline was strapped in the backseat of the huge vehicle, Savannah closed the door and pointed at the men on the sidewalk. "Are they all coming with us?" she asked Hack.

"One will stay to watch the apartment while we're gone," he replied. "One will leave first and drive several miles ahead of us." His attention shifted to the group of his employees still gathered on the sidewalk. He pointed at one, and the designated man climbed into a dark sedan and drove off down the street. "The other two will drive directly ahead and behind the Yukon."

Savannah frowned. "Do you think that Mario Ferrante has already tracked Rosemary here?"

"I'm not taking any chances."

To avoid further alienating Hack, Savannah said, "Whatever you think is best."

Hack opened the back door of the Yukon without comment. Savannah climbed in beside Caroline, and he closed the door firmly.

Once Hack was settled behind the wheel, he put in a DVD for Caroline. Then they sat in the vehicle for fifteen minutes.

Finally, Savannah leaned over the seat and asked, "What are we waiting for?"

Hack glanced at Caroline, who had the headphones securely over her ears, before he responded. "We need to give the lead vehicle an adequate head start."

"How long is 'adequate?'" Savannah was frustrated by the delay. Now that she had decided on a course of action, she wanted to get the inevitable confrontation with Dane over.

"Just a few more minutes," Hack replied.

Savannah frowned. "What will you do if that first car is attacked by Mario Ferrante's men?"

Hack's gaze didn't leave the road. "Take you and Caroline to General Steele."

She turned and searched the road behind them but found no trace of Doc's old Bonneville. "And what about Doc and Rosemary? They're supposed to come with us."

"A set of MPs will escort them out later—assuming you convince Dane to get involved with her."

Savannah was determined to think positively. "Will two MPs be enough protection for them?"

His eyes met hers in the mirror. "I can't guarantee anyone's safety, but Doc knew the stakes when he agreed to help you with this crazy plan."

Savannah fought instant panic. She hadn't meant to compromise Doc's safety. "It would be wise to request additional help from the general so you can give Doc more protection."

"The *wise* thing would have been to send Rosemary Allen straight to the police," Hack said.

The exchange with Hack distracted Caroline from her movie. After pulling off her headphones, she asked her mother, "Is Hack mad at you?"

Savannah didn't want to be dishonest, so she said, "A little, but he'll forgive me."

This seemed to satisfy Caroline. "Do you think Major Dane will be surprised to see us coming to visit so late at night?"

Savannah smiled grimly. "He'll be surprised, all right."

"What do you think he'll say when he sees us?"

"I'm not sure." Savannah kept her tone light with an effort. In less than an hour she'd be with Dane. The very thought nearly took her breath away.

"He might say hi," Caroline suggested. "Or Merry Christmas!"

Savannah ruffled her daughter's hair. "He might."

Caroline put her headphones back on and returned to her movie. Savannah turned to look out the Yukon's tinted window and let her imagination run wild. When she saw Dane again, maybe he'd be sitting in front of his computer, staring at the screen. The living room would be dark and lonely. Then he'd hear a noise at the door. He'd look up, and she'd be standing there. His eyes would register surprise and, fleetingly, welcome.

She smiled at the dark glass. This scenario would happen only in her dreams.

Maybe he'd be sitting on the couch when they arrived, watching the embers of a dying fire. She'd tiptoe up behind him and put her hands over his eyes. While her fingers luxuriated in the feel of his skin, she'd demand that he guess who she was. He'd cover her hands with his and say her name. *Savannah.*

A small sigh escaped her lips. This, too, was a little optimistic.

So she lowered her expectations even more. Maybe he'd be in the kitchen, making a pot of his special hot chocolate. Once he got over the shock of seeing them, he'd pull extra mugs out of the cupboard and pour them all a cupful. Then they'd sit around the old table talking and drinking hot chocolate—almost like a family.

This scenario seemed the most likely, and she considered asking Hack to stop for doughnuts, but his stiff posture convinced her that this would be a mistake.

Savannah's fingers moved to the locket at her neck, and she allowed herself to think back to the night years before when Dane had given it to her.

* * *

Dane and his special ops team had been training intensely in preparation for the overseas operation. When the day of their departure finally arrived, Savannah was glad. Their lives were on hold until after the operation was completed, so she was anxious for them to go—and come home. Then Dane could marry her. He had asked her out to dinner the night before he left, but a last-minute transportation problem forced him to cancel. He promised to stop by as soon as he got things handled so she could wish him luck.

But as the hours passed without word from him, she struggled to stay awake. Finally she fell asleep on her couch and was awakened in the wee hours of the morning by Dane knocking quietly on her door. As she let him in, she apologized for her appearance. She was still wearing the dress she'd purchased for their date, but by then it was a wrinkled mess.

He drew her close and nuzzled her neck. "You're the most beautiful sight I've seen in days."

She knew this wasn't much of a compliment, considering the company he'd been keeping, but she smiled anyway. "Can I get you something to eat?"

"Naw," he declined, "I've got to get back to the post. We leave at seven, but I couldn't go without saying good-bye."

She frowned. "You don't want me to come to the airport to see you off?"

He shook his head. "*It's probably better if you don't.*"

"*You think my presence would make Wes uncomfortable?*" she asked, referring to the third member of their now extremely lopsided threesome.

"*I don't want to rub my good fortune in his face,*" Dane acknowledged. "*And I don't want to show my softer side to the men I'm about to lead into battle.*"

"*I understand.*" And she did. But she was disappointed.

He pulled back and smiled. "*I've got something for you.*"

When he removed the small jewelry box from his pocket, her heart skipped several beats. He had told her he was going to wait until after the operation to buy her ring, but apparently he'd changed his mind. "*Oh, Dane.*"

He handed her the dark blue velvet box. "*I hope you'll like it.*"

Her fingers trembled as she struggled with the tiny latch. "*I'm sure I will.*" Then the box popped open, exposing not the engagement ring she was hoping for but a small silver locket on a delicate braided chain.

"*I've never given my heart to anyone before,*" he whispered, and she forgot all about her longing for a ring.

"*I'll take good care of it,*" she promised as tears filled her eyes.

He kissed her softly. "*I know you will.*"

After lifting the locket out of the box, she extended it toward him. "*Will you help me put it on?*"

He took the necklace, and she twisted around so he could secure the clasp behind her. When the locket was in place, she turned back to face him. She pressed the little silver heart against her own. "*Now our hearts will always be together—even when we're apart.*"

He put his hand on top of hers. "*Forever.*"

She didn't want their time together to end, but he looked so tired, and he was leaving in just a few hours, so she knew he needed rest.

"*I guess you'd better go,*" she said as the tears spilled from her eyes onto her cheeks.

"*Yes,*" he agreed. He shed no tears but his reluctance was obvious. "*I'll be back in a few days.*"

She kissed him once more and then stepped away.

After he walked off into the darkness, Savannah changed clothes and went to bed, but she couldn't sleep. She tossed and turned for a few hours and finally got up. She was sitting in the dim, early-morning light, waiting until it was time to go to work, when a thought occurred to her. If she left right now she could make it to Andrews in time to watch Dane and his team board the plane. As long as she kept out of sight, there wouldn't be any problem.

Energized by the thought of seeing Dane again, even briefly and even if he didn't see her, she stood and grabbed her car keys. Then she drove to Andrews Air Force Base and was standing in the shadows of a fueling station when Dane and the team walked out.

Unlike other soldiers who were transferred openly, Dane's covert unit left without fanfare. They had no crowd waving good-bye and received no applause. But Savannah's heart was filled with almost unbearable pride as she watched them. She thought she had successfully hidden her presence until Dane looked up and made eye contact. If he was surprised, his face didn't show it.

She raised her hand in a small wave. He was good at reading her thoughts, so she hoped he understood that she expected no personal time with him. His mission had begun, and he belonged to the Army for the next week. He was with his men, including Wes, and she couldn't be a part of that world. All she wanted was to see him one last time before he left.

To her amazement, he walked away from his men and crossed the few yards that separated them. She knew she should care about Wes and his reaction to her presence, but she couldn't tear her eyes away from Dane.

"I thought we said our good-byes at your apartment," he said gently.

She looked behind him and saw all his men watching them with interest. "We did. I didn't come here to stay good-bye, just to see you leave."

He smiled. "I've got to go."

It didn't occur to her to beg him to stay. It would have been like asking him to be someone else. "I know."

He took a step away from her and then seemed to reconsider. He turned and studied her for a few seconds. Finally he shrugged and said, "What the heck." He gathered her into his arms, and with his men whooping and hollering their encouragement in the background, he pressed his lips firmly to hers. "That's for luck," he told her before trotting back to his men.

Savannah stood on the tarmac waving until the plane disappeared into the clouds above. As she left the airport, headed for work, she wiped her tears away. She was sad but not particularly worried for his safety. He was Dane. He was invincible.

The operation was expected to last a week. She was concerned only about how she would make it that long without him. She still felt awkward around Wes, but she was optimistic that given time, things would eventually work out between the three of them. If she had only known . . .

* * *

Gradually Savannah became aware of her present surroundings. She was in the car with Hack and Caroline—headed to Dane's cabin. She stared at the locket. When she'd married Wes, she put the locket away in a box where she kept the few treasured relics she had from her childhood. When she moved to Ft. Belvoir, after her most recent encounter with Dane, she'd found the locket, had it cleaned by a jeweler, and started wearing it again.

"We're here!" Caroline squealed, and Savannah was tempted to hide the locket under her blouse. But it was time Dane accepted that whether he liked it or not, he was a part of her life. So she lowered her hand to her lap and watched anxiously as Hack slowed the Yukon and turned onto the well-maintained gravel road that led to Dane's cabin.

Savannah noted that there were two of Hack's huge armed guards posted near the road. By now she was familiar enough with Hack and the way he operated to know that if two of his men were visible, there were probably several more nearby whom she couldn't see.

The presence of the guards put an end to her hope of surprising Dane. Apparently Hack or Doc or both had ignored her request and warned Dane of their impending arrival. She tried not to be mad. Over the past couple of months, she'd learned to think of the men as her friends, and she trusted them not only with her own life, but also with Caroline's. However, it had been foolish of her to think that they would put her wishes ahead of Dane's best interest. Their first loyalty was to Dane—and it always would be so.

As Hack parked the Yukon, Savannah's eyes scanned the backyard in search of Dane. All she saw were more of Hack's men, standing guard at opposite corners of the cabin. The obvious show of manpower seemed a little excessive—even for Dane.

Hack opened the door for her, and she climbed out, vaguely aware that behind her Caroline was fumbling to release her seat belt. But Savannah's attention was concentrated on the cabin. She moved toward the house, squinting to improve her night vision. All was still. Dane was nowhere in sight.

Swinging her eyes away from the house, she surveyed the yard. Dane's nondescript gray sedan was not parked in its usual spot. And finally she accepted the sad reality. Dane was not at his computer or in front of the fireplace or making a tasty cup of hot chocolate. When he found out she was coming, he left.

The pain was swift and sharp. By now she should have been immune to disappointment where Dane was concerned, but apparently she wasn't.

She put a hand to her chest and rubbed as if the hurt she felt could be erased so easily.

Oblivious to her mother's distress, Caroline stepped up beside Savannah and said, "Where's Major Dane?"

Savannah was too grief stricken to respond. She knew that Caroline needed an explanation. Savannah knew that she should be trying to think of another way to help Rosemary—since apparently the Dane option was out. But she could only stare speechlessly at the dark cabin and massage her aching heart.

Over and over he had told her that he didn't love her—that he didn't want her to be a part of his life. She had ignored him, certain that he would eventually give in to the feelings she was sure were there. It looked as though the time had come for her to accept no as his answer.

After blinking back tears of loss and self-pity, she was trying to muster the courage to turn around and face Hack when the sound of an approaching car engine filled the cool night air. Her heart pounded with hope. Seconds later a gray sedan emerged from the woods and came to a stop a few feet away. The driver's side door opened, and Dane climbed out.

The moonlight illuminated his face, and Savannah couldn't control a gasp as she drank in the sight of him. His longish, brown hair that curled around his ears. The dark gray eyes. The worn flannel shirt. The old blue jeans. Her eyes clung desperately to his, and she hoped he couldn't read her thoughts.

His expression didn't convey unrequited love or barely controlled passion, as she would have liked. Instead she saw annoyed amusement. But there was tension in his stance, and she smiled. If he felt the need to guard against her, she would consider that a small victory.

She walked over to him, and when they were only a few inches apart, she whispered, "Surprise."

The corners of his mouth curled up slightly in something between a smile and a snarl. "Hardly."

"Have you missed us?" she couldn't stop herself from asking.

"How could I?" he returned. "You call me every day." His eyes dipped to the locket around her neck. "I figured you would have thrown that away by now."

She reached up, and her fingers caressed the small heart. "I can't. It has too much sentimental value."

Savannah was waiting anxiously for Dane's response when Caroline hurled herself at him. "Major Dane!" she cried.

Dane lifted Caroline off the ground and hugged her to his chest—probably as much to defend himself from the child's onslaught as to express affection.

"Hey, Caroline," he said.

"Did you make us some hot chocolate?"

"I haven't made any hot chocolate for a long time," he told her. "But when I heard you were coming, I went to the grocery store, and the first thing on my list was hot chocolate mix."

Caroline craned her neck to see over his shoulder into the car, where several white plastic bags were nestled on the seat. "Did you get doughnuts too?"

He gave her a reproachful look. "I wouldn't expect you to drink hot chocolate without doughnuts!"

Caroline laughed. "I'll bet you got the jelly kind."

"Of course I did." He lowered Caroline until her feet rested firmly on the ground. "Will you help me get this stuff inside?"

"Sure," Caroline agreed. Then she reached in and pulled out two grocery sacks.

Hack joined them, looking around like he expected an aerial attack momentarily. "I don't like this," he muttered—as if anyone seeing his dire expression would conclude otherwise.

Savannah felt brave enough to voice her feelings now that it was too late for him to refuse to bring her to Dane's cabin. "Rosemary isn't even with us. So if by some miracle Mario Ferrante has tracked her, wouldn't he attack Ft. Belvoir instead of here?"

"He might have used his daughter to find you," Dane said with a frown to match Hack's.

Her exasperation mounted. "I wasn't exactly hiding."

"No," Dane said. "But you were safely on the post. Now you're vulnerable. If that was Ferrante's plan, he's already been successful."

"I told her it was crazy to come here," Hack said.

She stepped closer to Dane and put a hand on his arm. Through the soft flannel, she could feel the muscles of his forearm tighten in response to her touch. She wanted to press her face against his chest and listen to the comforting beating of his heart. But instead she drew him aside and whispered, "If I could just explain to you how pitiful Rosemary is, you'd understand why I took the risk. She's worried sick and is painfully thin and terrified."

He raised an eyebrow. "Sounds like you when you came to visit me in the prison a couple of months ago."

Savannah made a face. "On my worst day I never looked as pathetic as Rosemary did tonight."

"Is that so?" There was challenge in his voice.

"She's eight months pregnant, and she'd been standing in the rain for hours," Savannah told him. "Who knows when she last had a decent meal or a good night's sleep . . ."

He lifted his hands in surrender. "Okay, the Ferrante girl is more pitiful than you."

She narrowed her eyes at him before adding, "And I've been taking a little better care of myself lately."

His lips brushed her ear when he whispered back, "I can tell."

Hack spoiled the moment by reaching around them and into Dane's car. He yanked out the remaining grocery sacks with one, huge hand. Then he started walking toward the cabin. "If there's anything more dangerous than leading Ferrante here, it's talking out in the open."

Dane pulled free of Savannah's grasp. "You heard Hack. Everyone inside."

"Hack didn't want to come," she whispered to Dane as they walked. "So don't hold our visit against him."

"I gave Hack permission to bring you here," Dane surprised her by saying. "Only to protect Caroline, of course."

"Of course."

"Your decision to leave Ft. Belvoir wasn't the wisest thing to do."

Savannah's heart sank.

Then he gave her a rare, genuine smile. "But then I'm not a big fan of the smart approach."

She smiled back. "That's why I'm here." *Among other reasons,* she thought to herself.

He raised an eyebrow, and she wondered, not for the first time, if he really could read her mind. Embarrassed, she took Caroline's hand and led the little girl into the cabin.

Hack was putting away groceries—or throwing them into the appropriate cupboard to be more accurate—when they walked in. Savannah sidestepped him and hurried Caroline toward the living room.

"I'll get a fire going," Dane said as he came up behind them.

"I can help," Caroline offered. She moved to the wood stacked by the hearth and selected three evenly matched logs. She took them to Dane one at a time, and soon they had a blazing fire.

After warming her hands, Caroline turned and surveyed the room. Then she frowned and said, "How come you don't have a Christmas tree?"

Dane seemed puzzled by the question, as if this thought had never occurred to him. "Christmas tree?" he repeated.

"It's almost Christmas," Caroline told him. "So why don't you have a tree?" She glanced up at the empty mantel. "Or any stockings either?"

Hack returned from the kitchen and remarked, "Santa doesn't visit bad boys."

"Santa visits everybody," Caroline corrected him solemnly.

"Santa visits children," Savannah pointed out. "And Dane doesn't have kids." She regretted this remark immediately, but it was too late to call it back.

Caroline's face relaxed into a smile. "I'm here now!" She turned to her mother. "Can we go back to Ft. Belvoir and get our tree to share with Major Dane?"

Savannah was touched by the magnanimous offer but shook her head. If they left now, there was no way Hack would bring them back. "No, the post is too far away."

Caroline thought hard. "Well, can we go to a store and buy him one?"

Anything that required her to leave the cabin, and the operation planning that she hoped was about to take place, would be out of the question. Savannah was about to suggest a tree-shopping trip the next morning, after they were firmly entrenched, when Dane surprised her by offering another alternative.

"Tomorrow we'll go out into the woods and chop down a Christmas tree," Dane said. "Just like they do in all the corny holiday movies."

Caroline's eyes widened in amazement. "Can we really?"

"We really can," Dane confirmed. "Now let's get you settled in the guest room."

"How long are we going to stay with you?" Caroline asked.

He glanced at Savannah over his shoulder. "Just for tonight. You and your mother are headed back to Ft. Belvoir in the morning."

Caroline put her hand in his. "After we get your Christmas tree."

"Yes, after that," Dane agreed.

"What about the hot chocolate and doughnuts you bought?" Caroline wanted to know.

"We'll have it for breakfast," Dane promised.

Savannah followed Dane and Caroline out of the living room. He stopped by the landing to the stairs and examined the overnight bags that were arranged neatly on the bottom stair.

"That's mine," Caroline pointed out. Dane picked it up with his free hand, leaving Savannah to retrieve her own suitcase.

"Where will Rosemary sleep when she gets here?" Savannah asked.

Dane looked more annoyed than usual. "This isn't a hotel, and I'm not exactly set up for a bunch of uninvited, overnight guests."

She wasn't sure if he was referring to the limited number of bedrooms or his frequent and violent nightmares, but she decided the space issue was the safest one to address. "Rosemary can have the guest room. Caroline and I will sleep on the couch."

Dane shook his head. "You and Caroline will stay in the guest room. We'll put Ferrante's daughter in my room." He leaned close and whispered. "And I'll just wander around aimlessly all night so I don't mistakenly kill someone in my sleep."

Hack came out of the kitchen, and Dane stepped away abruptly.

Hack looked between Dane and Savannah before asking Caroline, "You going to bed now?"

She nodded. "But I'm not tired."

"It's still bedtime," Savannah insisted, anxious to get Caroline settled so she could convince Dane to take Rosemary's case.

Caroline looked up at Dane. "When is my mama's sick friend Rosemary coming?"

"Whenever the doctor says she can," Dane replied. He put a foot on the first step and then turned to tell Hack, "I'll be back in a minute, and we can talk about all this."

"Yeah, I've got a lot to say," Hack responded grimly.

Savannah didn't want a discussion about Rosemary's predicament to take place without her. Hack was adamantly opposed to their involvement, and by the time Savannah got an opportunity to plead her case, Dane might already be hopelessly swayed against it.

"Why don't you go on upstairs and put on your pajamas," she suggested to Caroline. "I need to talk to Major Dane privately for a minute."

"Hurry," Caroline requested. Then she ran up the stairs.

Once the child was gone, Savannah said, "You should wait until I get Caroline to sleep, and then we can all talk about the situation together."

"Why wait?" Dane asked.

"That would be wasting time," Hack added.

"Well . . ." Savannah searched for a plausible reason—besides the truth. She settled for, "I might remember details of Rosemary's story that Hack doesn't."

Dane raised an eyebrow. "Unlikely."

"No way," Hack agreed.

"You need my input to make a good decision," she persisted.

Dane gave her a patronizing smile, clearly indicating that he didn't think she could contribute anything useful.

Annoyed, she said, "I've already established my worth as a member of the team. Remember, I'm the one who put the watch with GPS into Cam's pocket so you could track him."

If anything, Dane's expression became more smug and insultingly tolerant. "You did do that." He smiled at Hack over her head.

She narrowed her eyes. "What? Didn't Wes's watch help you track Cam?"

"It did," Dane confirmed, still amused.

She looked back and forth between the two men, searching for an explanation for Dane's more-superior-than-usual attitude.

Finally Hack took pity on her and said, "The only reason Dane gave the watch to Cam in the first place was because of the GPS."

This information was an unpleasant surprise. "You gave the watch to Cam so you could track him?" she asked Dane. "That was the plan all along?"

He nodded. "It was a good plan—until Cam decided to impress you by making a gift of Wes's watch."

"So by giving the watch back to Cam, I was just reimplementing your original plan," she said miserably. "Fixing what I'd messed up by taking the watch in the first place."

Dane smiled. "Don't feel bad. It *was* a good idea—even if you weren't the first person to think of it."

She felt a little stunned but wasn't completely ready to give up ownership of the successful idea. "But you told General Steele that it was my idea."

Dane shrugged. "I don't mind sharing the glory."

"He *did* mind sharing that watch, though," Hack divulged in spite of the warning glare Dane sent his way. "Only a drastic situation would make Dane part with something that belonged to Wes *and* had a connection to you."

"That's ridiculous," he claimed. "I'd been looking for a chance to get rid of that watch."

Hack laughed. "Why did you need a chance? You could have just thrown it in the garbage."

Savannah studied Dane. He was definitely annoyed, but there was something more—a vulnerability that he usually kept hidden. She instantly felt much better.

"Go on and get Caroline to sleep," he said more sharply than necessary. "And then hurry back so Hack and I won't have to manage without your valuable input for long."

She smirked at him.

"You know where everything is." He handed her Caroline's suitcase and gave her one of his signature, insincere smiles. "Make yourself at home."

"Thanks," she muttered as she hurried up the stairs.

When she reached the second-floor landing, her eyes were drawn to Dane's bedroom. She'd only been inside once, when he was having an awful nightmare. It seemed like just yesterday. She could almost see him in the bed pushed against the wall, thrashing around. She could almost feel his arm against her neck, preventing air from reaching her lungs. Touching her lips with her fingers, she remembered the kisses they'd shared. Then she frowned at the thought of Rosemary Allen sleeping there. Even though she knew it was unreasonable, she wasn't comfortable with another woman being in Dane's private space.

Pushing these thoughts from her mind, Savannah walked across to the guest room. Caroline had changed into her pajamas and was zipping up her overnight case.

"I'm ready to say my prayer." Caroline knelt down on the floor beside the bed near the window.

Savannah knelt beside her. "Go ahead."

Once the prayer was finished and Caroline had crawled into bed, Savannah stretched out beside her daughter. With the excitement of the past few hours, she expected it to take Caroline a while to fall asleep. But apparently all the drama had been exhausting, because minutes later Caroline had succumbed to peaceful slumber.

Savannah stood and tucked the quilt carefully around her sleeping daughter. Then she hurried back downstairs. Dane and Hack were sitting at the kitchen table, already deep in conversation. They fell silent when she walked in and turned to look at her. Annoyed that despite her request to the contrary they had started without her, Savannah pulled out a chair and sat down.

"So what have you been talking about?" she asked. *As if I don't know,* she thought.

"Rosemary Ferrante," Dane replied.

"It's Rosemary Allen," Savannah corrected. "She's married."

"She'll always be Rosemary Ferrante," he corrected. "Husbands notwithstanding."

Savannah decided not to argue this point in the interest of time. "Maybe we can just call her Rosemary."

Dane objected to this as well. "Too personal."

Hack raised his eyebrows and said to Savannah, "You know Dane avoids personal involvement, don't you?"

She knew that as well as anyone, but she couldn't let Hack distract her. So she cleared her throat and pressed on. "I guess 'Ferrante's daughter' will do. You're still concerned that Ferrante is a threat to our safety. Hack's over-the-top reaction tonight proves that."

Hack muttered something unintelligible under his breath, and Savannah didn't try to decipher it.

"Ferrante is still a threat," Dane confirmed.

"And Rosemary provides you with an opportunity to lure him out of hiding so he can be arrested," she said.

"Yes."

Savannah was pleased. "So you'll take the case?"

Dane nodded. "I can't pass up a chance like this."

"It's a trap," Hack said with certainty.

Dane shrugged. "We'll be careful."

"Ferrante is extremely dangerous," Hack argued further. "I'm not sure it's possible to engage him *carefully*. And if you get killed, Dane, then Savannah and Caroline are vulnerable."

"Ferrante will never get the best of Dane," Savannah said. "Dane's too well trained."

Hack didn't back down. "His training has taught him it's foolish to risk his life and the lives of others with a futile operation."

"I'm the commanding officer," Dane reminded them unnecessarily. "I've decided to take the case. There will be no argument on that point."

Savannah was thrilled, but Hack looked so unhappy that she tried not to gloat. "I knew you'd help Rosemary."

Dane shook his head. "I didn't say that."

Savannah frowned. "You said you'd take the case."

"I said I'd use Ferrante's daughter to facilitate his arrest," Dane corrected her.

"And in the process of trapping Mario Ferrante, you'll rescue Rosemary's husband and help them get into some kind of government protection plan so they'll be safe from her father."

Dane laughed without a trace of humor. "I challenge you to give me *one* good reason why I should."

"Besides compassion for your fellowmen?" Savannah tried.

"I'll definitely need more than that," Dane assured her.

"Amen," Hack added.

She stood and addressed Dane. "Can I see you in the living room for a minute?" She shot Hack an irritated glance. *"Alone."* Without waiting for a response, she walked out.

When Dane finally walked into the living room, he said, "So do you really have something private to say, or are you just trying to lure me in here with hopes of getting a kiss?"

Her eyes strayed to his lips, but she forced herself to say, "I want to talk."

"About what, Savannah?" Dane asked in obvious exasperation. "If Ferrante really is holding the husband against his will, there's nothing we can do to help him."

"When you were in the Russian prison, didn't you hope someone would come and get you?"

Dane regarded her with a practiced blank look. There was a time when she would have thought her words didn't move him. Now she knew better. "Blackmailing General Steele worked out so well last time that you've decided to try the emotional variety on me. Unfortunately for you, I'm not as easy to manipulate as the general."

"Admit that you wanted to be rescued," she demanded.

"Okay." He put his arms around her in a flagrant attempt to distract her. "I'll admit that. But I was a soldier, sent into Russia by my country. They had an obligation to rescue me. I don't owe Rosemary Ferrante or her husband anything."

The feel of his arms around her was intoxicating, and Savannah fought to stay focused. Although she had personal motives for coming to Dane's cabin and for enlisting his help, she had made a commitment to Rosemary, and she meant to keep her word.

"I promised Rosemary," she told him firmly. "I can't be a part of this operation if it doesn't involve rescuing her husband."

Dane's lips formed a thin, irritated line, but he nodded. "I can't make any promises, but we'll try to locate the husband."

Savannah felt weak with relief. "And if you find him, you'll try to get him away from Ferrante?"

He pushed away from her and walked over to stare out the window. "Against my better judgment, I'll include Chad Allen's rescue as part of the operation. But I do have conditions."

This came as no surprise. "Of course."

"First, you have to recognize me as the leader of the operation and promise to obey me without question."

"Honor and obey," she repeated. "That sounds remarkably like a marriage vow."

He gave her an impatient look over his shoulder. "It's a condition of employment. If you don't agree, I don't take the case."

"You're the boss," she acquiesced.

"Also, for the duration of this mission, neither you nor Caroline go anywhere without some of Hack's men for protection."

She was used to being followed everywhere, so this was easy. "Okay."

"And I want laptops in addition to the computer equipment we've already got. Chasing Ferrante may require changing locations, and I want our information systems to be portable."

"If General Steele won't buy new laptops, I will," Savannah promised.

"And active duty pay for my men for another six months."

She had expected no less. "Again, if the Army can't cover that cost, I'll take care of it personally."

Dane frowned. "You gave all Wes's money away."

"I have the proceeds from the sale of my row house. I'm saving it to pay for Caroline's education, but I'll gladly spend part of it to end the threat Mario Ferrante poses to her safety."

"Hopefully General Steele will be generous."

"Hopefully," she agreed. "So I accept all your conditions."

He gave her a smug smile. "Of course you do."

"But," she added, "I have some of my own. Terms of *your* employment so to speak."

The smile disappeared. "Such as?"

"You have to be honest with me. I want to know what is going on this time."

He nodded. "Okay."

She narrowed her eyes at him. "Are you lying?"

He nodded again.

She joined him at the window and asked, "Why won't you trust me with the details? I'm a member of the team now, just like Doc and Hack. I have a respectable security clearance and I've proven my loyalty. I deserve to know the plan!"

This seemed to amuse him. "What you deserve has nothing to do with it. Secrecy is a part of any covert operation, and I can't guarantee that I won't withhold things from you. I distribute information on a need-to-know basis only."

She tried to hide her disappointment. "All I ask is that you be as honest as possible with me."

Their eyes met and held. "I will promise you that much."

"Thank you," she whispered.

He leaned closer. "But that most recent blackmail attempt cost you any chance you had of getting a kiss from me tonight."

"That's a big price to pay," she returned.

He rewarded her with a little smile. "I guess we'd better go break the bad news to Hack."

As he turned and walked back to the kitchen, Savannah's fingers strayed to her lips, and she wondered how the evening would have gone if she'd chosen a different form of persuasion.

CHAPTER 2

When Savannah entered the kitchen, she was surprised to see Doc sitting at the table with Dane and Hack.

"Look who's here," Dane said.

"Where's Rosemary?" Savannah asked.

"I left her at Ft. Belvoir," Doc said. "They're still running tests to be sure the baby is okay."

It was unlike Doc to be so insensitive to the needs of others, and Savannah frowned. "I can't believe you left her there alone."

"Doc came here because he was ordered to do so," Dane said in Doc's defense. "And the Ferrante girl is far from alone. Doc arranged for a couple of female MPs, a volunteer from the USO, and an Army chaplain to keep her company. Doc can go back and get her when the doctors determine that her condition is stable. In the meantime, I wanted him here so that we can formulate the plan as a team." He pointed at an empty chair. "Take a seat, and let's get to work."

She narrowed her eyes at him. "Now you *want* my input?"

He pulled out the chair for her. "We couldn't possibly succeed without you."

Gritting her teeth, Savannah sat down. "So you told them we're going to rescue Rosemary's husband and try to catch Mario Ferrante in the process?"

Dane nodded. "They're thrilled."

Doc was regarding her with a worried expression, and Hack looked like he wanted to strangle her.

Savannah propped her arms up onto the smooth, cool surface of the wooden table. "So the first thing we need to do is find Rosemary's husband."

"Actually," Dane corrected, "the *first* thing we need to do is figure out how to safeguard everyone involved."

Hack made a derisive noise. "Like that's possible."

Dane didn't seem concerned by Hack's skepticism. "I'm open to suggestions for a secure place to keep Ferrante's daughter."

"I vote for here," Savannah said. She liked the idea of everyone staying together at the cabin the way they had before when they were looking for Caroline. At the cabin they had easy access to all the expensive computers the Army had loaned them—not to mention the cozy fire and the Christmas tree Dane had promised Caroline.

Dane shook his head. "That's not an option. I'm flirting with bad judgment by getting involved in this case at all. I'd have to be completely crazy to risk my property *and* my peace of mind too."

Savannah couldn't hide her disappointment, which seemed to irritate Dane even more.

"Don't give me that look!" he commanded. "I've agreed to help my fellowmen."

Savannah was going to point out that his help was grudging and came with a list of conditions, but Doc intervened first. "The cabin isn't a safe location to keep Rosemary," he said.

"Why not?" Savannah asked, keeping her wary gaze fixed on Dane. "Hack's men are already providing incredible security, and I'm sure General Steele would send some soldiers if you think more men are necessary." She waved a hand around to encompass the pleasant space. "It seems perfect to me."

Dane grabbed her hand and pressed it to the table. "Even if I was willing to let Ferrante's daughter stay at the cabin—which I'm not—it wouldn't be safe. We have to *hide* her, and since there's been a parade of folks coming here all night, this cabin is out of the question."

"The FBI might loan us a safe house," Doc suggested.

Dane released Savannah's hand. "I want to limit the FBI's involvement as much as possible. We already know Ferrante has employees there."

"Ferrante has employees everywhere," Hack said. "He even had Cam."

"True," Dane acknowledged. "And because of that, no matter who we involve, we won't share critical information."

"Need to know," Doc murmured.

Dane nodded. "In the most emphatic sense."

"Wherever we put Rosemary, there has to be an adequate medical facility nearby," Doc contributed. "She could go into labor at any moment."

"Great," Hack muttered. "This gets worse and worse."

"So where should we put the girl?" Dane asked.

"I still vote for here," Savannah told him stubbornly. "There's a nice hospital in Fredericksburg, and if we do a good job of staging an exit—Ferrante won't know we circled back."

Dane scowled in her direction. "Go ahead and vote for here if you want to waste your vote. I've already told you that's not happening."

"I have the right to *waste* my vote if I want to," Savannah said defiantly. "And if you'd ever consider my suggestions instead of automatically dismissing them, your operations might run smoother."

Doc cleared his throat nervously. "Savannah has cast her vote." He turned to Hack. "What do you vote?"

"I vote for taking her to the DC police and letting them deal with her and her father," Hack said.

"I think Ft. Belvoir is the best place for her," Doc voted quickly—in an obvious attempt to avoid further conflict. "The security and medical issues can be easily managed there."

Dane considered this. "We'd have to get General Steele's cooperation."

"We'll have to get that anyway," Doc said. "There's no way we can take on something like this without his okay."

"What about the McLaughlins' mountain?" Savannah asked. "The Brotherly Love Farm people owe us a favor. Maybe Rosemary could stay there."

Dane glanced briefly at his men before saying, "That may be the craziest suggestion I've ever heard."

Hack nodded in silent agreement. Doc looked sympathetic but didn't comment.

Savannah refused to back down. "The mountain can only be reached by helicopter. It would be easy to secure."

"Ferrante could get experienced mountain climbers in there on foot with no problem," Hack disparaged. "The hard part would be getting our men and supplies onto the mountain—not to mention communication equipment, since the farm folks don't believe in it. And then there's the issue of a hospital, which the McLaughlins don't have on their little hideaway from the world."

Dane held up his hand to stop Hack's negative tirade. "For now, Ft. Belvoir is Plan A for Ferrante's daughter."

Hack seemed mollified, and Savannah wondered if Dane had discarded her idea so quickly to obtain exactly that result.

"What about Caroline and me?" she asked. "Can we stay at the cabin?"

"No one stays at the cabin." Dane's tone was final.

Savannah wouldn't beg, so she said, "And how are you going to find Rosemary's husband?"

"There is one guy at the FBI that I trust. Agent Gray," he said thoughtfully. "He's the organized crime specialist from Atlanta. I'll ask him to help us determine Chad Allen's location and what role he plays in Ferrante's organization."

"Chad Allen doesn't have a role in Ferrante's organization," Savannah reminded them. "He's being held against his will."

The men exchanged another look before Dane said, "It won't hurt to check. Now we have to figure out how and where to set our trap."

Savannah was concerned. "How will you lure Ferrante into the trap without actually using Rosemary?"

"Since the girl's condition makes using her too risky, we'll have to bait the trap with a decoy," Dane replied. "We'll find a woman who looks like her and set a trap somewhere else."

"Who's going to find a look-a-like?" Doc wanted to know.

"Why waste time looking?" Hack said, a challenge in his tone. He pointed at Savannah. "She'll do."

Savannah gaped at him in astonishment. "Me?"

Hack nodded, his eyes still on Dane. "Why not? This whole thing is her idea. She should take risks just like the rest of us."

"It's okay with me," Dane agreed.

Savannah was even more astounded. "You're going to let me be a part of the operation?"

Dane shrugged. "Why not?"

Savannah was now speechless.

"She's about the right height," Hack said.

"Her hair's the wrong color," Doc pointed out.

"That's easy to fix," Hack countered. "And she's *available*."

"She is that," Dane agreed.

Savannah's surprise gave way to an undeniable thrill. Dane was going to allow her to participate actively in the operation. Would wonders never cease?

"She's already on the Army's payroll," Doc remarked. "So she won't cost any extra."

"And I do trust her," Dane cut his eyes over toward Savannah, "to a point."

Savannah pressed her hands against her flat midsection. "I'm not pregnant."

"We can get you a fake pregnant stomach at a costume shop," Doc told her. "And with some black hair dye, from a distance you would resemble Rosemary."

"So once I'm disguised, you'll put me someplace safe and let Ferrante know where I am," Savannah clarified. "Then we'll wait for him to come after me so you can arrest him?"

Dane nodded.

"This is our plan?" Hack nearly shouted.

"So far," Dane acknowledged.

Hack held out his hands in supplication. "Please tell me you're joking. We've never gone into anything this big and this dangerous with so little reconnaissance!"

"We can't wait," Dane's tone was firm. "The element of surprise is the only thing we have going for us."

"We're good at thinking on our feet," Doc said.

Hack shook his head, and his braids danced. "It's bad enough that we're taking on this mission at all, but to do it with haphazard planning is irresponsible."

"If we don't know what we're doing ourselves, how can Ferrante figure it out?" Dane quipped.

Hack wasn't amused. "I'm afraid he'll figure out our plan *before* we do and be waiting on us when we get wherever it is we're going."

Savannah tried to overlook Hack's pessimism. "How will we keep Ferrante from knowing it's a trap?"

"We may not be able to," Dane admitted. "In which case we'll have to hope he wants his daughter back bad enough to come anyway."

Doc refocused their attention on the matter at hand. "We'll need a place to set up the decoy operation."

Dane looked at Savannah. "Not here, in case that's what you were about to suggest."

"Where then?" she asked.

Dane shrugged. "Someplace where Ferrante doesn't have many resources."

"If there is such a place in the world," Hack said morosely.

"Well, someplace he's less familiar with than the DC area," Dane conceded.

"Assuming we were able to come up with such a place," Hack didn't sound confident, "how would we feed him only the information we want him to have?"

"And how will we monitor Ferrante's movements?" Doc asked.

Dane stared at the ceiling. "What we really need is an inside man—someone Ferrante trusts and would keep close by."

Hack laughed. "There's no way you'll turn any of his people, especially the ones close to him. Crossing Ferrante means death—not only for you but for your family and friends. There's nothing you could offer one of his top guys to make them risk it."

"I can think of one person who might be willing to sell Ferrante out," Dane said thoughtfully. "But only because he has nothing left to lose."

Everyone turned to stare at him.

Savannah said, "You can't seriously mean . . ."

"Cam," Dane finished. "Cam's military career is over. He feels responsible for Wes's death, and he may never see his kids again. All because of Ferrante."

"That's enough to make someone bitter," Hack agreed.

"But he's in prison at Ft. Lewis," Savannah pointed out.

This detail didn't seem to concern Dane. "That can be worked around."

"He kidnapped Caroline and tried to kill you," Savannah reminded him. "We can't *trust* Cam."

Dane nodded. "It's safer that way. When you trust people, that's when you set yourself up for trouble. Surely you've learned that by now."

Savannah still believed in trust and love, but she knew this wasn't the time or place to try to change Dane's cynical attitude toward both. So she kept her opinions to herself.

"Can you really get Cam out of prison?" The possibility seemed to encourage Hack.

Dane turned to Doc. "What do you think? Can you find a technicality and manipulate it in our favor?"

"I'll try," Doc said. "But this is another area where we're going to need the general's help."

"That shouldn't be a problem," Dane replied. "The general's going to love this plan."

"What plan?" Hack grumbled.

"The one I come up with by the time I present it to him," Dane replied.

"I still don't like the idea of involving Cam," Savannah felt it necessary to say. Her memories of their last time together were still fresh on her mind.

Hack glared at her. "That's the only part of this whole thing that I *do* like. We may not be able to trust Cam, but we do know him. Surprises can ruin the best plan, and this one sure as heck ain't the best."

"There's got to be another way," Savannah pleaded with them.

Dane looked up. "And as soon as you figure out the *better* way, we'll abandon this one. But until then, we'll plan on springing Cam from prison and reintroducing him into Ferrante's camp."

"Won't Mario Ferrante be suspicious if Cam is released from prison and shows up on his doorstep, anxious to work for him again?" Savannah tried. "Especially right after Ferrante's daughter disappears?"

Dane shrugged. "Probably. We'll take that into account."

Now Savannah was getting desperate. "How can you be sure that Cam will agree to be a part of the operation?"

Doc cleared his throat, and all attention turned to him. "I'm sure Cam will help us. He's anxious to make amends and earn a place on the team again."

Dane raised an eyebrow. "And you know this because . . ."

"Because I visit him," Doc explained simply. "In prison."

This announcement caused Dane to scowl and Hack to laugh.

"Doc, in a previous life I'll bet you were a mother," Hack said.

Dane's displeasure was obvious. "In this life he might as well be one."

"I hope Doc is right," Savannah said. "But if Cam won't agree to help us, what will we do?"

"We could use Cam without his knowledge," Hack suggested. "By planting a secret tracking or listening device on him. Or both."

"Keeping Cam out of the information loop would have its advantages," Dane said thoughtfully.

"Or we might try a combination," Doc proposed. "Ask for his help but plant a tracking device too. And only tell him what we want Ferrante to know."

Hack smiled grimly. "Loyalty insurance. I like that."

"Then that's what we'll do." Dane turned to Doc. "Look over Cam's case file for something we can use to get him out of prison. Hack, you talk to the spy folks at Belvoir and see what options we have for tracking Cam—with and without his knowledge."

Both men nodded.

"How are we going to pay for this?" Hack wanted to know. "An operation on this scale won't be cheap."

"You're all still on the Army's payroll, so it won't cost the Army anything to assign you to the case officially," Savannah said. "And the general wants to get Ferrante as much as we do, so he'll probably be willing to appropriate additional funds and equipment. I'll take care of any other expenses."

Dane looked at her. "Okay, I need you to make a list of things you'll be asking General Steele for when you call him."

"Why do I have to call him?" she demanded. "You're in charge of this operation. You should call him."

"Being in charge means you get to pass off the unpleasant jobs to someone else," Dane explained in his most condescending tone. "And do I need to remind you who dragged us all into this?"

She shook her head in resignation. "No."

"Or that you agreed to obey me without question or complaint?"

Savannah narrowed her eyes at him. "You have a bad habit of exaggerating."

"Are you going to support me as your commanding officer?" Dane pressed.

"Yes."

"Then start your list." Dane waited until she had a pencil and paper ready. "Ask General Steele to classify this as a sanctioned covert operation. That gives us legal and physical protection through the Army—but latitude when it comes to military procedure. Also see if he'll finance at least part of it. If not, Caroline's college fund can make up the difference. If we still come up short, I guess we'll do a bake sale."

Hack laughed, and even Doc, who tried hard not to side against Savannah on most issues, smiled.

"Very funny." Savannah tapped her pencil on her list.

"The general might be able to get us some financial help from the FBI too," Dane continued. "But any assistance the general gives us with getting Cam out of prison will have to be received with stealth. Cam's lawyer is paid by Ferrante, so his release needs to look completely legitimate, and there can be no hint of the Army's involvement. In fact, the general should probably make a public show of outrage when Cam is released."

"The general's good at outrage," Hack said.

"Tell me something I don't know." Dane stopped behind Savannah so he could read over her shoulder. He pointed at her last entry. "Tell the general that Doc will contact him as soon as he finds a legal loophole."

Savannah wrote frantically to keep pace with his demands.

Dane resumed his pacing. "And since we're short a man—thanks to Cam—we'll need to bring in someone else."

Savannah looked up. "Wigwam's already on the Army's payroll as a member of the team. How about him?"

Dane shook his head. "He's got a new baby, and this operation could be dangerous. It's team policy to keep family men out of the line of fire. I'm thinking Steamer."

"You couldn't lure Steamer away from his lucrative real estate business in Las Vegas before," Hack said. "What makes you think you can do it now?"

"Steamer doesn't believe in 'One for all and all for one'?" Savannah asked.

"Some team members are more committed to the concept than others," Dane said tersely. "And you'd better use that silly motto sparingly if you want me to work on this case."

Before Savannah could come up with a sufficiently scathing reply, Dane turned to Hack.

"If Steamer won't volunteer, General Steele will make it mandatory," Dane said confidently. "The only other thing we need from the general is our new laptops."

Hack perked up. "Laptops?"

Dane smiled. "Savannah has agreed to buy us all the finest laptops available if the general won't spring for them."

Hack grinned for the first time since they'd seen Rosemary Allen at Tulley Gate. "Sweet."

"Why don't you pick them out for us," Dane requested.

Hack's eyes were shining with excitement. "The spy guys at Belvoir have been working on a prototype laptop that's small, operates off of satellites, and, best of all, leaves no trace of forced entry."

"So it's easy to carry around, can connect to the Internet anywhere, and when you invade secure databases, you can do it invisibly," Dane summed up.

"Yeah," Hack confirmed. "It's like a work of art."

"See if you can get four of them," Dane said. "And while you're at it, get us all new satellite phones—with untraceable numbers of course."

Hack nodded. "Of course."

"And have them send the bill to Savannah at General Steele's office."

"Maybe I can get a military discount," Hack joked, and Dane laughed along with him.

"What's next?" Doc asked, gently nudging them back to the purpose for their meeting.

Hack's expression became more serious. "If Savannah goes to some yet-to-be determined place away from Washington, DC impersonating Rosemary to draw Ferrante out of hiding, what will we do with Caroline? She can't be anywhere near the trap location."

This was something Savannah hadn't considered, and she immediately forgot to be mad at Dane. "I won't be able to take her with me, obviously."

"Obviously," Dane agreed.

"We could leave Caroline at Ft. Belvoir with General Steele again," Doc suggested.

Hack shook his head. "If that's where we're keeping Ferrante's daughter, we don't want Caroline there. That would make it too easy for Ferrante to kill two birds with one stone." He glanced at Savannah. "Just a figure of speech."

She did her best to smile at him. "I know."

"What do you think about taking her to stay with her grandparents in Colorado?" Dane asked.

"Are you kidding me?" Savannah objected. "A few minutes ago that was the dumbest suggestion you'd ever heard."

"It was a dumb suggestion for where to put Ferrante's daughter," Dane corrected. "It would be a good, safe place for yours."

"What about the concerns you mentioned," she asked. "Like the lack of communication equipment and the difficulty in getting men and supplies in?"

"Caroline won't be a primary target, so she won't require a huge security force," Dane explained calmly. "And the fact that there are no communication capabilities actually works to our advantage. Fewer ways for Ferrante to collect information we don't want him to have."

"The McLaughlins already think I'm a terrible mother," Savannah murmured. "If we send Caroline back so soon, they'll be *sure* I'm a terrible mother."

"We'll take Caroline there ourselves and explain the situation," Dane consoled her. "Once they understand that the child might not be safe anywhere else, I'm sure they won't think too badly of you."

She smirked at him. "I feel so much better."

Before Dane could reply, Doc said, "I'll stay with Caroline on the mountain during the operation. I promise to protect her with my life."

Savannah knew that Caroline would be safe with Doc, but she was still annoyed with Dane, and just the thought of being separated from her daughter made her ill. She did her best to hide her feelings and nodded at Doc. "Thank you."

"That will work," Dane agreed. "As long as we get Steamer, I can spare Doc to watch over Caroline."

Savannah narrowed her eyes at him. "I really appreciate your generosity."

"What will we tell the farm people?" Hack asked.

Dane considered this for a few seconds. "We'll fabricate a threat scenario."

"Against the Brotherly Love Farm?" Savannah asked skeptically.

"Even loving people have enemies," Dane assured her.

"If you convince the farm people they are all in danger, we could bring in troops from Ft. Carson again," Hack said.

Dane nodded. "If we convince them that the danger is bad enough, they'll be begging us for protection."

Savannah shook her head in amazement. "Lies come so easily to you."

Dane smiled. "Thanks."

"I didn't mean that as a compliment."

"I know," he replied. "Lies come even easier to Steamer. We'll let him work out the details of the scam when he gets here."

Savannah decided to let this pass. "I'm going to call General Steele before it gets any later."

Dane turned to Doc. "You work on getting Cam out of jail. Hack, keep tabs on our security detail. I don't want to have to worry about whether we're safe here. Then dig into Ferrante's daughter and her story. I want to verify every detail."

Savannah hadn't expected Dane to trust Rosemary, and she wasn't surprised by this assignment.

"And I'll call Steamer and tell him that his life of luxury is coming to a temporary end," Dane concluded.

"It's about time," Hack muttered. "He's probably gotten all soft and lazy."

"Probably," Dane agreed. "But there's nothing we can do about that. Everybody get at least a few hours of sleep, and we'll reconvene in the morning."

The men stood as the meeting adjourned.

"What about Rosemary?" Savannah asked.

Dane looked annoyed. "What about her?"

"When is she coming?"

"Didn't I say that they were going to call from the hospital at Ft. Belvoir when she was ready?"

Savannah frowned. "Yes, that's what you said. But then, you don't always tell the whole truth and nothing but the truth. Especially to me."

Hack laughed. "She's got you there."

Dane pushed his chair under the table. "I swear on all I hold dear that I'll let you know the moment the girl gets here."

Savannah searched his words for deceit and his face for signs of guile. Finding neither, she finally nodded. "Thank you."

"Call the general and let me know what he says before you go to bed," he said over his shoulder as he walked into the living room.

Savannah scowled at his back and then waved good night to Hack and Doc before heading up the stairs.

Despite Dane's presumptuous attitude and his insistence that she call and beg the general for help, Savannah felt optimistic. It was good to be back in the cabin, working with the team, sparring with Dane. She turned right at the top of the stairs and opened the door to Dane's guest room. Caroline was sleeping soundly, tangled in the covers. Savannah straightened the old quilt and then dialed General Steele's private number on the cell phone. He answered on the second ring.

"I'm sorry to bother you so late," Savannah apologized, "but we have a situation, and we need your help. Is this line secure?"

"It is." There was a brief silence, and then the general added, "By *we* I suppose you mean you and Dane."

"Yes," she confirmed. "And Doc and Hack."

"I heard about the incident at the Tulley Gate," the general surprised her by saying. "So I'm sure this also involves Ferrante's daughter?"

"Dane has agreed to help rescue Rosemary's husband," Savannah said. "And in the process he hopes to capture Mario Ferrante."

"That's a pretty ambitious undertaking," the general remarked.

"And expensive," Savannah added. "We'll need your help."

"Putting Ferrante behind bars is very high on my priority list," the general said. "So I'll do whatever I can to assist."

Savannah sighed with relief. This was going to be easier than she had expected. "Dane wants to run it as a covert operation, so I won't give you any details at this point. But we'll need you to sanction the operation and officially assign Dane's special ops team."

"Consider that done."

"And we'll need your financial backing."

"Keep things reasonable," the general requested. "And I'll set up a support team here to serve as a hub for all data that is collected during the mission from surveillance teams, etc. They can also monitor Mario Ferrante and satellite phone calls between the operation's participants. I'll have shifts work twenty-four hours a day so information will always be available to Dane."

Savannah was impressed and grateful. "That sounds great."

"I'll get the support team's secure contact number to Dane once I have it set up."

"I'm sure he'll appreciate that," Savannah said. Then she added, "And I'll need some time off."

"You're on indefinite leave. As you need additional equipment or personnel, just let me know."

"Thank you," Savannah said with feeling. "And now there's just one more thing. Dane wants to get Cam out of the prison at Ft. Lewis."

The general laughed. "You saved the best for last. I don't see any possible way that can be accomplished—especially not within a tight timeframe."

"I don't see it either, but with Dane, nothing is impossible. Doc's working on it, and once he comes up with a loophole, we might need you to help—discreetly of course."

"Of course."

"Doc will be in touch with you when he has the details worked out."

"I'll be waiting anxiously to hear what Doc comes up with," the general replied.

"Thanks."

"Your gratitude is a little premature, since I haven't actually helped you yet."

"We appreciate that you're willing to help us," Savannah said. Then she told the general good-bye and closed the phone.

More than satisfied with the general's cooperation, Savannah changed into her pajamas. She collected her toiletry items and walked downstairs to the bathroom. During the entire process of brushing her teeth and washing the surviving traces of makeup off her face, she was thinking about Dane and how pleased he was going to be when she reported that she had gotten the general to give them everything on his list. Praise from Dane was rare, but this time she deserved it, and she was determined to bask in the moment.

Of course, she was going to have to find him first. She planned to begin her search in the living room. If Dane wasn't there, she'd try the kitchen and finally venture outside if necessary. After repacking her toothbrush, Savannah gathered her things and opened the bathroom door. Dane was standing there, glowering.

She couldn't control a startled gasp and almost dropped her makeup bag. "Well, I guess I don't have to search the premises to give you a report on my conversation with the general," she said, trying to mask the fact that he'd scared her to death.

He completely ignored her reference to General Steele and instead demanded, "Why are you running around in your pajamas? It's indecent!"

Savannah glanced down at her thick flannel nightwear. The pajamas were at least as modest as the clothes she wore during the day and in no way indecent. And she resented his trying to boss her.

She lifted her chin in defiance. "Since when is what I wear your business?"

"Since you're staying at my house," he retorted.

"I wore my pajamas around your house the last time I stayed here," she reminded him. "And you didn't object then."

"Before it was just you and me," he shot back.

She raised an eyebrow. "And we both know that you are completely immune to me, no matter how I'm dressed." She brushed past him and stalked up the stairs.

Caroline's sound sleep was the only reason Savannah didn't slam the door when she walked into Dane's guest room. Who did he think he was anyway? Ordering her around and accusing her of inappropriate behavior? She wanted to be mad, but when she climbed into bed and pressed her face to the pillow, it smelled distinctly of Dane. This caused her to wonder if in her absence he had been sleeping in the guest room—in *her* bed.

This was a fascinating concept that deserved much consideration. She planned to mentally explore the possibilities, but with her face against the cool, cotton fabric, savoring the surrogate contact with Dane, her eyes grew heavy, and she fell asleep.

CHAPTER 3

SAVANNAH WAS AWAKENED later by a noise outside her door. With sleep-blurred eyes she watched the doorknob to the guest room turn and a thin arc of light cut into the darkness. Dane was standing in the doorway, backlit by the light in the hallway. His face was shadowed, his stance stiff.

When he reached toward her, she couldn't control a squeal. "Dane!"

He jerked his hand back and whispered harshly, "What?"

She sat up in the bed. "I thought you were sleepwalking."

Even in the darkness she could see his disdain for her remark. "Well, I'm not."

At this point, Hack and Doc joined them. Flanking Dane, they looked around the room.

"We heard you scream," Hack explained.

"Is everything okay?" Doc asked a little breathlessly.

Hack flipped on the light switch, and Savannah held up a hand to shield her eyes. He looked first at Caroline, sleeping soundly despite the commotion. His gaze moved to Savannah, who sat clutching the bedcovers to her chest. His gaze finally settled on Dane. "I don't see a problem."

"There's no problem," Dane confirmed. "I just came in to check on Caroline and startled Savannah."

She didn't contradict him, although she knew his statement wasn't completely true. His reasons for entering the room may have involved concern for Caroline's safety, but he'd walked straight toward Savannah. This was something else to think about and savor later.

Dane addressed his men. "You two can go back downstairs now. I'll be there in a minute."

Once Hack and Doc had left, Savannah cleared her throat and asked, "Have you heard from Rosemary?"

"The doctors are afraid she might go into premature labor, so they are keeping her in the hospital at Ft. Belvoir. She's safe there."

Savannah shook off the last vestiges of sleep and swung her legs over the side of the bed. "But she's alone and afraid. I need to go and explain the situation and reassure her that we're working to get her husband away from her father."

"I don't want you anywhere near Rosemary Ferrante," Dane said.

Savannah walked over to stand in front of him. "And I don't want her to think I've deserted her. Why is what you want more important?"

His expression hardened. "Because I'm the commanding officer of this operation. If you visit Rosemary Ferrante, you will be disobeying a direct order. If you plan to be a part of the team, you need to remember who is in charge."

Savannah squared her shoulders. "How am I supposed to tell the difference between direct orders and suggestions?"

"From now on, assume everything I tell you to do is a direct order," he told her. "If I'm making suggestions, I'll be sure to specify that so we can avoid confusion."

Several sarcastic responses came to Savannah's mind, but before she could choose just one, Dane continued.

"I won't always have the time or the inclination to explain my orders, but in this case I have both. We have to be cautious in case this whole thing is a trap set by Ferrante to get you or Caroline or both."

The broader implications of his words became clear. "Rosemary was never coming here," Savannah said. "That's why we were separated at Tulley Gate."

Dane nodded. "It was a security measure Hack wouldn't compromise on."

"And why didn't you just tell me that?"

He expelled a long-suffering sigh, as if she required more of his limited patience than the average person. "We discussed this a little while ago. On every operation there is information that has to be distributed on a need-to-know basis. In this case, you didn't need to know my plans for Ferrante's daughter."

"So there are elements of this operation that Hack doesn't know?" she pressed, and he looked mildly uncomfortable. "And Doc?"

Now he had the decency to look ashamed.

"Of course not," she answered for him. "The need-to-know aspects apply only to me."

"Look at this as an opportunity to prove yourself," he suggested.

She hoped it was too dark for him to see the pain in her eyes. "Why do I have to prove myself?"

"Maybe that was a poor choice of words," he said. "But whether you like my decisions or not, for the rest of this operation I'll distribute information as I see fit. If you can't accept those terms, tell me now, and I'll get someone else to impersonate Ferrante's daughter."

She looked into his eyes. "I want to trust you."

"If you'll remember, trusting me worked out pretty well for you last time."

She glanced at Caroline. "Yes, you came through in the end." In her peripheral vision, she saw his expression relax slightly, and she turned back to face him. "Did you call the FBI about Rosemary's husband?"

His expression hardened again. "Agent Gray has an undercover guy inside Ferrante's camp. The plant doesn't have access to sensitive information, but he was able to confirm that Chad Allen is a high-level member of the organization and goes everywhere with Ferrante. So if we take Allen out, we'll be kidnapping him more than rescuing him."

"He wants to get away from Ferrante so he can be with Rosemary," she insisted. "He's just playing along until he gets the opportunity to leave."

"Savannah, you claim you want honesty and to be treated like a member of the team, but as long as you cling to naive fantasies, how do you expect to be taken seriously?"

"I do believe in love," she confirmed. "And I know how it feels to lose it. I want to help Rosemary get her husband back so she doesn't have to live with that same pain."

"That terrible pain of losing a husband?" he asked with an edge to his voice.

Savannah felt tears stinging her eyes, and she blinked them away. "Losing Wes *was* terrible," she agreed. "But I was referring to the loss of *love*. The loss of you."

Dane pulled her close and whispered, "I'd be willing to bet everything I have that this whole thing is a setup, and the husband has been in on it from the first."

She grabbed two fistfuls of his flannel shirt. "Please believe in love again, just this once. Just for me."

He scowled, but she saw his lips tremble and knew her words had penetrated his defenses. "How can you trust Ferrante's daughter?"

She shrugged. "I just know she loves her husband, and if you can get him away from Ferrante, maybe they have a chance for happiness."

He covered her hands with his. "You want me to ignore my instincts and years of military training in the name of love?"

"If you trust Rosemary's love now, I'm hoping that someday you'll be able to trust my love for you." She paused to lick her lips before adding, "And yours for me."

He pulled her hands away from his shirt and stepped back. "Don't count on that, no matter how this operation turns out."

"Please," she repeated.

He gave her a curt nod that she took as reluctant agreement and said, "We'll do our best to get the kid out—even if he doesn't want to leave. Now go back to sleep for a couple of hours. It's going to be a long day." He turned and walked out of the room, closing the door firmly behind him.

* * *

After Dane's interruption to her sleep and peace of mind, Savannah didn't expect to get any more rest. But she must have dozed off, because she was awakened three hours later by the sound of a knock on the door. She had just opened her eyes when Dane walked into the guest room.

"Time to get up," he announced.

Savannah sat and stretched her hands over her head. "You're doing your own dirty work now, I see."

Caroline rubbed the sleep from her eyes and crawled to the edge of the bed. "Good morning, Major Dane."

His expression softened immediately. "Hey, Caroline. I came to get you so we could watch the sunrise."

Caroline scooted over to make room for Dane on her bed. "I'm ready."

"I was thinking that we could watch it from the kitchen window," Dane suggested. "That way I can make hot chocolate at the same time."

Caroline sprang from her bed and grabbed Dane's hand. "Hurry and come down, Mama," she said to Savannah as she pulled Dane toward the door. "I'll save some hot chocolate for you."

Savannah watched them leave with a combination of confusion and wonder. It hurt that Dane found it so easy to express affection to Caroline and so impossible to do the same for her. Anxious to join them, she stood up and made the beds. Her hand lingered on the pillow as she smoothed it. She'd have to think of some way to trick Dane into admitting that he'd been sleeping in the guest room during her absence.

By the time Savannah arrived in the kitchen, the others were gathered around the old wooden table, eating doughnuts and drinking hot chocolate.

"Good morning," Doc greeted, and she gave him a smile.

Hack didn't even glance up, so she knew he was still mad at her. Dane looked rumpled and grumpy, and she felt sure he hadn't slept at all. So things weren't perfect, but they were all together, and Savannah decided to be satisfied with that for the time being.

"There's your cup," Caroline pointed out for Savannah's benefit. "And we have lots of doughnuts."

Savannah helped herself to a doughnut and sat down in an empty chair.

"The sick girl still isn't here," Caroline said. "What's her name again?"

Savannah took another bite of doughnut. "Rosemary."

"Where's Rosemary?" Caroline asked.

Hack made a growling noise under his breath.

"Ft. Belvoir," Savannah replied. "The doctor said she has to stay in the hospital."

The fact that Caroline's mouth was full didn't interfere with her ability to make conversation. "Is Major Dane going to help her find her husband?"

"Yes, helping Rosemary is the most important thing in the world to Major Dane," Savannah assured Caroline, earning a glare from Dane.

Doc picked up a box of doughnuts and extended it toward Savannah. "Would you like another one?"

She knew his offer was an attempt to avoid an escalation of hostilities, and to be cooperative, she selected a chocolate glazed with cream filling. "Thanks. These are my favorite."

Dane handed her a napkin. "You'll need this."

She frowned. "I can't possibly have chocolate on my face already."

"Just planning ahead," he replied.

She made an effort to eat the doughnut neatly, but in the end the napkin was necessary. Annoyed that once again Dane had been right, she was wiping the last of the glaze from her fingers when Caroline climbed down from her chair.

"I'm going to put on a coat," she said. "Then we can get our Christmas tree."

"I don't really need a tree . . ." Dane started to say.

"Everybody needs a tree for Christmas," Caroline said.

"Not everybody," Dane countered.

Caroline frowned. "You promised."

She'd found the magic words. He caved with a sigh. "Okay. But hurry. We've got a lot of work to do this morning."

Savannah followed her daughter upstairs and supervised the dressing process. Once Caroline was sufficiently swathed in warm clothing, they returned to the living room, where the men were waiting.

"This won't take long," Dane muttered. "Doc, be prepared to report on your assignment when I get back."

"Is there anything I can be doing?" Savannah asked.

"Just try not to distract Doc from his work."

"Yes, sir," she replied. "I know a direct order when I hear one!"

Dane gave her an impatient look and then stepped outside with Caroline and Hack close behind him.

After the tree-hunters were gone, Doc announced his intention to clean the kitchen. Savannah followed him there.

"I'm worried about Rosemary," she confided as she filled the sink with warm, soapy water. "Have you talked to anyone at Ft. Belvoir?"

"Her physical condition is good," Doc said. "Emotionally she's a little shaky."

Savannah remembered how lonely she felt after Caroline was born—without a mother or even a mother-in-law to help her. "Hopefully we'll have her husband back before the baby is born."

Doc nodded. "I hope so. But Ferrante is a formidable adversary."

When order had been restored in the kitchen, Doc set up his laptop on the table and went to work, presumably looking for a legal way to get Cam out prison. Savannah walked into the living room and curled up on the couch. Her full stomach made her drowsy, so she watched the fire and dozed until Caroline burst through the front door of the cabin.

"We got one!" she announced breathlessly. "Hack is nailing boards into the bottom so it can stand up."

Savannah smiled. "That's great!"

Caroline's cheeks were pink from the cold and her eyes were shining with excitement. "Major Dane let me pick the tree and it took me a long time."

Savannah walked over to help Caroline unbutton her coat. "I'm glad you didn't settle for a less-than-perfect tree."

Dane's cheeks were also pink, but his eyes reflected only annoyance. "It's a good thing we don't have anything *important* to do," he murmured crossly. "Like rescue a kidnapped husband and protect the country from a criminal mastermind."

She hung Caroline's coat on a hook by the door, which brought her very close to Dane. "Some things can't be rushed."

"Some things don't have to happen at all," he returned, and his breath stirred the hair around her ear.

She wasn't sure if he meant the tree or finding Rosemary's husband, but either way, Savannah decided it was best to ignore the comment. "Thank you for getting the tree. It means a lot to Caroline . . ." She paused before adding, "And me."

"You're welcome," he said as Hack walked in.

Hack held up the tree and asked, "Where do you want it?"

Caroline crossed the room. "Can we put it here?"

"I guess," Dane agreed. "But not too close to the fireplace. I draw the line at burning down my house in the name of Christmas spirit."

Hack put the tree in the corner near the fireplace and then turned it until Caroline was satisfied that the best side was facing forward.

"Now we need decorations," Caroline told Dane.

"Are you sure this isn't good enough?" His tone was near pleading. "I like the natural look."

Caroline shook her head. "It's not a Christmas tree until it has a star on the top and red balls and maybe some candy canes."

Dane looked over at Savannah. "Can you give me a little help here?"

Savannah shrugged. "What can I say? She knows what a Christmas tree is supposed to look like."

"Thanks a lot," Dane muttered.

"We have some extra stuff at our apartment you could use," Caroline offered. "If Hack will drive me there to get it."

Dane ruffled her hair. "You're not going anywhere, young lady." He turned to Hack. "Do you have a man you can spare for a quick trip to the nearest store that sells tree decorations?"

Hack pulled the keys to the Yukon from his pocket. "It will be easier to go myself than to try to explain this crazy errand to someone else."

"Hurry," Savannah encouraged. "We'll have Christmas on hold here until you get back."

Hack grumbled under his breath as he walked out the door.

Caroline stared after him. "I think Hack is mad at me, too."

"Hack loves you," Savannah promised her. "He's just a little crabby."

"Maybe he'll feel better when we have a nice Christmas tree," Caroline proposed hopefully.

Savannah smiled. "I'm sure that will make all the difference."

Dane moved closer to Savannah. "You may be able to get away with antagonizing me, but you should probably cool it with Hack. You really don't want to be on his bad side."

She shrugged. "I'm tired of him pouting because I want to help Rosemary. He can't always have things his way."

Dane raised an eyebrow. "*He* thinks he can, and there aren't many people who would have the nerve to tell him otherwise."

"You have the nerve," she said. "You boss everyone around—including Hack."

"That's what being a commanding officer means. I'm the boss, and sometimes I have to overrule him. Hack understands that. But I don't rub his face in it and torment him at every opportunity."

"No, you save all the torment for me."

He shrugged her comment off. "That's different."

"I'd like for you to explain how."

His lips turned up in one of his almost-smiles. "No time for that now. We need to discuss this new operation. Is there some way Caroline can entertain herself until Hack gets back?"

Savannah turned and addressed her daughter. "Caroline, would you like to watch a movie? I brought *The Santa Clause.*"

"That's my favorite Christmas show," Caroline told Dane.

"I'll set my laptop up here by the couch so you can stay near the Christmas tree," Savannah offered.

"And the fire," Caroline added.

"Just not too close to the fire," Dane qualified.

Once Caroline was settled, Savannah joined Dane at his desk. She pulled a chair up beside his and whispered, "Now, what did you want to talk about."

"Last night I researched possible locations for the trap phase of our plan," he said.

She studied his face and noted the dark circles under his eyes. "You were researching when you should have been sleeping."

He shrugged. "If I'd been sleeping, nobody else would have been able to because of all the screaming."

"You can't go without sleep throughout this operation."

"My doctor gave me some sleeping pills that knock me out to the point that I don't dream," he admitted. "But I don't like to take them, because they also knock me out to the point that I can't wake up. The effects wear off after about six hours, but that's a long time to be . . ."

"Vulnerable?" she supplied for him.

"I was going to say *useless*," he amended. "Anyway, there aren't many occasions when I dare sleep that hard or that long. But maybe once we get our trap set, I can risk it."

"So based on your all-night research, which location would be best?"

He leaned forward so that their noses were almost touching. "We need a place where we can slip in unnoticed. A place where people don't pay close attention to their neighbors."

"And this place is?"

"New Orleans," he confided softly. "It's always been a little wild and lawless, but it's even more so after Katrina. The reconstruction efforts provide added confusion that will help to hide us until the time is right."

"New Orleans," she whispered.

"I own a place in the French Quarter. It has limited access to the street and would therefore be fairly easy to secure."

"You have a house in New Orleans?" This came as a total surprise.

He gave her an impatient look. "It's not a *home*, just an old house I bought as an investment property several years ago with the intention of renovating it. But between prison stays I haven't made much progress. It won't be very comfortable, but it's vacant."

"And in a good location," she noted.

He nodded. "The first step is to get Cam inside Ferrante's organization. Then we'll take Caroline to the McLaughlins' mountain. I don't want to scare Caroline, so we'll wait until she's in Colorado before transforming you into a Rosemary look-a-like."

Savannah nodded again.

"Make no mistake, Savannah, this operation will be dangerous. We're purposely taunting one of the biggest criminals in America. I'll do my best to protect you, but . . ."

"I'll be fine." Savannah was confident. "And if we can catch Ferrante, we'll eliminate the threat to Caroline forever. That's worth some risk."

"I agree. Otherwise we wouldn't even be discussing it," Dane said as the front door opened.

Savannah turned, expecting to see Hack returning with decorations for the tree. Instead she saw a man wearing aviator sunglasses and a pink linen suit reminiscent of *Miami Vice*. His dark hair was slicked back into a tiny ponytail at the base of his neck, and his skin was tanned to an unnatural shade of brick-brown. He flashed them a very white-toothed smile and said, "Never fear, Steamer's here."

Dane seemed dumbfounded for a few seconds. Finally he managed, "What the . . ."

Doc walked in from the kitchen and asked, "Steam, is that really you?"

"You'd better believe it, baby," the sun-baked man in pink replied. "I'm here to save the day. As usual."

Dane stood and studied the newcomer. "Could you possibly have found a more obnoxious outfit?"

"In Vegas, baby, it's all about image."

"I don't even want to know what kind of image you were going for with that suit," Dane said. "And if you call me *baby* again, you're going to regret it."

Steamer pushed the sunglasses up onto his head and nodded. "Sorry, sir."

"You don't have to call me sir," Dane told him brusquely. "Just don't call me baby."

Steamer glanced around the room. "So what's shaking?"

"If by that you mean what is going on," Dane said with barely controlled impatience, "we're waiting for Hack to get back with some Christmas tree decorations. Then we'll have a strategy meeting."

Steamer looked at the tree. "That's a pretty pitiful specimen, there. It's like something you cut down yourself."

"We did cut it down ourselves," Caroline informed him from her position on the couch. "It was growing in the woods."

Steamer nodded. "That explains a lot. Now, who are you, baby?"

"I'm Caroline," she replied, "and I'm not a baby."

"Nice to meet you, Caroline," Steamer said. "And *baby* is just a figure of speech." Then he turned back to Dane. "If I had known you needed a Christmas tree, I could have brought the one from my office in Vegas. It's neon pink, and the green lights are permanently affixed. All you have to do is plug it in, and you got Christmas, baby!" Steamer realized his mistake immediately. "Sorry!"

Dane's jaw was clenched with irritation, and Savannah had to bite her lip to keep from laughing.

There wasn't a trace of humor in Dane's voice when he said, "If there's anything I don't need, it's a pink Christmas tree."

"I didn't know there was such a thing as pink Christmas trees," Caroline remarked.

"They make a lot of cool things in Vegas," Steamer told her. Then he walked over to the couch. "What are you watching?"

"*The Santa Clause,*" Caroline informed him. "It's about Christmas." She pointed, redirecting his attention to Savannah. "And that's my mom."

Steamer stared at Savannah for a few seconds, his antagonism obvious.

"Hey, Steamer," Savannah said finally.

He pushed the sunglasses back in place to cover his eyes. "Mrs. McLaughlin."

The cool reception hurt, although she knew it was unreasonable of her to expect Steamer to react otherwise. She was used to the camaraderie she now enjoyed with Doc and Hack. She had complete confidence that Steamer would come around, but it was going to take some time for her to win him over. Just like it had with the others.

"Thank you for coming," she added.

"General Steele didn't give me much choice," he replied.

The awkward silence that followed his remark was broken when Hack burst in through the front door carrying several plastic sacks.

"Well, if it isn't my old friend Hack," Steamer said.

Hack glanced in his direction. "Well if it isn't the Easter Bunny turned gangster."

Steamer laughed. "Don't be jealous."

"I'm not," Hack assured him.

Caroline trailed behind Hack as he carried his purchases across the room. "Did you get a star and red ornaments?" she asked.

Hack placed the bags on the floor in front of the tree. "You have to remember that I was shopping at a small store in Tylerton, and they didn't have much to choose from."

Caroline nodded solemnly, prepared for disappointment.

Hack reached into a bag and pulled out a star. Then he flashed Caroline a gold-toothed grin. "I got the star and a whole bunch of red ornaments."

Caroline threw her arms around one of his knees. "Thank you!"

He laughed and patted her head. Then she released him to dig through the bags. In addition to all the items she had requested were several boxes of icicles. She held them up high and asked, "What are these?"

"You don't know what icicles are?" Hack demanded as he ripped open a box and draped a handful of silver strands over a tree bough. "You put them on like this after you get all the ornaments on and it makes the tree real shiny."

Caroline nodded, her eyes wide with wonder. "Oh."

Dane looked at the clump of icicles and frowned. "I hate those things. They fall off the tree and get stuck to everything."

Hack placed another handful of icicles on the tree. "My mother always bought them when I was a kid."

"I don't believe it!" Steamer said.

Hack frowned. "You don't believe that we put icicles on our Christmas tree?"

"Naw," Steamer clarified, "I don't believe you have a mother."

Hack made a growling noise.

Steamer held up a hand. "Take it easy, big man. I was just kidding."

"I won't be ridiculed by a man wearing pink," Hack told him.

Steamer tugged on the lapels of his suit coat. "Only men who are very confident of their masculinity feel comfortable in pink."

Hack growled again.

Dane decided to intervene. "Steamer, you might as well go ahead and call Hack *baby* since apparently you want him to kill you."

"Baby?" Hack repeated.

"It's a commonly used form of speech in Vegas, but Dane here objects," Steamer explained. "Some guys just ain't cool."

Before Hack could respond, Savannah inserted herself into the conversation. "Well, now that Hack has gotten all these decorations, why don't we put them on the tree?"

"The lights go first!" Caroline said with authority.

Savannah picked up a box that, according to the label, contained a thousand stringed lights capable of running, blinking, and alternating colors.

Dane walked over and took the box from Savannah. "We need to continue our strategy meeting in the kitchen." He leaned a little closer. "After all, we are here to get Ferrante—not to celebrate Christmas, right?"

She wanted very much to celebrate Christmas here with Dane, but she nodded. "Right."

"So we can't decorate the tree?" Caroline looked close to tears.

Dane smiled. "You can decorate the tree while the rest of us have a meeting."

Caroline held up the star. "I don't think I can reach the top."

"That is a problem," Dane agreed. Then he turned to Hack. "Can you get one of your men to come in and help?"

Hack nodded and moved toward the door. Savannah waited until Hack returned with one of the huge security guards. Then she instructed Caroline to mind him before walking into the kitchen.

Dane was seated at the head of the table with a brand new laptop perched in front of him.

"You got the laptops already?" Savannah asked in surprise.

Hack nodded. "And the satellite phones. I drove into Ft. Belvoir last night and picked them up." He distributed identical laptops and phones to Dane, Doc, and Steamer. Savannah tried not to be bothered by the fact that she had been excluded electronically. Maybe they were just trying to save her some money in the event that she ended up paying for the new acquisitions.

Steamer was in the chair to Dane's right, and Doc was on the left. Doc stood and pulled out the chair beside him for Savannah. She accepted it with a smile. Hack joined them and sat at the foot of the table. Then he scooted his chair back until he could see into the living room.

"Afraid they'll get the icicles on wrong?" Steamer teased.

"No, I'm afraid Ferrante might come charging through the front door with a bazooka," Hack responded.

The smile disappeared from Steamer's face.

"It's probably a good idea to keep an eye on Caroline," Dane said mildly.

In an effort to be congenial, Savannah asked, "Where did you get your nickname, Steamer?"

He wasn't impressed by her friendly overture. "I don't remember."

"We call him Steamer because he irons everything," Hack provided, and Savannah was sure he was trying to aggravate Steamer more than inform her. "There's even a crease in his socks."

"I thought it was because he likes to blow off steam," Doc said.

"I thought it's because he's loud and flashy like a locomotive," Dane contributed.

Hack shrugged. "Apparently nobody knows where he got his nickname."

"And nobody cares," Dane said, putting an end to the discussion. "Now let's get started."

Steamer leaned his elbows onto the table and said, "I think the first order of business is to come up with a snappy name for the operation."

Hack made a derisive sound, but Steamer pressed on.

"I've come up with a few suggestions: Operation Hide and Seek, Operation Ready-Set-Go, Operation Sitting Duck, or, my personal favorite, Operation Where-Oh-Where-Can-My-Husband-Be."

"Those are all stupid," Hack proclaimed. "And way too long."

"You got a better idea?" Steamer demanded.

"Yeah, how about working on a plan instead of playing name games," Hack suggested. "And why don't you take off those ridiculous sunglasses. Only fools wear sunglasses indoors."

"Not fools—*cools*," Steamer corrected.

"Personally, I like the name Operation Hide and Seek," Doc offered.

"I prefer Sitting Duck," Dane muttered.

"I second that," Hack said.

"Then Sitting Duck it is," Doc decreed.

"Now on a less important topic." Dane cut his eyes at Steamer. "I've chosen the location where we'll spring our trap."

"Where?" Steamer asked.

"Like everything else relating to this operation, I'll divulge that on a need-to-know basis. And right now you don't need to know."

Steamer frowned, causing Hack to laugh. Savannah felt surprised, yet honored, that Dane had trusted her with information he wasn't even willing to share with his men.

"So," Dane continued, "I've chosen a location, and Steamer is here. I've talked to Agent Gray and confirmed that Chad Allen is with Ferrante at his estate in Maryland. That means I'm 100% for my assignments." He turned to Savannah. "Will you please report on your call to General Steele?"

She nodded. "He's agreed to sanction the operation and classify it as covert."

"So Dane can run it like he wants to," Steamer guessed.

"Without having to get permission from anyone," Hack added.

Savannah moved down her list. "He even offered to set up a support team, and he said he'll give Dane the contact number."

"He already did," Dane said as he distributed what looked like business cards to his men. "Here are the new phone numbers for each other and the support team at Ft. Belvoir. Memorize them and destroy the cards."

Savannah gave the cards a longing glance before continuing, "The general promised to provide additional men and some funding but requested that we keep the costs down. And he didn't sound hopeful about getting Cam out of jail."

"So Savannah is 100% too," Dane pronounced. "What about you, Hack?"

Hack leaned forward and lowered his voice in an obvious attempt to keep Caroline from hearing him. "The girl's story checks out as far as I can tell. She was a student at George Washington but withdrew suddenly. Chad Allen was also a student there—no obvious ties to Ferrante prior to marrying the daughter."

Savannah's heart swelled. She looked to Dane, expecting a positive reaction to Hack's words. But Dane was scowling. "Any relative of Ferrante's is someone I don't trust."

"Any relative of Ferrante's is someone I want to stay away from," Steamer embellished.

"I've already tried that argument," Hack told him. "Nobody's listening."

Dane interrupted this rare harmonious moment between Hack and Steamer. "How do you feel about security, Hack?"

"My men are handling things fine for now, but I'm glad we'll be getting some guys from Ft. Belvoir. Especially since we're splitting into three groups that will all need high levels of protection."

"So you're 100% too." Then he turned to Doc. "Okay, did you figure out a way we can spring Cam out of jail?"

Doc cleared his throat nervously and said, "I've looked through everything relating to Cam's arrest and the evidence against him to be presented in a court martial scheduled for next month. My assignment was to come up with some questionable aspect that we could reasonably magnify into an error or technicality and thereby obtain his release."

Dane nodded. "And?"

"And after a thorough search, I've come to the conclusion that there is no way we can work out a legal release for Cam in a timely manner."

Dane was obviously disappointed. "None?"

Doc shook his head. "Even if there was anything remotely irregular—which there isn't—it would take months to work through all the hearings, etc."

"We could try for a presidential pardon,"

"Cam can't be pardoned until he's convicted," Doc pointed out.

"And besides that," Hack interjected, "if the president of the United States takes the time to arrange Cam's release, Ferrante's going to smell a rat, big-time."

"So where does that leave us?" Dane asked Doc. "In order for this operation to work, we've got to have a way to monitor Ferrante and feed him information. The FBI's plant isn't placed high enough to help us. We need Cam."

Doc nodded. "Since we can't get Cam out through legal means, he'll have to *escape* from prison."

Savannah was astounded by Doc's suggestion, but nobody else even looked surprised.

"I like it," Steamer said.

"How?" Dane wanted to know.

"The first step is to get him off the prison grounds. The easiest way to do that is through a medical emergency. I've been trying to decide between a stab wound and a heart attack," Doc told them. "I think the heart attack would be best, since that can be faked with the use of drugs. Once the medication wears off, Cam will be fine. A stab wound would have to be real—if superficial—and that might limit Cam's usefulness during the rest of the operation."

"Makes sense to me," Steamer agreed.

"Although I wouldn't mind Cam getting stabbed," Hack contributed. "He deserves it."

Savannah felt she had to be the voice of reason. "Surely we are not seriously considering a prison break and stabbing someone."

Ignoring her comment, Dane asked Doc, "So assuming we go with the heart attack drugs, how will we administer them to Cam?"

"Timing will be important, so we can't use any haphazard method," Doc replied thoughtfully. "Since it's a military prison and we have General Steele's cooperation, it shouldn't be hard for us to get someone inside posing as a records inspector for the health department. After looking through the files, he'll pull out several inmates who need immunizations, including Cam."

"But Cam's shot will be special," Steamer said with a smile. Pointing to Doc, he said, "I guess you'll be 'our man' since you have medical training."

Dane shook his head. "I want Doc with Caroline, so Steamer, you'll have to pose as the records inspector."

Steamer nodded. "I can do that. But how do we actually get Cam out?"

Doc explained the details of his plan. "When Cam starts having chest pains, you'll express concern that they might be a reaction to the immunizations. So you'll stay at the clinic to be sure he's properly monitored."

"From a distance so Cam won't recognize me," Steamer added.

Doc nodded. "Definitely. When the timing is right, you'll say that his condition isn't improving and insist that they airlift him to Walter Reed. With all the bad press the Army's had lately over health care, I don't think they'll refuse. But General Steele can be standing by to encourage them if necessary."

"Then we'll send a helicopter to get him?" Steamer guessed. "With our own crew onboard."

"Yes," Doc confirmed. "We'll make it look like Cam recovered during the flight to Walter Reed, commandeered the helicopter, and made his escape."

"And he'll fly the 'stolen' helicopter straight to Ferrante?" Steamer asked.

Doc nodded. "After a brief stop to unload the pilot and nurse."

"I presume that during the short helicopter ride—after reviving Cam and before turning the helicopter over to him—our 'crew' will convince Cam to cooperate with us?" Dane said.

"Yes," Doc confirmed. "His cover story will be that he faked a heart attack to escape from Ft. Lewis, since after his conviction he'd be transferred to a more secure location like Leavenworth. He'll ask Ferrante to hide him and express a great desire to get revenge against us."

"And when Ferrante comes after his daughter, Cam will beg to come along," Steamer said.

"Ferrante won't be able to resist the chance to use Cam against us again," Doc said.

"I think you're overlooking a major obstacle," Hack interrupted. "Gaining Cam's cooperation might not be easy. The last time I checked, we were kind of on the outs with him."

"If Savannah asks Cam to help, I'm sure he'll agree. So Dane will fly the helicopter to the prison at Ft. Lewis, and Savannah will pose as the nurse."

"Whoa!" Dane held up a hand in objection. "I don't mind flying the helicopter, but there's no way Savannah's getting anywhere near Cam, even if he's having a drug-induced heart attack."

"He'll just be having heart attack symptoms," Doc felt it necessary to explain.

Dane waved Doc's comment aside. "Regardless, Savannah won't be on that helicopter. Don't you remember what happened the last time Cam had access to her?"

"I was there," Doc reminded him. "But Savannah's presence is essential if we want to push Cam's guilt buttons. And as far as the safety issue, Cam will be strapped onto a stretcher during transport. You won't free him until you're sure he doesn't pose a threat."

"What if we can't convince him to help us?" Savannah asked.

"Then take him on to Walter Reed," Doc replied. "After they check him out, they'll send him back to Ft. Lewis."

"No harm, no foul," Steamer said.

Doc turned to Dane. "I'm pretty sure Cam will jump at the chance to be out of prison and a part of the team again. But since you don't trust him, give him only the information you don't mind Ferrante knowing."

Dane raised his eyebrows. "That will be a short conversation."

"Which is good," Hack interjected. "That means a short helicopter ride."

"We want Ferrante to know you've got his kid anyway," Steamer pointed out. "So tell Cam you've got Rosemary and that you want him to help us trap Ferrante. If he turns on us, he'll really be helping our plan along."

Dane nodded. "But rushing our timetable."

"And what if you tell him our plan, and you're sure he's on our side?" Savannah asked.

"I'll never be sure of Cam's loyalty again," Dane replied. "Like Steam said, he'll know only what we want Ferrante to know."

"Cam really does believe in honor," Doc said quietly. "He made some bad choices . . ."

"He was a part-time assassin for Ferrante, Doc," Hack interrupted.

"He did things that were wrong," Doc continued doggedly, "mostly because he was afraid for his kids. Since they are out of Ferrante's reach now, he'll cooperate with us."

Dane gave Doc a sad smile. "I wish I had your confidence. But I have to protect the team against the worst possible scenario. So we'll plan on Cam betraying us. If he doesn't, that's a bonus."

Doc looked disappointed, but he didn't argue.

"In that case," Hack said, "we need two ways to track Cam—one he knows about and one he doesn't. Both will have to be installed quickly."

"Did you get any ideas from the spy folks at Belvoir?" Dane asked Hack.

"A few," Hack acknowledged. "The challenge we face is that Ferrante has equipment as sophisticated as anything the FBI's got. Which means any device we put on Cam, they can detect."

Dane didn't look happy about this news. "So where does that leave us?"

"The Army's spy guys have a few tracking methods that are basically untraceable. They can measure body heat distribution, speech patterns—even radiation. But these methods require close-range monitoring and sophisticated, bulky equipment."

"Which would be impractical," Dane said.

Hack nodded. "Right."

"So what will we do?" Savannah asked.

"Several things," Hack said. "First we'll try a high-tech but fairly standard device and hope Ferrante doesn't find it. The easiest way to install such a device is with a dental appliance—like a fake filling or a crown."

"I think it would look too suspicious if we have Cam receive an emergency crown and an unscheduled immunization on the same day," Dane said. "If we choose this method, I may have to put the crown on him in the helicopter."

"You know how to crown a tooth?" Savannah was surprised.

"I have a general idea," Dane replied.

"Are you kidding me?" Steamer said. "A crown has to fit just right, or it's very uncomfortable. If you're installing your first crown in a helicopter, you'll get it on crooked for sure. And when Cam wakes up, he'll guess in a heartbeat that we tagged him."

"What makes you think I'll get it on crooked?" Dane asked with a dangerous look in his eyes.

Steamer backed down immediately. "With all due respect, sir, the last time I checked, you ain't been to dental school."

Doc stepped in before Dane could respond. "I agree that any dental work should be handled by trained professionals. So if we're crowning one of Cam's teeth, it's got to be done at the prison."

"And the chances of us pulling off a dental emergency and a surprise inoculation are zilch," Hack remarked. "Not only will Cam get suspicious, so will the people at the prison."

"And no telling how many of them work for Ferrante," Steamer pointed out.

Dane abandoned the battle. "So if we can't install dental work, what else can we use?"

"The guys at Ft. Belvoir will give us three devices. One is adhesive and looks like a freckle. It can provide audio as well as location. It uses radio waves, so if Ferrante's surveillance guys aren't paying close attention, they might miss it. The 'nurse' who gives Cam his inoculations can install the device."

"That's good," Dane sounded pleased. "Do you think it will go undetected?"

"No," Hack said. "Ferrante's guys will find it pretty fast, but it will at least help us confirm that Cam makes it there."

Dane nodded. "What are the other two ways to track him?"

"We'll give him a capsule that contains an internal tracking device. Once he swallows it, we can track him for up to ten days until it works its way out of his system."

"Cam will know about this device?"

"Yes," Hack confirmed.

"Then Ferrante will probably have it *removed* from his system before it has time to work its way out naturally," Dane predicted. "So what's our final tracking method?"

"The final device is so new, they aren't even through testing it. It's so tiny that it's basically invisible. It will contain an M-CODE signal." He turned to Savannah. "This is the military equivalent of GPS and is so sophisticated it can only be picked up by special equipment."

"That Ferrante won't have." Steamer sounded pleased.

"We hope." Dane didn't seem nearly as confident.

"The spy guys said nobody has it. The only reason they've got it is for testing purposes."

"Where will they put this M-CODE device and how will it get there?"

"They recommend the ear cavity. The installation is painless and can be done during the course of a routine exam. It will seem like the nurse is just taking Cam's temperature with an ear thermometer."

"What if it comes loose or falls out?"

"They say it won't ever come out."

"Ever?" Savannah repeated.

Hack shook his head. "It will embed itself in the cartilage of the ear. It can later be neutralized with a chemical but never actually removed."

"So Ferrante will never find it, and we can track Cam anywhere in the world," Hack summed up.

"Assuming Ferrante doesn't kill Cam and dump him in a ditch somewhere," Steamer added.

Hack was philosophical. "That's a risk we're all willing to take."

Savannah was going to object to this, but Dane was already nodding. "That sounds good. Hack, I'll leave all the details to you."

"When is all this going to go down?" Steamer wanted to know.

"Time is on our side only if we act quickly," Dane said. "So I'd like the prison inoculations to take place this afternoon, assuming Doc can get all the arrangements made at the prison by then." He turned to Hack. "And assuming your spy guys can come through. Ask them if they can loan us a technician to act like a nurse and implant the devices on Cam. If we have someone experienced do it, we can limit the possibility of error."

Hack made a note and then said, "We should get Caroline secured *before* we get Cam out of prison."

Dane nodded. "There's no question about that. Steamer, I need you to create a panic at the Brotherly Love Farm."

Steamer looked up in confusion. "Huh?"

Dane briefly outlined his idea to make the peace-loving, cooperative farmers think that they were the target of hate crimes.

When Dane was finished, Steamer looked up from the notes he had taken and smiled. "Sounds like fun."

"I thought you'd like it," Dane said. "Agent Gray is willing to help you make a lasting impression on the farm people."

"Don't worry, *ba* . . . I mean sir," Steamer caught himself just in time. "In no time I'll have those farm folks begging for government interference."

"We'll need ground troops and aerial support from Ft. Carson," Hack told Steamer.

Steamer nodded. "I can have the Brotherly Love Farm locked down and fighter jets circling above in a matter of hours."

Savannah assumed he was kidding—about the fighter jets at least—but Hack said, "Good."

"One last thing, Steam," Dane continued. "During the rest of this operation, you're going to need to dress a little less . . ."

"Flamboyant?" Steamer provided with a smile.

"That wasn't the word I was looking for," Dane hedged.

"Ridiculous?" Hack said helpfully.

Dane smiled. "I was going to say *noticeable*. But anyway, Steam, you know the rules of a covert operation. Blend in, don't stand out."

"I got you." Steamer looked down at his pink suit. "It's a shame though—sacrificing all this style."

Hack muttered something under his breath.

Dane checked his watch. "I want to meet with the general and go over his plans for the support team."

"And make sure what he's got planned is up to your exacting standards," Hack guessed shrewdly.

"Yeah," Dane admitted. "I also need to arrange for a helicopter to pick up Cam, and Doc has to set up the fake health department raid at the prison. So Doc and I are headed to Ft. Belvoir. We should be back in three hours. I'll have a charter plane waiting to fly us to Colorado then." He turned to Savannah. "You and Caroline need to be packed and ready to go."

"We'll be ready," Savannah promised.

Savannah followed Dane and Doc as far as the back door. Then she stood and watched through the screen as they climbed into Dane's gray sedan. A few seconds later and they were gone. Reluctantly Savannah turned around. Steamer and Hack were still sitting at the table. Since neither of them was very happy with her at the moment, she said, "I think I'll go see how the Christmas tree decorating has progressed."

Without waiting for a response, she walked into the living room.

CHAPTER 4

DANE'S CHRISTMAS TREE was charming in a pitiful kind of way. The tree itself was imperfect with lots of drooping branches and plenty of gaps between boughs. Hack had purchased enough red balls to sufficiently decorate the tree at Rockefeller Center, and this was a further complication. To show her appreciation, Caroline was trying to use as many of the balls as possible—overpowering the poor little tree. And it was easy to identify which icicles Caroline had applied. All Savannah had to do was look for big clumps of silver.

But in spite of its shortcomings, Caroline was proud of the little tree, so Savannah searched for an honest form of praise. She settled on, "I'm sure Dane has never had a nicer tree here in his cabin." That, at least, was probably true.

Caroline pointed at the leftover decorations. "We couldn't get all the balls on the tree. We tried, but we were afraid if we put on any more, the branches would break."

"That was very wise," Savannah concurred. "And I don't think Hack thought we would need so many. He just wanted to make sure we had plenty, so we wouldn't send him back to the store."

"Major Dane doesn't have any presents," Caroline said. Then a frown creased her forehead. "Who will give him some?"

"I'm sure his parents will send him presents." Savannah tried to sound positive. Dane seemed to hold his parents at arm's length, and they were in Thailand, so exchanging gifts might not be possible. But there was no need to share these concerns with Caroline.

"We have presents at our apartment," Caroline reminded Savannah.

Savannah smiled, remembering the fun they'd had designing the T-shirts for the team. She could hardly wait to see the slogan he detested emblazoned on Dane's chest. "Yes we do."

"The tree will look much better with presents underneath. When will we bring them here?" Caroline seemed to be getting attached to the idea of Christmas at Dane's cabin, and Savannah didn't have the heart to tell the child that they would soon be leaving and she couldn't promise that they'd be back by Christmas.

"I'm not sure," she answered vaguely. "Later. But right now you need to go pack up your things. When Major Dane gets back, he's going to take us for a ride in an airplane."

Caroline's eyes brightened. "Where are we going?"

"It's a surprise," Savannah replied.

"I love surprises." Caroline ran toward the stairs. "Are we spending the night somewhere?"

"Maybe."

"Then I'll make sure I take my toothbrush."

Once they were repacked, Savannah insisted that Caroline eat a light lunch.

"Doughnuts are good, but they don't provide a lot of nutrition," she explained as she led Caroline into the kitchen. Hack and Steamer had their laptops set up on the table, and Savannah paused in the doorway. But Caroline barreled on in and pulled up a chair next to Hack.

She pointed at the laptop's screen and said, "Are you playing a computer game?"

Hack shook his huge head. "Nope, I'm working. Did you finish the tree?"

"Yep," Caroline confirmed. "My mom says it looks great. You want to see?" Caroline took one of Hack's large hands in hers and pulled. "Come on."

With a scowl at Savannah, Hack stood and allowed Caroline to drag him into the living room.

"You're invited too, Mr. Steamer," Caroline called over her shoulder.

Savannah trailed behind Caroline and Hack. Steamer joined them in front of the tree a few moments later.

"This doesn't look too bad," Hack said as he studied the tree. "The icicles shine just like I remember."

"Yeah," Steamer agreed. "This nice tree is getting me in the Christmas spirit. Now all I got to do is figure out what kind of costume to wear. I'm thinking maybe Dracula or Frankenstein."

"How about Tinkerbell," Hack suggested snidely.

Caroline laughed. "You only have a costume on Halloween—not Christmas."

Steamer frowned. "Are you sure?"

Caroline nodded. "I'm sure."

"Well, will you at least let me hide eggs?" Steamer requested.

Caroline giggled again. "You only hide eggs on Easter."

Steamer scratched his head. "So what do you do on Christmas besides have a tree?"

"You have presents, and Santa comes, and you read about Baby Jesus in the manger," Caroline itemized.

Steamer smiled at the child. "Well, I'm glad you can keep it all straight."

Caroline took Steamer's hand. "My mom is going to make us sandwiches for lunch. Do you want some?"

Steamer's smile faded when Savannah's name was mentioned. "I'm not really very hungry. I think I'll just stay here by the fire and work on my laptop."

"Well, I'm hungry." Hack waved to Caroline. "Let's go to the kitchen with your mom."

Once Savannah had the sandwiches ready, she prepared individual plates. She put Hack's beside his workstation at the table and sent Caroline into the living room with one for Steamer. When the child returned empty handed, Savannah silently claimed a minor victory in her battle to gain the newcomer's friendship. But not one to push her luck, she decided to give Steamer some space and ate her lunch in the kitchen.

It was after three o'clock before Dane called and told Hack to bring them to meet him at the airstrip. Savannah roused Caroline, who had fallen asleep while watching movies. Hack collected all their bags in one hand and led the way out to the Yukon. He supervised as they climbed in and fastened seat belts. Then he slipped behind the wheel and started the vehicle.

Two escort cars fell in line with them, one in front and one behind. Savannah couldn't resist a wistful glance back at the cabin. Steamer was standing on the porch, watching them leave. She waved. He didn't. So there was still room for improvement there.

During the short drive to the airstrip, Caroline asked endless questions about their destination. "Is it a fun place?"

"Sometimes," Savannah answered.

"Is it Disneyworld?"

"No."

Caroline asked, "Is it someplace I've been before?"

"Yes."

"Do I like it there?"

Savannah nodded. "I think so."

Hack checked his mirrors vigilantly, ever on guard against a surprise attack.

"Is it the beach?" Caroline continued.

"No."

"Is it hot there?"

"You're just going to have to wait and see," Savannah said as Hack slowed to turn onto the road that would lead to the airstrip. Her heart began to pound with anticipation. Ridiculous though it seemed, she'd missed Dane during the short separation and was anxious to see him again.

Hack drove slowly across the cracked tarmac, and Savannah's eyes searched for Dane. When Hack pulled to a stop beside a private jet, Savannah thought he'd made a mistake. The plane was easily four times the size of the one Dane had chartered for the trip to Colorado to rescue Caroline. But before she could question Hack, Dane ducked out the plane's door and descended the steps.

"It's about time," Dane said as he opened Savannah's door.

"This plane is much bigger than I expected, and certainly more expensive," she whispered, partly because she felt General Steele was trusting her to keep costs down but mostly because it gave her an excuse to move closer to Dane.

"Small planes have to make stops for fuel, and we don't have time for that today. This one will get us to Colorado before the sun sets there." He took their overnight bags from Hack and herded them toward the plane. "The pilot is ready to go. Everybody onboard."

Savannah followed Dane until she realized that Hack was still standing by the Yukon. "Aren't you coming too?" she asked him.

Hack shook his huge head. "I've got a trap to set."

Savannah turned to Dane.

"Hack has to go and secure the location we discussed," he said.

"Oh." She looked back at Hack. He'd been against the plan since the beginning, but he'd stood by her. Loyalty like that was rare, and she wanted to thank him, but finding words that adequately described her feelings seemed impossible.

"Hack knows you appreciate him," Dane said impatiently. "We don't have time for a long farewell."

Savannah gave Dane a smirk and then smiled at Hack. "Thanks!" she called. "For everything!"

He nodded.

When Savannah climbed onto the plane, she noted that one of Hack's men was acting as copilot. Doc already had Caroline strapped securely to a seat close to the cockpit. Savannah was about to sit beside Caroline, but Dane took her arm and guided her a few rows back.

"Once the plane gets in the air, we need to talk," he explained.

With his fingers clasping her arm, she could barely think, so she allowed him to lead her.

Caroline leaned around the edge of her seat and said, "Doc brought us snacks and coloring books. He says we just have to wait until we're flying."

Savannah sent Doc a grateful smile. "That was very thoughtful of you. Thanks."

Doc blushed. "It was no trouble."

"It was a *delay*, and that's why we're running late," Dane muttered as he motioned for Savannah to precede him into a row that contained two seats. "I hate it when things don't happen in a timely manner."

Savannah sat by the window and reached for her seat belt. "Sorry," she said, but she didn't mean it. She watched as he settled down beside her. Their arms brushed briefly, and she smiled. Danger seemed very far away at the moment.

Dane pressed a button on the overhead console and spoke to the pilot. "Let's get out of here." Then he leaned back and closed his eyes.

"You're tired." There was no question. His eyes were red-rimmed and surrounded by bluish circles of exhaustion. "You need sleep."

"I can't afford sleep," he replied.

"Why can't you sleep right now?" she asked. "If you start to scream, I'll wake you up."

His eyes flew open, and she realized it had been a mistake to mention his weakness. "Sleep is for sissies."

She frowned. "That's probably the dumbest thing I've ever heard you say."

Dane shrugged.

"Would it be okay for me to call Rosemary?" she asked. "I want to check on her and explain why I can't come to the hospital."

"The situation has been explained to her," Dane replied.

Savannah nodded. "I know, but I'd like to explain personally."

Dane looked annoyed but nodded. "Make it quick."

Savannah pulled her phone from her purse and got the hospital's number from post information. When Savannah was connected with Rosemary, the girl sounded very pleased to hear from her.

"Are you coming here soon?" Rosemary asked.

Savannah hated to disappoint the girl but had no choice. "No, I'm sorry. Something has come up, and I can't come there right now. But Dane has a plan to rescue your husband. I can't give you any details—for your own safety—but you can rest assured that he's doing everything he can."

"I appreciate that very much," Rosemary replied. "But I'm scared."

"You are safer there at the hospital. I'll be in touch as soon as I can."

"Okay," Rosemary agreed. "I trust you and Major Dane to get Chad."

Savannah smiled at Rosemary's assumption that she and Dane were a team. "We'll do our best."

"You'll call me again, won't you?" Rosemary's voice quivered.

"I'll try," was all Savannah dared promise. Then she closed the phone and was about to return it to her purse, but Dane extended his hand.

"I'd better take that."

"My phone?" she asked in alarm.

"For the rest of this operation, we don't want to use anything but the secure satellite phones."

Savannah surrendered the phone. Dane took it to the front of the plane and handed it to a member of the ground crew.

"Don't you think you're being a little dramatic?" Savannah asked when he returned.

"I'm being cautious," he returned. "A trait you should acquire."

Before she could respond, the pilot interrupted them by announcing that they were ready for takeoff. He asked them to double-check their seat belts and remain seated until he notified them that they had reached cruising altitude.

Savannah clutched the arms of her seat as they left the tarmac. Then she sat quietly, hoping the gentle vibrations of the plane and fatigue would lull Dane to doze. She was rewarded a few minutes later by the sound of his steady breathing. When Doc looked back to check on them, she put a finger to her lips and he nodded. The boss was asleep, and they would all do their best to keep him that way.

Dane slept for almost an hour, and when his eyes opened, they stared at her in accusation. "You promised you would wake me up if I fell asleep."

"No, I promised I would wake you up if you started *screaming* in your sleep," she corrected. "But except for a few little snores, you slept quietly."

His scowl deepened. "You knew I didn't want to sleep."

"I knew you needed to sleep," she replied. "And since you didn't *order* me to wake you . . ."

Doc appeared in the aisle and extended a grocery sack. "Would either of you like snacks?" he offered.

Dane shook his head. Savannah politely accepted a bag of skittles and a bottle of water. Doc returned to his seat beside Caroline, and Savannah opened her candy. While she was contemplating which color to try first, Dane held out his hand.

"You want some Skittles?" she asked.

"I do," he replied.

"So why didn't you take a bag from Doc when he offered you a snack?"

He regarded her dolefully. "Because I thought you'd be willing to share."

She poured several pieces of candy into his waiting palm. "I don't mind sharing. I just don't understand why you'd say you didn't want a snack when you did."

He reached for her water, and she watched as he drank almost all of it. "I never realized how stingy you are."

She sighed in exasperation. "You're the most irrational, incomprehensible man I've ever met."

"It's all part of my charm."

Savannah retrieved her water bottle and took a sip before asking, "How did the meeting with General Steele go?"

Dane popped the last of her Skittles into his mouth. "Fine. Steamer's hate-crime scheme for the Brotherly Love Farm worked great. After a few of Steamer's letters were faxed to the farm's office, Father Burnett begged for troops from Ft. Carson."

"Steamer's letters must be truly harrowing," Savannah murmured.

"I'm sure they are," Dane agreed. "Doc set up Steamer's visit to the prison at Ft. Lewis. He'll pose as a health inspector checking inoculation records." Dane glanced at his watch. "In fact, he should be arriving there now. By the end of the day, Cam will be experiencing heart attack symptoms. And I've got a helicopter ready and waiting to help Cam make his great escape."

"That will take place tonight?"

Dane nodded. "As soon as we can get back from Colorado. The prison clinic has a reduced staff at night, which will make the decision to send Cam to Walter Reed more reasonable. And finding the hijacked helicopter will be more difficult in the dark, so Cam's ability to elude the Army won't seem so miraculous."

"So we won't be able to stay on the mountain very long?" Savannah realized.

"Only an hour or so," Dane confirmed.

Savannah reached up and rubbed the little locket in anxiety. She hadn't been separated from Caroline for almost two months, and the thought of leaving her was frightening, even with the McLaughlins and Doc and Hack's men and an entire unit of soldiers.

"I hate to leave her." She turned to Dane, needing comfort and wanting nothing more than to bury her face in the crook of his neck. She knew a hug was unlikely in such a public setting, but she did expect at least a hand-pat or a smile.

Instead he frowned at the locket. "You don't have a picture of Wes in there, do you?"

She shook her head. "I wouldn't put a picture of Wes in your locket."

"Caroline?" he guessed, and she nodded. He relaxed. Apparently he was okay with that. "So you like the locket now?"

"I always liked it," she said. "I was just disappointed when you gave it to me, because I was expecting an engagement ring."

He sighed. "I know. I'm sorry."

She narrowed her eyes at him. "How do you always know what I'm thinking?"

"I've been trained to analyze people, and your face is very expressive."

"I wish I could read your mind," she mused. "I never know what you're thinking."

"That's because I've learned to control my emotions, my expressions, and my feelings. After years of altering myself to fit each new operation, sometimes I wonder exactly who I am and if I can really have genuine feelings anymore." He glanced at her. "You trust and love so easily."

"Just not wisely," she added with a self-depreciating smile. "Since few people love and trust me in return."

"People love you," he disagreed. "There's Caroline and Hack and Doc."

She raised an eyebrow. "That's a pretty pitiful list. My marriage was a disaster, my father deserted me, and my mother did too—emotionally anyway."

Dane looked away. "Wes loved you. And your mother dedicated her life to you."

"Maybe she shouldn't have," Savannah blurted out. "If the rumors that dogged us from one city to the next were true, and she really had an affair with a married man who wouldn't leave his wife, why didn't she just give me up for adoption? Then instead of the grim, lonely life she led, she might have found happiness. And I would have had a real family—a normal life."

"Even real families have their problems," he told her. "Maybe she was afraid if she gave you up, whoever adopted you wouldn't love you as much as she did."

Savannah didn't agree, but she also didn't want to argue. "Maybe."

Discouraged by the topic and the things Dane said and didn't say, Savannah closed her eyes. She didn't mean to fall asleep, but she did. She startled awake when Caroline leaned around the edge of her seat and yelled, "Out the window it looks like the mountains by where Grandma and Grandpa live!"

Savannah turned to Dane before she answered. He nodded, so she said, "It *is* the mountains by where your grandma and grandpa live. You are going to stay there while Major Dane and I look for Rosemary's husband."

"Are we going to stay for Christmas?" Caroline wanted to know.

"I'm not sure where we'll be for Christmas," Savannah said honestly.

"We have a tree at our apartment and at Major Dane's cabin too," Caroline pointed out. "So we could go to both places."

Savannah smiled. "Yes, we have plenty of options."

"If Grandma and Grandpa don't have a tree, Major Dane can cut one down for them."

Dane muttered something under his breath, and Savannah had to laugh.

"I'm sure he'd be glad to," she told Caroline.

Dane leaned close, and his breath stirred the hair around her ear as he whispered, "Keep it up and you might get a chance to try *your* hand at Christmas tree cutting."

She did her best to smirk, limited as she was by her heart pounding and her breath coming in short, lovesick gasps.

They landed at a small private airstrip a few miles from the farm and traveled the remaining distance in an Army van provided by the commander at Ft. Carson. Thanks to the fact that they gained two hours because of the change to Mountain Standard Time, they arrived at the farm before sunset. Captain Findlay, who had assisted with Caroline's rescue two months earlier, was there along with an impressive number of soldiers.

When the van stopped at the gates to the farm, Dane climbed out of the vehicle. He instructed Doc to stay in the vehicle. Then he lifted Caroline out and led her toward the administration building, where a group of soldiers and farm men were gathered—leaving Savannah to choose for herself whether to stay or go.

"I'll be back," she promised Doc. Then she got out of the van and closed the door behind her. The scene was uncomfortably reminiscent of the day she had come to the farm in hopes of finding her missing child. During that initial trip, the farm's leader, Father Burnett, had resisted their intrusion and the Army's presence. Now, because of Steamer's threatening—if artificial, letters—Father Burnett seemed glad to have the Army there.

Despite his obvious anxiety over the farm's safety, Father Burnett welcomed Caroline warmly. His greeting to Savannah and Dane was only slightly less heartfelt.

"You know we're always glad to have you here," he told them. "But I'm afraid you've picked a dangerous time to visit. The FBI has received letters from a group of terrorists who want to destroy the farm." Just saying the words seemed to cause him pain and confusion. "I don't understand it," he continued. "We don't do anything to attract negative attention—let alone hatred. We don't get involved in politics or social issues. We just grow our vegetables and live peacefully."

Dane shook his head in apparent sympathy. "It's a weird world we live in, Father—where some people hate for no reason."

Savannah narrowed her eyes at him. He gave her a warning look before saying to the father, "We won't stay long. Caroline just wanted to wish her grandparents a merry Christmas."

Father Burnett nodded distractedly. "Okay, well, please hurry. I can't guarantee your safety while you're here."

"Captain Findlay and the U.S. Army will take care of that," Dane spoke with confidence. "No need to worry about us."

Father Burnett seemed relieved to be absolved of responsibility for them. He took a few steps away and then turned back. "If I'm not available to tell you good-bye when you return from the mountain . . ."

Dane waved this aside. "We understand that you have a farm full of innocent people to comfort and protect."

Savannah resisted the urge to roll her eyes, but Father Burnett apparently didn't detect any deceit in Dane's words. He reached out and took Dane's hand in both of his. "Thank you."

Once the father was gone, Dane motioned toward the waiting Army helicopter. "You and Caroline get in." Then he flipped open his phone and spoke in to it. "Doc, come on quick."

Savannah was assisted into the helicopter by a soldier. Once she was safely inside, he handed Caroline up to her. There was a soldier in the pilot's seat and two more in the far back of the vehicle. Savannah was strapping Caroline into the helicopter when Doc climbed in. The medic pushed his glasses more firmly up onto his nose, smoothed his wind-mussed hair, and plopped into the seat by the door.

Dane swung up into the helicopter. The noise of the rotors made talking impossible, so Savannah strapped herself into the seat next to Caroline without asking permission. Dane crossed over and sat next to the pilot. After putting on a set of earphones, he nodded to the pilot, and they began their ascent.

As they rose above Father Burnett and the soldiers, Savannah's thoughts turned to the upcoming meeting with her in-laws. She wondered if Dane had notified the McLaughlins that they were coming. Her relationship with Wes's parents was tenuous at best. If Dane was keeping their visit a surprise, she hoped their unexpected arrival wouldn't tip the scales too much against her.

She glanced over at Caroline, who smiled back in youthful enthusiasm. Caroline had no concerns about what kind of reception she would get from the McLaughlins. Savannah turned to stare out the thick glass of the helicopter's window and tried not to let her anxiety show.

The snow-covered landscape sparkled in the setting sun as the helicopter touched down on the concrete pad near the McLaughlins' mountaintop home. When Doc slid the door open, Savannah could see both of Wes's parents waiting for them a few yards away. The intense wind created by the helicopter's rotors pulled at their hair and old-fashioned clothing.

The pilot cut the motor and jumped to the ground. He was followed closely by the two soldiers from the back of the helicopter. The pilot took up guard duty in front of his vehicle while the other two men began walking along the perimeter of the McLaughlins' farm.

Slowly the rotors stopped whirling, and the artificial wind ceased. Doc climbed out of the helicopter and lifted Caroline down. Then he trailed behind the child as she ran to greet her grandparents. Caroline hugged each of the McLaughlins in turn.

"We don't know if we can stay for Christmas," Savannah heard her say. "And we didn't bring any presents because we had already mailed them."

Wes's mother nodded. "We got your package. We're waiting until Christmas Day to open it."

"Do you have a tree?" Caroline asked.

The McLaughlins shook their heads in unison.

Caroline looked back toward the helicopter. "Don't worry. Major Dane will get you one."

Deciding that at this point facing the McLaughlins was safer than staying with Dane, Savannah climbed out and approached her in-laws.

* * *

Wes's parents weren't what Savannah would call friendly when they greeted her, but they were so pleased to see Caroline that they couldn't remain completely aloof. And they seemed genuinely fond of Dane.

"It's good to see you again, Christopher," Mrs. McLaughlin said.

Dane nodded. "You too, ma'am. Sorry to drop in on you like this."

Wes's mother smiled. "You are welcome anytime—especially if you bring Caroline."

Mr. McLaughlin's expression remained grim. He seemed to know that this was not a social call.

Dane introduced Doc as Lieutenant Moser and then suggested that Caroline take the medic to see her kittens. Caroline was happy to comply. She grabbed Doc's hand and pulled him toward the barn.

"When are we going to get my grandparents a Christmas tree?" she called over her shoulder to Dane.

"I have to make sure they want one first," Dane responded.

Caroline stopped and frowned at him. "Who wouldn't want a Christmas tree?"

"You go on, Caroline," Mr. McLaughlin said, kind but firm. "We'll worry about a tree later."

"Your kittens have grown so much, you won't recognize them," his wife added as encouragement.

"Come on, Doc," Caroline said. "Let's go find those kittens."

Doc followed without argument. Savannah was standing beside Dane, waiting to participate in his conversation with the McLaughlins, so she was surprised when he pressed his hand against the small of her back and propelled her forward.

"Why don't you go look at the kittens too?" he suggested.

She frowned at him. "I'd rather stay here with the *adults*."

"But it would be *better* if you go with Caroline and Doc," he insisted.

She gave him a look that left no doubt how she felt about being sent off like a child and then walked to the barn. Doc helped Caroline search for the kittens, but Savannah hovered near the door, her attention focused outside. She watched as Dane spoke to the McLaughlins, presumably telling them about Rosemary's situation and asking for their cooperation.

Finally Mr. McLaughlin nodded and walked to the front porch. He returned a few minutes later with an axe in hand and called to Caroline. "If you want to help us get a tree, you'd better come on, girl!"

Caroline dropped the two kittens she'd rounded up thus far and raced to join Dane and Mr. McLaughlin as they headed into the nearby woods. Wes's mother disappeared inside the small house.

Savannah turned to Doc. "So what are we supposed to do?"

Doc smiled. "We can either keep chasing kittens or offer our assistance to Mrs. McLaughlin."

"I suppose helping Mrs. McLaughlin would be the best option," Savannah muttered. "But not by much."

Mrs. McLaughlin had dinner preparations well underway. When they offered to help, Savannah was assigned to peel potatoes while Doc scraped carrots. The kitchen was warm and smelled wonderful, and Savannah found it hard to maintain a resentful attitude.

After a while there was a commotion at the front door. Savannah walked in the living room and watched as Mr. McLaughlin propped a small pine tree in the corner. Caroline was trying to shake snow from the tree's frozen branches, but Dane was nowhere in sight.

Caroline looked over at her mother. "Can we decorate it?"

"Maybe later," Mrs. McLaughlin said from the kitchen door. "Right now it's time for dinner. Everyone come into the kitchen and have a seat."

"Where's Dane?" Savannah asked Wes's father.

He shrugged, unconcerned. "Come eat before it gets cold."

Savannah didn't dare defy him, so she followed the others into the kitchen and sat at the table. Mrs. McLaughlin dished out bowls of vegetable soup and poured glasses of cold milk.

"These vegetables came from our garden," Caroline informed them. "And the milk is from our cows."

"It's very good," Savannah said automatically, her attention focused on the door.

Mrs. McLaughlin put some slices of homemade bread on the table and asked, "Where are you from, Mr. Moser?"

"I'm from Roanoke," Doc responded. "My parents died when I was young, and I was raised by my grandmother. She was a school teacher for over fifty years."

"That's very impressive," Wes's mother said with sincerity. "Roanoke is a lovely area." As Mrs. McLaughlin continued to engage Doc in gracious conversation, Savannah glimpsed the woman she used to be—a wealthy woman hosting society dinners and putting her guests at ease.

Savannah was just about to take a bite of soup when a horrible thought occurred to her. Dane had left her there. That had been the plan all along. She'd been a fool to think Dane would actually allow her to participate in an operation. He just made up the part about her impersonating Rosemary to gain her cooperation. Then he'd coaxed her to the mountain and dumped her there with Caroline before going off to do the exciting stuff without her. Savannah was unbearably saddened by the thought.

Caroline put her spoon in her empty bowl. "I'm finished!" She scooted out of her chair. "Doc, come and help me decorate the tree."

"Give Mr. Moser time to eat his dinner," Mrs. McLaughlin admonished.

"You can eat first," Caroline informed Doc graciously. Then she turned to her grandmother. "Do you have any red balls for the tree? We had extra ones at Major Dane's house, but we didn't bring them with us."

Mrs. McLaughlin shook her head. "I don't have any red balls, but I have some ribbon. Maybe we can tie bows and put them on the tree."

"That sounds pretty good," Caroline agreed hesitantly.

"And we can string some cranberries," Mr. McLaughlin suggested. "I used to do that when I was a boy."

"And tomorrow you can find some pinecones and paint them." Mrs. McLaughlin had really caught the Christmas spirit.

Caroline beamed. "I love to paint!"

Doc finished his meal quickly and stood. The McLaughlins abandoned their food and followed Caroline into the living room. Doc paused in the doorway and asked Savannah, "Aren't you coming with us?"

"I'll be there in a minute," she managed, still trying to compose herself.

Doc nodded solemnly and joined the others.

Once she was alone, Savannah put down her spoon and abandoned the charade of eating. She was overcome with despair and hopelessness. Just when she thought that she'd seen the worst Dane had to offer, he surprised her with more. She'd gotten over his other betrayals and deceits. But if he had truly left her on the mountain, she was afraid she had reached her misery limit.

She was contemplating life without Dane, or even the hope of seeing him occasionally, when the door opened and he walked in.

"What's wrong?" he demanded when he saw her face.

Relief overcame all her other emotions, and she said, "I thought you'd left me."

He stepped closer and whispered, "Not yet. But don't get too attached to me, Savannah."

Before she could respond, Mr. McLaughlin walked in.

"How is the tree decorating going?" Savannah asked him.

"They sent me for twine," Mr. McLaughlin replied with his usual economy of words. Then he walked out the back door.

Savannah turned to Dane. "So when are we leaving?" she asked, mentally determining not to let him out of her sight until whatever time he gave her.

"Right after you get Caroline to sleep," he said as he dished himself up a bowl of soup.

This would require her to trust him, which she still wasn't sure she could, so Savannah frowned. "Can I tell Caroline that we're leaving tonight?"

"Of course. What do you think? She's just going to wake up tomorrow, and you'll be gone."

She gritted her teeth. "I wasn't sure how much of our plan was *secret*."

He took a bite of soup and reached for a slice of homemade bread. "Caroline needs to know that you're leaving, and it will obviously be best if you tell her."

Dane was using that I'm-so-much-smarter-than-you-are tone again, but Savannah found it difficult to be mad at him while sitting in the McLaughlins' cozy kitchen, watching him eat homemade vegetable soup. He'd had the chance to leave her but didn't take it. Surely that meant something—no matter that he claimed otherwise.

When he finished his soup, he took his bowl to the sink and rinsed it. Then he waved toward the living room. "Let's see what they've been able to do with the tree."

* * *

Savannah was prepared for resistance when she told Caroline it was time for bed. But on the farm, they all retired early, so Caroline didn't argue. The excitement of the plane ride and seeing her grandparents and decorating yet another Christmas tree had been too much. So by the time Savannah was sitting on the edge of the small bed in the McLaughlins' guest room, stroking Caroline's hair, the child's beautiful blue eyes were drooping with exhaustion.

"I like it here, don't you?" Caroline murmured sleepily.

Savannah always felt on guard when she was near Wes's parents, as if they might suddenly demand to know the details of her unhappy marriage and Wes's untimely death. But she didn't try to explain that to Caroline. She just said, "It's a very lovely place."

"What are we going to do tomorrow?" Caroline asked around a yawn.

"You'll have to ask your grandparents that when you wake up. Major Dane and I are leaving tonight, but Doc will be staying here with you."

Caroline opened her eyes and frowned. "Will you be back in time for Christmas?"

Savannah didn't want to make a promise she couldn't keep, so she said, "I really want to be, but I don't know how long it will take for us to find Rosemary's husband."

Caroline wrapped her small, warm arms around Savannah's neck. "I'll miss you while you're gone."

Savannah clutched the child to her and tried not to cry. "I'll miss you too. And I love you." She felt a tremor run through Caroline's small body, and suddenly catching Mario Ferrante and helping Rosemary didn't seem so important. She wanted badly to go with Dane to New Orleans, and she wanted to end the threat that Mario Ferrante posed to her family. But how would she find the strength to leave her child?

She heard a noise behind her and looked to see Dane and the McLaughlins standing in a concerned little huddle near the doorway.

"I'll be right back," she told Caroline as she joined the others at the door. Her eyes sought Dane's, and for once she was glad he could read her mind since this eliminated the need for her to explain.

"She will miss you, but she'll be happy and safe while you're gone," he said softly. "And we'll be back as soon as we can."

"She doesn't want me to go," Savannah countered.

"You're a part of the operation," he reminded her. "We need you."

This admission was a monumental concession on his part, and under different circumstances she would have been honored. But at the moment she was too worried about Caroline to enjoy it.

"Caroline needs me," she said. It was unnecessary to add that Caroline took precedence over all other concerns.

Support came from an unexpected source. "Christopher," Wes's mother said, "how can you ask her to choose between a military operation and her child?"

Tears flooded Savannah's eyes again. With that one question, Mrs. McLaughlin had both validated her reluctance to leave and deemed her a good mother.

Dane nodded, and she was sure he was about to say that she should stay with Caroline. It probably wouldn't be too difficult for him to find someone else to impersonate Rosemary. The operation would proceed without her. She would not experience New Orleans with Dane. But Caroline wouldn't have separation anxiety.

After taking a deep breath, she waited for him to speak the words that would both relieve her of responsibility and break her heart.

Dane said, "As long as Mario Ferrante is at large, Caroline is in danger. This operation gives us the opportunity to capture him, but we need Savannah's help."

Wes's mother put a trembling hand to her thin chest and turned to Savannah. Her eyes reflected both sympathy and determination. "So you have to go. That is what will be best for Caroline in the long run."

Wes's father asked Dane, "You're certain that Caroline can't accompany her mother?"

"Yes, sir," Dane confirmed.

Mr. McLaughlin nodded. "Then the child will stay with us."

"Mama, I'll be okay here with Doc and my grandparents," Caroline said from her bed, and Savannah wondered how much of their conversation she had overheard.

Dane smiled. "That's because you're a good, brave soldier."

"No, it's because I have my favorite teddy bear that my mom sprays her perfume on. Anytime I get lonely or scared, I can just sniff him." She demonstrated by pressing the bear to her face and inhaling deeply.

And just that quickly the decision was made for Savannah. It was still going to be difficult to leave Caroline, but she didn't feel guilty.

Mr. McLaughlin gave Savannah an approving nod. "Putting your perfume on her teddy bear was smart. When it's time to separate young animals from their mothers, we give them a scrap of cloth that has their mother's scent on it. It makes the process easier for the babies."

"I'm not a baby," Caroline objected.

"Of course you're not," Savannah replied. "Your grandfather was just using the animal babies as an example. You keep that teddy bear close, and I'll be back before you know it."

Caroline snuggled down under her covers with the bear clutched to her chest. "Don't worry about Christmas, Mama," she murmured around a yawn. "I'll save it until you get back."

Savannah pressed a kiss to Caroline's forehead and hurried from the room, afraid at any moment she might dissolve into a sobbing heap.

CHAPTER 5

SAVANNAH DIDN'T EVEN try to stop the flow of tears as she strapped herself back into the military helicopter for the trip down the mountain.

"She'll be fine," Dane said as he swung up and into the copilot seat. "Doc will protect her with his life if necessary."

Savannah nodded. "I know."

"And you'll be back soon."

"I know."

He scowled. "Then quit being a crybaby. I need you alert and focused."

She knew that leaving Caroline was only slightly more difficult for her than it was for Dane and that hatefulness was his way of dealing with his own separation anxiety. But she was too miserable to be patient and understanding. "I'll cry if I want to."

They didn't speak for several minutes, but finally the desire for information forced her to ask him, "How often can we call them?"

"Any direct calls between our team and the mountain might lead Ferrante to Caroline." He pulled a little black box from his pocket that resembled the keyless entry to her Yukon. "This transponder uses radio waves and is virtually untraceable. The green light indicates that all is well on the mountain. If the light changes to red, we'll abandon all other aspects of the operation and converge here."

She bit her lip until it stopped trembling and then said, "So I won't be able to talk to Caroline at all."

"No."

Her hand moved automatically to the locket around her neck, and her fingers traced the delicate carvings to calm herself. She didn't need to open the locket. She had the picture memorized and could access it whenever she pleased. Just as she would always remember the sound of Caroline's voice even if she wasn't able to actually speak to her child for the next few days.

When the helicopter landed on the pad at the Brotherly Love Farm, Captain Findlay met them. Savannah looked around for Father Burnett but didn't see him. She considered that just as well since it meant they didn't have to mislead the man any more than they already had.

Captain Findlay arranged for a Jeep to take them back to the airstrip, where the plane was waiting to return them to Ft. Belvoir. Savannah slept during the flight, which made the time in the air pass quickly. And she felt rested by the time they landed at Andrews Air Force Base.

Thanks to the opposite effect of the time difference on the return trip, they lost two hours, and it was three o'clock in the morning when the plane touched down. Savannah rubbed her eyes as they bounced along the runway.

"What are the chances of getting a bath?" she asked.

"Zero right now," Dane replied without compassion. Based on his mood, she guessed that he hadn't gotten any sleep during the flight. "Those chances might improve after we take care of Cam."

They were picked up at Andrews by a driver from General Steele's staff. He took them to Ft. Belvoir and dropped them off in front of the administration building for the Intelligence Center. Dane asked the driver to wait and then led the way inside.

The building she was so familiar with felt strange, even a little creepy. Maybe it was just the early-morning hour and the fact that the fluorescent lighting couldn't completely dispel the shadows.

"Why are we here?" Savannah asked.

"A couple of things," Dane responded. "I want to check on the support team General Steele set up for us before we go to the hangar, where the emergency helicopter is waiting for the call from Ft. Lewis. And I need to get you checked for bugs."

She raised an eyebrow. "Bugs?"

He almost smiled. "The electronic kind."

"How would I have gotten bugged?"

Dane opened the door and stepped back for her to enter first. "The same way Cam did."

"What about you?"

"Hack checked the rest of the team, but trust me—you don't want him to search you."

Savannah couldn't control a little shiver. "I trust you—on that at least."

When she reached her office, Savannah stopped in the doorway. She stared at the files stacked on her desk for a few seconds before crossing the hall to the closet that had been converted into a room for Caroline. When she saw the scattered toys and abandoned books, she felt the old panic start to rise up inside her. She grasped the locket. Caroline . . .

"She's fine," Dane said from behind her. He pulled out the transponder, still showing green, as proof. He walked over to the desk positioned protectively in front of the door to General Steele's office. He picked up the picture Lieutenant Hardy had framed of herself and studied it. "So this is the secretary who took Louise's place."

Savannah made a face. "Lieutenant Hardy is General Steele's new secretary. Nobody could take Louise's place."

Dane raised his eyebrows. "She looks nice enough to me."

"She is nice," Savannah replied. "I just miss Louise."

"And you don't like Lieutenant Hardy," he guessed shrewdly.

"Actually, it's the other way around. She doesn't like me."

Dane raised his eyebrows. "How did you get on Lieutenant Hardy's bad side?"

"She took my attempt to blackmail General Steele personally for some reason," Savannah admitted with reluctance. "We get along better now, because she's crazy about Caroline. But at first things were a little tense."

Dane replaced the picture. "I'll make sure I'm extra charming when I meet the lieutenant."

Savannah rolled her eyes.

Dane checked his watch and then made use of Lieutenant Hardy's desk phone to call the general. After hanging up the phone he told Savannah, "The general said the guys in Technical Surveillance Detection are expecting you at three-thirty. That gives us a few minutes to check on the support team. The general put them in an empty office by his situation room."

Dane led the way down the hall, Savannah following. As they walked, Savannah heard a radio playing in the distance. Based on Dane's irritated expression, she assumed he heard it to. He continued to the end of the hall and stopped in front of the office where the music was the loudest. Then he jerked the door open.

The small room was crowded with computers, monitors, and other devices. Two soldiers wearing most of their blue service uniforms stood inside. One was dancing to the music coming from a small radio, and the other was talking on a cell phone. Both looked like they wanted to die when they saw Dane.

Savannah hovered in the doorway and watched the proceedings with interest. She was often angry with Dane but never afraid of him. Sometimes she forgot that in military circles, he was a force to be reckoned with. The unfortunate soldiers were now standing at attention, saluting for all they were worth.

Dane's tone was deceptively calm when he said, "Apparently I've found the break room. I was looking for the support team for Operation Sitting Duck. Maybe one of you men could direct me."

It was obvious that neither man wanted to answer, but finally the dancer stepped forward. While maintaining his stiff stance and fervent salute, he said, "Corporal Lyle Benjamin, *sir!* I am a member of your support team, *sir!*"

Dane raised an eyebrow and then looked to the other man. "And who are you?"

The terrified soldier slipped the cell phone into his pocket with his nonsaluting hand and said, "Private First Class Eric Ponder, *sir!*"

Dane let his eyes roam critically around the room. "I don't know what kind of military operations you're used to, but when you work for me, you do things right. I never want to see that radio again."

"No, sir!" Corporal Benjamin promised. "It's gone, sir!"

Dane turned to Private Pounder. "And no personal phone calls of any kind while you're on duty."

The private blushed crimson. "No, sir."

Dane's eyes moved to the McDonald's sack on a nearby table. "There will be no eating in here. If you are medically unable to make it an entire four-hour shift without food, let me know, and I'll have you transferred."

"We're fine, sir," Corporal Benjamin answered for both men.

"This is a dangerous covert operation," Dane continued. "You'll be monitoring several teams at once, patching through phone calls, checking security codes, and tracking individuals of interest. While you're in this room, I need your undivided attention."

"Yes, sir," Corporal Benjamin agreed. "We're sorry about the radio and all. But since the operation hasn't actually started yet . . ."

"The operation started for you when you walked into this room," Dane interrupted him. "From this moment forward I want you to conduct yourself like thousands of lives are counting on you, because they are. And pass that same message on to the others who have been assigned shifts in here."

The men nodded in mutual humiliation.

Dane focused on Corporal Benjamin. "I'm holding you personally responsible for the accuracy of the intelligence information my team receives. If one of my men dies because of your negligence, I'll personally come for you."

Savannah shivered, and the chilling threat wasn't even directed at her.

Dane moved toward the door. "I'd tell you to be *at ease,* but you're way ahead of me."

Savannah waited until they were back down the hall before saying, "Thousands of lives? Don't you think that was exaggerating a little bit?"

"I was making a point. And your life may depend on those guys, so you'd better hope it was a point well taken."

She nodded. "I think you got through to them."

When they reached the general's office, Savannah was surprised and not completely happy to see Lieutenant Hardy sitting at her desk. Despite the early hour, the general's new secretary was wearing a crisply pressed uniform, and every hair was in place.

The lieutenant stood as they approached. After introductions were made, Lieutenant Hardy addressed Dane. "The general asked me to come in and escort Savannah to the Technical Surveillance Detection unit." She didn't try to hide her lack of enthusiasm for this assignment.

Savannah didn't relish visiting this unit as a customer but knew arguing with either Dane or the lieutenant would be a waste of time. Besides, she really did want to be sure she wasn't bugged.

"I'll wait in your office," Dane told Savannah. "I can be making some calls there while you're getting checked out."

Savannah wasn't completely comfortable with the idea of Dane making himself at home in her office, but she didn't want to waste time with an objection, so she nodded.

Then Lieutenant Hardy moved toward the elevators. "Follow me," she instructed.

Savannah reluctantly obeyed. As they walked, Savannah stared at Lieutenant Hardy's stiff back and thought longingly of Louise. The general's former secretary had been very dedicated to her job and more so to the general, but she understood the separation between private life and career. If the general had called Louise before dawn and asked her to come in to work, she would have laughed. Savannah found this new generation of overachieving workaholics exhausting.

The TSDU was in the basement of the building. With metal tables and basins and X-ray machines, it looked more like a morgue than a part of the Intelligence Center. As she walked inside, Savannah was oddly grateful for Lieutenant Hardy's presence.

A technician led her to a dressing room. "You'll need to take everything off," he told her. "That includes removable dental devices, contact lenses, jewelry, and hair clips. It all goes in here." He handed her a large plastic bag with her name written in bold block letters. "There's a robe in there for you to put on during your full-body scan."

Savannah nodded and stepped into the little cubicle. She took off her clothes, thankful she didn't have any removable dental devices, and put everything into the plastic bag. Then she put on the thick cotton robe and stepped out of the cubicle. Lieutenant Hardy was standing by the door and went with Savannah through every step of the scanning process. When they returned to the little dressing room, Savannah was feeling a little more kindly toward the other woman.

"I'm glad that's over," Savannah confided. "And I hope I never have to endure anything like that again."

"Don't be so dramatic. It's just part of life in military intelligence," the lieutenant replied. Then she handed Savannah the bag that contained her personal itmes. "Hurry and get dressed."

Savannah's goodwill toward the lieutenant evaporated.

Dane was waiting impatiently by Lieutenant Hardy's desk when they returned. "It's about time," he said as he rushed her toward the entrance. "I thought you'd never get back."

"Believe me, I wasn't trying to extend my stay at the TSDU," Savannah assured him.

Dane laughed. "Well, at least the technicians didn't find any electronic devices embedded in your ears. That's something to be grateful for."

"If you say so," she muttered.

During the drive to the airstrip, she asked about Cam.

"Our plan is underway," he told her. "Cam's been having chest pains for several hours, and Steamer has helped the medical staff at the clinic at Ft. Lewis to come to the decision that he should be moved to Walter Reed. They are just waiting for us."

A weary-looking flight crew met them at the airstrip. Savannah eyed the helicopter with distaste. She was growing weary of military transport.

"When do we leave?"

Dane put a hand on her elbow. "Right now."

Most of the helicopter's interior space was dedicated to a stretcher and other medical equipment. This left little room for Savannah to maneuver. Dane slid into the pilot's seat and pointed to a bench at the back. "Sit there and strap yourself in."

"I probably could have figured that out all by myself," she retorted as he started the engine.

"Huh?" he hollered back

She shook her head. "Never mind."

Once he had lifted off the dark tarmac for the short trip to Ft. Lewis, Dane gave her more unnecessary instructions. "Stay back until they have Cam secured inside the helicopter. If he recognizes you before we get rid of the prison's medical personnel, our plan is ruined."

She nodded.

"Act like you're busy with some of that equipment, since you're supposed to be a nurse," he shouted, indicating that he didn't trust her to come up with appropriate activities on her own.

She fought her annoyance and asked, "What if Cam really does need medical care?"

Dane shrugged. Apparently this didn't concern him. He put on his radio handset and notified security at Ft. Lewis of his imminent approach. A voice crackled back through the radio, giving him landing instructions.

The minute the helicopter touched down, the side door was wrenched open. Savannah shrunk against an equipment cabinet in the back as two medics combined to lift a thrashing body onto the helicopter's stretcher. While one worked from the outside, the other climbed in beside Savannah. Together the men managed to strap Cam in.

Once this task was complete, the medic inside the helicopter turned to Savannah. "We haven't been able to stabilize him," the medic said. "And he's in considerable pain."

Savannah nodded as she watched the medic hook Cam up to the monitors and IV fluids inside the helicopter. She knew the medication in the IV would counteract the shot Steamer had arranged for Cam to receive earlier. What she didn't know was how long it would take to work.

The medic waved her forward. "You'll need to watch him closely during the trip."

Hoping to hurry his departure, Savannah stepped up beside Cam. She kept her face averted from the patient by pretending to read one of the several monitors. Fortunately the medic didn't ask her any questions or seem to consider her behavior suspicious. He turned to Dane and said, "Walter Reed is expecting you."

"On our way," Dane replied.

The medic jumped out and secured the door. Then Dane lifted the helicopter into the air. After a brief exchange with the Ft. Lewis security people, they were on their way. Dane pulled off his headset and turned to Savannah. "Double-check those straps. He'll regain consciousness in a minute, and we don't want him to get loose until we're sure how he feels about us."

She leaned over Cam. He was calmer, and the pain seemed to be easing. It was odd to see him in the prison uniform instead of his trademark camouflage. He was pale instead of tanned, and his military short hair had grown out into an unattractive tangle. In spite of the circumstances of their last encounter, she felt sorry for Cam as she tested the strap near Cam's chest. She gave the strap a firm tug and was about to report that her mission had been accomplished when Cam's hand slipped out from under the strap and grabbed her by the wrist.

The pressure he exerted was painful, and she screamed. His eyes flew open, and he whispered, "Savannah?"

Dane turned around to see what was happening, and the helicopter tilted.

Savannah prepared herself for certain death as Dane yelled, "Let go of her, Cam!"

"Dane?" Cam craned his neck to see behind him.

"Let go before Dane crashes this helicopter!" Savannah cried.

Cam released her suddenly, and she moved as far from him as possible in the crowded helicopter. Reassured that she was not in imminent danger, Dane returned his attention to flying and soon regained control.

"What's going on?" Cam asked.

"I'll explain in a minute," Dane called from the front of the helicopter. "I'm putting down."

The landing was less than smooth, and Savannah had to grab the wall for support. Seconds later Dane was beside her.

"We broke you out of prison," Dane told their patient.

"Why would you help me break out of prison?" Cam looked away in shame. "You must hate me."

"We're angry, but we don't hate you," Savannah said.

Cam twisted under the tight straps. "Where are my boys? Are they okay?"

"They're in the witness protection program," Dane replied. "Your wife and her boyfriend too."

"So they're safe?"

Dane nodded. "I check on them regularly."

Cam relaxed against the stretcher. "What happened to me?"

"Steamer came to Ft. Lewis today and organized the immunization check. He arranged for you to get a shot that made you have heart attack symptoms. Then he convinced the clinic to transfer you to Walter Reed, and we answered the call for an emergency helicopter."

"But why?"

"Ferrante's daughter ran away from him and came to Savannah asking for protection. We're going to use the girl to capture Ferrante, but in order for our plan to work, we need someone in his camp."

"You broke me out so I could spy on Ferrante?"

"Basically." Dane waved at Savannah, and Cam's eyes followed the gesture.

"Now that Wes is gone, Caroline is all I have left," she said, playing the guilt card as she had been instructed. "Until Ferrante is behind bars, there's always a danger that he'll try and harm her again."

"I'm sorry about Wes," Cam whispered, "and for helping Ferrante with the kidnapping."

Dane reclaimed his attention. "There's nothing you can do about the past, but you can help me secure Savannah's future. You owe her that much."

"Please," Savannah pleaded.

"If Ferrante figures out that I'm a traitor, he'll kill me," Cam said.

"That's true."

Cam closed his eyes for a few seconds and then nodded. "Okay, I'll do it."

"Good." Dane regarded the other man with satisfaction.

"Thank you," Savannah said.

"But you have to promise me something," Cam told Dane.

"And that is?" Dane asked.

Cam's eyes sought Dane's earnestly. "If something happens to me, you have to promise to look out for my boys."

Dane didn't have to think about this request. "I will."

"I want them to have a nice place to live," Cam continued. "A neighborhood with sidewalks and lots of trees."

"Okay," Dane agreed.

"I want them to go to college and get good jobs so they can support their families without having to break the law."

"Don't worry about that . . ." Savannah began, but Dane held up a hand to silence her.

"You have my word."

"And one more thing," Cam said. "If I live through this, I want to see my kids. Just for a few minutes. They don't have to see me. It might upset them. But before you bring me back to prison, you can take me by their house and let me watch them play or something."

Savannah felt tears sting her eyes as Dane nodded. "It's a deal."

Dane reached over and unhooked the straps that restrained Cam. Slowly he sat up on the edge of the stretcher.

Cam sighed in resignation. "Now tell me what you want me to do."

"Savannah and I are going to get off here, and you'll take the chopper to Ferrante's country estate in Maryland. We got a tip from the FBI that Ferrante is there. Your escape has to look authentic or Ferrante will be suspicious, so we can't protect you from pursuit."

Cam rubbed his chest. "Who will be coming after me?"

"The Army first, joined quickly by the FBI and probably the DC police. You'll need all your skills to elude them."

Cam smiled. "My skills have been getting rusty while I was sitting in prison. I'm glad for the chance to use them."

Dane held out his palm, revealing an innocent-looking capsule. "I want you to swallow this."

Cam narrowed his eyes at Dane. "It's a tracking device?"

Dane nodded. "It has audio capability within a limited range—probably a few yards." Dane shook a couple of aspirins into his palm beside the capsule. "If Ferrante detects it, tell him it was administered with other medication and let him remove it. If he thinks you knowingly brought in a tracking device, he'll kill you and then all this will be a waste of time. And make sure Ferrante knows you want revenge against me for ruining your life—but don't overdo it. He's smart."

Cam nodded. "I understand." He took the capsule and the aspirins and threw them all into the back of his throat.

After he swallowed, Savannah asked, "How do you feel?"

"I'm good," Cam said. "And I'll do everything I can to help Dane catch Ferrante."

She was touched and couldn't help saying, "You're taking a big risk for us."

"I *owe* you." Cam reached a hand toward Savannah, but she shrunk away from him involuntarily. There was acceptance in his eyes as his hand dropped down to his side. "You need to be careful. Ferrante was obsessed with Wes. In fact, I wondered if he recruited me just because of my connection to him."

"And you think Ferrante's obsession with Wes has extended itself to Savannah?" Dane asked.

Cam nodded. "Caroline too. There were other ways to get that disc, but Ferrante *wanted* to grab the kid." Cam's voice was pleading when he continued. "You gotta promise me you'll be careful."

"I'll be very careful," Savannah assured him.

"The team won't let anything happen to them," Dane added.

Cam seemed slightly relieved. "Just don't underestimate Ferrante," he said. "It would be a mistake."

"I don't take chances. You know that," Dane said.

Cam slipped off the gurney and walked gingerly to the open door. "What if I need to contact you?"

Dane jumped to the ground and then reached a hand up to assist Savannah. "Don't unless there's imminent danger to Savannah or Caroline. But if you have to, use the old emergency number. It will be answered by a support team at Ft. Belvoir, and they'll patch you through to me."

Cam looked down at them. "Sending all your intelligence information through Ft. Belvoir might not be the best idea. I can't prove it, but I think Ferrante has someone inside."

Dane frowned. "Ft. Belvoir? You're kidding me, right?"

Cam shrugged. "Like I said, I can't prove it."

"I'll take that under advisement." Dane opened the sliding door on the side of the helicopter. "Head straight for Ferrante's estate. At this point, nobody can protect you but him."

Tears filled Savannah's eyes as Cam gripped the helicopter door. In spite of all he'd done, she hated to send him into danger. "Thank you."

Cam gave them a little wave and slammed the door closed. Dane and Savannah watched as the helicopter lifted off the ground and was swallowed by the darkness. Then Dane took her by the hand and said, "Let's go."

He led the way across the field where he had landed the helicopter until they reached a gravel road. Then he took a phone from his pocket and made a quick call. After ending the call, he reduced their pace but didn't release her hand. Even though she knew this was probably more of a security measure than a sign of affection, she savored the feel of his fingers, wrapped around hers. And she gloried in the fact that for just a few minutes, she had him all to herself.

Too soon headlights approached from the north, and Dane released her hand. The same car that had chauffeured them earlier stopped, and they climbed in. The euphoria Savannah had experienced during their walk under the stars dissipated as she watched Dane pull out his phone. He slipped quickly and completely into "commanding officer mode" making one call after another during the drive to Ft. Belvoir.

Savannah was surprised yet grateful when the car stopped in front of her apartment. Dane climbed out and held the door for her, all without interrupting his phone call. One of Hack's guards was standing beside the front door. He nodded politely as Dane ushered her inside. Steamer was sitting on the couch watching TV. In accordance with Dane's instructions regarding his attire, he was now wearing neat khaki pants and a blue oxford button-down shirt. His hair was still long, but gel-free.

Dane ended his call. "Cam made it to Ferrante's estate."

"Yep." Apparently this wasn't news to Steamer. "Ferrante's men didn't shoot him on sight, and they are supposedly taking him up to see their boss."

"I told Hack to stay in contact with the support team and keep us posted," Dane said.

Steamer nodded. "Hack's on top of it." Steamer held up a sack with RITE-WAY PHARMACY printed across the front. Careful to direct his comments toward Dane, thereby excluding Savannah from the conversation, he said, "Here's the stuff you told me to get. And the box you ordered is on the kitchen table."

Dane walked into the kitchen and ripped open the cardboard box on the table. From the corrugated remnants he pulled a flesh-colored combination of foam, nylon straps, and Velcro. He gave it a cursory examination and then handed it to Savannah.

"This is a prosthetic that simulates pregnancy," he explained. "You need to put it on and keep it on until after this rescue operation is over. Wear it even if you think no one can see you. Think pregnant, act pregnant. Become one with the fake stomach. Sleep in it, eat in it, shop in it . . ."

She held up a hand to stop him. "I get the picture."

He ignored her. "You must be totally convincing as Rosemary. That means looking pregnant always."

She nodded. "I said I *understand*."

Dane frowned, indicating that he didn't have complete confidence in her. Then he retrieved the plastic pharmacy sack from its spot on the couch beside Steamer and dumped the contents onto the kitchen table. There was a box of Miss Clairol's natural dark brown hair dye, a spray bottle of Insta-Tan, and a package of Crest White Strips.

"The hair dye I understand," Savannah said as she surveyed the sack's contents. "But why the tanning spray and white strips?"

"So that the people at the drug store would think Steamer was buying this stuff for himself—to maintain that Las Vegas weirdo look he's got going," Dane replied.

Steamer's resulting scowl was directed toward Savannah, and she sighed. The drug store assignment hadn't helped her campaign to win Steamer's friendship.

"Have you ever dyed your own hair before?" Dane asked as he opened the box and removed two bottles, a tube, and a pair of latex gloves.

"No," she said.

He scanned the instructions. "It doesn't look too hard." He pointed to a kitchen chair. "Sit."

Nervously she obeyed.

"Come here, Steam." When the other man joined them in the kitchen, Dane extended the gloves toward Steamer. "Put these on."

"No way!" Steamer replied. "Sir," he added as an afterthought.

Grimacing, Dane pulled the gloves on his own hands and handed Steamer the instructions. "Okay, tell me what to do first."

"Well, *first* it says you have to do an allergy test forty-eight hours before you dye," Steamer read from the bright blue print.

"Skip that part," Dane said. "We don't have time."

Steamer was frowning. "I don't know. It says an allergy to the dye can be bad. Especially if you have tattoos."

Dane rolled his eyes, and Savannah had to work hard to control hysterical laughter. "I don't have any tattoos," she promised the unlikely pair of hair colorists.

"You're also supposed to do a strand test to see how the chemicals will react with her hair before you put it all over her head," Steamer informed Dane.

"We're not doing any tests," Dane said with ill-concealed impatience. "Now get on with it."

"I'm just trying to tell you how to do it right," Steamer said.

"We'll do it *right* when we open our own hair salon," Dane promised sarcastically. "For now we've got to do it *quick* so we can get out of here."

Steamer abandoned his attempts to protect her from chemical disaster. "Mix the color-blend activator with the color-blend formula and shake," he read. Savannah watched in fascination as Dane performed this function.

"What next?" he asked with a finger still covering the tip of the applicator bottle.

"Part her hair into small sections and apply color to the roots and any stubborn gray first," Steamer instructed.

Savannah was offended. "I don't have any gray, stubborn or otherwise."

"You probably will by the time we're finished with you," Dane muttered. He used the tip of the applicator to part her hair, and then she felt the cool liquid against her scalp. She closed her eyes. It was nice that he was running his fingers through her hair—even if his fingers were encased in plastic and applying chemicals that she might be allergic to.

"Don't rub the solution into her skin!" Steamer cautioned sharply. "That can cause irritation."

"I can think of something else that causes irritation," Dane said with a look in Steamer's direction.

"She won't be able to pass for Ferrante's daughter if she's bald," Steamer pointed out, and Savannah's eyes flew open in alarm.

"You won't be bald," Dane said with confidence. He continued to apply the dye with military precision until the bottle was empty. Then he set it on the kitchen table and asked Steamer, "Now what?"

"Now we time it for twenty-five minutes," Steamer read aloud. "It would be longer if she had stubborn gray."

"Finally we have something to be thankful for," Dane said as he checked his watch. Then he addressed Savannah. "Sit still here while your dye works."

She nodded as her eyes drooped closed. In spite of her nap on the plane, she was still tired.

"Watch and make sure she doesn't fall out of her chair, Steamer," Dane said. "I've got to check in with Hack."

Savannah wasn't sure how hard Steamer would try to prevent her from falling, so she forced herself to remain upright, although she did doze.

After exactly twenty-five minutes, Dane shook her shoulder. "Time for the next step," he told her.

She opened her eyes and looked around. "Where's Steamer?"

"I sent him on a little errand." Dane pressed his gloved hands onto her head, and his fingers massaged the dye through her hair.

"Have you heard any more about Cam?"

"He made it to Ferrante, but contrary to Doc's lofty predictions of loyalty and teamwork, Cam immediately spilled everything we told him in the helicopter, including the fact that he was carrying an internal tracking device."

Savannah was disappointed. It had made no sense to trust Cam, but she had. "Did Ferrante find the freckle device?"

"He found it," Dane replied. "They removed both devices, but we did hear their plans to cover up Cam's escape."

"They're going to crash the helicopter?" Savannah guessed.

Dane nodded. "After putting a body inside. Ferrante said to make sure the impact was intense enough to make identification impossible."

"Where will they get a body?" Savannah couldn't help but ask.

Dane shrugged. "Guys like Ferrante probably keep several on hand just in case."

Savannah shuddered at the thought.

"So now we're down to just the ear implant as a way to track him," Dane continued. "Which is all we really need. And as long as Cam is with Ferrante, the surveillance guys at Ft. Belvoir can track them both."

"At least they didn't shoot Cam on sight," Savannah said as she closed her eyes again and enjoyed the sensation of Dane's fingers massaging her scalp.

"I guess that's a good thing," Dane muttered. Then he lifted his hands from her head. "I think I've got it all worked in evenly."

She opened her eyes and asked wearily, "What's next?"

"Now you have to rinse the dye out of your hair," he said. He put a blue tube in her hand. "This is the conditioning gloss and according to the directions, its application is vital to a good color job. So I need you to go take a shower. Rinse the dye out, and put this stuff on. Wait three minutes and rinse again. Hopefully you'll be a brunette without bald spots or an irritated scalp."

"Hopefully," she agreed.

"My reputation as a hairdresser depends on it."

She rolled her eyes and headed toward the bathroom.

"Don't forget this." He handed her the fake pregnancy stomach and whispered with a smile, "Become one with the stomach."

"One," she repeated.

Since Dane was in a hurry to leave, Savannah took a quick shower, applying the conditioning gloss as he had instructed. When she faced her altered appearance in the steam-frosted bathroom mirror, she saw that the color Dane had applied was startlingly different from her normal high-lighted shade of blond. Straight and hanging on both sides of her face, the new hair made her look pale and thinner, like Rosemary.

It took Savannah a few minutes to get the foam lump strapped on to her stomach and even longer to find clothing that would stretch across her altered figure. She settled on a pair of sweat pants and an old, paint-splattered William and Mary T-shirt. Then she walked back to the living room, where Dane and Steamer were both waiting.

They studied her with critical expressions, and finally Steamer said, "That outfit is atrocious."

Dane nodded in agreement. "But with dark hair she looks enough like Ferrante's daughter to fool someone from a distance."

"A rich girl would never be seen in clothes like that," Steamer insisted. "Fortunately Dane sent me to get you some maternity clothes." He pointed to a hot pink sack with MAMA MIA'S MATERNITY BOUTIQUE printed in gold letters.

Despite the insult to her clothes, Savannah was pleased that Steamer was actually speaking directly to her. She crossed the room and looked into the sack. "Thank you, Steamer."

The man gave her a brief nod.

Then she asked Dane, "Aren't you worried that Ferrante will find out you had one of your men buying maternity clothes?"

Dane shook his head. "I want Ferrante to know I have his daughter. What I don't want is for him to know that I've disguised a decoy."

Savannah nodded. "I guess that makes sense."

"Go dress in some of those clothes," Dane suggested. "Steamer's right—that outfit is painful to look at."

With a smirk, Savannah carried the bag into her bedroom. Inside the bag she found four complete maternity outfits, pajamas, and a winter coat. She tried on a pair of velvet-trimmed pants and a lace blouse. She was pleased to see that in addition to having good taste, Steamer had also predicted her sizes perfectly.

She was surprised that Steamer had gone to the trouble of shopping at a high-end maternity boutique instead of buying one-size-fits-all clothes for pregnant women from a discount store. Maybe he was just trying to buy clothes he thought a rich girl would wear, afraid that cheap clothing would tip off an observer and put the operation in jeopardy. Or maybe he was actually trying to do something nice for her.

With effort, Savannah pushed Steamer and his motivations from her mind. Then she returned to the living room and did a full turn in front of Dane. She came to a stop very close to him.

"Don't I look cute?" she asked.

"You're definitely cuter now than you were in those baggy sweat pants," he allowed.

Even though she'd forced the compliment from him, she felt a blush rise in her cheeks. Anxious to hide the disturbing effect his words had on her, she looked over at Steamer. "You did an excellent job of guessing my sizes."

He shrugged. "It's a talent."

She turned back to Dane. "Thanks to Steamer, I look better, but if you don't want me to get cranky, I still need food."

"I can handle cranky," Dane replied.

She narrowed her eyes at him. "You have a tendency toward crankiness yourself."

Steamer had been watching the exchange between Dane and Savannah with a puzzled expression. "No argument there," he contributed.

Dane waved toward the kitchen table. "Steam, clean up the evidence of our dye-job, and take all the trash with you. We don't want to leave any traces behind."

Steamer nodded. "Will do."

"Wait with Hack, and I'll be in touch." Dane took the Mama Mia sack that contained the rest of Savannah's maternity wardrobe from her and stuffed it into her overnight case. Then he led the way outside.

The sun was just beginning to peek over the horizon and hadn't had a chance to affect the temperature, so it was still uncomfortably cold. Savannah requested that Dane remove the coat Steamer had gotten for her from her overnight case. He handed her the coat, and she pulled it on gratefully as he stowed their bags in the trunk of a black sedan parked by the curb.

Then he motioned toward a white SUV across the parking lot. Two men, who were almost certainly employed by Hack, emerged from the vehicle and joined them in the cold, damp Virginia air. "These are a couple of Hack's guys," Dane confirmed.

"Nice to meet you," she said.

Both men nodded, but neither spoke.

"They'll be traveling with us." Dane checked his watch. "If we don't hurry, we're going to miss our plane."

They got to their gate at Dulles International just as final boarding was announced for their flight. Dane rushed Savannah onto the plane, and they were settling into their first-class seats when Hack's men walked past them in to the economy section. They arrived in Nashville ninety minutes later.

Once they were settled in their rental car, Savannah asked, "Where are Hack's men?"

Dane checked the mirror. "They should be along soon."

Minutes later a pickup truck passed by. Dane pulled in behind it, and Savannah saw a van driven by their other bodyguard bringing up the rear of their little caravan.

"Here we go," Dane said.

Savannah put on her seat belt and tried not to worry. Dane seemed to have things under control.

Dane turned on the car's radio and changed channels until he found the local news. There was a report of an escape from the prison at Ft. Lewis. Dane turned up the volume, and they listened together until the voice moved on to a traffic report, at which point Dane turned off the radio.

Savannah glanced at him. "That's what you wanted the press to say?"

He nodded. "So far, so good." He pulled onto an entrance ramp to the interstate and joined the sparse group of travelers headed away from Washington, DC.

They'd been driving for about two hours when she asked when he planned to stop for something to eat.

He frowned. "You ate on the plane."

"That was breakfast, and it was terrible," she reminded him.

"We need to put a few miles behind us before we stop," Dane said.

"I might die of starvation before then!"

He cut his eyes over to her. "I doubt that."

She bit back a sarcastic reply and decided to turn the tables on him. Patting her stomach, she said, "Remember, I'm eating for two."

He gave her a look of annoyance. But he said, "You win. We'll stop at the next exit."

When they pulled up to the drive-through window at Burger King, Dane asked what she wanted.

"What are you getting?" she asked.

"I'm not hungry," he claimed.

She leaned across and spoke directly to the girl at the window. "I want two number ones."

His eyebrows arched. "Why two?"

"Because once we get back on the interstate, you'll decide you're hungry and try to eat my food."

Dane paid for their food and crammed his change into a pocket. Then he eased the car down to the next window.

Savannah saw their escorts parked along the road in front of the restaurant and asked, "Should we get something for Hack's men?"

"If we deliver food to them, it will pretty much ruin our attempts at keeping their association with us a secret," he pointed out.

"But they must be hungry."

"Since they aren't pregnant," Dane said with a meaningful look at her stomach, "they can wait."

When the food was passed in to them, Savannah put the drinks into the console between the seats and opened the bag to extract the sandwiches and French fries. She spread out two napkins on the edge of her seat and then arranged each combo meal on its own napkin.

"Remember," she said, "these are both mine."

Without comment, he reached over and picked up the closest hamburger and took a big bite.

CHAPTER 6

AFTER EATING HER lunch, Savannah curled sideways in the seat so she could gaze at Dane while he drove. Finally he looked over with a frown.

"Why are you staring at me?"

She smiled. "I can't help myself."

"You're making me nervous," he claimed, although she doubted he meant it.

"Sorry," she replied with an equal lack of honesty.

During the weeks of separation, she had dreamed of an opportunity like this—to observe him without interruption. To watch his expressions change and his moods shift. She resisted sleep, anxious to enjoy the view, but finally exhaustion overwhelmed her. She awoke with a start when Dane stopped the car in front of a Motel 4. She stretched and yawned then asked, "Where are we?"

"A few miles south of Birmingham, Alabama," he replied. "We'll spend the rest of the day here and then drive on into New Orleans under the cover of darkness."

She waved at the hotel. "I've heard of a Motel 6 but never a Motel 4."

"Apparently this chain is . . . less," he replied.

"Great," she muttered. When he made no move to get out, she asked, "What are we waiting for?"

"We're giving Hack's men a chance to check things out."

Savannah scanned the area but didn't see their escorts. "Will they get hotel rooms too?"

"No, Hack will rotate in fresh replacements," he replied. One of their escorts stepped out and nodded to Dane.

"All clear outside," he said as he opened the door. "Come on in with me so the hotel folks can get a look at you."

"We're leaving a trail for Ferrante to follow?" she guessed.

He nodded, and she climbed out of the car. She stood on the sidewalk while Dane retrieved their overnight bags from the trunk. Then they walked inside, and Dane led her to the hotel desk. He gave the clerk a credit card.

The clerk smiled as she scanned his card. When she returned his credit card, she asked, "When is the baby due?"

Savannah was caught off guard by the question but recovered quickly. "January."

The clerk beamed. "Congratulations to both of you! Isn't having a baby a wonderful experience?"

"It's been pretty amazing so far," Savannah agreed with a look in Dane's direction.

"Do you know if it's a boy or a girl?" the friendly clerk asked.

Savannah shook her head. "No."

"I'm pretty good at predicting." The clerk frowned at Savannah's midsection. "You're carrying it kind of high, so I'm going to say a boy."

Savannah put a protective hand on her stomach.

The clerk said, "You're such an attractive couple, I'm sure the baby will be beautiful."

Dane didn't return the woman's smile. "I'm not her husband, and that's not my baby. We'll need two rooms on the ground floor, please, adjoining if possible." The stunned clerk quickly typed this information into the computer and gave them the keys for rooms 22 and 24. Savannah could feel the woman staring after them as Dane led the way down the hallway.

Once they were out of the clerk's line of vision, Savannah said, "You didn't have to be so rude to that clerk."

Dane looked surprised. "I wasn't rude."

"Yes, you were," she argued. "And you didn't have to be so quick to deny responsibility for me and my baby."

"I was denying responsibility for Rosemary and her baby," Dane pointed out. Then he glanced down at her midsection. "You don't have a baby."

Savannah followed his gaze to her protruding stomach, unreasonably overwhelmed with sadness for the baby boy who didn't even exist. "Make up your mind whether you want me to *think pregnant* or not."

He gave her a long-suffering look. "I said what I did to the clerk to make an impression."

"So she'll remember us?"

Dane nodded. "When Ferrante comes searching for his daughter."

Savannah was appeased by this explanation and followed Dane down the hallway. He was walking fast, and she had to struggle to keep up. He stopped at the door to room 22 and inserted the plastic key. Then he pushed the door open and stepped back for Savannah to precede him inside.

Savannah looked around as Dane placed her overnight bag on one of the beds. It wasn't a luxurious room but seemed clean and comfortable. She couldn't help thinking how much Caroline would have enjoyed being with them, and a longing to be with her daughter momentarily overwhelmed her.

"She's having fun with her grandparents," Dane said, reading her mind as was too often the case. "You have to focus on the operation."

Savannah fingered her locket and blinked back her tears. "I'll try."

He walked toward the door. "When I get into my room, I'll unlock the adjoining door. You keep yours locked unless you need me. Don't open the hall door for any reason." He had his hand on the doorknob when he thought of another instruction. "Come lock the door behind me."

She went to the door, and when she reached for the knob, their hands touched. Fatigue hampered his ability to hide his feelings, and she saw a fleeting response in his dark brown eyes. He leaned down, and her heart pounded. His lips were only inches from hers when he whispered, "Don't answer the hotel phone either." Then he slipped out into the hall and closed the door.

To pass time, she put on another one of Steamer's maternity outfits. Then she styled her newly dark hair and carefully applied some makeup. As a final touch, she sprayed perfume on her wrists. The smell reminded her of Caroline and the teddy bear that was scented to provide comfort. She had another bad moment or two but turned on the television to distract herself.

The midday news was just beginning, and Cam's escape and subsequent "death" was the lead story. When Dane knocked on the adjoining door, Savannah pulled it open and pointed at the television. "The news is saying that Cam is dead."

"I saw the report." He took in her improved appearance with a scowl. "How many times are you going to change clothes today?"

"Steamer only got me four outfits, so I guess that will be the daily limit," she replied as if he'd been serious. "I like this outfit even better than the first one. What do you think?"

He tried a withering look but wasn't very successful. He thought she looked nice—she could tell. "They're both okay."

She smiled. "So what now?"

"We don't want to be on the road again until the sun goes down." He gestured toward the bed. "Try to get some sleep. I'll wake you when it's time to go."

She wasn't tired but knew he was exhausted. However, he would try not to sleep because of the nightmares. "I don't see how you're going to drive to New Orleans if you don't get some sleep."

He shrugged. "I'll make it."

She crossed the room and put her hands on his arms. His muscles tensed defensively. "I'll be safer and you'll be more able to run this operation if you're rested. So why don't you take half a pill and go to sleep. I'll keep watch over you for a change."

He raised an eyebrow. "You think you could take care of me?"

"Yes," she confirmed. "I know I could with a little backup from the men Hack has assigned to protect us." She propelled him through the door and into his own room. "I'll sit right here by the adjoining door, and if you start to have a nightmare, I'll throw something at you from a safe distance and wake you up."

He didn't ridicule this idea, so she knew he must be completely exhausted. "You promise you won't come in?"

She nodded. "I'll keep my distance."

He looked longingly at the beds. "What if I get a phone call?"

"I'll wake you," she lied. Nothing could be more important than his getting some sleep. She pushed him down gently on to the edge of the nearest bed. Then she captured his gaze and said, "I'm going to have to pull rank on you and insist that you rest."

He raised a weary eyebrow. "You're a civilian employee of the U.S. Army. You don't have a rank."

"I work for General Steele," she reminded him. "And I'm sure he'd back me up on this."

He leaned back on a pillow. "Well, if it's an indirect order from General Steele, I guess I don't have any choice but to obey."

Savannah smiled at this outrageous remark. Dane was never obedient. "No choice at all."

"It probably wouldn't hurt for me to rest, just for a few minutes," he murmured as his eyes fluttered closed.

"What about the pill?"

"I'm so tired I don't think I need one."

She pulled the bedspread over to cover him. Once his breathing slowed into a steady sleep pattern, she tiptoed toward the adjoining door.

He stopped her by saying, "Savannah."

She returned to the side of his bed. "Yes?" she whispered.

He opened his eyes and said, "Thanks."

She walked back over and took his hand in hers. After giving it a gentle squeeze, she went into her own room. She left the adjoining door open a crack and pulled a chair up close so she'd be able to hear him if he needed her. Then she began her watch—protecting her protector.

* * *

In the quiet, without Dane to distract her, Savannah gave the entire situation some thought. She wasn't surprised that Dane had agreed to take the case. He wanted to put Mario Ferrante behind bars, and Rosemary offered him a chance to accomplish that. But she was a little surprised by his willingness to include her as a part of the team. He'd had several opportunities to replace her or exclude her or leave her behind. But he hadn't taken advantage of them.

She considered the possible reasons for this. It was unlikely that he thought she was the best-qualified person to impersonate Rosemary Allen. A trained female soldier would have been much better prepared for the dangers that would almost surely be involved in the operation. And Savannah's resemblance to Rosemary was slight and that only after the home dye job.

Maybe Dane didn't trust anyone else to protect her. Or, even more attractive was the possibility that he was using the operation and her involvement as an excuse to be near her. He couldn't openly admit that he loved her. But maybe he could permit her to stay with him in the name of justice and the American way. While she obviously preferred these reasons, she knew it would be foolish to become attached to either one. Dane always accused her of being naive and overly optimistic. Maybe he was right.

It was probably something else altogether. Cam's warning as they left the helicopter sounded sincere. If Ferrante wanted revenge against Wes's family for some event in the past, maybe her presence really was necessary to the success of the mission. Deciding to stop hypothesizing, she turned on the television and muted the volume.

As the hours passed, she found her guard duty more difficult than she had expected. It was hard enough just to stay awake, and fighting the boredom was even more difficult. She alternately walked the confines of the small hotel room and tried to lip-read the silent television.

By four o'clock she was starting to get hungry and desperately wanted some chocolate. She remembered craving Hershey Kisses when she was pregnant with Caroline. She frowned as she smoothed the lacy material that covered the bulge at her midsection. Maybe the maternity clothes were messing with her mind. Or maybe she'd been thinking pregnant a little too hard.

But whatever the reason for her chocolate fit, by five o'clock she was considering the drastic measure of trying to get one of Hack's men to make a candy bar run. Then she heard a noise from the next room. It wasn't a scream, more of a rustle. She walked to the adjoining door and peeked through the crack.

Dane was sitting on the edge of the bed, rubbing his tousled hair. There was a sheet-wrinkle imprint on his right cheek. He scowled when he looked up and saw her.

"Well, I see that several hours of sleep didn't improve your mood," she teased.

He stood and stretched. "I'm going to take a shower and change into some clean clothes. By the time I'm done, it should be dark enough for us to travel. So be packed and ready to go in ten minutes."

She resisted the urge to salute and moved toward the door. Just before she crossed into her own room, he said, "Savannah?"

Trying to ignore the hypnotizing sound of her name on his lips, she turned and said, "Yes?"

"Did I scream?" he asked.

"I didn't hear a peep," she reassured him. "And I was listening for an excuse to throw something at you. Goodness knows you deserve it."

She saw the relief on his face as she stepped through the adjoining door and closed it firmly behind her.

Savannah repacked her overnight bag and then turned up the volume on the television. She surfed the channels, hoping for more details about Cam's escape from prison, but apparently that was now old news. She did see a weather report. The forecast called for damp and cold. With a shiver, she turned off the TV and pulled on her new coat.

When Dane came through the adjoining door, his hair was still damp from his shower, and his eyes were still puffy from his nap. He looked adorable, and Savannah resisted the urge to wrap her arms around him. She could almost feel the soft flannel of his shirt pressed against her cheek. Hear his heart beating . . .

Breathlessly she watched as he picked up her overnight bag. "Let's go."

She joined him at the door, and he led her down the hallway away from the front desk.

"Why are we going out this way?" Savannah asked as she trotted beside him.

"One of Hack's guys put our car on this side of the parking lot."

"Don't we need to turn in our keys?"

He gave her an irritated glance over his shoulder. "No, I just left them in the room. Why so many questions?"

She grabbed his arm and pulled him to a stop. "Because there are vending machines by the front desk, and I'm dying for some chocolate."

"You're kidding, right?"

She shook her head. "I'm not leaving without candy."

He ran his fingers through his hair in frustration. Then he turned and walked back to the front lobby. At the end of the hall, he leaned against the wall and pointed to the vending machines. "Go ahead and get your candy."

She dug out all the change she could find at the bottom of her purse on her way to the small concession area. Once there, she started pushing coins into the machine. She selected two plain Hershey bars and one with almonds. She also got a Kit Kat and two Twix bars. Then she inserted three dollars and received two Crunch bars, a bag of M&M's, and a box of Junior Mints in return.

"Exactly how many sweets are you going to need for a five-hour trip to New Orleans?" Dane whispered when she rejoined him in the hall.

She glanced up. "You haven't spent much time around pregnant women, have you?"

"No," he admitted suspiciously.

"Well, cravings come with the territory," she informed him. "And rather than fight them, I figure I'll just give in to them." Cradling the candy against her chest, she began walking toward the side exit. "I'm ready to go now."

Once outside, Savannah looked up and down the road that ran along-side the hotel. The white SUV was parked a few yards away, but she didn't see the pickup truck. Dane took her arm and led her across the parking lot. While they walked, she asked about their other bodyguard in the pickup truck.

"He switched the truck for a different vehicle," he told her. "That's standard procedure during a covert operation."

"What is he driving now?"

"I can't tell you *that*. It would be a breach of security."

Savannah rolled her eyes and scanned the parking lot. She spotted a Toyota Camry a few yards away. Through the windshield she could see a large, severe-looking man confined in the inadequate space.

"I hope you're not counting too much on Hack's men being inconspicuous," she said. "Because they are pretty easy to spot."

Dane squinted at the Camry. "I guess I'm counting more on their intimidation factor than their ability to blend in." He used a keyless entry to open the doors of an unimpressive silver sedan.

"Let me guess, we changed cars too?"

Dane nodded as he opened the front passenger door for her.

"Well, if we switch again, can I suggest that you get us a Chrysler 300 like Cam had—with seats that get warm and a DVD player and surround sound."

"You've got a lot to learn about covert operations." He closed the door and walked around to the driver's side.

Once he was settled behind the wheel, she opened a Hershey bar and took a big bite. "You want one?"

He gave the candy a distasteful look. "You know those things aren't healthy."

"That's a matter of opinion," she said as she took another bite. "Chocolate might be full of fat and carbs, but it nourishes the soul."

"Says who?"

"Says hormonal women everywhere."

"I guess I'll have to take your word on that." He alternately watched her and the road for a few minutes and finally said, "Give me one of those." It was more a demand than a request. "I'll eat it just to save you the calories."

She passed a Twix bar to him. "You're so good to me."

She finished her Hershey bar and stashed the rest of the candy in her purse, out of his reach. Then she leaned her seat back. "I'm exhausted from all those hours of watching you snore."

He smiled briefly but didn't comment.

"If I fall asleep, wake me up when we get close to New Orleans."

They drove for miles in the darkness. No towns lined the interstate— just a continuous series of trees. Wrapped in the cocoon-like safety of the car with Dane, Savannah felt relaxed and content. She wanted to stay awake so she could enjoy the imposed closeness with him, but before they had traveled very many miles, she fell asleep. She was in the middle of a wonderful dream when Dane shook her shoulder.

Her eyes flew open in alarm. "Is something wrong?" she asked.

"No," he said. "But I do need to ask you an important question."

She sat up straight, instantly alert. "What?"

"I want to be sure you're fully awake, because your answer could be important to my future."

"I'm awake," she assured him. "Now what is the question?"

"I need to know . . ." He paused for effect, and she waited anxiously.

"You need to know what?"

"Do I really snore?"

If he hadn't been driving, she would have slugged him. As it was, she settled for giving him a disgusted look.

"Yes, you snore," she lied. "And worse than that, you also drool." She closed her eyes again. After a few minutes, the vibration of the car lulled her back to sleep. She woke up later with Dane shaking her shoulder again.

"You don't drool," she muttered, hoping to end his interruption of her sleep.

"We're crossing Lake Ponchatrain," he said. "And you wanted to see it."

She sat up and rubbed the sleep from her eyes. The bridge stretched for miles into the distance, water lining each side. Ahead she could see New Orleans glowing in the cold, damp night.

"Wow," she whispered.

"It's even better at sunrise." He sounded proud.

She scooted to the edge of the seat and stared out the windshield at the display of lights and sparkling water. "It's hard to imagine anything more beautiful, but you are an expert on sunrises."

"December is not the best time of year for the old city either," he continued. "Spring is my favorite season, when all the azaleas and camellias are in bloom."

Savannah was intrigued by this rare personal reference and tried to figure out what the disclosures meant in terms of their relationship. Maybe he now felt close enough to her to share his feelings? Or maybe he just loved the city too much to hide his feelings. Or maybe he was just bored and would have shared the same observation with Hack or Doc or Steamer if they'd been his riding companion?

The bridge over the Ponchatrain went on for miles with the city of New Orleans remaining tantalizingly close but still in the distance. Finally they exited the bridge and for the first time in what seemed like hours were driving on solid ground. Dane pointed out the top of the Super Dome, and she nodded, although she couldn't really distinguish it from the other large shadows on the horizon. After staring at the lights for so long, the actual streets seemed dark and dreary by comparison.

And then, to her further amazement, Dane launched into a short history lesson. "The city was founded by the French in the early 1700s. It instantly became an important port city—not just because of its location but because even back then, Americans had a guilty fascination with anything European. That explains the name and architectural style of the Quarter."

She didn't speak, afraid she'd ruin his rare, talkative mood. She nodded to show she was paying attention.

"The Spanish governed the city for about forty years and left their influence as well. It became part of the United States through the Louisiana Purchase, but the people of New Orleans have always remained a little aloof. That's particularly true of folks from the French Quarter."

"Are *you* from New Orleans?"

"Not personally, but I have ancestors who lived here," he said.

"That's why you bought the old house in the French Quarter?" she guessed.

He nodded. "My grandmother's parents fell on hard times during the Depression and had to sell their house. It's always been a dream of mine to buy it and restore it."

"And you finally got your chance."

"To buy it anyway," he agreed. "Restoring it has proved to be more of a problem."

She was anxious to hear more, hoping for a glimpse into his complicated psyche, but before she could question him further, they entered the French Quarter, and she completely forgot about everything except her unique surroundings.

The street narrowed, and the sidewalks changed from concrete to brick. The buildings they passed varied in architecture, color, and style. Some were startlingly beautiful while others were in disrepair. Many had balconies, some porches. Most were elaborately decorated for the holiday season, and the effect was magical.

"It's like another world," she breathed.

"It's like no other place on earth," he agreed. "Things sound different, smell different—even feel different."

Savannah leaned forward and stared in fascination through the windshield. Despite the fact that it was almost midnight, there were people everywhere. All the businesses seemed to be open, and various types of music mixed together to form a pulsing backdrop for the night's activities.

"What time does the French Quarter close?" she asked.

He smiled. "It's a nocturnal society. Things are just starting to warm up about now."

"That might take some getting used to."

"You'll be surprised by how quickly you adapt," he predicted.

The further they drove, the more the streets became crowded with parked cars and pedestrians. They passed a busy bar with a street band playing Dixieland. Several couples were dancing to the lively music, and Dane had to use extra caution to avoid hitting them as he pulled to the curb and parked.

She was delighted when he said, "Let's leave the car here and walk the rest of the way."

Savannah climbed out of the car onto the brick sidewalk and experienced New Orleans for the first time. The air was heavy and cloying, the music loud and overwhelming, and the lights hypnotizing. It was almost as if the Quarter was a living entity, and she was being formally introduced to it.

Dane stepped up beside her and took her hand in his. "Welcome to the French Quarter."

She was helpless against the charms of the man and the city. "I love it."

He smiled and tugged gently on her hand, pulling her down the sidewalk.

She glanced back at the silver sedan. "What about our things?"

"We'll get them later."

She was too distracted to argue.

As they continued up the street at a slow stroll, Dane kept her hand in his. Even though she knew the public show of affection was calculated, intended to help them blend in with the French Quarter crowds, she liked to think he enjoyed the contact almost as much as she did.

They passed restaurants and specialty food stores and hotels and several clothing boutiques. She didn't see any bodyguards following them, and when she mentioned this to Dane, he amazed her by saying, "Hack has secured the area. You can be sure our every move is being monitored."

They walked past a restaurant advertising creole cuisine. A long line of customers waiting their turn to dine extended out the door and down the street. "This place must be good," she said to Dane.

He studied the specials listed on a chalkboard near the door and then nodded. "I'll take you there for dinner if we're here long enough."

She couldn't control a smile. Eating with Dane in a quaint creole restaurant in the French Quarter was the stuff dreams were made of.

As they passed a massage parlor, a beautiful Asian woman standing in the doorway called out to Dane, offering him a free sample of her skills. He declined with a polite smile.

The next establishment was a souvenir shop that seemed to be displaying most of its merchandise on clothing racks on the sidewalk in front of the entrance. Savannah eyed the 2 FOR $10 rack like a real tourist.

"Do you want a T-shirt?" Dane asked.

She nodded and started to open her purse, but Dane was quicker. He pulled out his wallet and extracted a five-dollar bill. He gave it to the sales clerk. Then Savannah watched with wonder as Dane checked the tags. "They're one-size-fits-most," he informed her.

"Then any shirt will do," she managed.

He removed a T-shirt from the rack and held it out to Savannah. She took it with near-reverence. She smiled as she fingered the thin material printed with garish gold-and-purple ink.

"It's been a long time since I've gotten a gift from you."

"It's not a gift," he said. "You owe me five bucks."

She laughed. "If it isn't a gift, you should have just let me pay."

"Then you would have been providing fingerprints and trace DNA to the sales clerk."

Savannah's heart pounded as she stole a furtive glance behind them. "Does the sales clerk work for Ferrante?" she whispered.

"No, the store clerk works for us," Dane whispered back. "But you shouldn't trust anyone—just in case."

Savannah was still considering this when an elderly man walked up and asked Dane if he wanted a shoeshine. "Not tonight, thanks," he replied.

Savannah watched suspiciously as the old gentleman moved off in search of another customer. Dane's comment about fingerprints and DNA had reminded her that anyone could be their enemy.

"Who else works for us?" she asked.

"I don't think that falls into need-to-know."

"Well, I do," she argued. "What if I get separated from all the members of the team and need help? How will I know whom to trust?"

"The chances of you getting separated from all of us are infinitesimal," Dane prefaced. "But since I don't take chances . . ." He leaned close and whispered in her ear. "The massage parlor lady and the shoeshine man also work for us."

She was unaccountably pleased that he had shared this privileged information with her. "Thanks."

They passed another bar, and again couples were dancing in the street to slow, sultry jazz. To her surprise, Dane pulled her into his arms, and they swayed in time with the music. She tucked her head under Dane's chin and rested her cheek on his shoulder. The night, she realized, had now gone from just pleasant to truly enchanted.

The magical mood was broken when several drunken Saints fans careened out of the bar—alternately shouting cheers and laughing uproariously. A policeman on a bicycle peddled over to evaluate the situation, and Dane stopped dancing.

The policeman leaned his bike up against one of the bar's pink exterior walls and spoke to the rowdy football fans. "Everybody head home unless you want to spend the rest of the night in jail."

Dane held Savannah's hand and led her down the street away from disturbers of the peace and the growing throng of onlookers who were all collectively ignoring the policeman's instructions to disperse.

"Can I trust the bicycle policeman?"

"Yes," Dane confirmed.

They walked for two blocks and turned onto Royal Street. At the next corner there was a small booth that advertised the services of Madame Leone. According to the ornately painted sign, the proprietor was able to read palms, exorcise demons, interpret dreams, and tell the future. Each service was available for the reasonable price of twenty bucks.

"That looks interesting," she said, pointing toward the booth.

He rolled his eyes. "If you're so anxious to give away money, you can give it to me."

"I'm just saying it might be fun."

"And which of Madame Leone's multitude of skills are you interested in?" he asked in a teasing tone that guaranteed he had no faith in the Madame's abilities.

Before Savannah could answer, an ancient yet lovely woman stepped out of the booth. She was wearing a gypsy-style gown, and her long, gray hair hung almost to her waist. There were several cheap-looking rings on her age-spotted fingers, and her ragged nails were rimmed with dirt. But her eyes were surprisingly clear and a gorgeous violet color.

Savannah watched in fascination as the fortune teller took her by the hand. "Twenty dollars is a small price to pay to know what the future holds," the woman said in a lilting accent. Then she turned to Dane. "Because it is my ability to tell the future that interests her."

Savannah couldn't control a little gasp. Perhaps Madame Leone really could read minds.

Dane gave the fortune teller an insincere smile and pulled Savannah's hand from the woman's grasp. "Thanks, but no."

As they started to move away, Madame Leone called after them, "I can prove my powers."

Savannah couldn't help but turn back. "How?" she whispered.

The old woman looked at Savannah's midsection. "There is no baby," she said softly.

Savannah's heart pounded, and she glanced up at Dane.

He shook his head. "All that proves is that you're wearing the fake stomach wrong and we need to get off the street. Come on."

"I take it she's not on the payroll."

"Not ours anyway," Dane replied.

Savannah looked back over her shoulder. The fortune teller was watching her with old, wise eyes. And at that moment Savannah knew that somehow she would find a way to come speak to Madame Leone when Dane wasn't there to prevent a deeper conversation. Because the old woman was right. She very much wanted to know her future. And what role Dane would play in it.

CHAPTER 7

THEY TURNED ONTO Toulouse Street, and there were no more stops at stores or dancing interludes. Their encounter with the fortune teller had upset Dane for some reason, and instead of ignoring it, Savannah decided to approach the subject head on.

"Do you think the fortune teller works for Ferrante?"

"Hack checked everybody out, and he couldn't find a connection between that scam artist and Ferrante, but I don't trust her." His eyes scanned the balconies above and the street ahead.

"So you're just annoyed because you don't believe she has mystic powers?"

He looked over at her. "I'm annoyed because you seem to think she does."

Savannah shrugged. "She looked authentic to me."

"There is no such thing as an authentic fortune teller," he insisted. "That woman is observant and clever, but she's no more mystic than I am. She probably touched your stomach briefly when she took your hand. You wouldn't have felt it through all that foam, but she would have been able to tell that you weren't really pregnant."

Savannah was disappointed but had to admit that his explanation made sense.

"I'm sorry to dispel more of your illusions," he said, although he didn't sound sorry at all. "But the only way to know the future is to wait until it gets here."

"That may be the only way to know the future," she conceded. "But what we do today affects the future. You might want to give that some consideration."

He raised an eyebrow. "If you're going to randomly spout question-able wisdom, I might have to start calling you Madame Savannah."

She held out her hand. "That will be fifteen bucks."

"Madame Leone charges twenty."

"I owe you five," she reminded him.

He rewarded her with a smile. Then he pointed at the white SUV parked a few yards away. "It looks like our security team has made it."

Savannah nodded. "No doubt there's a Camry nearby as well."

"We passed it a few minutes ago. You need to learn to pay attention."

Savannah glared at Dane's back as he stopped at a door that was really a piece of metal on hinges, like something you might find at an old ware-house. He pulled some keys from his pocket and inserted one into the lock. He twisted the key, and the metal door swung open. Then he stepped back, allowing her to precede him into a dark alley.

She couldn't control a shiver as she walked past him. The cobblestones beneath her feet were slick with condensation and almost obscured by a thin, swirling mist. Overhead an arched arbor covered with ivy provided a ceiling. The music from the bar down the street insinuated itself into the small space, but the bustling crowd seemed far away.

At the end of the alley, Dane unlocked another door and ushered Savannah into an impressive courtyard shared by four houses. If the French Quarter felt like another world, the courtyard felt like another century. The center was dominated by a tiered fountain. Water dripped gracefully off its fluted edges into a small pond below. Large planters full of flowers and manicured trees managed to invoke a feeling of serenity. It was old-fashioned and elegant, and she could easily imagine beautiful women in antebellum dresses pacing the balconies above.

But the strangest part of the courtyard was the fact that the fronts of the houses faced it and not the street.

"How odd," she said. "It's backward."

"It's ingenious," Dane corrected her. "The idea originated with some of the city's earliest settlers. By presenting their homes' worst side to the street, they understated their assets—thus reducing the chances of robbery. And because the courtyard is closed in on all four sides, the homeowners had a great deal of privacy."

"Except from their immediate neighbors."

"Yes," Dane agreed. "I guess they had to pick their neighbors care-fully."

Savannah looked around the courtyard. "So who are your neighbors?"

"I've never met them," he admitted. "But according to Hack's research, we're sharing the courtyard with a couple of lawyers, an interior designer, and a real-estate broker. Only the designer lives here year-round, and all of them have agreed to stay elsewhere during the operation. For now, Hack's men are stationed at strategic locations in each house."

This thought took away some of the courtyard's charm but did make Savannah feel safer. Each house had a different architectural style, and three of them were beautifully restored. Dane approached the door to the fixer-upper and produced yet another key. He inserted it into a rusty lock on the door that had been punished by years of extreme moisture. The hinges moaned in protest as he started to push the door open.

He turned back to Savannah. "Remember, the house is under renovation, so be prepared to deal with some inconveniences."

She stared at the peeling paint and rusted wrought-iron on the porch and felt a wave of trepidation.

"What kind of inconveniences? Are there rats?"

He smiled. "There might have been, but I asked Hack to have the place cleaned and set up for us, so I'm sure any rodents have been thoroughly eradicated."

Savannah said a silent prayer of thanks for Hack as they stepped inside together. Dane switched on a small chandelier in the entryway. Her overnight case and Dane's duffel bag were right beside the door.

"Some of Hack's men delivered them I presume?" she guessed.

"I presume so," Dane confirmed.

Savannah took in the scuffed hardwood floors, peeling plaster, and water-stained crown molding. "I'll bet this house was fabulous a hundred years ago," she said.

Dane glanced around. "My grandmother said it was—although that's kind of hard to believe, considering its current condition."

Her eyes moved to the old chandelier above them. "It just takes a little imagination."

Dane led the way past an impressive but treacherous-looking stairway, through a dining room, and into a parlor. The rooms were well proportioned with high ceilings and large windows. There wasn't a lot of furniture, but what there was looked at least antique if not original to the house. He crossed the room and knelt in front of an ancient radiator.

"The first order of business is to get some heat going."

While he turned dials, Savannah studied their temporary residence. Building materials and tools were stacked against the walls, indicting that Dane had plans to make not only cosmetic changes, but also handle structural problems as well. Based on the yellowed labels of the paint cans, there had been a significant passage of time since his "renovation" began.

As steam and smoke began hissing from the radiator, Dane muttered something under his breath, and Savannah moved over to a set of French doors. Ice etched the glass, giving her a distorted view of the charming courtyard. She reached up to open the latch, but it was stuck. When she removed her fingers, they were covered with tiny paint pieces.

"You really should move renovating back to the top of your priority list," she remarked as she wiped the paint particles from her hand. "A house like this deserves to be well cared for."

"Renovations on this scale take time and money," he pointed out. "I have to work for a living, and I'm not rich like the Westinghouses and McLaughlins."

She smirked at him. "The surviving McLaughlins aren't rich anymore. And if you don't have enough time and money to devote to the house, you should sell it and let someone else restore it."

"Well, lucky for you I'm not a quitter. Otherwise I wouldn't have a perfect place to hide you from Ferrante."

Savannah frowned. "I thought we were trying to attract Ferrante's attention."

"Not yet." Dane walked over to stand beside her at the window. "And I can't let this place go—it's a great way to get dates."

"Dates?" she repeated stupidly.

"Girls just love a man who owns a house in the French Quarter."

He was probably teasing her, but she found even the outside chance that Dane *dated* unnerving. She was dealing with the fact that he couldn't, or wouldn't, commit to a permanent relationship with her—for now at least. But the idea that he might find female companionship elsewhere was something she hadn't considered. A bleak, hollow feeling engulfed her.

"Do you have a girlfriend?" she managed.

He grinned. "No."

She was almost too relieved to be mad. Almost. "Of course, you don't. You're too annoying for any woman to put up with."

His smile didn't fade. "Let's take the grand tour, and I'll show you where everything is."

She was still shaken by the thought of Dane with a social life. So she followed, but she kept a few feet behind him to discourage conversation until she could pull herself together.

They walked down a hallway, the old wooden floorboards squeaking with each footfall. The first room was a bathroom. Dane flipped the switch, but the room remained dark. "Bulb must be shot," he said. "Unless it's the wiring."

Savannah fervently hoped it was just the light bulb as she walked into the room. There was enough moonlight streaming through the stained-glass window above the tub to give her a general impression of renovation work started but not finished. The marble floor had been dismantled, and old tiles were stacked in haphazard piles. The claw-foot tub appeared functional but needed to be reglazed.

"Will I be able to take a bath?" she asked hopefully.

Dane crossed the room and turned on the faucet mounted on the wall. After a few sputters, water ran freely into the tub. "I don't see why not, since we have water. And I'll tell Hack to get us some light bulbs."

Savannah nodded. "Thanks."

He walked back into the hallway and opened the door to a bedroom. Like in the other parts of the house, the walls here were water-stained, the floors damaged. A huge fireplace flanked by carved wooden panels took up an entire wall. Cases marked FLOOR TILE lined the wall on the far side of the room, and the only piece of furniture was an exquisite iron bed. The mattress was still wrapped in plastic, and on it were sheets, towels, and a thick-looking comforter.

Savannah fingered one of the towels. "Hack did a good job buying supplies."

"Hack always does a good job—at anything." Dane moved on to the next door. It opened onto another bedroom, but this one was filled with heavily carved, dark wooden furniture. A price tag was still attached to one of the bed's four posts. Savannah read it as she ran a hand over the satiny wood of the footboard.

"You could complete the renovation of this house quicker if you'd stop buying these expensive antiques."

He gave her a narrowed look. "You should stop complaining about our accommodations. We could be staying in a fleabag motel."

"Like the Motel 2?"

He nodded. "Or *less*."

She had to smile. "Give me a hand with these sheets, and we'll make the bed." Savannah moved the towels and comforter onto the dresser while Dane ripped the plastic covering from the mattress. Then he shook out the fitted sheet. She took up a position on the opposite side of the bed and caught the sheet's edge. Then she tucked it around the top corner of the mattress while Dane did the same on his side.

He leaned down to secure the sheet. She watched him with a combination of tenderness and longing. Making a bed was such a simple domestic process, but doing it with Dane was an uncommon pleasure. They put on the pillowcases and spread out the comforter.

Dane said, "Now on to the next room."

They met at the doorway, and both attempted to pass through at the same time. Pressed together in the small space, they stared at each other, the fake stomach between them. She rubbed a hand across the misshapen foam.

"Thank goodness it's not a real baby," she said, immediately regretting the words.

"Thank goodness," he echoed. Their eyes met for a few seconds, and then he stepped back into the bedroom. "Ladies first."

Savannah walked into the next room, and they repeated the bed-making process.

"Which bedroom do you want?" she asked when they were finished.

"I don't sleep much," he reminded her. "You pick."

She considered her options and finally said, "I'll take the one with the iron bed since it's closer to the bathroom."

He moved into the hallway. "Now that we've got that settled, let's check out the kitchen. I'm ready for you to make us dinner."

She raised an eyebrow. "You expect *me* to make dinner at *your* house?"

"I'm the commanding officer of this operation, and I make the assignments. So you're doing the cooking—and whatever else I say, for that matter. Those were the terms of our agreement."

"The terms of our agreement have already changed several times," Savannah reminded him. "I'll cook, but only because I'm starving." As they passed the stairs, she pointed upward. "Are the upper floors better, or worse?"

"Worse," Dane responded. "Not that it really matters. Hack has men stationed up there, so we'll be staying down here out of their way."

Savannah cast one last curious look up the stairs. Something about being told she couldn't go upstairs made her want to go up there more.

When they entered the kitchen, Savannah felt hopeful that Dane really didn't have a woman in his life. The kitchen was unquestionably in the worst shape of all the rooms she'd seen so far. Stacked with supplies and materials and empty crates, it seemed to be doubling as a storage room with meals as a sideline. All the cupboards were bare—literally. There wasn't even a plate or drinking glass. And the only food was a shriveled apple in the harvest gold–colored refrigerator.

Dane frowned. "That's not like Hack to ignore the food part of an assignment."

"I still have a few candy bars left, so we won't starve," Savannah told him.

"With your sweet tooth, they won't last long."

She couldn't argue that. "Since you let me have my choice of bedrooms, you can have the first pick of the remaining candy bars."

He gave her an impatient look. "You picked them all, which means you must like them all. So your offer isn't as generous as it sounds."

She poised her hand above the candy. "Hurry—it's a limited-time offer."

He picked up the last Twix and ripped the paper off.

Savannah unwrapped a Hershey bar and took a bite. While it melted in her mouth, she said, "I wish I owned this house. I wouldn't neglect it the way you have."

"Too bad you gave away all Wes's millions. With that kind of money, you might have been able to make me an offer I couldn't refuse."

She smirked at him. "Yeah, money is everything to you."

He gave her a half-smile.

She continued her examination of the kitchen. "If I owned this house, I'd renovate this room first."

"Why?"

He sounded genuinely interested, so she continued.

"Because the kitchen is the heart of the house," she replied.

"What would you do in here?" He waved to encompass the whole forsaken room.

"The kitchen is large and has a lot of potential," she told him. "I can picture cherry wood cabinets with glass fronts, granite countertops, and a big island in the middle where your girlfriend can prepare food for your guests."

"I told you—I don't have a girlfriend."

"You did say that," she acknowledged. "But we've established that you lie—a lot."

"My honesty aside," he said, "what else would you do?"

"I'd buy top-of-the-line stainless steel appliances."

"Sounds authentic," he murmured sarcastically.

"The other rooms can be period-correct with antique furniture and all," she said. "This room needs to be *functional*."

"So once you turned this kitchen into a modern masterpiece, what would you do next?"

"The bathroom. Then I'd move on to the front parlor." She pointed with what was left of her candy bar at the dining room. "It wouldn't take much to fix up the dining room. Once I had the main rooms done I could work on the bedrooms one at a time. And when this floor was done I'd move upstairs."

He stood and collected their candy wrappers. "Well, my plan is to tackle all the structural problems first—replace rotted floorboards, drafty windows, leaks in the ceiling. Little minor stuff like that. Then I'll worry about cosmetic improvements like granite countertops and cherry wood cabinets."

She resisted the urge to stick out her tongue at him. "Obviously the structural things would have to be done first. That wasn't even worth mentioning."

"Obviously."

She was still annoyed with him, but she was more fascinated with the house. "Maybe while we're here, we could do some renovating."

He raised an eyebrow. "You know how to restore old houses?"

"No, but supposedly you do." She pointed at the wallpaper peeling off the wall in the dining room. "And even I know that this wallpaper is going to have to be removed eventually. I could pull it off and actually accomplish something instead of just sitting here waiting for Ferrante to show up and kill us."

Dane smirked. "I definitely don't plan to sit around *or* get killed. And I don't want you trying to make home improvements. On an old project like this, even minor demolition can be dangerous. So you'll just have to think of another way to entertain yourself."

He was saved from her scathing response by the ringing of the doorbell.

"That will be Hack," Dane predicted as he stood and led the way toward the front door. "And he'd better have us some real food." When they reached the dining room, Dane motioned for her to wait there. Then he removed a revolver from the antique buffet table before approaching the front door with caution.

"Hack?" he asked.

"It's me," Hack's voice growled back.

Dane opened the door, and Savannah peeked out of the dining room to see Hack standing on the front stoop. He was carrying several plastic grocery sacks and wearing a scowl.

"It's about time," Dane greeted him.

If anything, Hack's expression became grimmer. "Have you ever tried to rush a cashier in New Orleans?"

Dane smiled. "That's why they call it the Big Easy. Nobody's in a rush down here."

"Well, I am," Hack informed them. "And all that laid-back, slow-down-and-smell-the-roses nonsense makes me want to kill somebody."

Savannah laughed as she stepped out of the dining room. "Hey, Hack."

He looked up and cursed under his breath.

She laughed and rubbed her stomach. "You don't like my costume?"

"Not much," he replied. "But I'll admit you sort of look like Rosemary Allen. Or at least how she probably looked before she ruined her hair with that Sun-In stuff. So if you're trying to attract a bullet, you'll probably get your wish."

Savannah frowned. "I'm sure Mario Ferrante wouldn't shoot at his own daughter."

"I'm sure Ferrante would shoot his own *mother* if it suited his purposes," Hack said. "Maybe he did already, for all I know."

Savannah was trying to think of an appropriate comeback when Dane asked, "How's Caroline?"

Savannah grabbed Hack's arm. "Have you talked to her?"

Hack nodded. "In a roundabout way. I talked to my guys on the mountain. The kid's fine."

Dane pointed at the grocery bags in Hack's hand. "What you got there? I've eaten so much candy, I'm starting to feel nauseated."

Savannah laughed. "Maybe it's morning sickness."

Hack had started toward the kitchen but turned around at this remark. "What?"

"Sympathetic pregnancy," she explained. "When a woman is pregnant, sometimes her partner will share some of her symptoms, like cravings and morning sickness."

She saw a grin on Hack's face for the first time in days. "If that's not the craziest thing I've ever heard."

"It *is* the craziest thing," Dane assured him. "She's not pregnant, and I'm definitely not sympathetic. Now let's eat."

On the way to the kitchen, Savannah said, "I hope you bought some frozen dinners since Dane has assigned me cooking duty."

"I got frozen dinners." Hack flipped on the light in the kitchen and added, "Is there any particular reason why we've got to stay in a hole?"

"Because no one will look for us here." Dane moved past him. "And I don't see why you're complaining. The refrigerator works, and there's a microwave. What more do you need?"

Hack dumped out the groceries on the plywood table. He pulled out three Lean Cuisines and handed them to Dane. "Since you're so crazy about microwave cooking, why don't you heat these up? I'll make a salad."

Savannah waited for Dane to refuse, but he picked up the frozen meals and walked over to the microwave. Hack's salad making consisted of pouring a bag of precut lettuce into a bowl along with grape tomatoes and a box of croutons. Savannah found a folding chair, forced it open, and placed it beside the table. When the microwave timer went off, Dane pulled out the first dinner and placed it before her.

"Thanks," she told him.

He nodded and returned to the microwave.

She speared a piece of chicken Florentine, blew on it for a few seconds, and then tasted it carefully. "It's good," she told Dane.

Hack brought her a bowl of salad. "Try this."

She put a forkful into her mouth. "Amazing," she complimented Hack.

"They say everything tastes better in New Orleans," Hack said modestly. "Maybe they're right."

Dane stabbed a grape tomato with a disposable fork and popped it in his mouth. "It's more likely the fact that you've eaten ten candy bars and your body is craving real food."

"Or it could be that I'm a great salad maker." Hack gave her a gold-toothed smile.

Savannah laughed, pleased that Hack was in a better mood. "I'm glad you're here. Dane's not a lot of fun. He wouldn't even let me get my fortune read."

Hack's expression became serious. "You shouldn't mess with any kind of occult stuff, especially in New Orleans. Down here they do voodoo and hoodoo and no telling what all."

Savannah controlled the desire to laugh. "I'll be careful," she promised. "The last thing I want is to get hexed."

Reassured on this point, Hack turned to Dane, and the men discussed the security precautions that had been taken throughout the rest of the meal. Savannah listened closely—impressed anew by their knowledge and skill at planning for every eventuality. Her food did taste particularly good, and she had to wonder if the location really did make a difference. Or maybe it was her overindulgence in candy bars. Or maybe it was the company.

Once they were through eating, Hack looked around. "I'd say we should clean up, but what's the point?"

"The point is you have to eat here again tomorrow," Dane said as he threw his dishes into a cardboard box. As Savannah added her microwavable tray to the makeshift garbage can, she caught a glimpse of her ankles and frowned.

"Does my ankle look swollen to you?" She lifted a foot toward Dane to give him a better view.

He stared for a second and then shook his head. "It looks fine to me."

Hack laughed. "It looks *fine* to me too."

Dane didn't seem amused as he asked Hack, "Don't you need to check for snipers or something?"

Hack shook his head. "No, I'm good."

Still scowling, Dane turned back to Savannah. "Now what's wrong with your foot?"

"Swelling is a common complaint in late pregnancy."

"Will you cut that out?" Dane insisted.

"What?" she asked with exaggerated innocence.

"Now that you mention it," Hack said with a sly smile in Dane's direction. "My ankles feel kind of tight too. Maybe we all have sympathetic pregnancy."

"You're both crazy." Dane walked out of the kitchen.

Hack followed Dane and waved for Savannah to come along.

Savannah smiled. It was nice to be back in Hack's good graces.

Dane led the way to the parlor. He sat on an old couch that had beautiful lines but was in desperate need of new upholstery. Hack chose an overstuffed chair that was in equally poor condition but looked sturdy. Savannah sat on the opposite end of the couch with Dane. Hack shoved an old ottoman toward her.

"In case you want to elevate those ankles," Hack explained.

She laughed and placed her feet on the ottoman, creating a little puff of dust. "So we're still tracking Cam with the ear thing?"

Hack nodded. His cell phone rang, and after glancing at it, he said, "I'll take this in the kitchen, where the reception is better."

After Hack was gone, Savannah stretched and yawned. "I'm tired."

"You slept all the way here in the car," Dane reminded her.

She covered her mouth to hide another yawn. "Maybe this sudden pregnancy is making me twice as sleepy—and twice as hungry."

Before Dane could respond, Hack walked back in.

"What did your lookouts have to say?" Dane asked.

"The coast is clear," Hack replied.

Dane stood. "Well, then, I'd better get going."

All the air left Savannah's lungs. "Going?" she managed.

"I've got to go check on other aspects of this operation," Dane confirmed.

Her initial shock started to give way to painful disappointment. "You're *leaving* me?"

He nodded. "I've got to check on the guys we've got watching Ferrante's house, make sure the support team isn't dancing to the radio and eating McDonald's again—that sort of thing."

She fought against panic. "But you've set me up as bait for one of the most dangerous men in Washington, DC!"

"Hack and his men are here to watch you," Dane pointed out unnecessarily. "I've trusted him with my life many times—you can too."

"Of course I trust Hack." She moved closer. "That has nothing to do with it." She begged him with her eyes, but his expression remained cold and remote. "I want to be with you," she finally said.

Hack cleared his throat. "I think I'll wait by the door."

Once he was gone, Savannah added, "Please."

Dane put his hands on her shoulders. "Don't make me hurt you, Savannah."

She tried to laugh but failed. "Too late."

"I've got a job to do," he said. "Surely you understand that."

She nodded again as a few tears escaped from her eyes. "I understand that my feelings aren't important to you."

He removed his hands from her shoulders and stepped away. "Act like a soldier. I'll be back when I can."

She followed him through the dining room door and watched as he consulted with Hack for a few minutes. Then he opened the door and stepped out into the night without a backward glance.

CHAPTER 8

AFTER DANE LEFT, Hack and Savannah stood awkwardly in the entryway.

"Being in charge of a spread-out operation like this is a big responsibility," Hack said, trying to make conversation.

Savannah gave him a smile for his efforts. "Good night, Hack." She retrieved her overnight bag and went to the bathroom. During Dane's tour of the house, the bathroom had seemed full of potential. Now it just looked old and dark.

She held the tears back while she brushed her teeth. But once she was under the covers in the big iron bed, she allowed herself a good cry. If only she and Dane had married before that mission to Russia. Then everything would be different. Dane wouldn't be bitter and unwilling to trust her. She never would have married Wes. Of course, if she'd never married Wes, there would be no Caroline. A fresh wave of tears engulfed her. Maybe, like her mother before her, she wasn't destined for happiness.

Slowly her tears dried, and anger replaced her sorrow. She was mad at Dane for misleading and abandoning her. But mostly she was mad at herself. Always where Dane was concerned she gave too much and got too little. She could live without him, and she had to stop giving in to the feelings he evoked in her.

Savannah closed her eyes as more tears leaked out onto the new sheets. She knew that the next time she saw Dane, she wouldn't be able to resist him any more than she had the first time.

* * *

It was dawn before Savannah finally fell asleep and three-thirty the next afternoon before she woke up. She decided to make best use of the daylight and took a long bath. Then she put on makeup and styled her hair before dressing in another new maternity outfit. But her heart wasn't in it, since Hack was her only audience.

She found her bodyguard in the kitchen. He had his new laptop set up and was alternately typing on the keyboard and eating doughnuts from a Krispy Kreme box.

"Is that breakfast?" she asked.

"You slept through breakfast and lunch. This is my afternoon snack."

She found a cream-filled doughnut and nibbled at it. "I'm not really hungry, but I guess I should eat—for the baby's sake."

Hack gave her one of his no-nonsense looks. "Save that crazy stuff for Dane."

She took another bite of doughnut. "I'm glad you care enough about me and this operation to risk your life protecting me—even if Dane doesn't."

Hack ignored her remark about Dane and said, "I care enough about you for sure, but I'm still not happy about this operation."

"Don't you agree it would be wonderful if we can trap Ferrante?" she asked.

"It would be wonderful," Hack agreed. "Like achieving world peace would be wonderful."

"You're saying it's not possible?"

He took the last doughnut from the box. "That's what I'm saying."

She valued Hack's opinion, but he had a tendency toward pessimism. So she didn't let his remarks discourage her too much.

"Can we walk around the French Quarter?" she asked. "I'd like to see it in the light."

Hack shook his head. "I'll take you out for a little while tonight."

She accepted this without argument. Hack had made major concessions—she could make a little one.

She pointed at the computer. "How are things going?"

"Caroline's fine, Doc's fine, Steamer's fine, Rosemary Allen's fine. Cam's a double-crossing traitor."

"And Dane?"

Hack shrugged his massive shoulders. "Dane doesn't report to me."

"Does Doc know about Cam yet?" she asked. "I mean . . . that he's working for Ferrante again instead of being a loyal part of the team?"

Hack nodded. "Doc knows Cam is cooperating with Ferrante, and he always knew Cam could never be a part of the team again. The way we work is as a unit—almost like one person—and trust is . . ." his voice trailed off as he searched for the right word.

"Essential," she provided helpfully.

"It's even more than that," he replied. "I was going to say *fundamental* or *intrinsic,* but maybe there's no word to really describe it. I trust the other members of the team like I trust my own arm." He demonstrated by clenching his fist. "There can't be any doubt."

"So Cam couldn't win back your respect and trust—no matter what?"

Hack shook his head. "Respect maybe. Trust never. And Cam knew that. I figure that's why he chose Ferrante."

"Ferrante trusts him?"

"No, but he never did. Cam will be on the same basis with him as he always was."

"I guess that's part of why Wes was so depressed right before he died," Savannah said. "He wanted it to be like it was before—but he knew it never would be."

"It won't ever be like it was."

Savannah felt the old guilt return. "It was my fault."

"Yeah," Hack agreed. "But you didn't mess things up on purpose. And if Wes had the capacity to betray Dane—which I would have sworn he didn't—it would have come out eventually. Maybe at a worse time, and the price we paid could have been higher."

She recognized that Hack was trying his best to absolve her. "Thanks."

He flashed her a gold-toothed grin. "I brought a little television and set it up in the living room. You can watch game shows and soap operas until it gets dark. Then I'll take you out to dinner."

"As great as that sounds . . ." She stood and stretched. "Instead of watching TV, I think I'm going to pull down some of the old, ruined wallpaper in the dining room."

Hack looked uncertain. "Dane might not like that."

Savannah shrugged. "All the more reason to do it."

Apparently Hack decided to let Dane fight his own battles, since he made no attempt to stop her. She pulled down wallpaper for a couple of hours. It was muscle-stretching, dusty work but surprisingly satisfying. And the knowledge that Dane would be unhappy when he saw what she'd done made it even better. She had almost an entire wall cleared by the time Hack came to get her for dinner.

He toed the pile of wallpaper shreds. "What are you going to do about this?"

"I figure the only way to annoy Dane more than pulling down wall-paper without permission is to leave the scraps on the floor."

"Yeah, let him clean it up." Hack gave her a quick, visual once-over. "We're eating at a nice restaurant, so you might want to dust your clothes off and pick the dried wallpaper paste out of your hair."

Putting her hands on her hips, she pretended outrage. "Are you saying I look terrible?"

He grinned. "You don't look too bad for a construction worker."

She smiled and walked to the bathroom. "Give me a couple of minutes to make myself presentable."

While she made repairs to her appearance, she could hear Hack on his phone lining up security for their outing. When they left the house, two of Hack's men were waiting on the front porch to escort them. Savannah looked around as they crossed the courtyard and walked down the ivy-covered alley. It was still beautiful, but it didn't seem magical the way it had when she first arrived. With Dane. A black sedan with tinted windows was waiting by the curb when they stepped from the alley onto the sidewalk. One of Hack's men opened the door for her. She smiled her thanks and climbed in the front seat. The guards got into the backseat while Hack circled around to the driver's side.

Savannah was pleased that she still found the French Quarter intriguing. Hack parked in front of a restaurant that boasted the best seafood in Louisiana. Savannah couldn't help but be glad they weren't eating at the creole restaurant Dane had half-promised to take her to the night before.

Hack led her up the steps and into the restaurant while the guards took positions at the entrance and back exit. A waiter took them to a table near a window that looked out over the street. He then distributed menus and offered to give them a few minutes to make their selections.

"What's good here?" Savannah asked after the waiter left.

"Everything," Hack replied. "They have huge shrimp—as big as my hand."

Savannah looked at his ham-sized fist with obvious skepticism.

Hack grinned. "Well, as big as your hand, anyway. The broiled lobster is great, and the crab cakes are out of this world. You should order a seafood platter so you can try some of everything."

"I could never eat a whole platter—even if I am eating . . ." She glanced down at her foam stomach. "For . . ."

Hack held up a hand. "Don't say it! And leftovers won't be a problem. I'll handle them for you."

So Savannah ordered a seafood platter, and Hack did the same. She sampled all the dishes except the oyster, which Hack begged her to try, but she was adamant.

"We've had a lovely evening and a delicious dinner," she told him. "Please don't spoil it by trying to make me eat something disgusting."

"If you'd try oysters, you'd like them," Hack challenged.

"The possibility of them tasting good is not worth the risk," Savannah replied. "I won't negotiate."

Hack abandoned the fight. "Well, if you won't eat them, I guess I'll have to."

Savannah passed her plate to him, and he ate all her leftovers, just as he'd promised he would.

During the drive back to the house, they passed the fortune teller's booth. Madame Leone was sitting in her window, looking out at the street. She smiled when she saw Savannah.

"Pull over, Hack!" Savannah said.

"Why?" he sounded both confused and wary.

"Please, I see something I want to buy."

He didn't seem happy, but he did as she asked. Once they were parked at the curb, she opened the passenger-side door and hurried over to Madame Leone. Knowing that if Hack got the chance to stop her, he would, she pulled a twenty-dollar bill from her purse as she walked.

When she reached the booth, she put the money on one of Madame Leone's outstretched palms. She heard Hack groan from behind her.

Madame Leone slipped the money into the bodice of her dress and said, "I thought you would be back."

Hack stepped up beside Savannah and put a hand on her arm. "I don't think this is a good idea."

But Savannah couldn't help herself. "I've already paid, Hack," she said.

Hack glowered at Madame Leone. "She'll give you a refund."

The old woman glared back at Hack, and Savannah wondered if Hack had met his match.

"She wants to know her future," Madame Leone told him.

"It will only take a minute," Savannah pleaded.

He muttered something unintelligible under his breath but nodded. "Hurry up."

Madame Leone clasped Savannah's hand and closed her eyes. "You are very much affected by the past but are hopeful of happiness in the future," she said in a dramatic tone.

Hack made a derisive sound, but Savannah ignored him.

"Is this happiness possible?" Savannah asked.

"Yes," Madame Leone replied, "but it will require endurance and patience. You know what you want—refuse to let go of your dream. The one you love will accept you into his life, but before that day comes, there is much darkness and pain."

The old woman opened her eyes and fixed Savannah with an earnest gaze. "You think you have to choose between the men you love, but you can love them both. In fact, you must. But be careful." Madame Leone leaned forward and whispered, "There is danger all around you. It is so hard to know who to trust. Follow your heart."

"That's enough," Hack said impatiently. He tried to pull Savannah away, but she resisted.

"Thank you," she told the old woman. No matter how illogical it seemed, she was completely sure Madame Leone knew about Dane and her love for him. And she hoped that the old woman's prediction was correct.

"You are welcome, child," Madame Leone said. "Now go and be safe."

"We're supposed to be keeping a low profile," Hack said. "Dane won't like it that you talked to her again."

"That makes me even happier that I did it," she replied.

The owner of the souvenir shop where Dane had bought her gift stepped out onto the sidewalk.

"I'm having a sale," he told her. "Tonight you can get *three* T-shirts for ten bucks."

She smiled but shook her head. "Thanks, but one is all I need."

They had just reached the car when Hack was accosted by the shoe shiner. "Your shoes could really use a coat of polish," the elderly gentleman said. "I'll make you a good deal. Only ten dollars for both shoes."

Hack's braids whipped around as he shook his head in the negative. "My shoes are fine."

The bicycle policeman rode up. "Is there a problem, sir?" he asked Hack, eying the shoe-shiner suspiciously.

"No problem," Hack replied.

The policeman touched the brim of his hat and nodded. "Well, you have a good evening then."

Hack jerked open the passenger door to the dark sedan, and Savannah climbed in without argument. They were quiet during the short ride back to the house. She knew Hack was annoyed with her, but she couldn't apologize for speaking to Madame Leone. Their short exchange had given her much-needed encouragement. And since nothing bad had happened during their little sidewalk excursion, she didn't feel that any harm had been done.

Once they were inside the house, she followed Hack into the kitchen and watched as he checked in with Dane on his laptop. Even this tenuous connection with Dane was enough to make her heart pound. When he closed the computer, she asked if the operation was on track.

"We're still in a holding pattern. Ferrante is staying put. He's probably trying to figure out where Dane took the girl. Hopefully they'll pick up the trail soon, and we can wrap this thing up."

"Caroline's okay?"

Hack nodded.

Savannah smiled. "I'm not really worried about Caroline. I know Doc and the McLaughlins will take care of her. I just don't like to be so far away."

Hack nodded his approval. "That's the way any mother would feel."

"I guess I'll go pull down wallpaper until I get sleepy." She stood and moved toward the door. "And the next time your guys make a run to the store, would you have them pick up some furniture polish? That way when I get tired of ripping off wallpaper I can polish Dane's antiques."

"Savannah." Hack's rare use of her first name surprised her.

"Yes?"

"I don't want you to get hurt."

She waved this aside. "Don't worry. Dane won't get too mad about the wallpaper. I mean, it's not like I could make this place look *worse*."

He shook his head. "I don't care about the wallpaper, but I do care about you. This isn't your house, and you can't base your life on the rantings of a fortune teller. That woman tells people what they want to hear so they'll keep coming back."

Savannah was grateful for his concern but unwilling to let go of her belief in Madame Leone. "But how did she know the things about me— like the fact that my past affects me and that I love two men?"

"She saw you with Dane last night and me tonight, so she made a lucky guess."

Savannah walked over and sat back down beside Hack at the kitchen table. "You're just trying to discredit her because you disagree with Madame Leone. You don't think I have a future with Dane."

"Unlike Madame Leone, I don't think I can predict the future for you or for Dane," Hack corrected. "And it's wrong for you to try and force things. Being with you reminds him of painful things in the past. It's up to him to decide if your company is worth the pain."

"You admitted that not all of the bad memories are my fault."

"It doesn't matter."

She was upset by the unfairness of the situation and determined to win Hack over to her side. "You, of all people, should understand how I feel. I love him and want to be with him. You do too."

"I love him like a brother," Hack agreed. "And I feel like my place is with him. But if he ever asked me to leave, I'd go."

All the hope she'd felt after her short talk with Madame Leone evaporated. "So I should forget about trying to help him love again?"

Hack nodded. "You've told him how you feel. Now let him choose."

Tears she'd promised herself not to shed stung her eyes. "I know if he'd give me a chance, I could make him happy."

"Maybe he isn't looking for happiness," Hack suggested. "Maybe all he wants from life is peace."

"Love is better than peace."

"I agree," Hack said. "But it's his choice."

"It's my life, too," she pointed out doggedly.

"But not your choice," he reiterated. "You chose to marry Wes. Now it's up to Dane whether he wants to take you back or not."

She bowed her head in miserable acceptance. "You're right. I should leave him alone. But I don't know if I can."

Instead of launching into another lecture, Hack smiled. "If you'll give him a chance to miss you—he might decide he can't live without you."

"But what if he doesn't?"

"Then it wasn't meant to be."

After a few minutes of silence, Savannah said, "I'm going to bed."

"I thought you were going to rip down wallpaper."

"I'm not in the mood anymore," she told him. "And the sooner I get back on a regular schedule, the better."

He nodded. "Good night then."

She smiled. "Good night, Hack."

Savannah brushed her teeth in the dark bathroom, changed into her pajamas, and climbed into the big bed. She lay on her back, rested her hands on her fake foam stomach, and stared at the water stains on the ceiling. She tried to think of happy times, like when she first started her job on General Steele's staff and when Caroline was born. But every happy moment had its dark side as well. They all brought her thoughts back to Dane.

Turning over, she focused on the plantation shutters that covered the room's only window. The happy music being played in the streets of the French Quarter made her feel even more sad and alone. She couldn't help but think of the brief dance she shared with Dane before he left her. Too miserable even to cry, she closed her eyes, letting sleep provide temporary relief from the memories.

Savannah startled awake sometime later. Sitting up, she stared around the room, unsure what had awakened her. Maybe she'd had a bad dream she couldn't remember. Or maybe all the seafood she'd eaten for dinner wasn't digesting well. Or maybe her body still hadn't adjusted to the schedule changes that had been inflicted on her over the past few days.

While trying to decide whether sleep was still a possibility or if she should get up and tear down old wallpaper, she heard a scraping sound near the window. The shutters prevented her from seeing outside. With her heart pounding, she burrowed down further under the covers and tried to convince herself that the noise she'd heard was a tree branch or a squirrel.

Her breathing was almost back to normal when she heard the sound again. This time it came from father down the alley, toward the courtyard. It took every ounce of courage she possessed to climb out of the bed. Once she was up and moving, she found it easier to run through the door and up the hallway. She found Hack standing by the arched doorway that led from the dining room into the entryway. He put a finger to his lips when he saw her. Then he waved for her to stand behind him.

She gladly took refuge behind his reassuring bulk. "Someone is out there?" she whispered.

He nodded. "We think it's Dane."

Savannah's heart resumed its pounding. "Dane?"

"Yeah, he likes to spring surprise inspections."

Savannah remembered the visit they'd made to the support team at Ft. Belvoir. Yes, Dane did like to surprise people. The question was why would he surprise them when he'd just left a few hours before?

After retrieving the gun from the buffet drawer, Hack approached the door with amazing stealth. The doorknob rattled, and Savannah clutched her throat. If Hack was wrong and it was Mario Ferrante on the other side of that door . . .

Hack reached down and jerked the door open.

Savannah couldn't control a tiny scream as a shadowy figure rushed inside. The fact that Hack didn't fire the gun was a good indication that the intruder was indeed Dane. But she didn't know for sure until Dane pulled the ski mask from his head.

"Surprise," he said with a smile.

"Not hardly," she replied, trying to sound uninterested.

"We've been tracking you since you came into the Quarter." Hack stepped between them and addressed his commanding officer. "We weren't expecting you back so soon."

Dane pulled off his coat and hung it on a nail by the door. "Just checking to be sure the security is adequate."

Savannah leaned around Hack. "I thought you had important things to do elsewhere. Much more important than me."

"Checking on this part of the operation is important," Dane defended his decision to return.

Hack narrowed his eyes at Dane. "Now that you know we're ready for anything, I guess you're headed to Ft. Belvoir."

"No," Dane corrected. "I'm going to take over Savannah-sitting and let you go to Ft. Belvoir."

"Savannah-sitting," she repeated. "If that isn't the most insulting thing I've ever heard!"

Both men ignored her.

"You know what I think?" Hack said to Dane.

"I don't care what you think," Dane responded curtly. "Keep your opinions to yourself, and go check on your men. That's an order."

Hack continued as if Dane hadn't spoken. "I think you missed Savannah. You changed the plans, shuffled the assignments, and possibly endangered the whole operation just so you could be with her."

"That's ridiculous," Dane scoffed. "Now get out of here."

Hack laughed and turned to Savannah. "Maybe that fortune teller was right."

"What fortune teller?" Dane demanded.

"The one that has that little booth out on Royal Street," Hack replied.

Dane frowned at Savannah. "You talked to her again?"

She nodded, still processing Hack's words.

Dane addressed Hack. "What did the old con artist say?"

Hack walked over and opened the door. "You'll have to ask Savannah about that. It was *her* fortune." He slipped out into the darkness and was gone.

Dane locked the front door behind Hack and then turned around to face Savannah warily.

"Did you really miss me?" she asked.

"Definitely not." His tone was firm, but she felt amazingly light-hearted. He had come back.

"Now that I'm sure the other elements of the operation are running smoothly, I came here, since keeping you alive is my responsibility."

She moved forward until there were only a few inches separating them. "So it was duty that brought you back?"

"Of course," he said without conviction. His eyes roamed from her mouth to her eyes and back again.

"I'm just glad you're here." She put her hands on his shoulders, and his arms went around her.

He pulled her as close as the foam stomach would allow and pressed his cheek to hers. Then he asked, "What did the fortune teller say?"

This question made her suspicious of his motivations for the embrace, and she drew back in annoyance. "She said that eventually the man I love will love me too. But she said I'd have to be patient and endure much pain before that happened."

"Much pain, huh?"

"I've had plenty of pain, so love must be right around the corner."

This earned her half a smile. "You know she's a total fake?"

"I know nothing of the sort." Deciding to throw caution to the wind, she put her hands on the sides of his face and pressed her lips to his. He was stiff for a few seconds, allowing the kiss but not really participating in it. But finally he relaxed and kissed her back.

When he pulled away, she looked down at her fake stomach and said, "I wish this was a real baby." She dragged her eyes up to meet his. "Our baby."

He shook his head slightly. "We're enjoying a moment of suspended reality, Savannah. Don't spoil it."

She wanted him to acknowledge that the kiss was more than a stolen moment, but mostly she didn't want their truce to end. So she removed her hands from the foam stomach and put them around Dane's neck. When his lips reclaimed hers, she knew she had made the right decision.

When the kiss ended, she asked, "So what now?"

"Now we just wait for Ferrante to make a move."

"Do you think it will happen soon? Christmas is only two days away."

He nodded. "While I was gone, I laid a more obvious trail for Ferrante to follow. He won't be able to resist."

She couldn't control a little shudder. "Have you figured out how to get Chad Allen away from Ferrante?"

"The FBI has agreed to help us get him, but they don't want to make a move until Ferrante has left the estate."

"On his way here to get his daughter?" she confirmed.

Dane nodded. "We should get word that he's left at any minute."

Trying to be brave, she pointed toward the window, where faint rays of light were penetrating the shutters. "The sun is coming up."

"It looks that way."

"So will you take me out to that creole restaurant today?"

"I hope that by the end of the day things will be settled with Ferrante," he said. "If so, I'll take you out to dinner tonight."

"And what will we do all day?"

He pointed at the little television. "I guess we can watch TV. Or we could tear off more wallpaper."

She felt a little guilty. "I'm sorry, and I'll clean up my mess."

He smiled. "You did a good job, and I'd be a fool to complain about free labor."

She looked around the room. "How long have you owned this place?"

"I bought it right before you asked me to marry you the first time."

Her breath caught in her throat, and she was overwhelmed anew with guilt and regret. "Oh Dane, I wish things were different."

"I don't want to talk about what could have been." His expression was stubborn. "It's pointless."

She knew better than to press him. "Then tell me about your New Orleans ancestors."

He leaned his head back on the couch. "I don't know much about the early ones, except that they were from France originally. When my grandmother's parents sold this place, they moved to Baton Rouge. That's where she met my grandfather. He was a shrimper like his father before him."

"Did your grandfather ever take you fishing for shrimp?"

"They call it 'shrimping,' and I worked with him every summer when I was a kid. That's what convinced me to get an education."

She raised an eyebrow. "Shrimping was too hard for you?"

"I could take the hard work. It was the smell that got me." He shuddered. "I still can't stand the sight of shrimp."

"Then don't go to a seafood restaurant with Hack. He likes shrimp as big as my hand." She made a fist to emphasize her point.

He smiled. "Thanks for the tip."

They were quiet for a few minutes, and then she asked, "Why don't you hire another contractor and continue with the restoration?"

He shrugged a shoulder. "My incentive ended when my girl married someone else."

Savannah swallowed a lump in her throat. "She's available now."

"No, that girl is gone forever."

"The woman she became loves you even more than the girl did."

He shook his head. "It's not the same."

She struggled to control her frustration "The young man I loved was happy and daring but full of optimism. He's matured into a difficult, often crabby, man. But I still love him." She turned and forced eye contact. "If you truly loved the girl back then, you'd love the woman now."

He was looking at her intently, and as she waited for his response, she began to hope that he would finally admit his feelings for her. Then he gave her one of his sarcastic smiles, and she knew there had been no breakthrough. "Yeah, I didn't really love you. I just wanted to win my bet with Wes and get that watch his grandfather gave him. It's so cool, with GPS and a knife and even that little fork."

She stared at him.

"And a watch can't break your heart."

"Or love you back," she said.

He frowned. "I think we've spent enough time strolling down memory lane. Fatigue has made me much more sentimental and fool-hardy than usual. If you play your cards right, you might get another kiss before I come to my senses. But if you keep talking about true love, you'll miss your window of opportunity. So do you want the kiss or what?"

If nothing else, life had taught her when to cut her losses and take what she could get. So she nodded. "I want the kiss."

This time as their lips pressed together, sad, hot tears escaped her eyes. And, as usual, long before she was ready for the kiss to end, they were interrupted by a phone call.

Dane pulled away, but he didn't answer the phone immediately. He smoothed back her hair and wiped the tears from her eyes. Then he gave her a rare, genuine smile before removing his cell phone from his pocket and checking the screen.

"It was Hack," he said as he returned the call. "What's up?"

Savannah watched as he listened to the response. When he frowned, she fought back panic. "Is it Caroline?"

He shook his head and covered the phone. "Caroline's fine." Then he spoke to Hack. "Come on back here as fast as you can." After closing the phone, he told Savannah, "Ferrante is on the move, and he's got Cam and Chad Allen with him." He sat down in front of his laptop and entered a series of commands. "We'll be able to track them using Cam's M-CODE signal."

Her mouth went dry as she saw a topographical map of the eastern United States appear on Dane's screen. Ferrante was coming. A little green light was flashing in Maryland.

She cleared her throat and asked, "That's Cam?"

Dane nodded.

"Since Ferrante has Chad Allen with him, the FBI's rescue plans are ruined."

Dane grimaced. "Ferrante probably plans to use him to encourage Rosemary to surrender herself. But it's not a big problem. If the operation plays out the way we've planned, we'll recover Chad Allen ourselves after we arrest Ferrante."

Savannah was relieved but nervous. "So now we wait?"

He nodded. "Let's go see what our breakfast choices are."

* * *

In the kitchen, he opened the refrigerator, and together they studied the supplies Hack had purchased. On one shelf there was milk and a case of bottled water. On the next was a wide variety of sandwich meats, cheeses, and breads. In the freezer was an assortment of frozen dinners.

"No breakfast foods," she said smugly. "I guess you'll have to take me out for croissants and hot chocolate."

He frowned. "That would be a security risk. You could just drink a glass of milk."

She pressed her hands on her foam-covered midsection. "The baby and I need something from *all* the basic food groups. And you know where Ferrante is."

"I guess we're safe from Ferrante for a few hours." He frowned. "But I'd like to know what nutrients you're going to get from croissants and hot chocolate?"

"Grain and protein," she replied promptly.

He was still reluctant. "We could get one of Hack's guys to run to the store for us."

"And leave a security checkpoint unmanned?" she asked in mock horror. "It would be much safer for us to sneak to a restaurant. We could wear disguises."

"You're already disguised!"

She couldn't argue this, so she tried another approach. "Since the folks in the French Quarter stay up all night, I'll bet there's not a soul on the streets right now. Even spies for Ferrante!"

"You're probably right," he conceded. Then he glanced down at her stomach. "About the lack of activity at this hour anyway. I'm not sure you're right about the food groups."

She knew he was weakening and smiled. "You'll just have to trust me on that."

"In fact, at this time of the day, the trick will be finding a restaurant that's open."

"There's no obstacle you can't surmount!"

He narrowed his eyes at her. "Don't overstate your case."

She tried not to look too excited. "So can we?"

He nodded. "I guess a healthy meal is worth the minimal risk."

The reminder that they were baiting Ferrante took some of the fun out of the excursion for Savannah, but not much. She was afraid to make Dane wait long for fear that he'd change his mind, so she quickly put on one of her cutest maternity outfits and pulled her dark hair back into a ponytail. She didn't want to take the time to put on makeup, so she dug a pair of sunglasses out of her purse and perched them on her nose.

"Now you look inconspicuous," Dane said when she joined him in the parlor.

She lifted the glasses to peer at him briefly. "Did you warn your guards that we were leaving so they won't shoot us?"

"I did," he confirmed, putting a guiding hand on her elbow. "Now behave yourself, or I'll be forced to reconsider the wisdom of this outing."

It was a beautiful morning. The sun was warm on her face, and a light breeze carried the heady scent of gardenia from the courtyard planters. Everything was better when Dane was with her. She wondered briefly if her dependence on his presence was a sign of emotional dysfunction. Then she decided that in true Southern-belle style, she'd worry about that later.

A few blocks up on Dauphine Street they found a small café that was open if not really ready for business. The owner seated them with a warning that their meal would be delayed until the cook arrived.

"We're not in a hurry," Dane said

Savannah's heart swelled with happiness. He didn't want their outing to end any more than she did.

After the owner walked away, he leaned forward. "We're safer in here than on the street."

Savannah's heart constricted slightly. Okay, so maybe he wasn't enjoying their extended breakfast *quite* as much as she was.

It took nearly an hour, but finally their table was covered with food. They had buttery croissants, a delicious mushroom omelet, a fresh fruit salad, and rich hot chocolate. He didn't eat much, mostly pushing his food around on his plate. When she remarked on this, he blamed his lack of appetite on pregame nerves.

"I'm always like this right before an operation starts."

Savannah took a sip from her second cup of hot chocolate. "This is almost as good as yours."

"Not even close," he disagreed. "But I do believe we've covered all the basic food groups."

She patted her stomach. "Yes, we're very responsible parents."

On the way back to the house, Dane didn't seem to be in a hurry. He allowed her to window shop and even bought her another T-shirt from the street vendor who was part of Operation Sitting Duck.

"To add to your collection," he explained.

She folded the T-shirt and put it in her purse. "Thank you."

When they turned onto Royal Street they discovered that despite the early hour, Madame Leone was already sitting in her booth.

"She must have an incredible work ethic!" Savannah exclaimed softly to Dane.

He scowled. "If that's what you call someone who hates to miss an opportunity to trick naive people out of their money."

Savannah lifted her glasses to glare at him. "I'm not naive."

"Yes, you are," he returned.

As they approached the booth, Madame Leone smiled. "I see he came back."

Savannah nodded. "He did."

Madame Leone turned her gaze to Dane. "Would you like me to tell your fortune?"

"There's no way I'd pay you twenty dollars to make up a bunch of nonsense about my future."

The fortune teller's smile broadened. "It's on the house."

Dane shook his head. "No, thanks." He tried to pull Savannah away, but she kept her feet firmly planted in front of the fortune teller's booth.

"She's offered to tell your future for free," Savannah said. "It would be rude to refuse, not to mention foolish." She lowered her voice and whispered, "Hasn't Hack warned you that it's dangerous to offend someone with mystic powers?"

"I think perhaps he is someone who can't handle the truth," Madame Leone remarked in blatant challenge.

Savannah stood in speechless horror and waited for Dane to flail the old woman with words. But instead of reacting the way she expected him to, he smiled and laid a hand on the fortune teller's outstretched palm.

"I'm not afraid of anything," he assured her.

Madame Leone's eyelids fell closed, and she leaned her head back as if entering a trance.

Dane looked at Savannah and rolled his eyes. She had to work hard to control a giggle.

"I discern that you are a brave man," Madame Leone droned. "One who often puts the welfare of others before your own."

Savannah stopped laughing and gave the fortune teller her rapt attention.

"You hold people at arm's length," Madame Leone continued. "You rarely let anyone into your heart."

"You're supposed to be telling my future, not assassinating my character," Dane reminded the old woman.

She cleared her throat and continued. "You must make peace with your past and face your fears about the future."

Dane sneered. "I told you. I'm not afraid of anything."

Madame Leone opened her eyes. "We're all afraid of something. You fear failure. Accept that like the rest of humanity, you are capable of making mistakes. This weakness, as you see it, does not make you unworthy of happiness."

Savannah was mesmerized by the exchange, but Dane seemed unimpressed. He pulled his hand from Madame Leone's and said, "I'm glad I didn't pay twenty bucks for that."

Then he grabbed Savannah's arm and led her down the street. Savannah turned back and Madame Leone waved at her.

"Don't believe a word of that," Dane muttered as they hurried toward the house.

Nothing he could have said would have made Savannah more interested in Madame Leone.

CHAPTER 9

DANE WENT INTO the parlor when they got back to the house. His mood was worse than usual, which Savannah attributed to their encounter with Madame Leone. She pulled wallpaper down for a while, covertly watching Dane through the parlor door as he alternately talked on the phone and typed into his laptop.

Finally she abandoned her renovation efforts and tried to watch Hack's television, but her eyes kept straying to the windows—wondering if danger lurked just outside. At some point she dozed off and was awakened by Dane's cell phone. Blearily she watched him answer the call.

When Dane closed his phone, he stood and moved toward the front entrance. "We have intruders."

Savannah jumped up to follow him. "Ferrante?"

"No," Dane replied as they heard Steamer's voice raised in strident tones. Dane opened the door as Steamer was threatening one of Hack's men.

"You just wait until I talk to your boss!"

The look on the guard's face was almost comically stoic. In fact, Savannah might have been tempted to laugh if Corporal Benjamin from the support team at Ft. Belvoir hadn't also been in the large man's grasp. The corporal's presence was completely out of context, and she felt sure it wasn't a good thing.

"Let them go," Dane commanded.

Reluctantly, Hack's hired giant released his captives.

Steamer straightened his clothes and shot the guard a resentful look before stepping into the house. "You'll be hearing from my lawyer."

The guard didn't react in any way.

"Thanks," Dane said to the guard. Then he closed the door and addressed their surprise visitors. "What in the world are you doing here?

You're supposed to be in Birmingham," he told Steamer. Then he turned to the corporal. "And you're supposed to be at Ft. Belvoir."

"I was in Birmingham," Steamer replied. "Until *he* showed up." He jerked his thumb in Corporal Benjamin's direction. "Operation Sitting Duck is in trouble."

Savannah was trying to figure out why Steamer had been in Birmingham when Dane said, "Steamer, I want an explanation, and I want it fast."

Corporal Benjamin cleared his throat. "Actually, sir, maybe I should be the one to explain."

Dane nodded his curt approval.

"Yesterday afternoon while I was working my shift on your support team for Operation Sitting Duck, my CO showed me a glitch they'd found on one of our computers. It didn't take me long to realize the glitch was caused by a relay."

"A relay?" Dane repeated.

"Yes, sir," Corporal Benjamin confirmed. "Someone had encoded a transfer program onto the hard drive so all the information was being forwarded to another computer."

"An unidentified computer," Steamer clarified.

The corporal continued. "The relay was transmitting all the cell phone transcripts, personnel reports, satellite photos—everything. I reported it to the CO, and he checked with General Steele. The word came back for us not to worry about the relay. The general said that it was set up that way so the data could be stored in a backup computer in case we had a power outage."

Steamer scoffed. "What are the chances of that?"

Dane disregarded Steamer's question and asked the corporal, "Who is your commanding officer?"

"Captain Foxglove."

Dane nodded. "He's rock solid."

"Yes, sir," Corporal Benjamin agreed. "I tried to accept the general's explanation, but it bothered me. I'm not smart about some things, but I know computers, and that relay wasn't kosher. I was afraid that if the information got into the wrong hands, the lives of your men might be in danger." The corporal stood a little straighter. "And in spite of what you saw the other night, sir, I really do take my responsibilities seriously."

Dane nodded. "I can see that."

"I wanted to warn you that you were being monitored by some unknown person. I couldn't call you on your cell phone, since the relay would pick that up. The only location I had for your team was the hotel in Birmingham. So when my shift ended, I got in my car and started driving. I made it to the Birmingham location early this morning."

Steamer took up the story. "When he told me that we couldn't trust the support team at Ft. Belvoir and that we shouldn't be using our phones or computers, I didn't see any choice but to come here and tell you in person."

Savannah was confused and horrified by this turn of events, but Dane just frowned. "We're very careful about what we say over the phone, and we have extra safeguards on our computers—so the damage should be minimal." He looked at Corporal Benjamin and asked, "When does your next shift start?"

The corporal checked his watch. "Tomorrow morning at seven o'clock."

"I need you to get back to Ft. Belvoir and disable that relay computer. You can fry it with a surge of electricity, you can infest it with a virus—whatever—but I can't have my operation monitored."

Corporal Benjamin nodded. "Yes, sir."

Dane pulled out his wallet and handed the corporal several bills. "That should cover the cost of your gas. I can't ever repay you for your dedication to duty."

The young man blushed at the praise. "You don't have to pay me for that, sir. But I appreciate the gas money. Corporals don't make all that much."

Dane smiled. "You'll be a big asset to me as a part of the support team, but if you feel you are in danger, get out of Ft. Belvoir."

"Go AWOL, sir?"

Dane nodded. "If it comes to that, I'll take care of any charges that are issued against you. From this point on you work for me."

Dane was asking the corporal to jeopardize his military career and possibly break the law. Savannah wasn't sure if the young man would be willing to risk so much.

"I'd be honored to be a part of your team, sir!" the corporal responded.

"It's good to have you onboard, corporal." Dane walked into the dining room and opened a drawer in the antique buffet. He returned to the entryway with a box that contained several walkie-talkies. He put one in his pocket and gave one to Steamer. "Use that for the rest of the operation."

Steamer pressed the speak button and said "roger" into the mouthpiece.

Dane opened the front door and handed the box with the remaining radios to the guard standing there. "Get these to Hack, and tell him to distribute one to each lookout team. No more cell phones for the rest of the operation."

The guard nodded as he tucked the box of phones under his arm.

Dane turned to Corporal Benjamin. "You head on back to Ft. Belvoir and take care of that computer."

The corporal saluted. "Yes, *sir!*"

Dane looked uncomfortable with the military formality but returned the salute. "We'll see you at the post soon."

Dane closed the door behind the corporal and walked into the parlor. Savannah and Steamer followed behind him.

"Why were you in Birmingham?" she asked Steamer.

Instead of answering her, Steamer glanced at Dane, his eyes full of misery, and said, "I'm sorry, sir."

Dane waved this aside. "It's okay. Savannah understands that a covert operation requires a certain amount of secrecy."

Savannah narrowed her eyes at him as she assimilated this comment. There were aspects of the operation that she didn't know about. "Why was Steamer in Birmingham?"

"We had another decoy team there," Dane said, a little too casually.

And then what should have been obvious sooner became clear. "The Birmingham decoy team is set up at the hotel where we stayed," she said. "The Motel Four where we made a point of drawing attention to ourselves and then left through the side door without actually checking out?"

Dane shrugged. "Backups are essential to any well-planned operation."

"It sounds to me like *we're* the backup and you intended all along for Ferrante to go to Birmingham. Admit it!"

"Yes, yes, yes!" He held up his hands in mock surrender.

She saw it all so clearly now. "This was never the trap. This was just an elaborate plan to keep me out of the way."

"No, this is Plan B," Dane told her.

She leaned closer and whispered, "Why didn't you just tell me about the other decoy team? It doesn't matter to me if I'm a part of Plan A or Plan B—but I would like to know where I stand."

"You didn't need to know which plan you were a part of."

She shook her head angrily. "That excuse is getting old. I'm honestly afraid to believe anything you say anymore."

He looked angry too. "Well, then you'd better stop dragging me into your personal problems, because discretionary distribution of information is a military reality."

Some of her righteous indignation subsided as the front door burst open and Hack rushed in.

"Steamer!" he bellowed. "You've really done it this time!"

Steamer stepped behind Dane. "I have a good reason for being here."

"Apparently all those months in the desert sun fried your brain!" Hack accused. "That was the worst covert approach I've ever seen."

"There were extenuating circumstances . . ."

"Save it for later," Hack cut him off. "We've got bigger problems. "Ferrante's on the way here."

"Here?" Steamer repeated. "Not Birmingham?"

Hack nodded. "A guy from a courier service was waiting by the gate when I got here. He handed me this."

Hack extended an envelope toward Dane. While Dane read it, Hack told the others, "It's from Ferrante. He said to have his daughter at the gate on Toulouse Street at five o'clock tonight, and he'll make a trade."

"Who is he planning to trade?" Steamer asked.

"Cam," Dane answered grimly. "He says if we don't turn over his daughter, he'll kill Cam."

Hack scowled. "Yeah, Ferrante knows we'll have to try and save Cam—even though he's a rotten traitor."

"That relay at Ft. Belvoir is sending information to Ferrante!" Steamer cried. "He's been monitoring our phone calls and knows we're here instead of Birmingham."

"Ferrante didn't have to glean this location from phone calls," Hack said. "All he had to do was follow you."

Steamer looked crushed. "He used *me* against the team?"

"Steamer was just trying to help." Savannah drew Hack's angry gaze toward her briefly. "He had to warn us."

Her clumsy defense of his actions seemed to make Steamer more upset. "I can't believe I fell for such an obvious trick. I ruined the whole operation!"

Hack continued to glower at Steamer. "I can't believe it either!"

But Dane was reassuring. "We can handle Ferrante here. Not quite as well as we could have in Birmingham." He cut his eyes toward Steamer. "But we'll manage. The important thing is to stop this bickering and get ready."

Hack sighed. "What do you want me to do?"

"If possible, I'd like to catch Ferrante when his plane lands. So we need to get intercept teams set up at the airport and any other major landing strips in the New Orleans area," Dane said while typing on his laptop. "How many men can you spare?"

"About fifteen," Hack said after a few seconds of consideration.

"That will have to do. Watch for Cam's M-CODE signal. It might give us some warning about the landing site."

"What if we can't get him at the plane?" Savannah asked.

"Then we'll handle him here," Dane said, but he didn't look happy.

"We could ask General Steele to get us some additional help from the Air Force or Navy," Steamer suggested.

"We could," Dane agreed. "But until we find out who the security leak is at Ft. Belvoir, I don't want to share sensitive information with anyone outside the team—even General Steele."

"You think the general could be working with Ferrante?" Steamer sounded as horrified as Savannah felt.

"Very few people had the knowledge and opportunity to set up the relay on the support team computer," Dane said. "General Steele was one of them."

"We can trust General Steele," Savannah said. Then she watched the men exchange a significant look, and she felt as if the world had tilted. Saying the words didn't make it true.

"Trust issues aside, I still don't want to ask the general to call in troops," Dane moved on. "We might scare Ferrante away with a show of force. We have a better chance of catching him if we can lull him into a sense of false security." He paused for emphasis. "But from now on until the end of this operation, we don't share information with anybody outside the team. Even General Steele."

The men nodded uneasily.

Satisfied, Dane continued. "Hack, divide your fifteen available men into five teams, and send them to these locations." He pulled a sheet of paper from his printer and extended it toward Hack. "We can't use our cell phones anymore," he added. "I gave some two-way radios to your man at the door."

"I got one, and the others have been distributed," Hack said. "I'll come back once I have the intercept teams in place. In the meantime, you might want to come up with an alternate plan—in case Ferrante doesn't run right into our outstretched arms."

Dane grimaced. "I'll have a plan if we need one."

Just as Hack slammed the door closed, Steamer cursed under his breath.

"What?" Dane demanded.

Steamer pointed at the laptop. "We just lost Cam's M-CODE signal."

CHAPTER 10

"WHAT HAPPENED TO the signal?" Savannah asked with dread.

"Hopefully there's something blocking the signal, and we'll reacquire it soon," Dane said.

"Unless Ferrante dumped Cam out of his airplane," Steamer remarked.

Savannah looked at him in horror. "Surely he wouldn't do that."

"He would," Dane said. "But he probably didn't. He needs Cam alive until he gets his daughter back."

Savannah didn't feel much better. "Since we know Ferrante is headed here, I guess the M-CODE signal isn't that important anyway."

"It might give us an idea of where Ferrante is planning to land, and since our manpower is limited, we need any edge we can get."

The reality of the situation was starting to sink in for Savannah. In theory, impersonating Rosemary had seemed like a good idea—a chance to prove herself to Dane. In reality, the thought of facing Ferrante was terrifying.

"Caroline is still okay?" she asked.

Dane pulled the transponder from his pocket. The green light was shining in reassurance.

Savannah put a hand to her pounding heart. "Thank goodness."

"Now that a confrontation with Ferrante is likely and imminent, we need to address the issue of Savannah's safety," Dane said to Steamer.

Steamer nodded. "We need to get her out of here fast."

Savannah stared at him in confusion. "You want me to leave?"

The men ignored her. "You take her somewhere safe," Steamer proposed. "I can handle Ferrante."

Savannah was touched by Steamer's offer and considered it an indication that he was starting to hate her less. "I'm disguised as Rosemary," she reminded them. "How are you going to bait your trap if you send me away?"

"You've served your purpose by luring him here," Dane said. "You don't physically have to be here during the confrontation."

"So get going," Steamer encouraged.

"No," Dane said. "I'm the commanding officer of this operation, and so I *do* need to be here. I need Hack to manage the intercept teams, so you'll have to take her, Steam."

As much as she dreaded staying, she hated the thought of leaving more. So Savannah squared her shoulders and faced Dane. "You can't just send me away."

Dane laughed grimly. "It's an order."

"I'll start obeying your orders when you start being honest."

He put his hands on her shoulders and turned her toward the hallway. "This is not negotiable, Savannah. Go pack your things." He gave her a little push.

Furious, she walked into the bedroom and slammed the door. She had initiated Operation Sitting Duck, and he had led her to believe that she was a vital part of the team. But now, when success was in their grasp, Dane was going to send her off. As if she needed any more evidence that she was completely unnecessary.

Fighting tears, she packed her overnight bag. Then she realized he couldn't physically make her leave. With newfound resolve, Savannah walked to the door and locked it. Then she worked quickly and silently to transfer the boxes of floor tile stacked against the wall. Ten minutes later, she was sweaty and exhausted, but she'd created what she hoped was an impenetrable barrier inside the bedroom door. She climbed atop her barricade and waited for Dane.

She didn't have to wait long.

"Savannah!" His voice was accompanied by an impatient rap on the door. "Quit pouting and come on. You need to leave right away so I can concentrate on Ferrante."

"I'm not leaving," she said. "My place is with you."

She could feel his anger and frustration even through the thick wood.

"This is not up for discussion. I'm ordering you to come out and leave with Steamer."

"I'm not going to obey that order. When we get back to Ft. Belvoir, you can court-martial me."

He grabbed the doorknob and pushed against it hard. "Unlock the door, Savannah."

"No."

She heard him muttering under his breath and sorting through keys. Finally he placed one in the keyhole and metal grated against metal. But the door remained tightly closed.

"Savannah," he said. "What have you done?"

"I came up with Plan C, and I can only give information to those who need to know. Unfortunately, you're not one of those people."

"Savannah, this is only delaying the inevitable and risking lives. Not just yours, but Steamer's, too."

"Steamer can go ahead and leave now," she said. "I'm not endangering him."

Dane was quiet for a few minutes, and Savannah was beginning to think that he had given up and left her, but finally he spoke. "You are the most exasperating woman I've ever had to deal with." His tone was kinder than she expected. "And I've known some difficult women."

She smiled and pressed her face against the door in an effort to be as close to him as possible. "You understand why I can't go?"

"I understand why you don't want to," he conceded. "But if anything happens to you, Caroline will be an orphan. The McLaughlins aren't emotionally fit to be parents, so I guess she'd be put in a foster home or . . ."

"You'd take care of her," Savannah said with complete confidence. "Or General Steele."

"Do you really want that?"

"Of course not," Savannah returned. "I want to raise her myself. But I want to do it without looking over my shoulder all the time. We have to get Ferrante."

"We can get him without you here."

"Maybe," she admitted. "But I started the whole thing, and I feel responsible. I want to stay just in case you need me."

"So we have a standoff," he said.

"It looks that way."

He tried another approach. "You know I'm wasting time here that I could be using to fine-tune my plan to trap Ferrante."

"I've made my decision. I'm not going to open the door. So go ahead and work on your plans."

"What if I promise to let you stay? Will you open the door then?"

She laughed. "If I open this door, you'll send me off with Steamer so fast it will make my head spin."

He didn't answer immediately, and she took his lack of response as an admission of guilt. Finally he just said, "Please."

"I'm sorry." She looked down at the boxes beneath her. "Even if I wanted to, I probably couldn't. It took every ounce of my strength to drag all the cases of tile in front of the door. It might be days before I can move them away."

She heard him sigh. "While you're in there, I guess you could be thinking of what color I should paint that room."

"So you're going to go ahead with the renovation?"

"I'm considering it. How do you feel about a soft green?"

"I like green," she said, looking around. "Or yellow might be nice."

"Yellow sounds kind of girly."

"Yellow is cheerful," she corrected as her eyes continued to tour the room. "But first you're going to have to hire someone to get this old wallpaper down."

"You could do it."

She smiled. "If you don't want to finish before the turn of the next century."

"So I'll hire somebody."

"The ceiling has water damage, the light fixture will need to be replaced, and the crown molding should be looked at."

"Are you trying to discourage me?"

"No."

"What do you think about the floor?"

She studied the old hardwood planks. "The floors need to be refinished, but I think they'll do. And I hope you can save the shutters. They're in bad shape, but they could be beautiful."

"Yeah, I always liked those shutters."

"So you're not mad at me?" she asked.

"I'm irritated but not mad."

Despite the thick wood that separated them, she felt closer to him than she had in years. She knew he still wanted her to open the door—that if she did, he would still send her away and he was still going to be mad at her when this was over. But he understood.

"Thank you," she whispered.

"Savannah . . ."

The only warning she had was the sound of an old board squeaking. Then one of the wooden panels beside the fireplace slid open, and Steamer burst into the room. She covered her mouth to muffle the scream she couldn't control.

"That's one of the things I love most about this house," Dane said through the door. "It's full of hidden doors and passageways." He raised his voice and added, "Move the boxes, Steam. We've got to get her out of here."

Savannah watched in stunned dismay as Steamer made short work of the barricade she'd so laboriously built. She felt angry and betrayed, but mostly she was afraid. For the first time since she'd admitted to herself that she still loved Dane, she began to wonder if they would be able to work things out between them.

More than anything, she dreaded the moment when she would come face to face with Dane after this latest act of treachery. But there was no way to avoid it, so she stood by the door. Steamer worked steadily with an occasional sympathetic look in her direction. But when the moment of truth came, and Steamer swung the door open, Dane wasn't standing in the hall, waiting as she'd expected. She could hear him in the parlor talking to Hack.

"You should probably bring your suitcase," Steamer said almost kindly. "And you don't need that anymore." He pointed at the fake stomach.

Once she was alone, she unhooked the straps and pulled the foam out from under her expensive maternity shirt. The feeling of loss she experienced surprised her. She held the foam close to her chest for a few seconds and then slowly put it on the bed. The game was finished. Picking up her overnight bag, she hurried from the bedroom.

When she walked into the parlor, Dane and Hack were talking in quiet tones. They both looked up.

Dane moved forward. "I'm sorry about the hidden door thing."

She nodded, trying to give the impression that she didn't care and knowing she failed.

"If you'd obeyed me like you'd promised to, it wouldn't have been necessary."

She shrugged, not quite willing to concede that much.

"I have what I think you will consider good news."

She raised an eyebrow doubtfully.

He leaned close and whispered, "You can stay."

Her lips trembled with emotion, but she was grateful she hadn't thanked him when he continued. "Hack has convinced me that I can safeguard you better here than Steamer can in an unsecured location."

Savannah turned to Hack. "Thanks."

"Don't thank him too soon," Dane advised. "If you end up shot, you'll wish you'd left like I'd told you to." He pointed at her flat stomach. "What happened to the baby?"

"There never was a baby," she reminded him without a trace of humor.

Steamer stepped between them awkwardly. "Since you said you weren't going to let her impersonate Rosemary anymore, there didn't seem to be much point in wearing the fake stomach."

She lifted a handful of dark hair. "The next chance I get, I'm going to have my hair changed back to its natural color."

"Don't be in a big rush," Dane said. "I like it dark."

She wasn't flattered. "Then a trip to the hair salon just moved to the top of my priority list."

Dane ignored this and waved toward the couch. "Let's sit down and talk this through."

Once everyone was seated, Dane said, "Hopefully we'll catch Ferrante when his plane lands. But we need to have a backup plan in case he eludes us."

"We'll have to meet him at the gate down on Toulouse Street?" Steamer guessed.

Dane nodded. "Steam, I figure we can dress you up like Rosemary Ferrante. You'll wear a hat and a coat, and hopefully it will be dark enough by five o'clock to keep your real identity from being obvious."

"Steamer won't fool anyone," Hack objected. "Especially not the girl's father."

"It only has to work for a few seconds," Dane insisted. "Once we have Cam in our sights, we can move in, grab Ferrante, and it will all be over."

"I just can't believe we'll be able to get Ferrante so easily," Hack argued. "Why is he coming in here, where he knows we're fortified? Why doesn't he insist on a neutral meeting spot?"

"Because he's arrogant," Dane replied. "And he wants his daughter so badly he's not thinking clearly."

"I smell a rat," Hack warned. "We need to proceed with extreme caution."

"We'll have snipers posted all around with instructions to take Ferrante out if necessary. I'd rather have him dead than not at all."

"And how will we get Rosemary's husband?" Savannah asked.

"That will have to wait until after we have Ferrante."

"You promised," Savannah reminded him.

"My first priority is capturing Ferrante. My second is recovering Cam. Then we'll attempt to rescue Chad Allen."

Savannah was disappointed.

"It should be a lot easier to get the girl's husband after we have Ferrante in custody," Steamer pointed out, making Savannah feel a little better.

For the next hour they waited anxiously. Savannah offered to heat up frozen dinners, but no one was hungry. While the men conferred and calculated and stared at the computer screen, Savannah prayed for Rosemary and her husband and their baby. She prayed for Caroline and Doc and the McLaughlins. She prayed that General Steele was the trustworthy man she'd always believed him to be. And she prayed the operation would end without bloodshed.

She had just finished her long prayer list when Dane put his hand on her arm. "We've reacquired Cam's M-CODE."

She swallowed and asked, "Where is he?"

"About fifteen minutes from here—headed this way."

"So Ferrante eluded all our intercept teams?" she guessed.

Dane nodded. "He slipped through, so we'll have to handle him here."

"So what do we do now?" She wasn't sure she wanted to know.

"Steamer's getting ready to impersonate Rosemary Ferrante."

She turned to see Steamer dressed in a long, black woolen coat and a knit beret. "You don't look anything like Rosemary."

"It's getting dark," Dane pointed out. "And Steamer will be careful to stand in the shadows." He urged her forward with his hand. "Follow me."

Dane led her down the hall. When he reached the wooden panel at the end of the hallway, his fingers moved along the edge until he found the hidden latch. The panel slid open, revealing a small open space about the size of a closet. He waved for her to step inside and once she complied, he said, "Hack's going to stay here with you. If something goes wrong, he knows how to get you out."

Someone cleared their throat, and Savannah looked up to see Steamer and Hack standing behind Dane in the opening created by the displaced panel. "Uh, me and Hack have been talking about that," Steamer said. "And with all due respect, Major, we've decided that you should be the one to stay here."

Savannah gaped at the two men in the hallway. From the corner of her eye, she could see her astonishment reflected on Dane's face. She wasn't sure what surprised her most—Steamer's use of Dane's rank, which made the remark sound ominously official, or the fact that Hack and Steamer had been discussing things behind Dane's back.

When Dane spoke, his voice was so cold it sent a shiver up her spine. "I don't care what you and Hack have decided," he bit out. "I'm the commanding officer, and I make the assignments. I'll be running the operation, and Hack will be here."

Savannah noticed that Hack was staying in the background, allowing Steamer to take all the heat, and she was a little disappointed in him. But she didn't have time to dwell on this as the confrontation between Dane and Steamer escalated.

"I know you're in charge of this operation," Steamer said. "That's just another good reason for you to stay out of the line of fire. And the team rule has always been that men with families stay back, *sir*," he added either as an afterthought or a lifesaving measure.

"I don't have a family," Dane snarled.

Steamer glanced at Savannah. "Let me and Hack handle the front lines on this one."

"I've made the assignments," Dane replied. "There will be no more discussion."

"Yes, sir," Steamer replied in that same odd, respectful-yet-distant tone. She looked into his eyes, expecting to see anger or defiance or maybe even relief. Instead she saw remorseful determination. Before she could analyze Steamer's expression, Hack reached up and used one of his lethal hands to karate chop Dane on the neck.

Dane crumpled like a rag doll. Steamer stepped forward and caught him under the arms before he hit the floor. Then he dragged Dane into a corner of the closet and put him down gently.

"What have you done?" Savannah whispered as she stared at Dane's prone form.

"It was for his own good," Hack said from the hallway. He turned to Steamer and extended a roll of duct tape. "I don't know how long he'll be out, so you'd better tape him up."

Savannah watched as Steamer bound Dane securely. Once this job was done, Steamer joined Hack in the hallway.

Hack stared down at Dane. "When he wakes up, he'll have a headache but no permanent damage."

Savannah scooted forward in the small space and pressed a hand against Dane's forehead. "Are you sure?"

Hack nodded. "I've used that same chop many times. Not on Dane—of course," he clarified.

She pushed Dane's hair from his eyes. "He's going to be furious."

"Oh yeah," Steamer agreed. "I figure if we catch Ferrante, he'll forgive us pretty quick. But if Ferrante gets away . . . I'll be on a plane headed for Vegas so fast it will make Hack's ugly head spin."

Nobody laughed.

"We might have to make adjustments to the original plan as we go along," Hack told her. "If Dane comes charging out into the action once it's underway, he'll risk not only his life but ours. So if he wakes up, you can't untape him."

"You'll be saving his life by refusing," Steamer concurred.

"And when it's all over, he'll blame us, not you," Hack added. "So none of this will affect your relationship."

She gave him a small smile. "I don't know if what I have with Dane qualifies as a relationship, and I'm sure he won't be at all upset with me if I refuse to help him get free."

"It's important that he stay here," Hack insisted. "We can handle this without him."

She sighed. "Okay. If he wakes up, I won't undo the tape."

Satisfied, Hack backed into the hallway.

As Steamer slid the panel closed, he said, "Don't open this door for anyone."

Left in near-darkness with Dane, Savannah stroked his face and tried not to be afraid. She dreaded his reaction to Hack and Steamer's assumption of control. But she was selfishly glad they forced him to do the safe thing. More than anything else, she wanted Dane alive.

For several minutes he rested peacefully. She strained her ears, trying to hear something from outside her refuge, but all was silent. Eventually Dane became restless, and she assumed that he had slipped from unconsciousness into sleep—which for Dane usually meant nightmares. Steamer's restraints kept him from moving much. She held him a little closer, prepared to provide comfort if necessary.

She expected his first wakeful words to be an angry demand that she untie him, but when he spoke he said, "I was dreaming."

"Was it a nightmare?" she asked.

"No, I dreamed I was in heaven." He gave her a weak smile. "That's how I knew for sure it was a dream. Me in heaven—no way."

"Why don't you tell me about it," she suggested, hoping to delay the moment of truth.

"Maybe I will someday." He turned his face toward her. "You smell good," he murmured. "I can see why Caroline is comforted by a teddy bear that smells like you."

He dozed for a few more minutes, and then his eyes opened suddenly, and she knew there would be no discussion of perfume or dreams this time. He blinked and focused on the closed panel that provided access to the hallway.

"Hack knocked me out." He sat up and stared down at his hands and feet. "They tied me up."

"They did it to protect you," Savannah offered as an excuse.

Dane gave no indication that he had even heard her but shook his bound hands. "Get this tape off."

"Hack told me not to untie you," she explained. "He made me promise."

Dane fixed her with a glare. "And who are you going to obey, me or Hack?"

She swallowed nervously. "Hack said if I let you go, I'd be risking your life."

"It's my life to risk."

"He also said it would jeopardize the operation. They may have made changes to the plans that you don't know about, so if you go charging down there . . ."

"I won't go *charging* anywhere," he interrupted. "Now untie me."

"I can't. I promised."

Dane switched tactics relentlessly. "Hack and Steamer are both good soldiers, but I'm better. They need me—even if they don't realize it. Without me, the operation will fail, and people will die."

She didn't want anyone's death on her conscience, but she was afraid. "If you go down there now, the person who dies might be you."

He nodded. "That doesn't matter. The team and the operation are both my responsibility."

"Duty and honor," she whispered. "You love them more than life."

"Much more than my life," he agreed.

"What about my life and Caroline's?" she countered.

He smiled. "The kindest thing I could do for both of you would be to remove myself permanently from your lives."

"That's not true." She wiped at tears. "And it's definitely not funny."

"No, I'm sorry." He did sound repentant. "This situation is very serious. I don't want to die, but I can't stay here knowing my men are in danger. I have to go. Please, Savannah."

She closed her eyes and tried to block out his pleading face. She tried to remember Hack's stern directive. Dane's safety depended on her.

Finally he said, "If you love me, let me go."

She opened her eyes. "That's not fair."

"No," he agreed.

"Please don't ask me to do this."

He shook his hands again. "I'm sorry. But you need to hurry."

She turned away, unable to bear his calculated expression. He was using her and her love for him—just as he would any other available resource. She'd wanted him to define their relationship. Maybe he had.

Swallowing a lump of sorrow, she went to work on the layers of tape that bound his hands. She felt his gaze on her but wouldn't return it. When his hands were free, she stood back while he unwound the tape that restrained his feet.

After stretching to restore his circulation, he took a step toward her. "Savannah, I know what this cost you and I can't thank you enough . . ."

She shook her head. "Just do what you have to do."

He regarded her for a few seconds. She saw a flash of uncertainty in his eyes and wondered if he was finding this betrayal more difficult than the others. Then his expression hardened, and she knew he had made his decision. He had chosen duty over her.

He put his hands on the panel, but before he could push it open, they heard footsteps in the hallway. He froze and placed a finger on his lips. Once she nodded, confirming that she understood the need for silence, he pressed his ear to the panel.

The footsteps stopped right outside the secret closet, and Savannah put a hand over her mouth to muffle the sound of her breathing. Seconds later, when hands slammed against the wood and rattled the panel, she was grateful for this precaution since it kept her involuntary gasp from being audible.

The panel remained tightly closed, and a voice from the other side cursed before saying, "I can't figure out how to open this. Just bring me that sledge hammer."

More footsteps approached them, and Savannah didn't even try to hide her terror as she turned to Dane. She expected him to pull out a gun or make a quick call requesting reinforcements. Instead he reached behind him, and the back panel of the closet slid silently open. Dane stepped through into a shadowy passageway and waved for her to follow.

Once they were in the dark, damp space behind the closet, he closed the panel and then grabbed her hand. As they ran down the hidden corridor, they could hear the sound of a sledgehammer splintering the beautiful old wood. Savannah blinked back tears as anger mixed with fear. That panel had survived for over a hundred years only to be destroyed by Mario Ferrante. Mario Ferrante was here. And he had sidestepped all of their defenses.

She was trying to figure out all the terrible implications of this apparent fact when Dane came to an abrupt halt, and she ran into his back. She put her hands on his waist to steady herself and pressed her cheek against the soft fabric of his shirt. He tripped the latch to another panel and it slid open. Then he led her into the room she had slept in since their arrival in New Orleans.

The banging of the sledgehammer had stopped. Apparently the intruders had found the closet empty. Whether they would continue their demolition on the back panels of the closet remained to be seen.

Dane closed the panel and held up a hand indicating she should stay where she was. Then he moved with impressive stealth to the door. After cracking the door open enough to peer into the hallway, he returned to Savannah. He leaned very close and whispered, "I'm going to go out and see what the situation is. If I don't come back, leave through the panel and turn left. Eventually you'll reach a door that opens onto the street."

He took her fingers and pressed them along the outside ridge of the panel. She felt a small lump. He pressed it and the door slid open. "Got it?"

She nodded.

He closed the panel and crossed the room. After another quick peek into the hallway, he pulled open the door and slipped out.

Savannah stood anxiously by the wall. The panel that led to the hidden passageway blended so perfectly with the others she was afraid to step away from it for fear she wouldn't be able to find it again if she needed to escape. Of course, if the man with the sledgehammer had found the passageway, it might only be a matter of time before he came crashing through the panel into her bedroom.

Running her hands up her arms to ward off chill and panic, Savannah looked at the door to the hall. She willed Dane to walk back in, but it remained tightly closed. Then she heard a thud from the front of the house. It could have been the sound of a door closing. It could have been the sound of a sledgehammer dropping onto a threadbare rug. It could have been Dane's body hitting the ground.

Savannah inched closer to the door. If there was a chance that Dane might need her, she had to go. Following Dane's example, she cracked open the door and checked to be sure the hallway was empty before she stepped from the relative safety of the bedroom. Then she pressed herself into the shadows along the wall and moved toward the front of the house.

She had just reached the dining room and was stepping around the pile of wallpaper scraps when she saw the bodies lying by the front door. She concluded that the man closest to her was employed by Hack, based on his size. The other man was smaller in stature and wearing all black. He was equally motionless. Her eyes moved to the sledgehammer that had fallen beside him, and she shuddered. She closed her eyes briefly and tiptoed toward the parlor.

She heard them before she saw them. The sound was faint, like wind rustling, but enough to stop her progress. She squatted down beside the antique buffet and then leaned forward to see into the parlor where Dane and another black-clad man were locked in a deadly martial arts dance.

Dane seemed to be handling the attack from a purely defensive posture. When the other man would lash out, Dane would react, but he didn't strike back. She didn't doubt that Dane was well-trained, but she was afraid his bad leg might give his attacker the advantage. Dane needed help, and all he had was her. Savannah didn't want to make things worse by providing the intruder with a hostage, so she remained hidden, watching for an opportunity.

She reached up and slowly pulled open the buffet drawer that she knew contained a gun. As her fingers closed around the cold metal of the barrel, she prayed for the courage to actually use it if shooting the intruder became her only option.

Dane took a foot to the head. He fell back, and the other man jumped on top of him. Dane grunted in pain, and Savannah quickly regained her resolve. She could do most anything to save Dane. After pulling the gun from the drawer she released the safety as Dane had taught her to do years ago on the firing range at Ft. Belvoir. Then she leaned forward, pointed the gun at the stranger, and fired. The bullet missed the man's head by over a foot and embedded itself in the old plaster wall on the far side of the room. But the shot distracted the intruder long enough for Dane to land a punch on the man's jaw.

The man's head snapped back, but he recovered quickly and rolled off Dane. He ran for the front door, and seconds later he was gone.

"Are we going to chase him?" she asked Dane.

Instead of answering her question, Dane lunged toward the old radiator.

"Open the French doors," he called as he adjusted the dials.

His tone didn't encourage discussion, so she walked over and rattled the handle. "They're stuck closed with years of paint."

"Break them," he commanded. "If we don't get some of these gas fumes out of here we'll pass out—or worse."

Savannah didn't try to think of what could be worse. She picked up a nearby paint can and hurled it through the panes. Antique glass shattered and cold air rushed in. She heard Dane break a window behind her, and soon an uncomfortably cold cross breeze was moving through the room. She was shivering when Dane grabbed her and pulled her to his chest.

"I owe you one," he said with a smile.

She resisted him. "I'm still mad at you."

His smile broadened. "I know."

She blamed the cold for her quick surrender as she pressed her face against the soft fabric of his shirt.

CHAPTER 11

THE EMBRACE WAS short-lived. Dane gave her a quick hug and moved away.

She looked nervously at the front door. "Do you think that man will come back?"

He shook his head. "He's expecting the place to blow up any second, so he's long gone by now." Dane walked to the entryway and knelt beside the larger guard. "He's alive," Dane told her. "But probably just because they planned for everyone in the building to die when the gas exploded." He moved over to the man dressed in black. "He's still alive too. Go get me that duct tape out of the closet." He glanced up and added, "Please."

She hurried down the hall and cringed when she saw the splintered wood that had once been a beautiful wall panel. She picked up the roll of tape and hurried back to Dane.

While binding up the man, he asked, "How much damage did they do?"

Savannah decided that the truth was best, even if it hurt. "One panel is completely destroyed, and the one beside it is nearly as bad."

She saw his jaw tense, and he pulled the man's hands together more tightly than necessary. Once the unconscious intruder was secured, Dane stood and said, "Come with me." Then he began a quick search of the house and found it empty, except for another of Hack's men lying motionless in the back bedroom.

"Should we call an ambulance?" she whispered.

"We'll have to wait until the meeting with Ferrante has played out," he said.

Savannah frowned. "What if they can't wait that long?"

"More lives will be at risk if we act impulsively. They're breathing. That will have to be good enough for now." He waved for Savannah to follow him. They walked back to the entryway, and Dane started up the stairs that had whetted her curiosity when they first arrived. He put a finger to his lips in an unnecessary request for silence and continued up the steps. She trailed quietly behind him.

Dane stopped at the small landing on the second floor. Savannah stepped up beside him. The upstairs space was divided into a wide hallway with several rooms on each side.

Dane crossed the scuffed hardwood floors to a room at the far end of the hall. Another of Hack's men was on the floor in front of a large window. Dane checked the man's pulse and nodded at Savannah. Then he pried apart two wooden slats on the shutters and looked out. She stepped close beside him, dividing her attention between the fallen guard on the floor and the limited view of the street below.

Despite the relatively early hour, Toulouse Street was teeming with people. Dane watched intently. Savannah stared at the street below, too, but she couldn't see anything out of the ordinary. The owner of the bakery was sweeping the sidewalk in front of his shop. The T-shirt salesman was adding merchandise to his already-crowded clothing racks. Madame Leone had a customer. A bicycle policeman was weaving through the peaceful crowd.

Below them, standing against the metal gate that led from the courtyard of Dane's house to the street, stood Hack and Steamer. The latter was wearing the coat and hat in a minimally effective impersonation of Rosemary Allen.

Dane pulled the two-way radio out of his pocket. He pushed a button on the side and said, "Since you've taken over command of this operation, I thought I should report my new position."

Savannah could only imagine Hack's reaction to this, but when he responded, his tone was mater-of-fact. "Roger that."

"I'm at the upstairs window with direct view of the street. The three men you left inside the house are down but alive. One intruder is tied up in the entryway. The other one escaped. And a wooden panel in the hallway is destroyed."

Savannah didn't know if Dane included this information to alert Hack that the intruders had known about the secret closet or if he just wanted to warn Hack that he had additional grievances against him.

"Roger," Hack replied. "Operation Sitting Duck is proceeding as planned. Bait is on display. We'll move in as soon as our target is located."

"Roger and out." Dane put his radio in his pocket and returned his attention to the street below.

Savannah kept her gaze on the street. Hack had snipers stationed around the area. Maybe Ferrante had snipers too. The minutes ticked by without any action.

Finally Dane stiffened, and she followed the direction of his gaze. She saw two men emerge from the bar across the street. One had a muscular build and was wearing combat fatigues. He was leaning awkwardly, maybe involuntarily, against the other man as they made slow but steady progress toward the street.

"Cam?" she whispered.

Dane nodded.

She squinted for a better view. "It looks like his hands are tied behind his back."

"They probably are."

Savannah watched as Steamer and Hack stepped away from the gate on the other side of the street. Just as Cam and his escort reached the curb, two drunken men came staggering out of the bar waving beer bottles and laughing. One of the drunks staggered and fell down, which his companion seemed to find extremely funny. The fallen man yelled and hurled a beer bottle in the other man's direction. The man laughed harder.

Savannah resisted the urge to wring her hands as the bicycle policeman rode up to reason with the apparent drunks. In what seemed to be an effort to clear the bar's exit, the policeman led the rabble-rousers to the side, and soon they were very close to Cam. Steamer and Hack stepped forward just as the two drunks lunged for Cam. Shots rang out, and Savannah saw one of the drunks pull Cam into the shadows, out of the line of fire.

Dane pressed the button on his radio. "Do you have Ferrante?"

"Not yet," Hack replied breathlessly. "But we've got the area sealed off. There's no way out. While my men conduct a thorough search, Steamer's bringing Cam to you."

"Don't let Ferrante get away," Dane urged.

"Roger that. Hack out."

Dane took Savannah's hand and pulled her toward the stairs. They descended at what Savannah considered an unsafe speed—especially on questionably sound wood. They reached the front door just as Steamer burst in, dragging Cam behind him. The men who had pretended to be drunk brought up the rear.

"Is Cam okay?" Savannah asked.

"He might be okay," Steamer said. "But he ain't Cam." Steamer leaned down to pull back the hood of a camouflage jacket, revealing the face of a young man—definitely not Cam.

Savannah was stunned, but Dane didn't seem surprised.

"Rosemary Ferrante's husband?" he asked.

Steamer nodded as he allowed the man to slide onto the floor. "That's what he says."

"And why does he have Cam's M-CODE signal?" Dane wanted to know.

Steamer shrugged. "No clue."

"Pat him down," Dane said as he pulled out his radio and pushed the button. "We've got a problem here, Hack. The bait wasn't Cam."

"Roger," Hack replied. "And that's just one of our problems. We can't find Ferrante anywhere. It looks like he gave us the slip."

Before Dane could respond, Steamer said, "I think I can answer the question of why this guy has Cam's M-CODE signal." He waited for Dane to turn and look at him. "Cam's ear is in his coat pocket."

The room reeled, and Savannah felt Dane's arms encircle her waist to prevent a fall.

Dane spoke into the radio again. "Hack, have your men continue to look for Ferrante just in case. Come here, quick."

"Cam's dead?" she whispered.

"Cam can live without an ear," she heard Dane say. "But apparently Ferrante discovered the device and decided to remove it in a dramatic way. Probably to prove a point with me."

"But we can't track him anymore." Steamer sounded muffled and far away.

Savannah felt Dane lift her. She clutched his shirt and nuzzled the warm skin of his neck. He placed her on the couch in the cold parlor and tucked a thick, soft comforter in around her shoulders.

Hack arrived, and she heard the men discussing ambulances and hospitals but didn't want to be a part of it, so she kept her eyes closed and gave into unconsciousness. Mario Ferrante had cut off Cam's ear. And it was her fault.

* * *

Savannah was in the middle of a wonderful dream when a cold rag touched her face. Reluctantly she pried one eye halfway open. Hack was staring down at her in concern. Steamer was beside him, also looking worried. But when Madame Leone's face moved into her field of vision, Savannah smiled and closed her eyes again. Apparently she was still dreaming.

"Are you okay, my dear?" a lilting voice asked as a warm hand grazed Savannah's forehead.

"Hmmm," Savannah murmured and burrowed deeper into the comforter.

The voice spoke again, "I know you've been through quite an ordeal, but try to open your eyes and take a little sip of water . . ."

Dane's voice cut into the pleasant creole cadence. "Wake up now, Savannah. I don't have time for this."

Savannah obeyed Dane's unsympathetic command and found herself staring once again into Madame Leone's lovely, violet eyes. "You're not a dream?" she whispered.

The old woman smiled. "No, dear, I'm very real. And I told my grandson that you'd better not suffer any permanent effects from all this or he'll answer to me."

Savannah looked between Dane and Madame Leone. "You're *his* grandmother?"

"Yes," Madame Leone confirmed.

Savannah frowned. "He told me you were dead."

Madame Leone seemed surprised. "Well, that was insensitive of him. People my age don't appreciate being rushed into the grave."

"I did not say you were dead," Dane said crossly. "I just didn't correct her when she made that assumption."

Savannah fixed her disappointed gaze on Dane. "I guess that explains why Madame Leone was able to tell such compelling fortunes about you and me." Then she turned to his grandmother. "I believed in you."

"I'm sorry, dear," Madame Leone said softly. "I didn't want to mislead you, but Christopher said it was necessary for your safety and ours. I hope you'll forgive me."

Savannah glanced up at Dane. "Don't worry about it. Lying to me is a tradition in your family."

"That's enough," Dane interrupted gruffly. "Sit up."

Savannah lifted her head and bit back a wave of nausea.

"It's too soon, Christopher," Madame Leone insisted. "She needs to rest."

"We don't have time for her to rest," Dane responded. "She's in more danger now than she was before."

This caught Savannah's attention. She sat up and looked around the room.

To her left was the policeman on the bicycle who had broken up the fight on her first night in the French Quarter. He had been nearby when she'd gone to the seafood restaurant with Hack and again during the showdown with Ferrante. Beside him was the elderly shoe shine man. Next to him stood the T-shirt vendor. Near one of the broken French doors was the Asian massage therapist.

"Ferrante got away?" she said.

"Yes," Dane confirmed.

Savannah looked back at Dane's grandmother. "What should I call you?"

"My name really is Leone," the old woman said. "Just without the Madame."

"Leone," Savannah repeated.

"I hope you'll come back and visit us again when we can all be ourselves," she invited. "We'll tell you all sorts of embarrassing childhood stories about Christopher."

Dane didn't look pleased by the invitation, so Savannah smiled. "I might just do that."

Dane stood. "We've got work to do, so I'm going to have to ask everyone to leave for now."

"What about our salaries?" the massage therapist wanted to know.

"My grandmother will come and pay you tomorrow," Dane promised.

"Yes," Leone agreed. "And thank you all for your help." She led Dane's temporary employees to the door, continuing to promise payment the next day.

She glanced at Hack. "Are your men okay?"

He nodded.

"What happened to the guys who broke in here?"

"One got away, the other we turned over to the police," Hack said.

"And Rosemary's husband?"

"He's fine. The FBI took him for questioning."

Savannah found this news alarming. "But he'll be sent to Rosemary at Ft. Belvoir soon?"

Dane shrugged. "Eventually."

Leone returned to the parlor, and before Dane could object to her presence, she said, "You can't keep secrets from me—at least not in what used to be my house."

Dane nodded his permission, although he didn't look particularly pleased. He turned away from his grandmother and addressed his men. "The first order of business is to get new cell phones. Hack, will you send one of your men . . ."

"The first order of business," Leone interrupted, "is to warm this place up. Christopher, relight the pilot light and turn on the radiators. Hack and Steamer, there are some boards in the cellar that we use to protect the windows during hurricanes. Will you get a couple so we can reduce the amount of cold air coming in from outside?"

No one even considered disobeying Leone. She led Steamer and Hack to the cellar door while Dane worked on the radiator. Savannah swung her legs over the edge of the couch and turned to watch Dane. Then she asked about Caroline.

"She's okay." He pulled the transponder from his pocket and showed her it was still glowing green.

Hack and Steamer returned carrying large pieces of plywood. They nailed them in place under Leone's direction, and soon the room was something less than freezing.

"Now can Hack send one of his men to get us new cell phones?" Dane asked his grandmother.

"He may. And I'm going to see what I can come up with for us to eat. After a good meal, everyone will feel better."

Savannah knew that a magician couldn't prepare a *good* meal with the contents of this particular kitchen, but she kept that to herself.

Once Leone was in the kitchen, Dane turned to Hack and Steamer. Hack met his gaze steadily, but Steamer stared at the floor. "Now, to recap. We did not get Ferrante. We did not get Cam. We did let intruders into my house, where they destroyed an antique wall panel and almost kidnapped Savannah. So I guess you could say, Operation Sitting Duck was a total bust."

In an attempt to help Hack and Steamer, Savannah said, "There's no guarantee that the operation would have been successful if you had remained in charge."

When Dane turned his angry eyes to her, she regretted her decision to interfere. But it was too late to back down.

"I'm just saying that you can't blame them for all of it," Savannah continued.

"No," Dane agreed. "I blame you."

"Me?" She had wanted to defuse his anger toward his men but hadn't expected to draw the fire herself.

"You question my decisions and undermine my authority and inspire insubordination." He swung back toward Steamer and Hack. "You make the most reasonable, loyal men do the most illogical and dangerous things."

"She didn't make us do anything," Hack disputed. "I take responsibility for it all—the insubordination, the failure of the operation—even Cam's ear."

Dane ran his fingers through his hair in obvious frustration. "Since I am the commanding officer of this team, I have to take the responsibility—whether I deserve it or not."

Savannah felt a little bad for him. He was proud of his nearly perfect record of successful covert operations.

"No one can take all the responsibility for the failure," Steamer said.

"We each own a part," Hack agreed.

"And things are not completely hopeless," Savannah said. "Operation Sitting Duck might still lead us to Mario Ferrante."

Dane lifted an eyebrow. "How do you figure that?"

"We still have a man inside Ferrante's organization, even if we don't have a way to track him," she said.

Dane turned on her with unusual venom. "Cam is *not* our man. He is unquestionably working for Ferrante."

She frowned. "I just can't give up hope that he'll decide to be loyal to the team."

"Yes, but then you're not a very good judge of character—especially when it comes to loyalty and trustworthiness," Dane pointed out. "The list of people you've tried to trust is a long one—starting with your husband, Westinghouse. Then you add your old boss, Doug Forton, and your personal assistant, Lacie Fox, and—last but not least—our friend Camouflage. If you'll remember, Cam kidnapped Caroline, tried to kill me, and would have turned you over to Ferrante if he'd had the chance. Grow up and lose the Pollyanna attitude," he finished harshly. "It's getting old."

Savannah was shocked and hurt by the intensity of his response. Blinking back tears, she asked, "And what about you?"

He held her gaze as he nodded. "You're right, I should be on the top of your *Don't Trust List*. And yet you keep coming back."

"Christopher!" Leone said from the kitchen doorway, and all eyes turned to her. "You were raised to behave better than that!"

He didn't apologize for his words, but he nodded at his grandmother. "Yes, ma'am."

Apparently satisfied, Leone returned to the kitchen.

Savannah decided to take advantage of Leone's support and ask, "Why didn't you tell me that she's your grandmother?"

Dane's eyes narrowed at her, but before he could answer, Hack stepped in. "If you're going to be a member of this team, you need to learn to read between the lines."

"Read between the lines?" she repeated.

"Some things don't need to be said. You should be able to figure them out," Hack explained.

"How could you miss the resemblance between Dane and his grandmother?" Steamer added.

Savannah had no defense for her blind stupidity, so she just shrugged.

Dane turned back to his men. "As bad as I hate to, I guess we'd better talk about this catastrophically unsuccessful mission."

"Basically, Ferrante outsmarted us," Steamer said, beginning the conversation on a negative note.

"How did he get away?" Savannah asked.

"He never came to the French Quarter," Hack guessed.

Dane nodded. "I'll bet he never even left his plane."

Savannah frowned. "So Mario Ferrante didn't expect us to trade his daughter for Cam?"

Hack shrugged. "Either that or he saw through Steamer's clever disguise."

"I think we can safely assume that Ferrante knew from the start that we'd use a decoy," Dane said.

"So his plan was to distract us with the whole exchange-in-the-street thing while those karate guys came into the house to get his daughter?" Steamer asked.

"It looks that way," Dane agreed.

"Those guys he sent to take Savannah were good," Hack remarked. "They were able to get a drop on three of my best men—and that just doesn't happen."

"Ferrante wouldn't send amateurs." Dane said with confidence. "What we need to figure out is how he knew that there were secret closets in this house."

"Are you sure the guys who broke in knew about the sliding panels?" Steamer asked.

"Positive," Dane confirmed. "But they didn't know how to open them—that's why they used a sledgehammer. If Savannah hadn't untied me, we'd have become the true sitting ducks of this operation."

Hack sighed. "Sorry."

"We'll settle that score later," Dane promised.

Savannah wanted to help Hack, so she claimed Dane's attention. "Who knew about the secret panels?"

"My family," Dane replied. "And I told Hack and Steamer."

"Did Cam know?" Savannah asked.

Dane shook his head. "No."

"What about General Steele?" Steamer asked.

Dane nodded. "Yeah, the general knows."

While they were all contemplating the dire implications of this, one of Hack's men walked in carrying a handful of cell phones. Dane distributed them to everyone, including Savannah. She knew he only gave her one because he had extras—and he probably wanted to make up for his harsh remarks earlier—but she was pleased just the same.

Savannah barely had time to determine the phone's basic features before Leone joined them and announced that dinner was ready.

"It's not up to my usual standards since the resources in the refrigerator were limited," she told them. "But it's better than nothing."

Dane waited until Leone had returned to the kitchen and then stood. "Hack, round up a few of your men and let them eat whatever my grandmother has prepared so she doesn't get her feelings hurt. Then go back to Ft. Belvoir and nose around a little. Maybe you can figure out where our security leak is or find a lead on Ferrante's new whereabouts."

"What about me?" Steamer asked.

"You'll come with me and Savannah. We'll drive to Ft. Polk tonight and fly from there to Denver in the morning. We've got to collect Caroline and get her home for Christmas."

Upon hearing this announcement, Savannah forgave him for his harsh words earlier.

"You're not going to let me eat before we go?" Savannah asked with a longing look toward the kitchen. "It's a long drive to Ft. Polk."

He almost smiled. "Not here. We'll pick something up on the way. Now get your bag and let's go."

* * *

Savannah brushed her teeth, repaired her makeup, changed into her least maternity-looking outfit, and then rushed out to the parlor, where Dane was waiting.

She said good-bye to Hack and Leone while Dane stood by impatiently. Hack uncomfortably endured a hug, and Leone reiterated her invitation to come back to New Orleans under better circumstances. Finally, Dane took Savannah's hand and pulled her toward the door.

"We've got to go."

Once they were outside, Dane led her to a minivan that was comfortable if not sporty. She noted that Steamer was already sitting behind the wheel as she settled herself in the backseat. After double-checking that the street was clear, Dane swung in beside her.

"Are you really hungry?" he asked.

"Starving," she confirmed.

"But no more cravings?"

She pressed a hand against her flat stomach. "No."

Dane turned toward Steamer. "You know where to take us."

Savannah watched out the window as Steamer maneuvered through the crowded streets. Finally, he turned down an alley and came to a stop. Savannah peered up at what appeared to be the back of a restaurant. "Where are we?"

"This is Constantine's—the restaurant you expressed an interest in the night we arrived," Dane said. "We don't have time to go in and eat, so I've arranged for some spectacular takeout."

As if on cue, the back door opened, and several waiters emerged carrying a variety of Styrofoam containers. Steamer climbed out of the van and helped them stack everything inside. Savannah blinked back tears. It was so unlike Dane to be thoughtful. And the food smelled divine.

The entire transaction only took a couple of minutes and they were driving again. Steamer put on headphones and sang softly along with the radio.

"He's trying to give us some privacy," Dane explained as he opened one of the containers.

Savannah smiled. "That's sweet." Then she felt guilty. "He's probably hungry too. Shouldn't we share?"

"He can't very well eat and drive," Dane replied. "But we'll make sure he gets something to eat later."

Savannah still felt bad about eating in front of Steamer, but she didn't argue.

"I had them give us a double serving of everything. Are you willing to share with me?"

She smirked. "Like I have a choice."

In the first container were two small bowls of turtle soup. Savannah was hesitant, but at Dane's insistence she tried a spoonful and loved it. When her bowl was empty, Dane leaned toward her and whispered, "Have I told you how much I like your dark hair?"

She nodded, a little wary of this new, charming Dane. "Several times."

"No wonder you're able to make my men do crazy things—like knock me unconscious and lock me in a closet, thereby ruining a well-laid plain."

Savannah frowned. "I didn't make your men do anything. And you acknowledged that this operation might have failed even if Hack and Steamer hadn't taken over."

"I did say that, although I don't believe it. If I hadn't been ambushed by my own men, Ferrante would be in custody right now."

She narrowed her eyes at him. "Do you promise that you're telling me the whole truth and nothing but the truth?"

He gave her another little smile. "Cross my heart and hope to die."

She sighed in exasperation. "Will you take official action against Hack and Steamer when we get back to Ft. Belvoir?"

"The matter will have to be addressed, but I haven't decided exactly how," he said.

"They were only trying to protect you."

"Mostly they were trying to protect you and your unreasonable notion that the two of us can live happily ever after."

"Call me crazy," she muttered.

"Your sanity aside," he continued, "I can't have my men disobeying orders or tying me up when they think I'm in danger."

"Maybe the situation won't ever come up again if you follow the team rules," she suggested.

"Rules?"

"About men without families taking the more dangerous parts of a mission."

Charming Dane disappeared. "I don't have a family, and it's not up to Hack or Steamer to enforce the rules."

She looked down. "Go easy on them. Please."

He frowned. "I can understand you pleading leniency for Hack, but when did you and Steamer become friends?"

She thought a few seconds and then said, "I think it was when you sent him through that secret panel in the bedroom while you were distracting me with a color scheme discussion."

In an obvious attempt to avoid an uncomfortable discussion, he said, "I'll take your request under consideration when I decide on the appropriate punishment."

She decided to be satisfied with this. "Thanks. And you have to give Hack a little credit, since his karate chop gave you some much needed sleep."

"I'm not giving Hack any credit for chopping me on the neck."

She took a flaky roll from an open takeout container and broke off a bite. "This would be a good time to tell me about your dream."

He looked up sharply. "My dream?"

"The one Hack is responsible for . . . where you were in heaven," she clarified.

He was silent for so long she had given up all hope of getting an answer. But finally he said, "Wes was there. He's been on my mind a lot lately. I guess that's why I dreamed about him. The guy I starved to death in the Russian prison was there too."

She wanted to correct his terminology but was afraid if she interrupted him, he might rethink his decision to confide.

"I wanted to apologize," Dane continued, "but he was too far away. Then Wes walked up, and I was surprised to see him there. I don't know why I thought he'd have a harder time getting into heaven than me."

She smiled. "What did Wes say?"

"He asked for my forgiveness."

"Did you give it to him?"

"I didn't want to," Dane remembered. "All the pain he caused me seemed very fresh again. But finally I did. It was an interesting dream." His tone sounded final, and Savannah knew he didn't want to discuss it anymore.

"But what about the man from the Russian prison?" she pressed.

"I didn't get to talk to him."

This vague response convinced her that there was more he wasn't sharing. "But something happened between you?"

He looked down at her. "I felt him staring at me. When I turned, our eyes met and he nodded."

"He didn't say anything?"

"No, he just nodded."

"He forgave you?" Savannah guessed. "Because you forgave Wes."

Dane looked away. "It was just a dream, Savannah."

"I believe in dreams, remember?" she told him gently. "Along with fairytales and love and happily ever after."

"Sometimes I wish I did," he said as the sound of a cell phone interrupted them. Dane pulled the phone from his pocket and spoke into the receiver.

"Dane here."

"The FBI managed to lose the Allen kid," Hack reported.

Dane frowned. "What do you mean they *lost* him?"

"He got away, disappeared, whatever you want to call it. He's gone."

Dane sighed. "He might try to visit his wife. Keep an eye out for him."

"Roger that," Hack promised.

Dane returned the phone to his pocket

"Do you think Ferrante got him back?" Savannah asked, dreading the answer.

"It's possible. Goodness knows he has enough contacts within the FBI. But maybe the kid just ran away."

"If he does go to see Rosemary, will you arrest him?"

"We need to question him, but if he cooperates, we won't press any charges."

Savannah smiled. "You're turning into a real romantic."

"I'm turning into an idiot," he countered. Then he lifted the next takeout container.

They shared crawfish étouffée, corn casserole, and spicy red beans with rice. Everything was delicious, and Savannah ate until she was far beyond full. Finally Dane opened a box that contained a huge piece of chocolate cake.

Savannah stared at the culinary masterpiece. "I can't eat that."

"You *must* eat that," Dane countered. "It's called Doberge cake, and it's a French Quarter classic." He took a bite, analyzed it, and said, "Perfect."

Savannah ate a few bites, and it was wonderful, but she really was full, so she pushed what remained toward Dane. "I'm done."

"Me too." He closed the box and put it on the seat behind them.

She frowned at the row of empty food containers "I don't want our date to end."

He pulled her close. "Who says our date is over? We've got the whole drive to Ft. Polk."

"More moments of suspended reality?"

"Hours of suspended reality," he corrected.

She smiled as the lights of the French Quarter faded behind them. In the darkness, with Dane's arm around her shoulders, Savannah found the courage to voice her worst fear. "Do you really think General Steele could have been working with Ferrante?"

She felt Dane shrug. "I don't want to believe that, but someone inside is definitely working for Ferrante—setting up computer relays, etc. I've looked at it from every direction, and the possibilities are few."

"Who else could it be besides General Steele?" Savannah searched her mind for other possibilities. "What about the support team at Ft. Belvoir?"

"None of them knew about the secret passageways in my house."

Savannah was starting to feel hopeless. "You really think General Steele is working with Mario Ferrante?"

"I'm not accusing the general of anything, but I have to be cautious."

She lifted her head from his shoulder. "Maybe it was the general's secretary, Lieutenant Hardy."

Dane raised an eyebrow. "I thought you said the two of you were friends now."

Savannah fingered the locket at her neck. "I said she tolerates me because she likes Caroline, but I'd much rather her be the traitor than the general."

Dane smiled. "Even if Lieutenant Hardy has treacherous tendencies, she didn't know about the secret closets either."

"I wish we could think of someone else besides the general who knew about your house and its hidden passageways," Savannah said. "Anyone else."

"Wes knew."

"Wes is dead," she reminded him.

"We were told by the Army that Wes is dead," he corrected. "Sometimes there is a lot of distance between what the Army says and the truth."

She looked up sharply. "You can't be serious."

"I'll admit the theory is a reach—bordering on desperate," Dane allowed, "but we're looking for a mole within Army Intelligence, somebody who has all the codes and knows all the procedures and knew about the unique design of my grandmother's house. Wes meets those requirements."

"If Wes is alive, that changes everything." Savannah tried to imagine the possibility. "I'd welcome the chance to talk with Wes again, to apologize for some things and explain others."

"Savannah, you need to understand that if Wes is alive, he's your enemy."

She shook her head. "No."

"If he's alive, he was involved in Caroline's kidnapping."

This was an unbearable thought. "I can't believe that."

"I hope it's not Wes, but I have to consider the possibility."

"If Wes is alive," Savannah forced herself to say the words, "do his parents know? Are they *helping* him? Because if they're involved, then Caroline isn't safe with them . . ."

Dane caught both her hands in his. "Caroline is safe, and Wes is almost surely dead. I shouldn't have mentioned it."

She couldn't stop tears from gathering in her eyes. "You were right to mention it. If there's a chance that Wes is alive, I definitely *need* to know."

He stroked her dark hair. "Poor Savannah."

She pressed her face into his neck. "In spite of the circumstances, I loved my time in the French Quarter."

"It's like no other place on earth."

"Promise me you'll bring me back someday."

His lips brushed her ear as he said, "I promise. Now why don't you try to get some sleep?"

Obediently she closed her eyes and tried to forget that Dane wasn't always a man of his word.

CHAPTER 12

WHEN SAVANNAH AWAKENED, they were still driving in the minivan, headed toward Ft. Polk. Steamer had removed his headphones and was engaged in a conversation with Dane. The men stopped talking when she sat up.

"Are we there yet?" she asked.

"About another hour," Dane told her.

Steamer met her eyes in the rearview mirror. "How was dinner?"

"Fabulous," Savannah replied. Then she looked at Dane reproachfully. "You said you'd let Steamer get something to eat."

"Yeah, there's a truck stop with a diner a few miles up the road," Dane said. "We'll stop there so Steamer won't starve to death."

When they reached the truck stop, everyone got out to stretch and make use of the restrooms. Then Dane and Savannah returned to the van while Steamer went into the all-night restaurant.

Once they were settled in their seats, Savannah's fingers touched her locket. "I'm anxious to see Caroline."

"Me too," Dane agreed. He pulled the transponder from his pocket, and Savannah was comforted to see the green light.

He returned the transponder to his pocket and opened his laptop. "You should try to go back to sleep."

She curled sideways in her seat and watched him work on his laptop.

Finally he looked up with a frown. "You're staring at me."

"Sorry," she lied with a smile.

He almost smiled back.

"Are you trying to figure out a new way to trap Ferrante?"

"No, I'm closing down this unsuccessful operation, and then I'm going to try and forget it ever happened."

"Well, do you have to shut it down right now?"

He narrowed his eyes at her. "Why not now?"

"Because I have something I'd like to talk about."

He closed the laptop. "Go ahead."

She took a deep breath and said, "I've been thinking a lot about what happened in Russia."

Dane groaned. "I take it back. I don't want to talk."

She ignored this. "What if the situation between you and Wes had been reversed?"

"I presume you mean how would I have reacted if you had chosen Wes over me?"

She shook her head. "No, how would you have felt if Wes had betrayed you first? Would you have felt justified in leaving him the way he left you? Would you have sacrificed friendship and honor and duty in the name of revenge?"

He frowned. "I don't know."

"I do," she told him with confidence. "Duty is everything to you, no matter what the personal cost. You would have completed the operation and returned with all your men—even the disloyal ones. Even a dead one."

He didn't deny this but said, "You make dedication to duty sound like a bad thing."

"Honor and duty are definitely good things. But the question that haunts you is how could an honorable man, a dedicated soldier, a man who loves God, take a sick man's food."

"Savannah."

She knew she was causing him pain, but he needed to hear what she had to say, so she steeled herself against sympathy.

"You'd been abused physically and mentally for weeks. They were starving you and depriving you of sleep and torturing you—"

"I presume you have a point here somewhere?" he cut in harshly.

"You *always* put the welfare of other people before your own."

He laughed at this remark. "Not always—as you know since you're the one who's determined to talk about that Russian prison."

She persevered. "You weren't yourself when you were in that prison. You weren't responsible for actions any more than a drugged person would have been."

"Unfortunately," Dane's voice was dripping with sarcasm, "you don't get to decide who is responsible and who isn't."

She'd come too far to back down now. "What did the Army say about it? Did they hold you responsible?"

"No," he muttered.

"What about the numerous psychiatrists and therapists you said you talked to?"

He shook his head. "They used more technical terms, like temporary psychosis—but the idea was the same. The situation I was in made me crazy and therefore unaccountable for my actions."

"But you don't agree?" she asked.

"It's just an excuse."

"If your doctors said it, that makes it a medical diagnosis," she countered.

"Can we please stop talking about my craziness?" he pleaded.

She hated to cause him more pain, but she'd come too far to give up. "Nobody holds you responsible except *you*. Even the man who died has forgiven you."

"That was just a dream."

"You're not dreaming now," Savannah pressed the issue. "Do you forgive Wes for what he did to you?"

Dane spread his hands in supplication. "Please."

"Give me an answer, and I'll leave you alone."

"Yes," he whispered. "I forgive Wes."

"If you can forgive Wes for the unforgivable, God can forgive you too."

"I thought you said you'd leave me alone," he reminded her crossly.

She was satisfied with the progress they'd made, so she didn't press him further. "Do I have to be quiet or just change the subject?"

The corners of his lips turned up slightly. "Let's just sit here quietly." His eyes dropped to her lips, and her heart pounded. But the moment was interrupted by Steamer returning from the diner.

"Okay, I'm full and ready to hit the road again." He climbed behind the wheel and started the car.

"I really need to finish up the paperwork on Operation Sitting Duck," Dane said.

Savannah shrugged. "Then I guess I'll sleep. It's the only way I can guarantee I'll be quiet."

"Sweet dreams," Dane whispered.

"No doubt," she assured him. Then she closed her eyes and leaned against the van's upholstered seat.

* * *

Savannah was awakened by the sound of Dane's voice. "Come on, Sleeping Beauty," he coaxed. "You've got to get up."

She opened her eyes to find him leaning over her. Still befuddled by sleep, she put her arms around his neck. "I may leave my hair dark after all," she murmured. "I've gotten more compliments from you in the past few days than in all the years I've known you."

He disengaged himself from her embrace. "We can discuss your appearance later. Right now you need to wake up. We'll be at Ft. Polk in a few minutes."

Savannah sat up straight and looked out the van windows. The first pink light of morning was visible on the horizon. Both Dane and Steamer looked tired—a consequence of staying awake all night. She, on the other hand, had slept long and well and felt quite refreshed.

When they parked at the airfield at Ft. Polk, Dane put the takeout containers in a nearby dumpster while Steamer unloaded their meager luggage. When Dane returned from his self-imposed garbage duty, Savannah pointed at the Mama Mia bag full of maternity clothes and said, "I'm not sure what to do with this stuff."

Dane looked confused. "Well, I certainly don't want it."

She gave him a well-deserved smirk. "I thought you might want to save it for a future operation."

"Sometimes we do save things," Dane acknowledged. "But I can't imagine ever needing maternity clothes again—especially in your exact sizes. So just give them to the Goodwill."

"We could save them in case Savannah decides to remarry and give Caroline a little brother or sister," Steamer suggested, earning himself a glare from Dane.

"Do whatever you want with them," Dane muttered. "I don't care."

Steamer winked covertly at Savannah as he handed her the bag. "If Dane doesn't care, you might as well keep them. They cost a fortune."

She stuffed the sack into her overnight case, mostly just to aggravate Dane.

"Since it's Christmas Eve, Ft. Polk is running an abbreviated flight schedule," Dane said as they walked across the tarmac. "So if we miss this plane, we won't be able to get another flight."

Savannah picked up her pace. She was determined to spend Christmas with her daughter.

Once they were settled, Savannah wished that they had missed the flight. Not intended for passengers, the plane was old and drafty, and the bench she was sitting on could have qualified as a form of torture. She wanted to complain, but Dane was talking on the phone during the entire boarding process. Then the pilot announced that their departure would be delayed for at least an hour due to technical difficulties, and Savannah felt close to tears.

When Dane finally put his phone away, she asked, "How long do you think we'll have to wait here?"

"Long enough to be sure the plane is fit to fly," he replied. "A delay is bad, but a crash is much worse."

"She couldn't argue with his logic, so she asked, "Is Hack back at Ft. Belvoir?"

"Not yet."

She made a face. "He must be taking the long way there—like us."

Dane smiled. "He had a few stops to make along the way."

"Did Mario Ferrante go back to his estate in Maryland?"

Dane shrugged. "I don't know. We haven't reacquired him yet." He leaned across her to ask a question, but Steamer was talking on his phone, so Dane sat back. "Let me know when Steamer ends that call. I have something I need to tell him—"

Steamer held up his hand in an uncharacteristic assumption of command. "Quiet!"

Savannah cringed, waiting for Dane to react to this. But instead of reprimanding Steamer, Dane waited in silence. Finally Steamer whispered, "Roger," and closed the phone. In spite of his artificial tan, he seemed pale.

"What's wrong?" Dane demanded.

Steamer cleared his throat, and Savannah thought he purposely avoided her gaze. "Hack just got a call from the Kansas City airport. Ferrante's private jet stopped there to refuel a couple of hours ago, and the flight plans the pilot filed say Denver."

"Why is Ferrante going to Denver . . ." Savannah began.

"Caroline," Dane whispered. Then he pulled the transponder from his pocket. As they all looked on, the light turned from green to red.

CHAPTER 13

AFTER A FEW seconds of shocked silence, Steamer said, "How could Ferrante possibly know where Caroline is?"

Savannah grabbed Dane's arm. "Ferrante's going after Caroline?"

Dane pulled her close. When their noses were almost touching, he whispered, "I won't let anything happen to Caroline."

Savannah clung to Dane as fear threatened to paralyze her. "I don't think I could survive it if he took her again."

"Before you were alone," Dane reminded her. "Now you have Doc and Hack and Steamer." He shook her gently. "And me."

Tears blurred her vision and. "But . . ."

"Trust me." He spoke so softly that she wasn't sure if she actually heard the words or if she'd read his lips. But either way, she understood. And she did trust him—at least where Caroline was concerned. So she nodded.

He set her aside and addressed Steamer. "Get General Steele on the line and explain the situation."

Steamer nodded and started dialing. "You realize that if the general's working for the other side, by asking for his help we'll be tipping him off."

"If the general's working for the other side, he already knows we're on our way to Denver," Dane replied grimly. "And if the general is on our side, he can arrange for us to get to Denver fast. It's a risk I can live with."

While Steamer made his call, Dane pressed the transponder into Savannah's palm. "You keep this and let me know if there's any change."

She looked down. The malevolent red light glowed, taunting her. At least now she had an assignment.

When Steamer ended his call, he nodded. "The general says he'll take care of it."

And he was true to his word. In less than thirty minutes they were in the air, headed toward Denver. Savannah was barely aware of her surroundings. All she could do was stare at the red light on the transponder and pray for Caroline's safety.

Dane sat up in the copilot's seat during the flight and was constantly either on the radio or conferring with the pilot. Steamer sat beside her, but they didn't talk. There was nothing to say.

Finally Dane pulled off his headset and turned around. "We'll be landing in a few minutes. The pilot was able to get clearance to land at an airstrip just a few miles from the farm. There's an Army helicopter waiting there to take us up to the McLaughlins' mountain."

"Are all the soldiers from Ft. Carson still at the farm?" Savannah asked.

"Yes," Steamer confirmed.

Savannah glanced at the transponder. "How did Ferrante get past them?"

Dane shrugged. "It doesn't matter now."

"Cam helped him," Steamer guessed. "He's the best at stealth approach."

Dane nodded. "And Cam does know the farm's layout."

"I'd like to get my hands on Cam," Steamer muttered.

"Hack can handle Cam when he gets there," Dane said.

Savannah leaned a little closer to Dane. "What is your plan?"

"I'm going to rely on my military prowess." His tone was glib, but his expression was serious.

"Please be more specific," Savannah requested.

"I'd tell you if I could," he promised. "But I'm making it up as I go along."

She clasped her hands together to keep them from shaking. "Dane . . ."

"Don't worry," he said. "We're a special ops team—remember? We've done covert operations all over the world, and our success rate is spectacular."

Savannah couldn't refute this. She rubbed her temples where a headache was forming. "I'll be so glad when this is over."

"We all will be," Dane assured her.

"Landing strip is coming up," the pilot called over his shoulder.

Savannah looked out the window to see an alarmingly short runway. As the ground rose toward them, she closed her eyes. The landing was smooth, considering the circumstances, and Savannah was only too happy to unfasten her seat belt and climb off the plane. Captain Findlay himself was waiting with the helicopter.

Savannah pushed her fists into the pockets of her jacket. She stared at the mountains in the distance and had a nauseating sense of déjà vu. Caroline was near. Soon she would have her child back. Again.

Dane shook hands with the captain and said, "Thanks for meeting us personally."

"No problem," the captain replied. "I brought my best pilot for you."

"I'd rather fly the helicopter myself," Dane told the captain. "If you don't mind."

Captain Findlay shrugged. "Okay by me. Just take good care of my copter. It's hard to get replacements these days."

"I'll bring it back in one piece." Dane waited until Steamer was inside the helicopter, then he lifted Savannah up.

Her hands were shaking so badly that Steamer had to help her secure the seat belt.

"Thank you," she whispered.

"Everything will be fine. Dane's the best."

She couldn't quite manage a smile, but nodded.

As they made their ascent, Savannah leaned forward and yelled into Dane's ear. "I hope Wes *is* working with Ferrante."

Dane frowned. "Why?"

"Because I know he wouldn't let Ferrante hurt her," she explained.

"Wes would be a formidable opponent. He's almost as good as me."

Savannah turned to Steamer. "How do you feel about Dane's theory that Wes might still be alive?"

"I wouldn't mind if old Wes were still breathing," Steamer said. "That would give me a chance to kill him myself."

Savannah assumed he was kidding, but before she could clarify his comment, Dane pulled the helicopter up and began a slow descent.

"We're almost there," he said.

Steamer checked his gun in preparation for what lay ahead. As she watched him, Savannah was overcome with tenderness. He was risking his life for Caroline even thought he barely knew her.

"Be careful," she whispered.

Steamer nodded as Dane put the helicopter down on the concrete pad.

Savannah peered through the thick, tinted glass at the McLaughlins' cabin, hoping to catch sight of her in-laws or Caroline. But she saw no one.

Dane cut the engine and turned to her. "We're going to get out and see what the situation is. I need you to stay here in the helicopter so I don't have to worry about you."

Savannah fixed Dane with a penetrating look. "I'll stay here as long as we agree that Caroline is the most important concern. If the only way to save her is for me to go with Ferrante, then you'll make the trade."

He nodded. "Caroline is the priority."

"Okay," she whispered, "I'll stay here."

Steamer opened the door and jumped out of the helicopter.

"I'll be back as quick as I can," Dane promised her.

She leaned forward and pressed a kiss to his lips. "For luck."

He caressed her cheek before swinging to the ground. After he was clear, she pushed the helicopter door mostly closed. Through the small opening she watched Dane and Steamer advance toward the McLaughlins' house.

When they were a few yards from the front door, Dane yelled, "Hack! Is everything secure?"

Savannah watched in amazement as Hack stepped out of the house. Along the perimeter of the McLaughlins' farm, at least a dozen soldiers emerged from the woods with their guns drawn. "All clear, sir," Hack reported.

Savannah's relief was profound. Hack was there. Everything was under control. She had been right to trust Dane.

"Where are the others?" Dane asked.

"Inside," Hack told him.

Dane turned back to the helicopter and waved to Savannah. "It's safe."

Savannah pushed open the door and jumped gracelessly to the ground. Then she hurried over to Dane.

"Hack came here instead of going to Ft. Belvoir?" she asked.

"Yes," Dane confirmed. "This was Plan C for capturing Ferrante."

"How did you know he'd come here?"

"He seemed to know everything about the operation—so if he had an inside man, we decided to use that against him. We led him to believe that Caroline was here . . ."

"So he'd come, and you could trap him," Savannah finished the sentence for him. "You are a military genius!"

He smiled. "Thanks."

Then her heart started to pound. "But Caroline . . ."

"Is *not* here. She's safe," he promised. "I'll tell you the details later." Dane put a hand on the small of her back and propelled her forward. "Let's go meet Ferrante."

Savannah had no desire to meet their nemesis face to face, but she didn't want to stay outside alone either. So she accompanied Dane into the house.

The McLaughlins' small living room was crowded with soldiers. Dane led the way into the kitchen, which was equally crowded. Cam was sitting in one of the old caneback chairs. His hands were bound in front of him, and his head was wrapped with a sloppy bandage—apparently someone's half-hearted attempt to protect the wound left when his ear was cut off. He was staring at the wood plank floor, and he didn't look up when they walked in.

Savannah's eyes moved across the room to the handcuffed man standing near the window. He was flanked on each side by Hack's guards—emphasizing how dangerous they deemed him to be. Mario Ferrante in person was something of an anticlimax. In spite of all she knew about him, he didn't look like the embodiment of evil. In fact his appearance was so commonplace that under other circumstances she probably wouldn't even have noticed him.

Then Savannah saw Chad Allen standing beside Ferrante. His hands were also bound, and she looked at Hack in confusion. "I thought he got away."

"He did," Hack confirmed. "And he ran straight to his boss, Mr. Ferrante here."

Savannah's disappointment was profound. She'd encouraged Dane to trust in Rosemary and her husband. Apparently he had been right all along. But before she could pursue the subject, Ferrante himself spoke to Dane.

"So we finally meet."

"For what I hope is the first and last time," Dane replied. "Unless I'm asked to testify at your trial. I wouldn't mind helping to put you behind bars."

Ferrante seemed genuinely amused. "You flatter yourself, Major Dane. I'm not going to jail, and you certainly don't have the ability to send me there."

"There's no way out this time," Dane assured him. "Your days of murdering people and kidnapping innocent children are over."

Steamer waved his revolver at the mafia boss. "Give me an excuse to kill you, *please.*"

Ferrante ignored Steamer and turned to Savannah. He nodded at her like they had just been introduced at a dinner party. "Mrs. McLaughlin."

"Leave her out of this." Dane stepped in front of Savannah, blocking her from Ferrante's view. "But I would like to talk about my old friend Wes. In fact, I'd like to talk *to* him."

Ferrante grinned. "Then you'll have to arrange a séance."

"I've got my doubts about that," Dane said. "And if you tell me the truth, I'll ask the authorities to go easy on you."

"That's a lie," Ferrante accused. "You'd never do anything to help me."

Dane didn't deny it. "Is Wes really dead, or was his accident an elaborate scheme you cooked up with the Army's help?"

Ferrante looked bored. "You're wasting your time with that line of questioning."

"Well, I certainly don't want to waste your time," Dane said sarcastically as they heard the sound of a helicopter overhead.

"Were we expecting company?" Hack asked.

Dane shook his head while keeping his eyes on Ferrante. The other man was smiling. "Hack, go check it out. Take a few men with you—just in case."

Hack nodded and walked toward the front door.

Savannah watched Hack leave with growing anxiety. She just wanted to get off the mountain and find her daughter.

Hack returned a few minutes later. "It's the FBI—come to give us a hand."

"What would we do without them?" Dane muttered.

Savannah watched as the door to the McLaughlins' cabin opened and a man wearing a suit, accompanied by two uniformed soldiers, stepped in. He nodded to Dane.

"Agent Gray," Dane said when the FBI agent entered the kitchen. Dane extended his hand, and the agent shook it firmly. "To what do we owe this unexpected honor?"

Agent Gray smiled. "I'm here to take Ferrante off your hands."

Dane controlled his reaction well, but Savannah knew he was surprised and displeased. "Our orders were to bring him in to Ft. Belvoir and turn him over to General Steele," he replied casually.

The agent shrugged. "Orders change."

Dane pulled out his cell phone. "I'll need to check this out with the general."

"Of course," Agent Gray acknowledged.

Dane turned away to give himself a degree of privacy in the crowded room. Savannah heard him speak in muffled tones, and then he closed the phone and turned back to address the FBI agent. "The general confirms the change in orders. We are supposed to give Ferrante to you."

Hack cursed under his breath. "Why would the general let the Feds waltz in here and take Ferrante away from us?"

"Does this mean the FBI will get credit for his arrest?" Steamer asked.

"I don't care who gets credit," Dane said. "And I don't know why the general has decided to handle it this way. But orders are orders." He looked over at Hack. "Turn him over to Agent Gray."

Savannah watched with mixed feelings as the transfer of custody was made. She was sorry that the team wasn't going to have the pleasure of turning Ferrante over to the general—but honestly she was glad to be rid of him.

Once the FBI was officially in charge of the prisoner, Ferrante shook his bound hands at Agent Gray. "I want these off immediately. Chad's too."

Agent Gray walked over to Dane. "I need that handcuff key." Then he lowered his voice and whispered, "I'm sorry, but like you said—orders are orders."

"Whose orders?" Dane managed to ask.

"The White House," Agent Gray said softly. "Ferrante made a deal."

"Give him the keys," Dane said, and Hack relinquished them with obvious reluctance.

Then Savannah watched in horror as the FBI agent unlocked both sets of handcuffs. Once Ferrante and Chad Allen were free, the agent turned to Dane. "I really am sorry."

Dane gave the agent one curt nod.

Ferrante rubbed his wrists and then said to Dane, "I'll be sure to complain to my friends in high places about your rough treatment."

Dane smiled without a trace of humor. "If I'd known you had a White House deal in the works, we'd be turning your corpse over to the FBI right now."

"Careful," Ferrante warned. "I'd hate to have to add a harassment charge to my list of complaints."

"That's enough," Agent Gray said gruffly. "Let's go."

As they started for the door again, Cam looked up. "What about me? Did you get me a deal too?"

Ferrante laughed. "You've exhausted your usefulness. I'll leave you to the discipline of your *team*."

"Please!" Cam called out, a desperate quality to his voice. "Don't leave me here with them!"

Savannah was ashamed for him.

"You'd think that when he was working out a deal with the FBI that he would have included his loyal employee, Cam," Hack mused. "I guess you just can't trust anybody these days."

"Yeah, he's thrown you to the dogs," Steamer agreed. "Us."

Ferrante laughed.

"Aren't you going to try and stop them?" she asked Dane.

He shook his head, looking defeated. "No, if he's made a deal with the White House, it's not my place to interfere."

"But Ferrante is a horrible person," Savannah argued.

"The White House must have its reasons," Dane didn't sound convinced, but he was going to obey his orders. "Hack, will you follow them out and make sure Ferrante gets on the helicopter?"

Hack nodded.

Savannah fumed with frustration. It was so unfair. She moved forward and called, "Agent Gray!"

The FBI agent and Ferrante both turned.

"I want to ask him a question." She gestured toward Mario Ferrante.

The agent nodded. "Make it quick."

Mustering all her courage, Savannah addressed the mafia boss. "Is Wes alive?"

Ferrante gave her a malicious grin. "Isn't one Army hero enough for you?"

"Answer her question," Agent Gray demanded.

With an annoyed look at the FBI agent, Ferrante said, "If you're smart, you'll forget all about your husband. Asking some questions can be dangerous to your health." Ferrante looked up at Agent Gray. "That's all I plan to say on the matter. Get me out of here."

The agent nodded and once again started toward the McLaughlins' living room with Mario Ferrante and Chad Allen in tow.

Savannah thought her heart would break, but she had accepted defeat.

Suddenly Cam lunged forward and wrapped his handcuffed hands around Mario Ferrante's neck. Savannah watched as Ferrante's eyes bulged and his hands clawed ineffectively at the handcuff chain. Then the room seemed to explode into chaos.

Bullets flew, screams filled the cool mountain air, and Dane tackled Savannah to the ground. Her head hit the wooden floor with such force that she was rendered unconscious for a few seconds. When she opened her eyes, the shooting had ended. Dane rolled off of her, and she heard Hack yell, "All guns are down. Area secure, Major."

Dane pulled her up, and in dismay she surveyed the carnage. Cam lay motionless near her feet, a bullet wound in his chest. Even without the benefit of medical training, Savannah knew his chances of survival couldn't be good. Chad Allen also appeared to be gravely wounded.

Savannah noted that Mario Ferrante had survived the ordeal but that Cam's handcuffs had left a bright red stripe of raw flesh across the mafia boss's neck. No one else seemed harmed, but the kitchen was a mess.

Hack and Steamer took positions on opposite sides of the room, guns drawn, expressions grim.

"What happened?" Savannah whispered.

"That psycho tried to kill me!" Mario Ferrante stabbed a finger toward Cam.

"A couple of guys panicked and fired," Steamer added. "One got Cam and the other got the Allen kid."

Mario Ferrante interrupted the explanation by saying, "I want to get out of here right now before one of these military maniacs shoots me. Have one of your men get my son-in-law, and let's go."

Agent Gray looked at Chad Allen's prone form. "I'm pretty sure he's dead, and if not, he definitely needs immediate medical attention. Why don't you leave him here—"

"I said bring him along," Ferrante snapped.

Agent Gray instructed one of his men to lift Chad Allen. Rosemary's husband didn't make a sound, which Savannah considered a very bad sign.

"I'm sorry about your man," Agent Gray added, pointing in Cam's direction.

Dane absolved the agent with a quick nod. "Just get Ferrante out of here. The sight of him makes me sick."

Ferrante started toward the door and then turned to Dane. He lifted his hand in salute and said, "We'll meet again."

Dane stepped closer and whispered, "If we do, nobody will be able to save you—not the FBI or the White House or God himself."

The sound of Mario Ferrante's taunting laughter echoed through the room as Agent Gray rushed him out of the house.

After they were gone, Hack returned. "You want me to follow them and take him out the first chance I get?" he asked Dane.

Dane smiled. "No. I can't afford to have another one of my men sent to prison."

A couple of medics from Ft. Carson rushed in. Savannah watched them assess Cam's condition. The examination was short, and when the medics were through, they covered Cam with a white plastic sheet.

"He's dead," Savannah whispered as she pressed her cheek against Dane's shirt.

"Yes," he confirmed, stroking her hair in an attempt at comfort.

Dane waved for Hack. "Get a couple of your guys to take Cam out to the helicopter."

Hack nodded and assigned a couple of men to the task of transporting Cam.

As Savannah watched them carry his body out, she whispered, "Poor Cam."

"At least he died better than he lived," Steamer said.

Savannah blinked back her tears and squared her shoulders. There was one last battle to fight on Cam's behalf, and she prayed she'd have the fortitude to win it. "We were here and witnessed Cam's death. So now we get to choose."

"Choose?" Dane repeated.

"Choose whether Cam was with us or not," Savannah explained, bravely meeting his gaze. "I think Cam was a part of the team again. I think he was just pretending to work for Ferrante, waiting for the moment when he could be of the most benefit to us."

"You're entitled to your opinion," Hack said.

"This is important," she insisted. "It determines whether Cam died as a hero and deserves a full military funeral or whether he died as a penniless escaped convict with ties to the mob." She was gratified to see that she had their attention now. "I'd like to put it to a team vote. All those who believe Cam was loyal, raise your hand." She raised both of hers and waited.

Dane frowned. "Why are you voting twice?"

A few tears leaked out of her eyes, and she wiped them from her cheeks with her sleeve. "I'm voting for me and Doc."

Slowly Steamer raised his hand. "I guess there's no danger in trusting a dead man."

"All for one and one for all," Hack muttered as he raised a hand.

Savannah beamed at them and then turned to Dane. "The majority has spoken, but I'd like for the vote to be unanimous."

Dane nodded. "I agree. Cam's been with us since we broke him out of prison."

Savannah was pleased but confused. "Are you serious?"

"I am," Dane confirmed. "I knew Cam was loyal when Ferrante's guys had to use a sledgehammer to open the secret panels in my house. Cam did know about them. In fact, they fascinated him. If he'd been cooperating with Ferrante, those guys wouldn't have needed a sledgehammer. They would have known exactly how to open the hidden doors."

Savannah felt the grief within her lighten. "Cam was with us."

Dane gave her a little smile. "You were right about that."

"Then why did you insist, adamantly I might add, that Cam was working for Ferrante *after* the sledgehammer incident?"

"We knew we had a security breach," Dane began. "We knew it was someone with access to very sensitive information—which limited the possibilities. We were suspicious of everyone—even Wes."

"And . . ." Savannah prompted.

"And after Ferrante's men bashed in my secret panel, I knew it wasn't Cam or General Steele or even Wes. It had to be someone who knew everything else but didn't know how to open the panels."

Savannah frowned. "Who?"

"You," he said gently.

Her lips trembled. "I would never betray the team." And as she said the words, she realized it was true. Even to save herself or Caroline, she would remain loyal. There were things more important than life. She'd seen Cam and Lacie try to sacrifice honor for their families, and they ended up losing both. "You can trust me."

He reached out and stroked her cheek. "I know." His hand dropped to the locket around her neck. "I believe Ferrante had someone plant a tiny listening device in your locket. That's how he's been able to stay right in step with our investigation."

"I've been bugged?" she repeated. "This whole time?"

He nodded.

"And why didn't the technicians at Ft. Belvoir find it?" Savannah asked.

"Because that's when the bug was placed," Dane replied. "Right after they documented that you were bugfree."

"I'm going to be asking those TSDU technicians a few pointed questions when I get back to Ft. Belvoir," Hack said. "It won't take me long to get the answers we need."

Savannah almost felt sorry for the guilty party. "So once you realized I was wearing a bug, why didn't you remove it?"

"We decided it would be better to use the device to feed Ferrante the information we wanted him to have." Dane's fingers traced the gold chain to the latch at the back of her neck. She shivered as he unfastened the latch, and the locket fell into his waiting palm. "Hack, will you take care of this?"

Hack opened the locket, and they all stared at the tiny picture of Caroline sitting beside Dane on the bridge at the cabin. Savannah looked at Dane, but he was facing away, and so she couldn't see his reaction.

"Somewhere in here is a little marvel of technology that has kept Ferrante informed about our operation," Hack said. "It sure will be a pleasure to destroy it."

"You won't destroy the locket, too, will you?" Savannah glanced back at Dane. "It has sentimental value."

"I'll be careful not to damage the locket," Hack promised. "And I'll return it as soon as the listening device has been removed."

After Hack left, Savannah asked, "Now can you tell me where Caroline is?"

"She's at my cabin," Dane replied. "With Doc and half the U.S. Army."

Savannah frowned. "You made a huge point of saying that your cabin was not to be used as any part of this operation."

He grinned. "That's what made it the best place for Caroline." Then his smile faded. "By now she's probably got the whole cabin full of ugly Christmas trees."

Savannah smiled. Caroline was safe and happily ensconced in Dane's cabin, waiting for Christmas to arrive. "I hope so."

Dane held out a hand to her. "Let's get out of here."

She stood and took his hand in hers. "If we hurry, we can get back to your cabin before Christmas."

CHAPTER 14

DANE WAITED UNTIL all the other team members were inside the helicopter before he climbed in. He winced as he swung into the seat beside Savannah, and she noticed the blood on his shirt.

"Are you hurt too?" she demanded.

"It's nothing serious," he said, but she wasn't sure she could believe him. "Just a scratch from a stray bullet."

"You were *shot?*" She was incredulous. "And you didn't say anything to the medics?"

"I think the bullet that killed Cam passed through and nicked me. It's no big deal."

She studied the stain on his shirt. "You lost quite a bit of blood."

As the helicopter lifted off the ground, he said to Steamer, "Will you look around for the first aid kit before I bleed to death from this scratch on my stomach?"

Steamer laughed as he handed the kit to Dane. "You got hit?"

"Not even worth mentioning," Dane insisted.

Dane took a roll of gauze out of the kit and tore the foil covering off with his teeth. Then he lifted his shirt and told Savannah, "Wrap a few layers of this around me."

Thankful that the dim light inside the helicopter kept her from seeing too much of his new wound or all the scars that already marred his skin, Savannah wound the gauze around his midsection. As she leaned close, the helicopter lurched, throwing her against him. If the contact had hurt him, he gave no indication.

Finally, she tucked the end of the gauze in and surveyed her haphazard attempt at first aid.

"Not bad," he said.

"It's terrible," she said, "but it will do until we get to the farm, where a professional can look at it."

"It's fine. You're making me look like a sissy in front of my men," he hissed.

"They've seen your scars," she told him. "They don't doubt your ability to suffer."

As they approached the helicopter pad in front of the administration building of the Brotherly Love Farm, Savannah strained to see out the window. It was hard to make out individuals through the thick window glass, but she didn't recognize Wes's parents among the waiting crowd.

She turned to Dane and asked, "Where are the McLaughlins?"

"At my cabin with Doc and Caroline," he replied.

"They left not just the mountain but the entire farm?" Savannah asked in wonder. The McLaughlins had been in self-imposed seclusion on the mountain for over ten years. "I can't believe it."

Dane shrugged. "Love confined them to the mountain, and I guess love gave them the courage to leave."

She narrowed her eyes at him. "I thought you didn't believe in love."

"I never said that," he corrected. "I just said people can't be trusted."

"You're impossible," Savannah told him in exasperation.

When they landed, Captain Findlay was waiting for them, and he delivered the bad news that Chad Allen had died during transport to the hospital.

"Thank you for letting us know," Dane told the captain.

"And is it true that all of this was for nothing since Ferrante got away with a little help from his friends in the FBI?" the captain asked.

"He did get away, but his friends were more important than FBI agents," Dane said.

The captain studied the makeshift bandage around Dane's midsection. Then he called over one of the medics. "Major Dane needs some attention."

Dane looked annoyed, but he didn't refuse treatment. "It's just a scratch."

"Scratches like that can kill you," the medic told him.

Dane reluctantly submitted to an examination. While the medic prodded his wound, Dane told the captain, "I hate for the McLaughlins to come home to that mess. Could you send some guys up to clean their house?"

The captain agreed with a nod. "I'll take care of it."

The medic completed his examination and let Dane's shirt fall back into place. "This is going to need a couple of stitches. You can go to the clinic here at the farm, or I can do it in my van."

"I'm in a hurry," Dane said. "Show me your van."

Ten minutes later, Dane was pale but stitched and ready to go.

"I gave him a pretty strong painkiller before sewing him up," the medic told Savannah. "So he might act a little loopy for the next couple of hours."

The thought of Dane loopy made her smile. "Thanks for the warning."

Dane rolled his eyes.

"Just don't let him drive or operate heavy machinery for a few hours," the medic said as he walked away.

Captain Findlay offered to drive them to the landing strip where the jet was waiting to take them to Ft. Belvoir. Once they were settled in the Jeep, Savannah leaned close to Dane and whispered, "You'd better make a full recovery, or I'll never forgive you. I'm determined to prove to you that there is such a thing as happily ever after."

He leaned his head back against the seat. "If you truly want to live happily ever after, you'll forget you ever met me."

"I may have to live without you, but I'll never forget you."

He closed his eyes. "And all this because I'm such a good kisser."

When they reached the landing strip, they climbed out of the Jeep, and Dane thanked Captain Findlay for his assistance.

The captain waved aside Dane's appreciation. "The only thing I want from you guys is a promise that we won't get another visit from you anytime soon. Nothing personal."

Dane nodded. "I understand."

The pilot had the plane ready to go, so minutes after they boarded, they were underway.

"I wish Doc were here with a bag of snacks," Hack said. "I'm starving."

"Me too," Steamer commiserated.

Dane wasn't sympathetic. "Hopefully you'll live until we get to Ft. Belvoir."

Savannah was hungry, too, but based on Dane's comments to Hack and Steamer, she decided to keep it to herself. She reclined against the uncomfortable seat and smiled. With each passing minute, she was getting closer to Caroline.

"What's funny?" Dane asked.

"Nothing," she replied. "I'm just glad to be going home."

"So," Steamer rubbed his hands together, "are we going to make use of this time to go over the operation?"

"I'm too tired, and discussing this operation would be too depressing," Dane muttered and closed his eyes.

"And he is under the influence of strong pain medicine," Savannah reminded Steamer. Then she turned to Dane. "But the operation wasn't a total disaster."

He opened one eye. "How do you figure that?"

"Well, we got Cam back," she said.

"Cam's dead," Dane reminded her unnecessarily.

She nodded. "But he proved his loyalty. Although, knowing he was part of the team again at the end makes his death even sadder."

"I've wanted to kill him for weeks," Steamer concurred. "But now that he's dead, I sort of miss him."

"And I can't help feeling responsible for his death," Savannah told them.

"That's ridiculous." Dane didn't bother to open even one eye.

"But Cam wouldn't have been in danger if it hadn't been for me," she insisted. "I'm the one who dragged you all into this."

"General Steele approved the operation," Dane said. "So if you have to blame someone, blame him."

"Cam agreed to help of his own free will," Steamer added.

"And Cam died in combat," Dane pointed out, "protecting his country and ensuring domestic tranquility—as he had sworn to do."

"You probably shouldn't argue with him while he's under the influence of a strong painkiller," Steamer advised Savannah.

Hack gave her a gold-toothed grin. "Yeah, the doctor warned us he'd be *loopy*."

Dane opened his eyes and sat a little straighter. "I'm not loopy, but I did make promises to Cam about his kids. I need to go see his ex-wife so I can personally explain what happened and make arrangements for their future."

"I talked to General Steele while you were getting your side stitched up," Steamer said. "He's already informed Cam's ex-wife and said he'll make sure she gets full death benefits."

"No matter what arrangements the general has made, I'm still going to see Cam's family," Dane said stubbornly. "He was a member of my team, and I'm responsible for them now that he's gone."

Steamer smiled. "I'll bet the major here will offer Cam's ex all kinds of death benefits for those kids."

Hack smiled back. "Yeah, college at least—maybe graduate school and a tour of Europe."

"Sky's the limit," Steamer said.

"It's a good thing the wife already has a boyfriend, or he'd probably marry her to fulfill his duty," Hack predicted, and Steamer's smile widened.

"I thought we agreed not to upset Dane," Savannah reminded them.

Hack wiped his eyes. "He knows we're kidding."

"Mostly," Steamer hedged. "When it comes to honor, the major knows no bounds."

"Why don't you guys go lie down in back and try to get some sleep?" Dane requested. "I could use some peace and quiet."

Savannah was pleased that he didn't dismiss her along with his men. Once they were alone, she said, "I wonder what Caroline is doing right now."

"Probably trying to convince Doc to take her fishing."

Savannah reached automatically for the locket, but her neck was bare.

Dane's eyes followed the action. "I'll get your locket back to you soon."

"What about us?" she asked.

He was instantly wary. "There is no us."

"I mean the team," she clarified quickly. "Can we spend Christmas at your cabin?"

"I suppose," he agreed with obvious reluctance.

"And after Christmas?"

"I'm probably going to take Hack and Doc with me to New Orleans. We'll hire some contractors and work on my house. Steamer will go to Las Vegas and resume his lucrative real estate career. You'll take Caroline back to Ft. Belvoir. When I get the house finished, the two of you can come visit."

She pushed past the hurt of being excluded. "Maybe Caroline and I will come with you to New Orleans now. I'm getting pretty good at tearing down old wallpaper."

"No."

"Why?"

"For all the reasons I gave you before," he said irritably. "Separation is best for you and for Caroline—probably for me too, although that's not important."

Savannah frowned. "And what if I told you that I think Wes is alive and working with Ferrante so I'm afraid for my life?"

"I'd say that I'm way ahead of you. Hack is assigning extra men to protect you, and when I get through with the surveillance guys at Ft. Belvoir, the term *high security* will have a whole new meaning to them."

"And what if I told you that I love you and can't live another day without you in my life."

"I'd give you the number for my psychiatrist." He closed his eyes. "Now be quiet. Please. I'm tired."

Accepting defeat, she said, "Would you like me to stand guard while you sleep again?"

He shook his head. "I'm just going to doze, but it probably would be safer if you moved across the aisle—just in case I fall asleep and try to strangle you."

Savannah put one seat between them. "There, that will be our buffer zone."

He nodded, and a few minutes later he was sleeping peacefully.

CHAPTER 15

DANE WOKE UP as the plane touched down at Andrews Air Force Base. He looked around him—disoriented and maybe a little afraid.

"I've been asleep?" he asked Savannah.

"You have," she confirmed. "For almost three hours."

"And I didn't scream?"

"Nope. You didn't try to kill me either," she reported. "I think we need to get the name of that painkiller the medic gave you and keep some on hand so you can get some rest occasionally."

He made a face. "Great, in addition to my other faults, you want to turn me into a drug addict."

She ignored this. "How do you feel?"

"Good," he admitted as he stretched. "It's amazing what three hours of sleep can do for you."

"Imagine how good you'd feel if you actually slept for a whole night like most people."

"I'm not like most people," he said with a smile. "I'm much better."

She yawned and looked out the window. "Caroline is probably already asleep."

Dane shrugged. "There's no law against waking her up."

Savannah smiled. "For once you are absolutely right."

After leaving the plane, Dane gathered everyone together and made assignments. "I've got Doc working on funeral arrangements for Cam," he said. "Hack, I need you to go to the Intelligence Center and interrogate the TSDU technicians who we suspect planted the bug in Savannah's locket. I've had the MPs pick them up, and they're waiting for you."

"My pleasure," Hack accepted.

"Steam, I have just one last assignment for you, and then you can head back to Las Vegas and make another fortune in real estate."

"I'm not really in any big rush to get back to Vegas," Steamer told him. "What do you need?"

"I thought you said you could be making millions if you were back there selling houses," Hack said with a scowl.

"Don't you watch the news?" Steamer demanded. "There's no market for houses anywhere right now."

"You two can fight about real estate later," Dane interrupted. "We need groceries for our Christmas dinner, but that's going to require all your impressive shopping skills since most stores close early on Christmas Eve."

"I'm good for the challenge," Steamer said.

"I'm sorry that you guys won't be spending Christmas with your families," Savannah apologized.

"We don't have what you'd call real families anyway," Hack replied.

Savannah wasn't sure if that made her feel better or not. "Well, it's nice that most of the team will be together for Christmas anyway."

"The team is our family," Hack said and then he frowned. "But I don't have a Christmas gift for Caroline." He turned to Steamer. "Pick something up for me while you're grocery shopping. But make sure it's nice."

"Sure," Steamer said. Then he looked at Savannah. "What kind of stuff does she like?"

"She'll be happy with anything," Savannah assured him. "She asked Santa for a 'Real Baby'—a doll that eats and drinks and has to have diaper changes. If that helps."

Steamer frowned at her. "She actually wants a doll that does all that?"

"She does," Savannah confirmed. "And it comes with a stroller and high chair. Santa got it weeks ago. But it needs to be transferred from my apartment to the cabin."

"We'll get it," Dane promised.

"And I'll come up with something for Caroline from the guys." Steamer turned to Dane. "You can go in with us, too, if you want."

Dane shook his head, and Savannah was hurt until he said, "I've already got her something."

Savannah turned to him, but he wouldn't meet her eyes.

"I'm going to take Savannah to her apartment so she can pick up Caroline's Santa stuff," Dane said in a professional tone. "Then we'll come to the Intelligence Center and see if Hack's had any luck with the TSDU techs. Steamer, meet us there when you're through shopping, and we'll drive on out to the cabin."

At the apartment, Dane watched television while Savannah took a shower. Then she put on some of her own clothes for the first time in days. When she rejoined Dane, she said, "I enjoyed having Steamer buy clothes for me. I wonder if he'd be interested in a job as my personal shopper."

Dane turned off the TV and stood. "That's not something every soldier would consider a compliment."

She smiled. "I'll bet Steamer would."

Savannah collected Caroline's Santa gifts and the presents under the tree. Once it was all safely stashed in Dane's car, they headed to the Intelligence Center.

At the Intelligence Center they walked down the empty halls, their shoes echoing on the institutional tile floor. Dane suggested that she wait in her office while he checked on Hack's interrogation session. They parted ways, and she walked toward her office. She was surprised—if not entirely pleased—to see Lieutenant Hardy still sitting at her desk in front of General Steele's office, guarding it like a maladjusted pit bull.

"Hello," Savannah greeted. "I'm surprised to see you here so late on Christmas Eve."

Lieutenant Hardy gave her a doleful look. "The general asked me to come in and provide Major Dane with anything he needs. Are you back from your unplanned leave?"

Savannah knew Lieutenant Hardy would have preferred to say "unauthorized leave" but didn't quite dare.

"No," Savannah replied. "I'm still vacationing."

Lieutenant Hardy's disapproval was obvious. "The regulations state that the Army is not required to hold your position if you take a leave of more than four weeks," she informed Savannah. "That's something you might want to keep in mind."

Savannah gritted her teeth. "I will."

At this point, Dane joined them. Lieutenant Hardy stood, blushed, and looked uncharacteristically flustered.

"Hello, Major," she said, extending her hand to him.

"Nice to see you again, Lieutenant," he returned.

"Is there anything I can do to help you?" Lieutenant Hardy offered.

He smiled. "No, go on home and enjoy what's left of your holiday."

Lieutenant Hardy looked uncertain. "If you're sure . . ."

"I am," Dane replied. "Merry Christmas." Then he turned to Savannah and pointed at her office. "We need to talk."

Once they were settled in her office with the door closed, she asked, "So has Hack convinced one of the technicians to confess?"

Dane shook his head. "No."

"So what do we need to talk about?"

"Nothing, I just wanted to get away from Lieutenant Hardy. I think she likes me."

As Savannah smirked at him, there was a knock on the door. Assuming Lieutenant Hardy had thought of a reason to interrupt them, she opened the door with trepidation. But instead of Lieutenant Hardy, she found General Steele and Rosemary Allen standing in the hallway. Rosemary's hair was dark again, and at the sight of her bulging midsection, Savannah felt an odd sense of loss.

"Hello, General, Rosemary." Savannah pulled the door open to admit them. "I'm so sorry about your husband," she told the girl.

"Thank you," Rosemary said softly.

Savannah glanced at Dane, unsure how he would react to the unexpected visitors.

"And I'm sorry about Ferrante's release," the general told Dane. "That was out of my hands."

"I understand," Dane said, but he didn't sound convinced. "We didn't expect to see you here."

The general grimaced. "I didn't plan to be here so late, and my wife is probably going to kill me. But I had to get Rosemary settled."

"Settled?" Savannah repeated.

"Rosemary is about to enter the FBI's witness protection program," the general said. "But she wanted to thank you both personally first."

Rosemary took a step toward Savannah. "I can never apologize enough for putting you and your daughter in danger." She glanced at Dane. "And Major Dane, too, of course."

"Of course." Savannah pointed at Rosemary's distended stomach. "Are you feeling okay?"

"Yes, fine."

There was an awkward silence, finally filled when Savannah asked, "So you're going into the witness protection program?"

Rosemary nodded. "It's the only way to keep my father away from my baby."

Savannah knew how difficult raising a baby alone could be. So she said, "I'd like to keep in touch . . ."

"No way." Dane put an end to this idea from across the room.

Rosemary blushed as she risked a quick glance at Dane. "I know you don't trust me because of my father . . ."

"I don't trust anyone," Dane said, and the words fell heavily in the room. "But trust aside, keeping in contact with Savannah would be dangerous for you and Savannah and your child. Your father watches her, and if you contact her, he'll find you. And your baby."

Rosemary nodded. "I see that it's for the best that we part ways."

Then the general moved toward the door. "Well, I guess we're ready to go." His expression was a little too bright. He knew Dane had doubts about his loyalty, and it broke Savannah's heart to see the friends at odds.

As Savannah walked them to the door, Rosemary leaned over and whispered. Savannah listened carefully and nodded. Then she watched as Rosemary left with the general.

Once they were gone, she turned to Dane. "So do you think Rosemary will be able to hide herself and her baby from Mario Ferrante?"

"It's unlikely," Dane said. "If he doesn't find her, she'll probably return to him of her own free will. Even a criminal grandfather is better than no family at all."

Savannah remembered her mother's beautiful, unhappy face. Although she didn't know the challenges her mother had faced or the reasons for the choices she made, Savannah had to wonder if her mother had made the right decisions. Surely there was family somewhere who could have helped her to raise her child, even if Savannah's father couldn't or wouldn't be a part of their lives.

Dane yanked Savannah from her reverie by saying, "If you and the Ferrante girl exchanged cell phone numbers during that little whisper, it was a waste of time. One of the first things I plan to do is get you a new phone with a secure number. And if you gave her any details about your life at Ft. Belvoir, you'll have to move to another post."

Savannah was offended by his assumption that she had breached security and was irritated that he thought he could boss her around.

"Rosemary asked if I'd take her baby if something happens to her. She said if I agreed, she'd put it in writing and leave the paperwork with General Steele."

"Great," Dane said. "As if you needed another way to attract Mario Ferrante's attention."

"I was honored," Savannah said, "that she would choose me to raise her baby if she can't."

"Let's hope—for all your sakes—that she doesn't have to leave her child to anyone."

"Of course I hope Rosemary lives a long happy life and raises her own child." She glared at Dane for implying otherwise. "And I'll change my phone number and address only if *I* feel it's necessary."

"You won't endanger Caroline to prove a point with me," Dane responded with annoying certainty. "And while I don't think Rosemary Ferrante has what it will take to defy her father in the long term, I'll admit that I admire her determination to try."

Savannah smiled. "I'm proud of her too. And I think she just might make it. A child is a powerful incentive."

Dane wouldn't meet her eyes. "I guess."

Savannah frowned. "You're getting cranky again. You need another nap."

"No time for naps. Let's go check on Hack."

She immediately regretted her decision to accompany Dane into the general's situation room. The technicians were sitting in chairs on opposite ends of the room with their hands tied behind their backs. Hack was standing over one in a threatening way. Both men were sweating profusely. Although there was no evidence of physical mistreatment, they were obviously terrified.

"I think I'll wait in the hall," she said and retreated back out the door.

Dane joined her a few minutes later. "We're headed to my cabin," he said.

"Is Hack coming too?"

He nodded.

"What about the technicians?"

"We're leaving them in a lockup. Maybe after spending Christmas here, they'll be more cooperative."

She pointed at the door to the general's situation room. "Is that really necessary?"

He answered with another question. "Do you really want to see Ferrante behind bars?"

She looked at the ground. "Of course."

"Then it's necessary." He started down the hallway. "Let's go see if Steamer is back from his shopping spree."

Steamer was back. The Jeep he had commandeered from the air force was parked in a space reserved for the Inspector General. When he saw them, he climbed out and met them on the sidewalk. "Man, I'm good."

"You were able to find stores that were open?" Savannah asked.

"No, but I found a Super Target with a manager who hadn't left yet. And I convinced him to let me in. That's my new favorite store. They have *everything*."

Savannah smiled. "You'll have to give me the manager's name so I can send him a thank-you note."

Steamer looked mildly embarrassed. "Actually, I told him you'd be sending him more than that. I promised him a big check for a fundraiser they're doing to benefit local charities."

Savannah laughed. "I guess it's worth it for a nice Christmas dinner."

Hack joined them, and Steamer asked, "Any luck?"

The big man shook his head. "Naw, whichever one is working for Ferrante is still too scared of him. But he'll soon learn to fear me more."

Savannah shuddered. "Let's not talk about the technicians on Christmas Eve."

Dane checked his watch. "It's almost Christmas Day."

"Any chance that it will snow?" Steamer asked.

Dane shook his head. "None."

"White Christmases are overrated anyway," Steamer muttered.

They all got into the Jeep with Steamer, and when they approached Tulley Gate, Savannah's thoughts went back to the night when she had met Rosemary for the first time. Since then so much had happened. She'd met Steamer and added him to her circle of trusted friends. Cam had rejoined the team, costing him his life. Ferrante had been captured and subsequently released. The McLaughlins had found the courage to leave their mountain—at least temporarily. Rosemary had gained her freedom but had lost her husband. One thing, however, remained the same. Savannah was still not sure where she stood with Dane or what hope they had of a future together.

Two cars fell into place in front and behind them as they left the post. Savannah didn't have to ask if they were driven by Hack's men. She just knew.

When they turned onto Dane's gravel driveway, Savannah's heart started to pound. It had only been a few days since she'd seen her daughter, but it seemed much longer. Until she actually held Caroline in her arms, she wouldn't be sure that all was well.

Doc was waiting for them on the back porch. Savannah hurried toward him and clasped his hands in hers. "I can't think of words sufficient to express my appreciation."

Doc smiled. "No thanks necessary. I enjoyed spending time with your daughter."

At this point Savannah noticed the McLaughlins standing shyly on the edge of the porch.

She smiled at them. "I can't believe you left the mountain!"

"It was difficult," Wes's mother admitted.

"We're anxious to get back," her husband added.

"But we had to," Mrs. McLaughlin said finally.

"For Caroline," Savannah whispered.

The McLaughlins nodded.

"You left her in our care," Mrs. McLaughlin said. "We had to be sure she was safe."

Any fears Savannah had had about them being involved in the kidnapping plot with Mario Ferrante disappeared. "Now that you know you *can* leave the mountain you'll have to come visit us often."

Mrs. McLaughlin gave her a tremulous smile. "I'm not sure we can do it again—certainly not often—but we'll try."

"You're very brave," Dane said.

Wes's father shrugged. "We love Caroline."

"I'm glad she has you in her life," Savannah told them.

Wes's mother stepped back. "Well, I know you want to see Caroline."

Savannah smiled. "I do. We can talk more tomorrow."

The McLaughlins exchanged a look, and Doc said, "As soon as we got word that you were on your way back, I booked them on a flight for Denver. It leaves in a few hours. They were just waiting for you to get here before heading to the airport."

Savannah was a little disappointed but too grateful to complain. "We'll come see you soon," she promised as she hugged her in-laws. Mrs. McLaughlin hugged her back. Mr. McLaughlin only tolerated her embrace—but considering the reception she'd gotten from him at their first meeting, this was progress.

Then Savannah hurried inside and up the stairs toward the guest room. Dane was right behind her. She pushed open the door and saw Caroline asleep in the bed closest to the window. Moonlight illuminated her face, and she looked like a little angel. Caroline was curled around her favorite teddy bear—the one that smelled like Savannah's perfume.

They stood in the doorway together for a few seconds, absorbing the sight. Then Dane nudged her forward.

Savannah crossed the room and sat on the edge of the bed. She stroked Caroline's soft cheek and slowly the child's eyes opened.

"Mama!"

Savannah swallowed the sobs that threatened to choke her. "Caroline."

"Is it Christmas yet?"

Savannah nodded. "It is."

"Has Santa come?"

"No, but I think he'll be here soon."

Caroline pulled back and squinted at her mother in the dim moonlight. "Your hair is brown."

Savannah decided to skip explanations and just said, "Do you like it?"

"Mostly," Caroline decided after brief consideration. Then she noticed Dane, standing in the shadows by the door. "Hey, Major Dane."

"Hey," he replied.

"Is it time to get up?"

"No," Dane told her. "You need to go back to sleep."

Savannah lay down beside her daughter. "I'll stay here with you for a while."

"Stay here until morning," Dane suggested. "The guys and I will take care of . . . everything."

Savannah raised an eyebrow. "Are you sure you and the guys can handle . . . everything?"

He gave her an incredulous look. "I've created international incidents in most of the countries around the world. I think I can handle . . . everything."

He turned to go but Caroline yelled, "Major Dane! You didn't kiss me good night!"

He smiled then leaned over and pressed a kiss to Caroline's forehead.

"How about Mama?" Caroline prompted.

After a brief pause, Dane kissed Savannah's forehead too. Then he left them alone.

Savannah changed into her pajamas and snuggled with her daughter. With Caroline in her arms and the fresh memory of Dane's kiss on her mind, she smiled in contentment and closed her eyes. All was right with the world.

CHAPTER 16

ON CHRISTMAS MORNING, Savannah woke up early. She lay in the bed in Dane's guest room for a few minutes, relishing the sunrise and the closeup view of her daughter. While stroking Caroline's hair, she thought about the past few days. Had she been wrong to try and help Rosemary? Had she been foolish to drag Dane's team into the operation? Was she responsible for Cam's death? No answers came, and finally she abandoned her attempts to make sense of it all. She climbed out of bed, stretched, and prepared to face the day.

From her suitcase she pulled out her favorite pair of jeans and the blue cashmere sweater Wes had given her on their last Christmas together. It was beautiful, but she'd never worn it. He suggested that she try it on as soon as she opened it, but she had declined in passive protest against their loveless marriage. She regretted that now—denying him such a simple pleasure. Her mind started to drift back to that day.

She could smell the evergreen tree. She could hear the carols playing on Wes's state-of-the-art stereo system. She could see Caroline, just a tiny girl, opening gifts with wild abandon. She could feel the tension between herself and Wes.

Then she stopped the memory and opened her eyes. She wouldn't go back. The past was gone. It was time to look to the future. So today she would finally wear the blue sweater. And she hoped that Wes, wherever he was, would somehow know that she appreciated his gift.

Savannah turned just as Caroline's eyes opened. The child looked around the room and then whispered, "Did Santa come?"

Savannah smiled. "Let's go downstairs and see."

Caroline sprang from the bed and ran toward the door.

Savannah did her best to keep up with the excited six-year-old, but Caroline entered the living room well ahead of her. When Savannah arrived, she saw that Hack, Doc, and Steamer were all assembled in the small room. They all greeted her absently, but everyone's attention was focused on Caroline. She circled the room, giving hugs while her eyes strayed longingly toward the stocking above the fireplace and the presents under the tree.

"Where's Major Dane?" Caroline asked.

"Here," he said from the kitchen. "Making some Christmas hot chocolate."

"Can I drink it after I see my presents?"

He nodded. "Of course."

Savannah felt Dane's eyes on her, and when she looked up, his expression was anything but absent. She smiled at him and silently thanked Wes for the beautiful sweater. Then she crossed the room and sat on the couch between Doc and Steamer.

Caroline ran toward Dane. "I haven't hugged you good morning yet."

"Be careful. Major Dane has stitches," Savannah cautioned.

"It's just a scratch," he downplayed.

"I'll be careful." Caroline hugged him gingerly. Then she ran to the large stack of neatly wrapped gifts. "Did Santa bring all this for me?"

"Well, we know Major Dane hasn't been a good boy this year," Steamer replied with a wink. "So I think we can safely assume that none of them are for him."

Caroline laughed.

Dane narrowed his eyes at Steamer. "If the real estate market is so bad, maybe you can try stand-up comedy."

"What's that?" Caroline asked.

"Never mind," Savannah said. "Just open your gifts."

"There are tags on the gifts, telling you who they're from," Dane said.

"I can open them now?" Caroline confirmed.

Hack nodded. "You'd better. The suspense is killing me."

Caroline studied all her options and finally said, "This one says TO CAROLINE FROM MAJOR DANE, so I think I'll open it first."

Savannah was surprised. "You're going to open it before the ones from Santa?"

Caroline was already tearing the paper. "I'll do Santa's gifts second," she promised as she exposed a Lionel Electric Train starter set. The box boasted twenty feet of track with impressive features like a drawbridge and mountain with a tunnel. At first Savannah was concerned. It seemed like an unusual present for a six-year-old girl, and she wasn't sure how Caroline would react. By purchasing the gift, Dane had gone out on an emotional limb, and Savannah wanted Caroline to be overjoyed with it.

She needn't have worried.

Caroline transferred her eyes from the box to Dane and solemnly declared, "I've been wanting one of these." She looked at her mother. "Major Dane had a set like this when he was a little boy, and he used to play with it all the time. It was one of his favorite things to do."

Savannah was mildly unnerved by this declaration. She knew that Dane loved Caroline, but it was strange to think that he had shared memories and feelings with Caroline that he'd never mentioned to her.

"After breakfast I'll help you put it together," Dane offered.

"You can put it around the tree," Doc suggested.

Caroline frowned. "But what about after Christmas? It's pretty big. I don't think we have room at our apartment."

"You can put it back in the box and save it for next Christmas," Steamer proposed.

"Or maybe we can just keep it here in this corner by the fireplace, and I can visit it sometimes," Caroline said.

Savannah held her breath. Caroline was asking for personal space in Dane's home, and she didn't know if he'd be willing to share—even with Caroline.

After just a momentary pause, Dane nodded. "That corner is the perfect place for a train."

Savannah blinked back tears.

"My parents get to call me from Thailand today since it's Christmas," Dane continued. "I'll ask my mom where she stored my old train set. Then we can combine them and have longer tracks and twice as many cars."

Caroline considered this. "Or we can have two trains and do races."

Dane smiled. "That sounds even better."

Savannah watched the two of them in amazement. Caroline looked so much like Wes it was as if the old threesome was back together again . . . almost.

"You've got more presents," Steamer reminded Caroline.

"Although it's unlikely that anything will top a train set," Savannah murmured.

"Do I detect a trace of jealously?" Dane asked.

"Definitely," Savannah admitted, giving him a smile.

Caroline reluctantly left her train and studied the tag on another box. "This one is from Hack, Steamer, and Doc."

"I thought you were going to open your Santa gifts," Doc reminded Caroline.

"It's okay," Savannah said. "You can open them in any order you please." Then she watched as Caroline unwrapped a kid-friendly laptop. Caroline was ecstatic. Savannah was horrified. "That must have been so expensive!" she scolded the men.

"We split it three ways," Doc said.

"It was within my price range," Hack assured her.

"Money's no problem for me," Steamer added.

"Last night you said the real estate market in Las Vegas was depressed," she whispered.

"Yeah, but things are looking up now that I've been put back on the Army payroll, isn't that right, Dane, baby?"

"Don't make me kill you on Christmas," Dane warned.

"It's purple!" Caroline informed them as she pulled the computer from its box. "Can you show me how to work it?" she asked Hack.

"I can," he agreed. "But you have a few more gifts to open first."

Caroline reluctantly put the computer aside and opened her Real Baby doll. "I love it," she told her mother, but her eyes kept returning to the train set.

Santa also brought Caroline some new clothes, including a winter coat with faux fur around the hood, which she promptly put on. Finally the stack of gifts had been reduced to a pile of crumpled wrapping paper. Caroline looked a little sad that the excitement was over, so Savannah reminded her about the gifts they'd gotten for the guys.

Caroline's face brightened immediately. "I almost forgot." She collected the gifts from under the tree and distributed them. "These are all from me," she announced proudly. "My mom helped make them, but I wrapped them myself." Eventually Doc, Hack, and Dane all had a present. But Caroline frowned when she realized that they didn't have one for Steamer. "We didn't know you were coming when we made these," Caroline told him.

"It's okay, baby," Steamer assured her. "I got tons of presents back in Vegas."

"But I want you to have one here," Caroline replied stubbornly. She turned to her mother. "What can we do?"

"Well, we could wait until tomorrow to open gifts, and that will give us time to go shopping for Steamer," Savannah suggested.

"But I want him to match," Caroline said.

"Steamer can have mine." Dane tossed his gift across to Steamer. "I've already got enough T-shirts anyway."

Caroline's eyes widened in surprise. "How did you know it's a T-shirt?"

"I can read minds," Dane told her then cut his eyes to Savannah. "It's a talent that drives some people crazy."

"I wish I could read minds." Caroline was obviously impressed. "And I still wish I had a present for you—even if you don't like T-shirts." Then her face brightened. "I'll be right back." When Caroline returned, she was clutching her favorite teddy bear. She handed it to Dane.

He accepted the gift and held it up to his nose. "It still smells like your mother."

Caroline smiled. "She puts her perfume on it. I hope you like it."

Hack laughed. "If it smells like your mama, I *know* he likes it."

Dane scowled at Hack and then returned his attention to Caroline. "This is a pretty big sacrifice. Are you sure you can do without your bear?"

"I don't get scared too much anymore," Caroline said bravely.

Dane took another sniff. "I never get scared, but I appreciate the gift just the same."

Apparently satisfied that the gift shortage dilemma was solved, Caroline instructed the others to open their packages. As Dane had predicted, each man received a T-shirt with the team slogan ALL FOR ONE emblazoned across the front. There was also a picture of the Three Musketeers. With assistance from Doc, who was the team's unofficial photographer, Savannah had Photoshopped the faces of Dane, Hack, and Doc onto the bodies of the Musketeers.

"Do you like it?" Caroline asked the men.

Steamer held Dane's shirt up against his chest. "I do like it, but I'm much more muscular than Dane, so I hope this fits me."

Hack put his shirt on. "If I can get my shirt over all my muscles, you shouldn't have a problem."

Doc gave Caroline a hug. "Thank you. It was the perfect gift for all of us."

Caroline beamed at them. "Now let's see what's in my stocking."

She had just poured the entire contents of her stocking onto the floor when Dane called them in to breakfast.

They feasted on doughnuts and hot chocolate while the guys took turns telling outrageous stories of Christmases past. Savannah gloried in the opportunity to learn more about all of them, especially Dane.

"One Christmas," Dane shared, "my sister got a new dress. She's ten years older than me, so she was about fifteen. I was trying to watch television, but she kept standing in front of the TV saying, 'Don't you like my new dress, Christopher?'" he said in a falsetto to impersonate his sister, and Caroline laughed uproariously.

"How long did that go on?" Savannah asked.

"Until I poured my glass full of red Kool-Aid down the front of her new dress," Dane replied.

Caroline squealed, and Savannah put a hand over her mouth.

"That'll teach her," Hack said with approval.

"What did your sister do?" Steamer asked.

"She screamed and cried and said I ruined her new dress. My parents whipped and lectured me." Dane looked up with a smile. "But my sister never stood in front of the TV when I was watching a show again."

"She learned her lesson," Caroline said, to which everyone laughed, especially Dane.

"But pouring Kool-Aid on someone is not the best way to handle a conflict," Savannah felt obligated to say.

"I know," Caroline assured her. "Besides, I don't even have a sister."

Before Savannah could start feeling too guilty about this, Dane stood and announced that it was time to assemble the train. Savannah sat on the couch and watched as the team members, all highly trained soldiers, crawled around Dane's living room floor snapping together track pieces and arranging bridges, mountains, trees, and a railroad crossing.

Once it was finished, Dane gave Caroline the remote control, and she sent the train off on its maiden voyage. Then she passed the controller around and let everyone have a turn.

"I'm going to have to get me one of these," Hack said as he watched the train pass through the mountain and head toward the bridge.

"You can play with mine sometimes," Caroline offered generously. But she reclaimed possession of the remote.

"Okay," Dane said. "It's time to start making dinner. And in keeping with military procedure, as commanding officer of this covert operations team, I will make assignments. I'll take the turkey, since that is obviously the most important part of the meal."

"I like the mash potatoes best," Caroline chimed in.

"That's because you've never tasted a turkey roasted by me," he told her. "Now, Caroline, you will be responsible for making Christmas cookies."

Caroline's cheeks turned pink with pleasure. "I get a responsibility?"

"Of course," Dane replied. "You're a member of our team." Then he turned to Savannah. "You're assigned the rolls."

Savannah nodded and hoped she didn't look as embarrassingly happy as Caroline about being included.

"Hack, you've got the pies. I tried to put everything I thought you'd need on the list I gave Steamer, but if I forgot something, there's a convenience store in Tylerton that stays open on holidays."

"And if they don't have what you need, I can intimidate another Target manager," Steamer offered.

"You didn't *intimidate* the last one," Hack corrected. "You *bribed* him—with Savannah's money."

Steamer shrugged. "I'd be willing to try that again."

"Steam, you've got mashed potatoes," Dane interrupted. "And remember—that's Caroline's favorite part."

Steamer winked at Caroline. "The potatoes are in good hands, baby."

"Doc, will you take the dressing and maybe a couple of vegetables— just to round out the meal?" He glanced at Savannah. "Some people think it's important to hit all the major food groups."

Savannah smiled, and Doc nodded.

Dane rubbed his hands together. "Okay then, everybody get busy."

Savannah had assumed that her assignment would involve mixing and kneading, but she was pleased to discover that Steamer had purchased frozen yeast rolls. So all she had to do was put them on a buttered pan and allow them to rise. This gave her plenty of time to assist Caroline, which she realized was probably part of Dane's master plan.

The Christmas cookie dough, too, was already made and cut into little chunks. Caroline just had to put them on the cookie sheet, and after a few minutes in the oven, they were ready to decorate.

Space in the kitchen was at a premium, so Steamer took his potatoes into the living room and peeled them in front of the fire. Hack appropriated half the kitchen table for his pie making and allowed Savannah and Caroline to have the other half. The downside of this was that while the cookies were baking, he drafted them for picking the shells off pecans.

Doc made use of the counter space by the sink to prepare the dressing and vegetables. Dane seasoned and basted the turkey while the cookies were baking. Once the cookies were done, he took possession of the oven.

"It's pretty small." Caroline eyed the turkey suspiciously as Dane placed it in the oven.

"I told Steamer to get a little one so it would cook faster."

"I hope there's enough meat for everyone to get a bite," Hack contributed morosely.

Dane patted Hack's massive shoulder. "Don't worry, big man, nobody leaves my table hungry."

They worked together throughout the rest of the morning and into the early afternoon. There was an easy camaraderie and plenty of laughter, and Savannah couldn't remember the last time she'd enjoyed a holiday as much.

Finally everything was ready, and Dane assembled everyone around the table. He asked for a volunteer to say a blessing on the food.

"Since you're the commanding officer in charge of this operation, seems to me like you should do it," Hack said.

Savannah held her breath, waiting to see how Dane would handle this challenge.

Finally Dane shrugged and bowed his head. It was a short prayer, but Savannah felt sure it was the first he'd said in years, and she was thankful to Hack for having the nerve to push him into it.

When the prayer was over, they began passing dishes and filling their plates. Caroline tasted the turkey and the potatoes. Then with her mouth still full, she announced, "This is really good turkey, but I still love the potatoes best."

Dane reached over and ruffled her hair. "That just shows how much you know."

"This is much better than the holiday dinners my mom used to make," Hack told them. "She always burned everything."

"Then how did you get so big?" Caroline asked.

"Caroline!" Savannah gasped. "That's not a polite question."

The child looked crushed. "I'm sorry, Hack."

Hack gave Caroline a gold-toothed grin. "I'm proud of my size, and I'm thankful that I learned early in life about fast food and frozen pizza."

"My grandmother was a good cook," Doc said, "but it was just the two of us—so our holidays weren't very festive."

"I was raised by my aunt," Steamer told them. "And she loved to try new recipes, so on special occasions we always had weird food like oyster stuffing and poached green beans."

Caroline made a face. "Yuck."

"Sometimes it wasn't too bad," Steamer said. "She made a mango chiffon pie once that was delicious."

"How about you, Savannah?" Hack asked. "How does this Christmas dinner stack up against the ones from your childhood?"

"My mother always took me to Denny's," Savannah told them. "The food was lousy, and there was no festivity at all. So this is unquestionably better."

"At least you didn't have to wash dishes afterward," Steamer pointed out.

Savannah smiled. In this collection of dysfunctional misfits, her strange childhood seemed almost normal. "True."

"Gotta look on the bright side," Steamer added. Then he pointed to the potatoes. "Pass me some more of those better-than-turkey spuds, please."

After their meal, Hack and Steamer offered to help Caroline play some games on her new laptop while the other adults cleaned up the kitchen.

Savannah stayed with Dane and Doc. While they were clearing the table, they heard the sound of the train's whistle. Savannah frowned. "I thought they were going to play computer games."

Dane raised an eyebrow. "The best computer in the world can't compete with a Lionel Electric Train."

By the time they had order restored in the kitchen, Caroline was sleeping on the couch while Hack and Steamer took turns with the train set. Savannah sat on the couch and pulled Caroline into her arms. Dane sat beside her, close but not touching. Doc took a chair near the fireplace.

"Are we going to go over the particulars of Operation Sitting Duck now?" Doc asked.

"I'm sure there's a lot of what not to do that we could learn from reviewing this operation," Dane agreed. "But I don't want to ruin what's left of Christmas. So let's talk about something else."

Savannah tried to give the situation a positive spin. "While it's true we didn't accomplish all we meant to with this operation—" she began.

Dane rolled his eyes. "That's an understatement."

"If nothing else, we remembered that we are soldiers," Steamer said. "And it feels good."

Savannah smiled her appreciation. "You're an amazing team, and it seems like a shame to waste all this collective talent."

"We are like a well-oiled machine," Steamer agreed.

"You could ask General Steele for another assignment," Savannah proposed.

"Not until we settle the question of who betrayed us during this last operation," Dane said. "If the general was involved in Ferrante's White House deal, I'll never work for him again."

Savannah wouldn't give up. "You could set another trap for Ferrante."

Hack growled.

But Dane nodded. "We will go after him again, but we'll wait for the right opportunity."

Savannah didn't want to be sent back to her dull life at Ft. Belvoir, so she chose her next words carefully. "What if you had a civilian client who was willing to pay you to find someone?"

Steamer nodded. "More time on the Army payroll means a better cash flow for me."

"I'm sorry that your business is slow," Savannah said.

"Me too," Dane added. "But we don't have a client, civilian or otherwise."

Savannah took a deep breath and then said, "I'd like to hire the team."

"You?" the men chorused.

"I want you to find my father."

"Your father?" Dane repeated.

"Why?" Hack asked.

"How long has he been missing?" Steamer wanted to know.

Savannah was not as interested in finding her father as she was in prolonging her time with Dane, but she had to make this convincing. She turned to Steamer first.

"I've never known him. He was gone before I was born, and my mother wouldn't even talk about him." Then she looked at Hack. "I think it's natural that I would be curious."

"So that's all this is—just a curiosity thing?" Steamer asked.

Savannah shook her head. "I grew up without roots—not knowing anything about my family. I don't want it to be that way for Caroline." She turned to Dane. "Especially after I met your grandmother. Maybe I'm related to someone like that and don't even know it."

Dane cautioned her, "You might not like what you find."

She nodded. "I know that my father is probably dead. But even extended family would be good for Caroline."

"You have the McLaughlins now," Hack pointed out.

"I'm grateful for that," she acknowledged. "But they may never be able to function in the world like regular people. If there's someone else . . . well, I'd like to know. For myself and for Caroline."

"And knowing the names of biological relatives could even be important to Caroline's survival," Doc contributed. "If she ever develops a genetic disease."

Dane raised an eyebrow. "Any genetic diseases discovered so far?"

"Not yet," Savannah admitted. "But no sense in waiting until the last moment."

"Sounds like a case for a private investigator," Dane said. "Not a covert military operations team."

"I've already tried private investigators," Savannah told him. "Several in fact. All of them were well-qualified and came highly recommended. They couldn't find anything."

"Nothing?" Steamer sounded slightly intrigued.

"No," she confirmed. "The last one told me the only way to explain the total lack of information on my father was a government coverup."

"You want us to uncover something the government has purposely buried?" Hack clarified.

"Yes. If anyone can do it, this team can," Savannah said.

"The question is why should we?" Dane asked.

"Because you don't have anything better to do," Savannah pointed out.

She was beginning to think Dane wasn't going to respond when he finally said, "If I agree to take on the investigation, are you going to pay for our services or talk the general into funding it?"

"I'll arrange with the general to borrow the team, and I'll pay the costs," Savannah replied promptly. She'd already thought this through.

"How do you guys feel about it?" Dane asked.

"It sounds okay to me," Steamer said.

"My business pretty much runs itself." Hack cut his eyes over at Steamer. "And we definitely want to keep Steam from going bankrupt."

"How about you, Doc?" Dane asked.

"I'd like to help Savannah if we can," Doc said.

Dane exhaled heavily before addressing Savannah. "Since we don't have anything better to do, I guess we'll take the case. But with the understanding that if an opportunity arises for us to get Ferrante, we'll put your father's search on hold and take it."

"Thank you!" Savannah accepted his terms exuberantly.

"Don't thank me yet," Dane cautioned. "By the end of this, you may be sorry you started it."

She refused to be discouraged. "I'm sick of wondering. I'd rather know the truth, even if it's bad."

Dane got his laptop. "Okay, I'm going to ask you some questions so I can make assignments."

"Actually, the first order of business is to come up with a name," Steamer interrupted.

"This isn't an official military operation," Dane pointed out without looking up. "So I think we can skip the naming step."

"I can't perform to my best ability without a name," Steamer said firmly. "How about Operation Missing in Action? Or Operation AWOL?"

"I like Operation AWOL," Savannah said in an effort to avoid an argument.

Dane turned to Savannah with flagging patience. "Operation AWOL it is. Now, the questions." Dane slipped into interrogation mode, and for the next thirty minutes, she divulged everything she could remember about her childhood. She told him the cities where she lived, the schools she attended, and the people she knew.

Finally Dane said, "You know so little about your father. I find it hard to believe that you never pressed your mother for more information."

"I did when I was young," Savannah admitted, "but my mother was a very fragile person, and whenever I asked about my father, she got so upset. I hated to see her cry, and gradually I just stopped asking. Then a neighbor girl in Lexington told me she'd heard a rumor. She said my mother had had an affair with a married man. When she got pregnant, she thought he would leave his wife and marry her, but he wouldn't. So her parents wanted her to give me up for adoption." Savannah paused. It was still difficult for her to say. "But she wouldn't, so they kicked her out. She spent the rest of her life going from one job she hated to another, trying to support me."

"Did your neighbor have any evidence to back up this story?" Dane asked with surprising gentleness.

Savannah shook her head. "It's just what she'd heard her mother say."

"Then it's worthless," Hack pronounced.

"Sometimes neighborhood gossip has at least a trace of truth," Doc pointed out.

"We need more than traces," Hack said.

Dane looked at Savannah. "Anything else?"

"One day when I was about five, I asked my mother if she thought I'd be tall. She slipped and said, 'Your father was tall.'"

"Was?" Hack confirmed.

Savannah nodded. "She definitely used the past tense."

"But that doesn't mean he was dead," Steamer said. "Maybe she just meant that he was out of your life."

"Maybe," Savannah agreed. "Then about a year later, I was looking through my mother's closet to see if she'd been able to buy me the new shoes I wanted for Christmas."

Hack frowned at her reprovingly. "And I thought you were an angel."

She smiled. "I am, most of the time. Anyway, I found a small box tucked away in the corner of the closet. I opened it, hoping to find my shoes. But all I found were a few girlish mementos, like a movie ticket and a Valentine card. And a badge."

"A badge?" Dane asked with interest.

"CIA, FBI? Local police?" Hack wanted to know.

"I don't know," Savannah said.

Steamer leaned his elbows onto the table. "Was there a name on it?"

"No," she said. "I think there was a number on it—but I can't remember it."

"Did you ask your mother about it?" Hack asked.

Savannah frowned. "I didn't have to. She caught me going through the box."

"Uh-oh," Steamer said in sympathy.

"Yes, it was terrible. She didn't cry like she usually did when I asked about my father. She just went completely white, and I was afraid she was going to faint. Then she told me to get out. She didn't speak to me for a couple days." Tears burned Savannah's eyes. The memory was still painful.

"Did you ever see the box again?"

"No, it was years before I got up the courage to look. I conducted searches about once a year after that, but I never found it. When my mother finally died, I went through everything, and it wasn't there."

"She destroyed it?"

Savannah nodded. "I suppose."

"How significant do you think the badge is?" Dane asked her.

"The way she reacted to it and the fact that it disappeared makes me sure that it was important and related to my father. I hated the story the neighbor girl had told me about my mother and the married man,"

Savannah told them honestly. "So as I got older, I made up fantasies about him. The badge usually featured prominently in these scenarios. It was much easier to think that he had left us out of duty to his country than because he just didn't want us."

Doc nodded. "Your fantasies sound normal and even healthy. It's better to be optimistic than bitter."

Savannah continued. "I became pretty attached to the idea of my father as an agent. It seemed to explain a lot of things—like the fact that my mother never dated, that we moved often and never made friends."

Dane nodded. "I agree. So that's where we'll start." He turned to Hack. "What do you think?"

Hack frowned. "The P.I. Savannah hired said it looked like a government coverup. That's usually what they do with a problem, not a hero."

"Yeah, that's true." Dane's expression was more grim than usual.

"The government didn't extend protection to you and your mother after your father's death or disappearance—that's a bad sign too," Steamer told her. "Assuming he was an agent."

"In fact, it's possible that the government actually had your father *removed*," Doc added with obvious reluctance.

"You mean killed?" Savannah clarified.

Dane nodded. "That's exactly what he means."

Savannah squared her shoulders. "Any scenario where my father left us for some other reason than just not wanting us is a good one as far as I'm concerned."

"Now that's what I call looking on the bright side." Steamer sounded proud.

"If we're going to pursue this," Dane began, "we need to concentrate our initial efforts on trying to figure out which agency or department your father worked for."

"That won't be easy," Hack warned. "Government agencies are stingy with information about their employees—particularly the ones who go bad."

Dane didn't deny this. "It will be a challenge."

Steamer waved their concerns aside. "We're used to challenges."

"We'll do our very best to find your father," Doc promised.

Dane sighed. "What happens after that is anybody's guess."

"And what exactly are we looking for?" Hack asked.

"An agent who disappeared about twenty-eight years ago," Dane replied.

"And remember—he's tall," Steamer added with a wink at Savannah.

"How could we forget that?" Hack muttered. "It's our only clue."

"Too bad we can't ask for the general's help," Steamer said. "He's good at getting cooperation from other government agencies."

"As far as the general knows, the team is on hiatus while I recuperate from the scratch in my side," Dane said firmly. "No one breathes a word of this new operation to him."

"Operation AWOL," Steamer contributed.

Dane rolled his eyes.

"Once we start making inquiries, the general will know we're working on something," Doc pointed out.

"By the time he does, I'll have a plausible excuse ready," Dane said.

"You mean a lie?" Savannah asked.

"Exactly," Dane confirmed. "And since we don't want to set off any alarms, avoid calling people at home on Christmas Day to ask questions about an agent who has been out of commission for nearly thirty years. Just do what you can with computer networks today. Personal contacts can wait until tomorrow."

Hack nodded. "Okay, so what's my assignment?"

"Take the whole Department of Defense, in case Savannah's father was a military intelligence officer. Steamer, you take the FBI. Doc, since you've got friends at Langley, you take the CIA. I'll see what I can find out about Savannah's mother."

"Sure, take the easy job," Steamer complained. "The one where you actually have a *name*."

Dane smiled. "The privileges of rank."

"What do you want me to do?" Savannah asked.

Dane's smile broadened. "You'll be helping me, of course."

* * *

Savannah had just settled down beside Dane's desk to begin researching her mother when Caroline woke up from her nap. She was hungry and wanted someone to play with, so Dane changed Savannah's assignment.

"Spend some time with your daughter," he said. "I can handle this."

Savannah felt guilty for leaving him, since she had asked him to take on the assignment. But she'd missed Caroline. So she allowed the child to drag her into the kitchen. After making sandwiches for a spur of the moment picnic, Savannah packed a handful of Christmas cookies and followed Caroline outside. Hack was sitting on the back steps, typing away on his laptop.

"How's your assignment coming?" Savannah asked him as they settled on the steps beside him.

"Considering it's Christmas—pretty good," he replied.

Caroline offered him a sandwich, and he accepted.

Once Hack had closed his laptop, Savannah said, "I want to thank you for helping with Operation Sitting Duck. You were opposed to it and . . . you were right. The operation was doomed from the start."

"It wasn't the fact that I thought the operation was doomed to failure that bothered me," Hack told her. "I became a soldier to protect and defend the innocent against evil. It goes against all I believe to *invite* trouble."

"And that's what you felt like we were doing—asking for trouble?"

"By taunting Ferrante?" Hack said as he polished off his sandwich. "Oh yeah. We were going needlessly into danger."

"That makes me appreciate your involvement even more." She gave him a cookie and then asked, "And how do you feel about this new case?"

"Basically the same."

"You think we're asking for trouble?"

Hack nodded.

"But you're with us?"

He grinned. "All for one and one for all."

* * *

That evening they ate Christmas dinner leftovers, and once Caroline was in bed, the team gathered to discuss progress on Operation AWOL— which was minimal.

"I asked my friend at Langley to see if your father might have been a CIA agent," Doc told her. "He said that if it was a government coverup they aren't going to want it uncovered—especially not by one of their agents while on the federal payroll."

"That's understandable," Savannah admitted.

"I don't want him to lose his job, so I told him just to do what he can without making waves," Doc continued. "He said he thinks he can get us the names of all the agents who became inactive during the five-year span before and after Savannah's birth."

"We can't ask for more than that," Dane said.

"I'm running into similar problems at the FBI," Steamer acknowledged. "They aren't quite as stingy with information as the CIA, but almost."

"I'm not even trying to get cooperation from the Defense Department," Hack reported. "I know the military systems well enough to just hack in. I'm doing it in small sessions, so hopefully nobody will see my footprints in their files. I've got a couple of possibles. I'll let you know if they pan out."

"In my investigation of your mother," Dane began, "I was able to follow your school records back to Tampa."

"Where I was born," she said.

"That's what your birth certificate says anyway," Dane agreed. "I was able to find addresses for all the apartments you lived in."

Savannah felt embarrassed. "Cheap places in lousy neighborhoods."

"I even found most of the places where your mother worked," Dane continued.

"Crummy jobs."

"Crummy *life*," Steamer interjected.

"It wasn't great," Savannah acknowledged. Then she narrowed her eyes at Dane. "Why do I get the feeling that my crummy life is a clue of some kind?"

"If you'd been in a witness protection plan with *any* agency of the Federal government, you would have lived better," Doc explained for Dane. "They arrange for good jobs and even help with housing if necessary."

Dane handed Savannah a printout. It was a grainy photograph of her mother. "She was very beautiful," he said softly.

"Looks just like Savannah," Hack remarked.

Doc, the amateur photographer, frowned. "The photo quality on that picture is terrible."

"It's the only one I could find," Dane said. "Despite her beauty, she was apparently camera shy."

"That's true," Savannah realized. "She hated having her picture taken. I only have a couple, but they're better than this." She handed the printout back to him.

He tucked the poor-quality picture under his laptop. "I'd like to get copies of the photos you have."

She nodded. "They're in my apartment at Ft. Belvoir. I had hoped to find more when I went through my mother's things after she died. But there were no pictures. In fact, there wasn't much of anything."

"Now *that* sounds like government involvement," Hack said.

"Yeah," Steamer agreed. "They may have sent somebody in to sort through your mother's things before you got there."

"That would be like the FBI or CIA," Hack complained. "They don't help the wife of a rogue agent survive, but then they paw through her stuff when she dies to make sure there's nothing that would incriminate them."

"And a last-minute search would explain the dearth of pictures," Steamer remarked.

Hack frowned. "Dearth?"

"It means scarcity, baby," Steamer informed him.

Hack's hands clenched into ham-sized fists. "So why didn't you just say scarcity?"

"Anyway," Dane interrupted, "keep working on your assignments. Tomorrow morning I'm flying out to meet with Cam's ex-wife."

Savannah was disappointed that their Christmas holiday was coming to such an abrupt end. "So soon?"

Dane nodded. "I want to get that taken care of. I'll come back in time for the funeral on Saturday. And immediately after the funeral, Savannah, Caroline, and I will be making a little trip."

When Savannah realized that he intended for their separation to be temporary, she smiled with relief. "Where are we going?"

"To the only clue your mother left us," Dane said. "Savannah, Georgia."

Everyone was silent for a few seconds. Then Savannah whispered, "You think that's where she's from?"

"I know it is." Dane turned his laptop around so she could see the screen. It was a page from the Savannah, Georgia, Department of Motor Vehicle archives. Savannah was concerned about the legality of hacking into secure databases until she saw her mother's young, happy face.

Savannah felt tears sting her eyes.

"That's her," she confirmed. "But the name is wrong."

"Different, not wrong," Dane corrected. "I've hired a P.I. in Savannah. He'll start working on a background check tomorrow. Maybe by the time we get there, he'll know why she changed her name." He glanced around the room. "But as far as the general knows, we're just going on vacation."

* * *

Savannah went up to check on Caroline, and when she returned, Dane was sitting on the couch in the living room, staring at the fire.

She sat beside him and asked, "Where are the guys?"

"At a hotel in Fredericksburg," he said.

"You must be exhausted," she said. "Why don't you go up and sleep?"

He shook his head stubbornly. "Not with Caroline in the house."

"I've seen you sleep several times, and you weren't violent," she pointed out. "In fact, I think I have a calming effect on you."

"It's not worth the risk." He was so stubborn.

"You could take a pill."

"And wake up on New Year's day?"

She rolled her eyes. "Take half a pill then."

"I'm fine," he insisted.

With a sigh, she gave up on convincing him to sleep. "So tomorrow you're going to see Cam's ex-wife."

"Yes."

"But you're not going to marry her, are you?" Savannah hoped it sounded like a joke.

He shook his head. "No."

"Can Caroline and I come?" She felt him stiffen and saw his expression close. "Just to the airport to see you off," she clarified.

Dane relaxed and nodded. "I guess that would be okay. Hack is going to the post early to check on his suspects. But I'll arrange for Steamer and Doc to go with us so they can escort you back here."

"After we leave the airport, I'd like to go by Ft. Belvoir. Since Lieutenant Hardy informed me that the general isn't obligated to keep my job open, I think I should ask him personally about extending my leave."

"The general won't fire you." Dane sounded certain. "But I'll tell Doc and Steamer to take you by the post."

Savannah took a deep breath and said, "I know you don't want to talk about Operation Sitting Duck . . ."

Dane groaned.

"But I just have a few questions." She waited until he nodded his reluctant cooperation. Then she continued. "From the beginning, Caroline was never in any danger from Ferrante?"

"No," he confirmed. "The president of the United States was less secure."

"And you never intended for me to be in danger either."

"No."

She decided to consider this a declaration of love. "And once you figured out that I was bugged, you didn't tell me or remove the device so you could lure Ferrante to the McLaughlins' mountain, where you had a trap set for him."

"Yes."

"And it would have worked if the FBI and the White House hadn't gotten involved."

Dane frowned. "Why do you sound so surprised? I'm a highly decorated, very successful covert operations officer. This type of thing is what I do."

"I know. But it's hard to conceive that there's someone as smart as you are."

"I am one in a million." He put his arm around her shoulders, and she knew he was trying to distract her.

But she had more to say. "I can't stop thinking about Cam."

He removed his arm and fixed his eyes on the dancing flames. She knew his retreat was her punishment for bringing up a painful topic.

"He did so many bad things—unforgivable things—but he redeemed himself to some extent in the end by risking his life for the team."

Dane turned to stare at her.

"It makes me wonder if that would work for you."

"You want me to die to make up for my sins?"

He was being obtuse on purpose, and she resisted the urge to shake him. "No, I want you to forget your sins and live well. You can't change what happened in the Russian prison, just like Cam couldn't change the mistakes he made. But if you do everything you can to live a good life from this point on, don't you think that will mean something to God?"

He looked away. "I'm afraid to hope that it will."

Dane rarely let his guard down, and she knew this was a significant moment. "The only other choice is to throw the rest of your life away. And I can't believe God wants you to do that."

He didn't agree, but he didn't argue, and she decided to be satisfied with that. "Well, if you won't sleep, I guess I will."

He reached a hand out to stop her from standing. "But I haven't given you your Christmas gift yet."

She wasn't expecting anything from him and suddenly felt vulnerable and uncertain.

"Hold out your hand."

Once her hand was outstretched he dropped the locket onto her palm.

"Bug free," he said with a smile.

"Thank you. It's the nicest Christmas present I've ever gotten *twice*."

"I'm glad you still like it," he said. "But that's not your gift." He leaned close and whispered in her ear. "When I got word that Rosemary Ferrante was at Tulley Gate trying to involve you in her personal problems . . ."

"Yes," she prompted breathlessly.

"I was holding my cell phone, trying to think of an excuse to call you."

Savannah's heart started pounding so hard she was sure he could here it. "Are you trying to tell me that you love me?"

He winced. "No. I just needed to get that train to Caroline."

She pulled his face close to hers. "The only time I'm *sure* your lips aren't lying is when you're kissing me."

When the kiss ended, she whispered, "You love me."

Obviously still conflicted, he replied, "Wes will always be between us."

"No, Wes will always be *with* us," she corrected. "There's a difference."

Then she rested her head on his shoulder, and together they watched the fire blaze.

CHAPTER 17

SAVANNAH HAD PLANNED to wake up early the next morning to be sure Dane didn't leave for the airport without her. But once she finally went to bed, she slept long and hard, and the sunrise was well over by the time she opened her eyes. Caroline's bed was empty, so Savannah pulled on her robe and rushed downstairs. When she walked into the kitchen, she was relieved to see Caroline perched on the edge of a kitchen chair, eating a jelly-filled doughnut. Steamer and Doc were there too. She presumed Hack was already at Ft. Belvoir, browbeating the TSDU technicians, but Dane's absence was unexpected and alarming.

"Where's Dane?" Savannah managed to ask around the lump of disappointment in her throat. "He said we could go with him to the airport."

Doc nodded. "He told us. He just had to run some errands before his flight."

Weak with relief, Savannah sat down in the nearest chair.

"Want a doughnut?" Caroline invited.

Savannah shook her head. "No thanks."

A few minutes later they heard footsteps on the back porch, and all eyes turned to watch Dane enter. When Savannah saw him, she was thankful that she was already sitting down. He stood before them in full dress uniform. His hair was cut to regulation, and his hat was tucked under his arm. He was a stunning sight, rendering Savannah speechless.

Steamer and Doc didn't comment, which she presumed meant they weren't surprised by Dane's appearance. And she realized she shouldn't have been. Of course when going to see Cam's ex-wife on official Army business, he would need to dress the part.

Caroline squealed and leapt from her chair. "You're beautiful!"

Dane smiled as he accepted her embrace. "Be careful not to mess up my badges and ribbons. It took me years to earn them all."

Caroline released him and smoothed the front of his uniform. "I'll be careful."

"You want a doughnut?" Steamer offered.

Dane shook his head. "No, I don't want to get crumbs on my badges."

Savannah was still gawking stupidly at him and couldn't seem to stop herself. He was beautiful. And a military uniform always stirred her patriotic feelings. But finally she decided it was the glimpse of the old Dane, the man he used to be, that held her spellbound. Seeing him this way gave her hope that he could be that man again.

"You're staring," Dane said to her. He glanced down at his highly decorated chest. "Is something crooked?"

"No," she assured him. "It's just been a long time since I've seen you in uniform."

"It's been a long time since I've *been* in uniform," Dane admitted. "So long, in fact, that I had to pay a tailor in Fredericksburg a ridiculous amount of money to alter it for me this morning."

Steamer pointed at Dane's short haircut. "And how much did it cost to get someone to scalp you?"

"Less," Dane replied, rubbing the crisp, short hair along his neckline. Then he waved at the doughnuts on the table. "If anyone hasn't had breakfast, you need to hurry. We're leaving in ten minutes." He glanced at Savannah. "And you might want to put on some clothes."

This snapped her out of her admiring trance. She smirked at him and said, "Come on, Caroline. We'd better get ready so Major Dane won't leave us."

Caroline ran toward the stairs, and Savannah followed at a more sedate pace.

"Ten minutes," Dane reminded her.

Slowly she looked over her shoulder. "If you leave me, I'll call the airport and tell them your plane has a bomb on it."

His eyebrows rose. "That's illegal."

"And the illegal call will be made from your home phone, so I suggest you wait." With that, she turned and walked leisurely up the stairs.

In spite of her passive defiance, Savannah had herself and Caroline ready within Dane's ten-minute deadline. Caroline insisted on wearing her new coat, even though the temperature outdoors was a balmy seventy-three degrees. So by the time they arrived at Dulles International Airport, the child's cheeks were pink, and Savannah was getting worried about heat exhaustion.

Dane wasn't checking any luggage, so they proceeded straight to the security screening area. Savannah was already grieving over the impending separation and didn't want to let Dane out of her sight.

They drew many stares as they walked, which Savannah attributed to Dane's uniform until Steamer said, "A guy asked me if we were actors making a war movie, and I figured there was no harm in playing along. Boy, did that news spread like wildfire!"

Dane rolled his eyes. "Just don't start signing autographs."

By the time they reached the security checkpoint, they had a sizeable crowd following them. Dane looked behind them and said to Steamer, "I'm holding you responsible for this."

"Give me a break," Steamer begged. "Girls love movie stars."

Dane gritted his teeth and spoke to Doc. "I have something I need to discuss with Savannah. While Steamer pretends to be an actor in order to get girls, please take Caroline over there to watch airplanes take off." He pointed at a wall of windows a few feet away. "And keep a close eye on her. All these people make me nervous."

Steamer resumed his flirting while Doc took Caroline to the windows.

When Dane looked back at her, Savannah said, "I wish you didn't have to go."

He nodded. "Believe me, visiting the survivors of fallen team members is the worst kind of duty."

"Hurry back." She leaned close and whispered, "There's still the matter of 'best kisser' to be decided."

He grinned. "There was never any real question in your mind."

She couldn't deny it. "No."

Before he could respond, his flight was called.

Steamer broke away from his gullible groupies and warned Dane, "If you don't get through security now, you're going to miss your plane."

He waved for Doc and Caroline to join them, and they walked together to the security screening area. There was no time for long good-byes, so Dane hugged Caroline, shook hands with his men, and gave Savannah a brief but very public kiss before merging with the line of travelers waiting to be X-rayed.

"Is Major Dane your boyfriend?" Caroline asked her mother as they watched Dane snake through the maze of partitions.

"I'm not sure," Savannah replied honestly. "Maybe."

"I hope so," Caroline approved.

Savannah couldn't bear to take her eyes off Dane's retreating figure and didn't have a response, so she just squeezed Caroline's hand.

When Dane emerged from the other side of the security checkpoint, he turned and waved. They all waved back. Savannah watched until he disappeared from sight. Then she had to control the urge to run screaming after him, begging him not to go. Only the certain knowledge that security personnel would stop her long before she could reach him prevented her from making the attempt.

As if sensing her distress, Doc stepped up and put a hand on her arm. "He'll be fine. But we'd better head on to Ft. Belvoir."

Savannah only nodded, afraid that if she tried to speak, she'd dissolve into a sobbing spectacle.

"It's only for a couple of days," Steamer reminded her.

"I know," Savannah managed. She wasn't bothered so much by the length of the separation as by the timing. Just when she and Dane seemed to be bridging the obstacles that had kept them apart for years, he had to fly across the country, adding distance to the list of barriers.

Caroline pulled on her mother's hand. "If it will make you feel better, we can go fishing when we get home."

Savannah wasn't sure what affected her most—Caroline's attempt at improving her mood or her reference to Dane's cabin as home.

"I'm fine," she promised. "And I'm not very good at fishing. Maybe that can wait until Major Dane gets back. Now let's get to Ft. Belvoir. After I talk to General Steele, we can go out to lunch."

"Okay," Caroline agreed readily, and Savannah wished she had the optimism and resiliency of her child.

Savannah was edgy during the drive to Ft. Belvoir. She stared out the window and wondered if her uneasiness was a premonition. Maybe Dane's plane was going to crash. Or maybe when he met Cam's ex-wife, he'd change his mind and decide to marry *her*.

She pulled her eyes from the window and saw Doc watching her with concern.

"I'll just be glad when he gets back," she whispered to him. *Without a wife,* she added in her mind.

When they reached the Intelligence Center, they walked to General Steele's office. This time Savannah was not surprised to see Lieutenant Hardy at the receptionist's desk. If she'd work late on Christmas Eve, the day after Christmas was pretty much a given.

Lieutenant Hardy gave Savannah a pleasant, professional smile, but was more animated when she greeted Caroline.

"It's so good to see you," she told the child. "Did you have a nice Christmas?"

Caroline propped her elbows on the edge of Lieutenant Hardy's desk. "I got a train and a doll and a computer." She pulled on the fake-fur that encircled her sleeve. "And this coat."

"I'm not surprised you got so much good stuff," the lieutenant told Caroline. "After all, you are a very good girl."

Caroline nodded in complete agreement. Then she pointed at Steamer and Doc. "These are our friends."

Lieutenant Hardy nodded a vague greeting to the men. Then she reached under her desk and pulled out a box wrapped in bright-colored Christmas paper. "I have a gift for you too."

Caroline accepted the gift reverently. "Can I open it now?"

Savannah nodded her permission, and Caroline ripped aside the paper to expose an art kit.

"There are watercolors and oil paints and even charcoal to make sketches," Lieutenant Hardy listed off.

"I love it," Caroline said politely.

"You draw such lovely pictures," Lieutenant Hardy said. "I thought this would help you develop your artistic talents."

"Can I be an artist?" Caroline asked her mother.

"That sounds like a great idea. Why don't you go in my office and practice drawing while I talk to General Steele." Savannah smiled at Caroline's babysitters. "Have fun, boys."

"I love to color," Steamer said.

Once Caroline and her escorts were headed down the hall, Savannah turned back to Lieutenant Hardy. "Is the general in?"

"He's in the building but not in his office."

"Do you know when he'll be back?"

"No."

Savannah was losing patience. "Do you know where he is?"

"Yes."

Savannah narrowed her eyes at the lieutenant. "I just need to ask him a question. It will only take a few minutes. Now where is he?"

"In a meeting." Lieutenant Hardy's expression was smug. "And I'm afraid I'm not at liberty to disclose his location. But you're welcome to sit here until he comes back." She waved at the row of seats across from her desk where visitors waited for an opportunity to speak to the general.

Savannah was annoyed that Lieutenant Hardy was treating her like an unwelcome guest instead of a coworker.

"Or I'd be glad to take a message if you'd prefer," Lieutenant Hardy added. Savannah detected a sly tone to her voice.

She didn't trust Lieutenant Hardy to deliver her message, so she said, "I'll wait."

As she sat in one of the visitor chairs, the phone on Lieutenant Hardy's desk rang. The lieutenant turned away before answering the call, in an obvious attempt to keep Savannah from overhearing her conversation. Savannah gritted her teeth and looked into the hallway, hoping to convey her total uninterest in anything the lieutenant had to say.

Lieutenant Hardy concluded the phone call and stood. "That was General Steele," she informed Savannah. "He said they are taking a fifteen-minute break, and if you come immediately, he can talk to you."

"Where are they meeting?"

The lieutenant just waved and said, "Follow me."

Anxious to see the general and be done with Lieutenant Hardy, Savannah obeyed.

Savannah followed Lieutenant Hardy to the elevator, concentrating more on Lieutenant Hardy's stiff, disapproving posture and thinking how much she disliked the woman. When they exited the elevator on the basement floor, Savannah was confused.

"Where exactly is this meeting being held?" she demanded of Lieutenant Hardy's back.

"Just up here," the lieutenant responded.

Savannah continued to follow until they reached an exterior door. Lieutenant Hardy quickly entered the security code into a keypad and stepped out onto a loading dock.

"Almost there," the general's secretary said a little breathlessly.

Savannah frowned as she joined Lieutenant Hardy on the concrete platform. "I can't believe that General Steele is having a meeting out here . . ."

The lieutenant hurried to a dark sedan—obviously an official Army car—and told her to get in. "You're in danger," Lieutenant Hardy announced. "And I'm taking you to safety."

"How do you know I'm in danger?"

"During my conversation with the general a few minutes ago, he mentioned your name and used the code for imminent danger. Protocol requires me to take you to the nearest MP station."

Savannah's heart was pounding. "What about Caroline?"

"The warning didn't include her—she's safe in your office with Major Dane's men."

Savannah knew that was true but still didn't want to go. She didn't really trust the general and certainly didn't trust Lieutenant Hardy. "I think I should wait . . ."

The lieutenant gave her an impatient look. "I don't really care about you or your safety, but I know Caroline will be upset if something happened to you, and I'm obligated to follow the general's orders. So get in the car, and let me take you to a secure location before you get yourself killed. By staying here, you're endangering yourself *and* Caroline!"

Savannah reluctantly opened the passenger door of the sedan and was about to climb in when someone called her name.

"Mrs. McLaughlin!"

She turned back to see Corporal Benjamin running out of the building, his arms waving in distress.

"Don't go," the corporal pleaded breathlessly. "She's working for Ferrante!"

Lieutenant Hardy turned on him "How dare you accuse me of such a thing. If anyone works for Ferrante, it's you! That's why you begged the general to include you in the support team. Then you pretended to warn Major Dane when really you were leading Ferrante right to him!"

"She's lying!" the corporal promised. "She has access to everything the general knows. She used that information to help Ferrante and incriminated the general in the process."

"I would never do such a thing," Lieutenant Hardy appealed to Savannah. "You know how I feel about General Steele. He's stalling for time, waiting for more of Ferrante's men. You are risking your life with this conversation."

"She's dangerous," the corporal warned. "I knew she was bad, but I had no proof. I've been watching her for weeks, trying to catch her stealing information. When I saw her lead you off, I knew something was up, so I called Major Dane. He's on his way here. He told me to tell Doc and Steamer to take your daughter to his cabin for safe-keeping. That's where I'm supposed to take you."

"But Dane is on a plane," Savannah replied. "You couldn't have talked to him."

"I told you he's just trying to trick you," Lieutenant Hardy said with a nervous look over her shoulder. "Get in the car! Maybe we can still get away—or at least draw the danger away from Caroline before Ferrante arrives."

Savannah only had a few seconds to make a decision. She thought about the lieutenant's abrasive personality, her determination to belittle Savannah at every opportunity. She thought of the corporal's valor in trying to warn them in New Orleans and his willingness to disable the support team's computer that was relaying information—at the risk of his career. She thought about Dane and how nothing was ever as it seemed. Then she made a decision.

Jumping into Lieutenant Hardy's car, she said, "Hurry."

The Lieutenant slid under the wheel and turned the key in the ignition. With Corporal Benjamin running behind them, they screeched out of the loading dock area and onto the street that ran behind the Intelligence Center. Savannah watched the corporal through the rear window. He had stopped running and was now just staring after them as the lieutenant put more distance between them and the Intelligence Center.

With a sigh, Savannah turned around and settled into the seat. She was uneasy about her choice until she saw the gun in Lieutenant Hardy's hand pointed directly at her. Then she knew she had made the wrong decision. She had trusted the wrong person again.

Savannah stared at the gun in resignation. "You do work for Mario Ferrante?"

"Of course," Lieutenant Hardy said with loathing.

"Why?"

"Because he appreciates me and my service more than the Army ever did."

Savannah felt desperate and confused. "What does he want?"

"He wants Major Dane, and he needs some bait. He told me to bring Caroline, too, but I've seen the way the major looks at you." The lieutenant didn't try to hide her disgust. "You'll be bait enough, and Caroline won't be placed in danger."

"Caroline," Savannah felt the familiar light-headedness threaten, but she fought it. Dane and Caroline needed her. She had to be strong.

Driving with her right hand, Lieutenant Hardy angled her left arm across her lap and kept the gun pointed directly at Savannah.

"You were the one who planted the listening device in my locket,"

Savannah realized. The technicians hadn't been the only ones with access to her locket after it was scanned. Lieutenant Hardy had been there, on the pretext of escorting her.

"Yes," she agreed. "And I kept the bug from being detected by TSDU. I just slipped the locket in my pocket while they scanned the rest of your things. Then I returned it with no one the wiser."

"Two innocent TSDU techs have been interrogated for hours and were forced to spend Christmas away from their families because of you."

"Like I care." Lieutenant Hardy drove fast, in an obvious effort to reach Tulley Gate before Corporal Benjamin was able to convince someone in authority to shut down the post.

Savannah took a deep breath and tried to think. Lieutenant Hardy was working for Mario Ferrante. Ferrante was going to use Savannah to lure Dane into danger. Savannah could not be the means of his destruction. So she had to get out of the car, even if she didn't survive the attempt.

What would Dane do? she asked herself.

Dane wouldn't be in this position in the first place, because he never would have trusted Lieutenant Hardy.

Pushing this discouraging thought aside, she concentrated on the task at hand. Ignore emotion. Become a machine. Analyze the situation to find a weakness and then turn weakness into opportunity. Caroline, Savannah realized, was Lieutenant Hardy's weakness. If the lieutenant had brought Caroline as Mario Ferrante had instructed her to do, she would now have two hostages and could afford to kill Savannah. But with Caroline out of reach, the lieutenant would be reluctant to shoot. That gave Savannah just the smallest advantage.

At Tulley Gate, the MPs checked every vehicle coming into the post but only gave those exiting a cursory glance. And once they were off the military post, Savannah's chances for a successful escape diminished drastically. So she had to act now.

As a distraction, Savannah pretended to cry and saw the lieutenant's look of patronizing aversion. She had expected no better. In between sobs, Savannah peeked out the window at the familiar landmarks. Tulley Gate was just ahead. The lieutenant would have to slow down as she approached the gate. That was when Savannah would have to make her move.

The first step was to convince Lieutenant Hardy that she was incapable of aggressive action, so Savannah clutched her midsection and wailed, "I'm going to be sick!"

"Don't you vomit on me!" Lieutenant Hardy commanded. She shook the gun. "I'll shoot you."

Savannah reminded herself that this was an idle threat and continued to thrash around. "I'm so ill."

"You are a disgrace," the lieutenant spit out.

Savannah moaned louder and let her head loll to the side—toward Lieutenant Hardy and the all-important steering column.

"Shut up!" Lieutenant Hardy hissed.

"I can't help it that I'm sick." Tears pooled in her eye and dripped onto her cheeks.

"I don't know what in the world Major Dane sees in you," the lieutenant said snidely. "You're just a sniveling soldier wannabe."

Savannah's determination to bring Lieutenant Hardy to justice solidified. She would prove Lieutenant Hardy wrong. She would make Dane proud. If it was the last thing she ever did . . .

"Oh I'm really going to be sick." Savannah was now leaning into the space between the two front seats. She saw Lieutenant Hardy shrink away in anticipation of an eruption. And that was her final mistake.

Savannah moved her hands away from her mouth and grabbed the gear shifter. Then she pulled down with all her might. There was a horrible screech and the car went into a skid.

Savannah was peripherally aware of Lieutenant Hardy fighting with the steering wheel for control. Savannah made use of this opportunity to yank the handle on the door and throw herself out of the car. When she saw the gravel shoulder coming up toward her face at an alarming rate, she wondered if she'd made another mistake. She hit the ground hard.

* * *

Savannah opened her eyes and saw a bright light shining above her. Squinting, she tried to determine if she'd died and gone to heaven. Then Dane leaned over her, blocking the light. Since she knew Dane wasn't dead, she assumed she wasn't in heaven. But since he was on a plane headed to see Cam's ex-wife, she guessed she must be dreaming. His dark gray eyes were grim and his soft, full lips were pressed into an angry line. She wanted to reach up and touch his cheek, but her arms felt so heavy.

"Savannah," her Dream Dane said. "You're going to be okay."

She smiled and nodded, hoping she didn't wake up any time soon. "I love you."

The Dream Dane reacted exactly the way the real one would have to such a comment. He frowned. "Try not to say too much. You've had a blow to the head, so you're not thinking clearly."

Slowly she became aware of other things. The sounds of traffic passing by. The syncopated flashing of red lights. The smell of warm asphalt.

"I'm awake?" she whispered.

Dane nodded. "Yes."

"But you're on a plane."

He shook his head. "I *was* on a plane. But just as they were about to close the door I got this overwhelming feeling that I shouldn't go."

Savannah's eyes widened. "I had the same feeling. I wanted to chase you, but I was afraid I'd get shot."

He gave her a brief smile. "I was already on my way here when Corporal Benjamin called me."

Savannah winced. "I should have trusted him."

Dane nodded. "Yes, but you didn't know."

"Caroline is safe?"

"Completely," he assured her. "Doc and Steamer have her at the cabin."

"How did you find me?"

"Thanks to Corporal Benjamin's phone call, I was waiting at Tulley Gate, prepared to shoot out the tires to stop the car when the door opened and you came flying out." He shuddered. "It was one of the worst moments of my life."

Savannah tried to smile but her face was too stiff. "And you should know about bad moments."

"I do," he confirmed.

"Did you get Lieutenant Hardy?"

Dane nodded. "The MPs have her."

Savannah tried to concentrate. "So you had a feeling that I was in danger, and you left the plane."

"Yes."

Tears stung her eyes. "You chose me over duty."

He had to think about this for a few seconds. "I guess I did."

"Oh, Dane," she whispered. "You do love me. And more than that, you got a warning from God and you *listened!*"

Dane cringed. "If you don't want to be checked into the psych ward the minute you get to the hospital, you'll take my advice and stop talking!"

She frowned. "I'm going to the hospital?"

"Yes," Dane's voice was almost tender. "You broke your arm, and the paramedics think some of the cuts you got from the gravel may need to be stitched."

"You'll come with me, right?"

He nodded. "I'm never letting you out of my sight again."

She smiled at him and said, "I should have thrown myself out of a moving vehicle weeks ago."

EPILOGUE

A pair of paramedics from DeWitt Army Hospital insisted that Savannah ride in the ambulance to the emergency room for evaluation, even though she assured them that such extreme measures were unnecessary.

"My injuries are fairly minor, and I'd rather ride in the car with Dane."

"There's no way to be sure how severe your injuries are," one of the paramedics argued. "You've sustained a head trauma, and we have to take precautions."

"It's policy, ma'am," the other paramedic explained as he collapsed a stretcher beside her.

"This is silly," Savannah complained. She turned to Dane. "Tell them I don't need an ambulance."

"Their policies are designed to protect their patients, so just do what they ask you to," Dane said. Then he stood by and watched while she was carefully transferred from the gravel shoulder onto the stretcher.

Although she still felt the precautions were excessive, her head was starting to pound, and the thick foam pad on the stretcher was much more comfortable than the rocky ground had been, so Savannah discontinued her objections. The paramedics lifted the stretcher and rolled her to the waiting ambulance.

Dane followed them step for step, and once she was settled inside, he climbed up and sat on the stretcher across from hers. "How are you feeling?"

"Numb." Her fingers gingerly explored the lacerations on her face. "Do you think I'll have scars?"

Dane shook his head. "I hope not."

"I wouldn't mind having a few war wounds of my own."

He raised an eyebrow. "I've never heard anyone sound so excited by the prospect of a scar."

She smiled. "I'm just trying to fit in with the rest of the team."

"You don't need scars to fit in," he assured her. "Jumping out of a moving vehicle was enough to prove you're as crazy as the rest of us."

Savannah felt so pleased. "So when are you going to see Cam's ex-wife?"

"I'm not," Dane surprised her by saying. "I sent Hack."

She couldn't believe she'd heard him correctly. "You sent someone else to do your official duty as commanding officer of the team?"

He leaned close and whispered, "Taking care of wounded soldiers is an official duty, too. As commanding officer, I get first pick of the available duties."

"And you chose to stay with me?"

He nodded. "I didn't dare trust your safety to anyone else."

She narrowed her eyes at him. "Admit it. You *wanted* to stay with me."

"I'll admit that." He gave her a wicked smile. "I never did like Cam's ex-wife much."

The ambulance stopped while she was trying to think of an appropriate response. Seconds later, the back doors flung open, and the paramedics waved for Dane to climb down. They pulled out Savannah's stretcher and rolled her into the hospital's emergency room.

"We're taking her to triage," one of the paramedics told Dane. He pointed to their left. "You can fill out her paperwork at the desk."

"I'll be right back," Dane promised her. Then he was gone.

The paramedics parked Savannah in a tiny cubicle, and a weary looking nurse gave her a quick examination and started an IV.

"You're going to need an orthopedist to set your broken arm and a plastic surgeon to stitch up the cuts on your face," the nurse said as she worked. "The longer we wait on the stitches, the more chance of scarring, so I'm going to try to set it all up fast."

Savannah decided she really wasn't all that attached to the idea of being a scarred soldier, so she thanked the nurse.

Once the IV fluids were dripping slowly but steadily, the nurse stepped out of the cubicle. She was back a few minutes later with news. "An operating room is being prepared for you now, and the anesthesiologist should be here soon to put you to sleep."

"I'm going to an operating room?" Savannah repeated. "Just to set a broken arm and stitch up a few cuts?"

"Both procedures would be very painful if you were awake," the nurse explained. "And the plastic surgeon prefers to work on patients who won't move while he's stitching. It's the best way to handle the situation."

Savannah didn't relish the idea of being put to sleep or being in an operating room for that matter, but she kept her uneasiness to herself.

"Where's Dane?" she asked instead.

"The major who came in with you?" the nurse clarified.

Savannah nodded, which sent shooting pains through her head. She closed her eyes to block out the light, which was aggravating her headache.

"Try to hold still," the nurse advised unnecessarily. "I think the major is at the admissions desk filling out forms. Here's the anesthesiologist. I'll leave you with him and go check on the major."

"Thank you," Savannah whispered, careful not to move her head.

She opened her eyes just enough to see the doctor walk in, swathed in disposable surgical gear. He moved around in the room opening drawers and reorganizing equipment. Then he stepped up to the bed and put a new bag on the IV pole.

"It will just take a couple of minutes for this medication to take effect," he said, his voice partially muffled by the surgical mask. "You'll fall asleep quickly, and by the time you wake up, it will all be over."

"That's good," she replied with difficulty. Her lips were already slack, and she was starting to feel very drowsy.

The doctor leaned down over her. "Don't worry about a thing," he said. Then he pulled down his mask so she could see his smile.

The last thing Savannah saw before she lost consciousness was the face of Mario Ferrante above her hospital bed.

ABOUT THE AUTHOR

BETSY BRANNON GREEN currently lives in Bessemer, Alabama, which is a suburb of Birmingham. She has been married to her husband, Butch, for twenty-nine years, and they have eight children, one daughter-in-law, two sons-in-law, and three grandchildren. She loves to read—when she can find the time—and watch sporting events, if they involve her children. She is a Primary teacher and family history center volunteer in the Bessemer Ward. She also works in the office at the Birmingham Temple. Although born in Salt Lake City, Betsy has spent most of her life in the South. Her writing and her life have been strongly influenced by the town of Headland, Alabama, and the many generous and gracious people who live there. Her first book, *Hearts in Hiding*, was published in 2001, followed by *Never Look Back* (2002), *Until Proven Guilty* (2002), *Don't Close Your Eyes* (2003), *Above Suspicion* (2003), *Foul Play* (2004), *Silenced* (2004), *Copycat* (2005), *Poison* (2005), *Double Cross* (2006), *Christmas in Haggerty* (2006), *Backtrack* (2007), and *Hazardous Duty* (2007).

Find out more about Betsy Brannon Green and her books on her website: www.betsybrannongreen.net